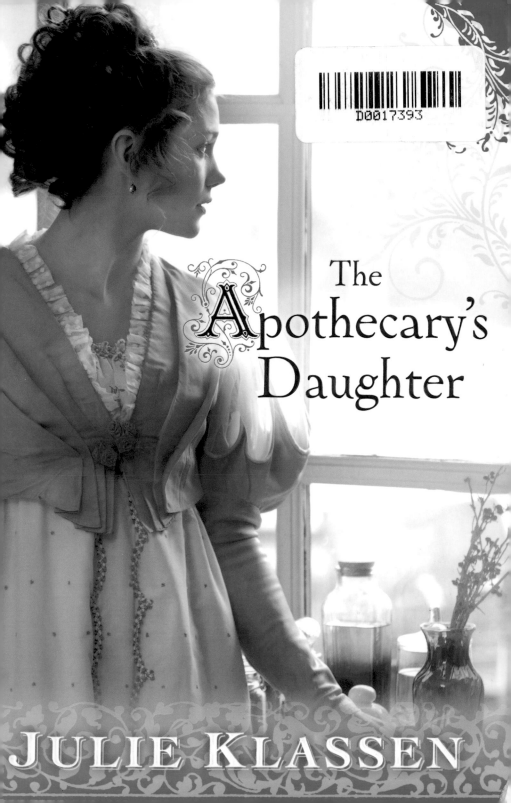

The
Apothecary's
Daughter

JULIE KLASSEN

Praise for Julie Klassen's first book,
Lady of Milkweed Manor

"Both readers of faith fiction and general readers of historical romance should enjoy this lovely first offering from Klassen."
—*Publishers Weekly*

"Klassen has written an amazing historical novel. Her style may remind readers of Jane Austen and Lawana Blackwell, and she handles a 19th-century taboo with grace, style and respect."
—Patsy Glans, *Romantic Times*

"It's a rare book that forces me to press the pause button on my life and simply devour the story—this is one such book. Well-written, emotionally charged, unexpected plot twists, and an amazing balance of foreshadowing with backstory all lend to a remarkable debut novel by author Julie Klassen. The tension builds throughout and keeps the reader guessing until the last page."
—Michelle Griep, *Novel Reviews*

"This was an excellent first novel and one of the best historical novels I've read this year. I am looking forward to Julie Klassen's next book. HIGHLY recommended."
—Deborah Khuanghlawn, *Books-Movies-Chinesefood*

"A delightful first novel. Julie Klassen weaves a compelling story . . . fully imagined. I loved it!"
—Beverly Lewis, *New York Times* bestselling author

"The characters are strong—the writing excellent—and the love that blooms for Charlotte, in many ways and with many characters, will leave you immensely and blissfully happy that good things actually do come to good people after their dues have been paid."

—Amy Lignor, *Once Upon a Romance*

"Ms. Klassen has penned an exquisite first novel that echoes the era of Jane Austen in both setting and style. . . . This novel engaged me from the first page, and I can highly recommend *Lady of Milkweed Manor* to anyone who delights in Regency romance."

—Tamela McCann, *Historical Novels Review*

". . . not only a beautiful tale but a fascinating study of women's roles in a time not so terribly distant. I'd say bravo on a fine debut, and here's hoping for another finely crafted historical from Klassen soon."

—Violet Nesdoly, *Blogcritics*

"*Lady of Milkweed Manor* is beautifully crafted with characters that will live on in your heart long after you've closed the last page."

—Kim Vogel Sawyer, bestselling author

"A strong and entertaining story that you'll finish with a sigh. Read it and tell your friends to buy it too."

—Lauraine Snelling, bestselling author

"This is truly one of the most emotionally gripping novels I've ever read and it is sure to make my best of 2008 list. My heart pounded with anticipation so many times I lost count. . . . This story is so full of passion that it will make your heart sing."

—Michelle Sutton, *Edgy Inspirational Author*

The Apothecary's Daughter

JULIE KLASSEN

BETHANY HOUSE PUBLISHERS
Minneapolis, Minnesota

Published by Bethany House Publishers
11400 Hampshire Avenue South
Bloomington, Minnesota 55438

Bethany House Publishers is a division of
Baker Publishing Group, Grand Rapids, Michigan.

Printed in the United States of America

Library of Congress Cataloging-in-Publication Data

Klassen, Julie.
    The apothecary's daughter / Julie Klassen.
        p. cm.
    ISBN 978-0-7642-0480-7 (pbk.)
    1. Young women—Fiction. 2. Villages—England—Fiction. 3. Fathers and daughters—Fiction. 4. Family secrets—Fiction. 5. Pharmacy—Fiction. 6. London (England)—Fiction. I. Title.

    PS3611.L37A66   2008
    813'.6—dc22

                                                                    2008041671

In memory of my funny, creative, hardworking father

H<small>AROLD</small> "B<small>UD</small>" T<small>HEISEN</small>

OCTOBER 1937 – AUGUST 2008

SHEPHERD'S PURSE

This plant is a remarkable instance of the truth of an observation
which there is too frequently room to make, namely,
that Providence has made the most useful things most common
and for that reason we neglect them. . . .

—CULPEPER'S COMPLETE HERBAL & ENGLISH PHYSICIAN

PROLOGUE

I remember it clearly, although it was years ago now. For I remember everything.

The year was 1810. I was a girl of fifteen, standing on the arched Honeystreet Bridge—which I often did when I was not needed in Father's shop—gazing upon the brightly painted boats that floated past. There a blue barge, and there a yellow-and-white narrowboat. In reality, I was searching. Searching the face of every person on every narrowboat that passed by on the newly completed K and A Canal. There were not many women, but a few. For though men worked the canals as pilots, navigators, and merchants, entire families sometimes lived aboard—as wives and children made for less costly crews.

My mother had disappeared on one of those narrowboats two months before, or so the villagers whispered when they thought I could not hear. I suppose I hoped she would return as she left, declaring her absence a lark, an adventure, a mistake . . . anything. How many hours had I stood there? How many boats had I seen pass beneath that bridge—boats with names like the *Britannia*, *Radiant*, or *Perseverance*?

Where had they come from, I always wondered, and where were they bound? What cargo did they bear—spices from the West Indies, perhaps, or tea from China? Coal from the Midlands or timber from as far away as Norway? How often I dreamt of stowing away and leaving Bedsley Priors for the bright unknown beyond.

That day, however, I watched the yellow-and-white narrowboat for another reason. A gangly boy with a cinched bag slung over his shoulder climbed unsteadily from the moored boat. My father, standing on the bank, extended his hand in greeting, just as the boy leaned over and was sick.

I winced. Not a very propitious beginning for a new apprentice. Father's shoes were likely spoilt.

I sighed. I knew I should go down to them. Father had not seen me there or he would have called for my help. He always did. With Mother gone and my only brother slow of mind, many responsibilities for both the household and shop fell to me.

But no. I would wait and meet young Mr. Baylor later, once he'd had a chance to collect himself. I would brew ginger tea for him and find an old cloth for Father's shoes. But first I wanted a few more moments on the bridge.

Several minutes later, a red-and-blue narrowboat approached from the west, from as far away as Bristol, perhaps, on its way to the Thames and then to London some eighty miles east. A man led one boat-horse along the towpath. A lone person sat in the curved bow deck. Far behind, aft of the cabin, two crewmen stood on the tiller deck.

As the boat drew nearer, I saw that the figure in the bow was a woman, head low, as if in prayer. Or perhaps she was reading. A wide bonnet concealed her face from the sun, from me. My heart leapt. Something about the woman's posture and tilt of her head struck me as familiar. *Mother loved to read.*

I leaned across the wide brick ledge, peering hard, heart beating. The boat drew closer. I saw that the man leading the horse was deeply tanned and broad-shouldered. *The man she left us for?* As he led the boat-horse along the strip of land beneath the bridge, he disappeared from view. The bow of the boat reached the shadow of the bridge, and one of the crewmen gaped up at me. I barely saw him. Instead I read the vessel's name painted in decorative lettering on the side, *The Gypsy*, and I thought, *How apt.* Still, I could not see the woman's face.

I whirled and raced to the other side of the bridge, hoping my angle would be better, that I would see her from that side as they passed.

Perhaps she does not even realize where she is, I thought, engrossed as she was in her reading. *Should I call to her?*

I only stared, afraid to be a fool before this woman, before the men labouring at the nearby timber mill. *If only I could see her face. . . .*

I squinted. Tried to focus. Dimly, I heard a voice. Someone was calling my name.

"Lilly!"

The boat passed further down the canal and she began to disappear all over again. *Look up!* I urged silently. *See me.*

The woman stood and looked up, but away from me—ahead toward the man and horse. The back of my mind registered pounding footsteps. The voice grew urgent. *Is she calling me?*

"Lilly!"

"Here I am!" I called.

The woman turned around. She held a hand to her forehead, shielding her eyes from the sun. Her brow wrinkled in perplexity as she stared back. I raised my hand and waved.

The woman slowly, tentatively, raised her own hand. Not in greeting, but in somber salute. The motion revealed her face—a stranger's face—kind and plain. In her hand, not a book but a rumple of cloth. Mending.

A hand shook my shoulder. "Lilly?"

Numbly, I tore my eyes from the fading sight of the woman and turned. My younger brother, Charlie, stood before me, clearly agitated and breathing hard. "I called you. Why did you not answer?"

"I . . . thought . . ." I blinked away the pathetic vision of what I had thought and in its place saw his wide eyes, his frightened tear-streaked face. "What is it, Charlie?"

" 'Tis Mary. Oh, how she shakes! Father sent me. He needs—" He paused, eyes searching the air above me.

"He needs what?" Pulse accelerating, I grasped him by both arms, frustrated at his limited ability to focus, to remember.

He winced and bit his pronounced lower lip.

"Valerian?" I prompted. "Hyssop?"

He shook his head, still squinting in attempted concentration.

"Musk pod? Peony?"

"Peony!" he shouted. "Yes!"

I was incredulous. "But we have syrup of peony on the shelf. The jar marked *S: Poeniae.*"

"Father says 'tis empty!"

Dear Lord, no.

"Oh, Lilly! How she jerks about! Will she die?"

"No," I bit out. Running from the bridge, I yelled over my shoulder, "Tell Father to set water to boil!"

I knew of only one place to get peony root. One nearby garden where it grew. I began perspiring—not from exertion, but from fear. Fear for my oldest friend. Fear for myself. For to trespass in this garden was to break the law and risk *his* wrath. But he was far away at university, was he not? *Lord, let him be far away. . . .*

I ran.

I had always loved to run, across the vale, or up the chalk hills beyond Bedsley Priors. But this time I felt no pleasure in the exercise. I ran because I had no other choice—it would take far too long to return home and hitch up the gig. True, Mrs. Mimpurse had often admonished me not to go running about the village, that I was practically a young lady now and ought to behave as such. But I knew our kindly neighbor would not blame me for running this time. For Mary was her daughter.

I ran up the Sands Road and veered right onto the High Street, nearly colliding with a man coming out of the wheelwright's.

"Sorry, Mr. Hughes!" I called, without breaking stride.

I sprinted across the village green, around the enclosed churchyard, past the Owens' farm, and up the lane to Marlow House. Once there, I darted around the stone garden wall, ducking to keep out of sight as I ran toward the closed garden gate. Fear gripped me, but I had only to imagine Mary, writhing in pain, and I pushed the gate open, wincing at its high-pitched screech. Rushing across the path to the gardener's shed, I threw back the door and grabbed the first spade I saw. Dashing to the cluster of staked peonies—the late Lady Marlow's *prized* peonies—I swallowed, realizing I had no time to be neat or exacting.

As I lanced the soil with the spade, I heard the first cry of alarm. A man yelled "Stop!" but I shoved the spade in again, deeper now. I heard footfalls and cursing on the other side of the wall. Mr. Timms, the surly gardener, I supposed. Another few seconds and I would reach the roots. I put all of my slight weight on the spade and jerked the handle back and forth. *Come on. . . .*

Just as I pulled up the plant by its roots, a man's head and shoulders appeared over the garden wall. Not surly Mr. Timms. Worse.

"Stop where you are," the young man ordered. "Those are my mother's."

Steady . . . I tried to find my voice, to explain, but found I could not speak. I knew Roderick Marlow put peony blossoms on his mother's grave every spring. I knew he was infamously cruel.

"I need one . . ." I finally croaked out, "for a friend."

"Do not move! I am calling the constable."

I had no time to explain and no time to wait for the constable. I darted across the garden, and again I heard him curse. Over my shoulder I glimpsed him hauling himself up and over the garden wall. Heard his feet hit the ground and pebbles fly as he bolted after me, his long stride stretching no doubt twice the length of my own. I ran through the garden gate and slammed it closed with all my strength. His exclamation of pain and anger chased me across the lawn. There I glimpsed a groom leading out a tall black horse—already saddled.

No.

The gate screeched open behind me. Roderick Marlow whistled and shouted, "Bring my horse. Quick!"

Immediately, I changed course. I knew that if I followed the open road as I had come, he would overtake me seconds. I could not let that happen. Instead I headed for the wood, pushing past branches that scratched at my arms and legs. Horse hooves beat the ground behind me as I wove through the trees. I left the wood and ran across a narrow pasture—a sheep fence crossed the landscape ahead. I vaulted over it, stumbled, but ran on. Behind me horse and rider cleared the fence without pause. One chance left. Ahead of me stood the tall privet hedge around the churchyard. And beyond it, the village. My pursuer galloped closer. *Does he plan to run me down?* I wondered wildly. *For a simple plant Father will happily repay him for?* He would, I did not doubt.

I ran along the hedge, and there it was. I stopped abruptly, my back to the seemingly impenetrable wall of privet. Far too tall to jump. Too dense to push through. Roderick Marlow leapt from his horse and came striding toward me, anger in his eyes and riding crop in hand. I swallowed, suddenly grateful that my long frock covered the bottom reaches of the hedge behind me. *Wait until he is a little further from his horse. One second more. . . .*

Suddenly I turned and dove into a hole in the privet, the tunnel barely large enough for a child to wriggle through. Dug, I knew, by the vicar's hound. Terror gripped my heart as I felt Roderick's hand trying to grip *me*. Fingers clawed at my skirt hems as I scrambled through the hedge and stumbled to my feet on the other side. He swore in frustration, and I knew he was not giving up. *If only the horse would bolt.* But I doubted such a well-trained beast would dare. At least it might take a second or two for him to regain his mount. I dashed across the churchyard and out its front gate, and ran down the High Street. I saw the sign for my father's shop ahead, just as I again heard pounding hooves behind. *If I can just make it inside and deliver the root, he can do what he likes with me then. Just let me reach Mary in time.*

I ran through the door and gave it a shove. But Roderick Marlow caught it and pushed in behind me, the shop bell jingling crazily. He grabbed my arm before I could hand the plant to my startled father.

Roderick raised the crop in his hand.

"Roderick Rupert Marlow!" Maude Mimpurse commanded. "Put that down and unhand the girl. Lillian Grace Haswell. What have I told you about running through town like a stray?"

Roderick froze, and I was stunned to see him lower his arm in mute submission. *That's right,* I remembered to my immense relief. Our robust, dark-haired neighbor had once worked as the Marlows' nurserymaid. Her powers of persuasion were legendary.

"She is a vandal and a thief!" the furious Marlow shouted. "She trespassed upon our garden."

"I sent her for peony root, young sir," Father explained, concern straining his features. "It was an emergency. Miss Mary has had her worse case of falling sickness yet."

The rest of the room came into focus then. I spun about and, through the surgery door, saw my dear friend lying still on the cot. Deathly still.

"Am I too late? Is she . . . ?"

"The fit has finally passed," Father said. "I believe the valerian took effect after all."

"She's fallen asleep, poor lamb," Mrs. Mimpurse said, her voice returning to its customary softness. "So exhausted was she."

I held up the peony—stalk, root, and all. "Then . . . I stole this for nothing?"

"Stole? Good gracious." Mrs. Mimpurse tutted. "We are all neighbors, are we not?"

"I will reimburse your family, young sir," Father offered, reaching up to lay his hand on the young man's shoulder. "We still need to distill a batch of syrup in any case. Or we can endeavor to replant the peony, if you prefer."

Roderick Marlow shook off Father's hand. "No. Just stay away from our gardens." He aimed his blazing glare in my direction and a chill ran through my body. "And away from me."

I would obey that command for almost three years.

Not nearly long enough.

Part I

The apothecary's house should [have an] inner chamber,

wherein he may prudently observe through some lattice window

whether his apprentices spend their time idly or faithfully. . . .

—C. J. S. THOMPSON, *MYSTERY AND ART OF THE APOTHECARY*

❧

Thou art gone from my gaze like a beautiful dream,

And I seek thee in vain by the meadow and stream.

—GEORGE LINLEY, COMPOSER

LILY OF THE VALLEY
Strengthens the brain, recruits a weak memory,
and makes it strong again.

—CULPEPER'S COMPLETE HERBAL

CHAPTER 1

K nowing she faced a long day indoors, Lilly Haswell arose early
to take in the crisp, fragrant air of a Wiltshire autumn morning.
With a quiet greeting to Mrs. Fowler, already busy at the stove, Lilly
left by the rear garden door and walked sedately out of the village. As
soon as she rounded the corner of the vicarage, however, she picked
up her pace. When she reached the hill just beyond Bedsley Priors,
she began a loping climb, tripping over turf grass from time to time,
relishing the burning in her legs and lungs. She did not stop until she
crested modest Grey's Hill. As she leaned over to catch her breath,
her long russet brown hair fell around her shoulders. She'd not taken
the time to pin it up properly, though she knew she should, especially
now that she was eighteen years old.

She straightened, taking in the view across Pewsey Vale, with its
rolling chalklands, scant trees, and in the distance, the newly carved
white horse on the ridge between Milk Hill and Walker's. She had

heard that the rector of Alton Barnes often took his telescope up to Adam's Grave, the ancient mound atop Walker's Hill, and with it could see as far as the Salisbury Cathedral. Lilly wished she might climb that hill for herself some Sunday after services when she had the entire afternoon to herself. She would like to see the Salisbury spire. She would have given just about anything to see such places in person—and far more besides. She wondered what sights and delights her mother was experiencing, wherever she was, now these three years gone.

Lilly forced her gaze down to the village at the foot of the hill, with its Saxon churchyard, sleepy streets, and rectangular village green dotted with grazing sheep. How peaceful Bedsley Priors looked. How small and insignificant.

When her mother had first disappeared, Lilly had felt a roiling tincture of emotions—bewilderment, grief, guilt—certain her leaving was due to something Lilly had said or done. But in her secret heart, she had also felt a shameful thrill. Something had changed. Change begot change, she knew, and she longed for more. Though Lilly still prayed fervently for her mother's return, somehow she knew that had her mother not left, her life would go on as it always had. She would ever be trapped, working in an inconsequential shop in an inconsequential village. And Lilly was certain that would never be enough.

Sighing now, Lilly began the jarring downhill slog home. Back to the endless duties of an apothecary's daughter.

Again rounding the vicarage, she slowed to a stroll, passing the butcher's, the chandler's, and the coffeehouse. Inside, Mary looked at her through the window and motioned for her to wait. Lilly paused as her friend hurried to the door. Her friend who had thankfully not had a fit in nearly a year.

"Morning, Lill." Mary thrust a warm, paper-wrapped bundle into her hand. "I insist. You need sustenance after your long . . . *mmm*, walk." Mary's grin was all too knowing, and her pale blue eyes gleamed beneath faint strawberry brows.

Lilly smiled and accepted the scone. "Thank you. Currant?"

"What else? Now, go on. I shall see you later."

She gave Mary a mock bow and continued across the mews to her father's shop. She noticed the sign bearing the apothecary's rose and *Charles Haswell, Apothecary* was looking worn, and the white paint of the many-paned bowed window was beginning to flake. She would have to suggest Father hire someone to repaint it.

For a few moments she stood there, peering through the shop-window as a customer might, while she ate her scone.

Upon the inside ledge of the bowed window stood her grand-father's tall, ornate apothecary's jar, bearing the Haswell coat of arms. Around it were displayed colorful carboys and ready-made remedies with gilded labels: *Royal English Drops, Gaskoin's Powder, True Venice Treacle*, and many more.

Three walls of the shop were lined with shelves of blue-and-cream Lambeth delftware pottery. Upon each was inscribed its contents in Latin: *C: ABSINTHII*—conserve of wormwood, useful for dropsy. *O: VULPIN*—oil of fox, distilled in spring water, good for chest complaints.

And below these shelves were rows of knobbed drawers for small simples, such as leaves, seeds, and roots.

The front counter was clear for pressing tablets, and rolling and cutting pills. The rear counter held the tools of the trade. Open for reference were several books, such as Lewis's *New Dispensatory*, and Culpeper's *Complete Herbal*. Mortars and pestles of various sizes stood at the ready, as did scales, syrup jars, scarificators and bowls for bleeding, and leeches in their jar of water, always kept hungry.

To the left of the rear counter was the door to the laboratory-kitchen, where her father heated and distilled physic through snaking copper pipes. To the right was the door to her father's surgery, the private office where he consulted with or bled patients.

Already, the shop was busy and full of life. Father had his hand on Arthur Owen's shoulder, talking to the old pig farmer in gentle admonition. Her brother, Charlie, three years her junior, dusted the shelves. Her father's seventeen-year-old apprentice, Francis Baylor, stood behind the front counter, busy with mortar and pestle. She was pleased to see both young men engaged in such industrious fashion.

She pushed open the shop door, barely hearing the familiar bell. The usual rush of voices and aromas greeted her. Treasures from distant lands and nearby meadows, dried, crushed, and distilled, filled the air with powerful, exotic appeal. It was only during these moments, coming in from the windy hills, that she could really smell their complex and ever-changing fragrance.

From the beams that striped the ceiling, strings of poppy heads, chamomile, sage, and mint hung in bunches to dry. An ancient alligator hung among them in macabre pose, teeth bared. Several missing teeth rendered him less menacing.

Once inside, Lilly realized the probable cause of the apprentice's unusual dedication. He was serving the flirtatious Dorothea Robbins, whose father owned the timber mill and the new barge yard in the neighboring hamlet of Honeystreet.

"It is not for me, of course," Miss Robbins was saying. "For I am perfectly well."

Francis Baylor shook his head in near wonder. "As I plainly see."

The girl giggled and Lilly rolled her eyes. Francis glanced up and, seeing her expression, had the decency to flush. "If you will excuse me one moment, Miss Robbins?"

"Of course."

The gangly young man walked around the counter and paused beside Lilly. Quietly, he said, "You might wish to change your frock, Miss Lilly. You would not want Mrs. Mimpurse to catch you with muddy hems."

She looked down. "Oh! I did not realize . . ."

But a glance told her pretty Dorothea Robbins *had* realized. The honey-haired girl in a charming bonnet was regarding Lilly's frock with a condescending smile.

The sound of shattering pottery brought Lilly around. Charlie stood frozen, feather duster in hand.

"Suds!" He sank to his haunches and began picking up the sharp pieces of a broken ointment jar. "Not again . . ."

Lilly hurried to his side. "It's all right, Charlie. Only an accident. I shall help you clean this up. Mind your fingers."

Dorothea Robbins strolled past them, a small parcel in gloved hand and an aloof smile on her pretty lips. Francis nearly tripped over them in his hurry to open the door for her.

Shaking her head in disgust, Lilly carried the broken pottery through the rear door into the laboratory-kitchen, where Mrs. Fowler was washing up the breakfast dishes. She thought to dash upstairs to change her frock and pin up her hair, but she had barely dumped the pieces and wiped her hands when she heard the shop bell jingle, announcing the arrival of another customer.

"Good day, Mrs. Kilgrove," she heard Francis call. "And welcome to Haswell's."

"You need not behave as though you own the place, young man," the old matron reprimanded. Mrs. Kilgrove was known for her sharp tongue, which she seemed to wield on everyone save Charlie.

"Of course not, ma'am. I am only grateful to be apprenticed to such a respected apothecary. Now, how may I help you?"

"You? I'd not tell *you* my troubles for all the prince's ponies. Nor give you leave to sell me a single lozenge. Where is Miss Haswell?"

Lilly sighed. So much for changing her frock.

That afternoon, while Francis used the cork borer to fashion bottle stoppers, Lilly was bored indeed. She cleaned the front counter, all the while daydreaming about some gentleman traveler—wounded, ideally—falling into the shop, and in love with her. She had just reached the part where he begged her to run away with him when her cloth reached the bear-shaped pottery jar on the counter's far end. She paused, fanciful images fading. She wondered once more why her father insisted on stocking the useless remedy.

"Have we sold any bear grease lately?" she idly asked.

Francis paused in his work. "Yes, to several gentlemen yesterday."

"Would you try it, had you the need?"

He grimaced. "Why would I? I have a full head of hair."

A bit too full, Lilly thought, taking in his brown, wavy mop of hair.

Her father came in and stood, arms crossed, before his apprentice. "Mr. Baylor," he demanded sternly, "did I not ask you to compound another batch of Pierquin's Diuretic?"

Lilly saw the young man blanch.

"Right. Sorry, sir."

"You *do* recall the instructions I gave you only last week?"

Lilly held her breath.

"Of course I remember, sir. It was, after all, only last week." He stole a glance at Lilly, the plea for help evident in his wide eyes.

Stepping away from the counter with the cleaning cloth, Lilly said with as much nonchalance as she could muster, "That one is simple at least, as it has only three ingredients."

"Three, right," Francis parroted. "Very simple."

Lilly felt her father's gaze on the back of her head as she began polishing the shopwindow. "I cannot bear to compound Pierquin's," she continued, keeping her eyes focused upon her task. "It is"—she wiggled her fingers dramatically, hoping Francis was watching— "a *thousand* times worse than any other."

Behind her, Francis caught on. "Which of course it would be, with all those . . . millipedes."

"Exactly," she replied casually. "Which is why I am so relieved Father asked *you* to prepare it."

Glancing over her shoulder and seeing that her father was again facing Francis at the counter, his back to her, she breathed on the window glass and with her finger wrote *berry*. "I have not had to do so since *June*." She then held up her little finger, miming the act of drinking daintily.

After watching her surreptitiously, Francis announced, "Pierquin's Diuretic: macerated millipedes and juniper berries boiled in tea."

"In white *wine*, Mr. Baylor," Charles Haswell said between clenched teeth. "Tea, indeed. You had better study harder, young man, if you want to excel as my pupil." He threw Lilly a flinty look of two parts irritation to one part paternal pride. *"Professor Lilly* will not always be on hand to rescue you."

"Right. Sorry, sir."

Shaking his head, her father left them, taking the day's post back to the surgery to do a bit of reading and, she guessed, a bit of napping.

Francis looked at Lilly, shoulders drooping. "How do you do it? I must read and reread things ten times over before I remember them. It all comes so easily to you."

She shrugged. "It is in my blood, I suppose."

"It is more than that. Is there nothing you cannot remember?"

She strolled over to the old globe on its stand in the corner. Foregoing the cloth, she ran her fingers over its surface. "Probably a great many things."

"I do not believe it. Quick—Godfrey's Cordial."

"Francis. That one is easy. You know it is so popular we must prepare it every week—sassafras, aniseed, caraway, opium, sugar . . ."

"Stoughton's Bitters?"

She traced her finger over the West Indies. "Gentian root, orange peel, cochineal powder . . ."

"On what page in Culpeper's *Herbal* would you find, say, *saffron?*"

"I don't know. . . ." She glanced up. "Maybe, one hundred forty-four?"

"And what is listed after *saffron?*"

"Do you not wish to check my answer?"

He shook his head, waiting.

She sighed. "Well, *meadow saffron,* of course, then *scurvy-grass* in all its varieties, *self-heal, sage, saltwort* . . . It is in alphabetical order for the most part after all."

He stared at her, shaking his head. "You should be the apprentice. Not I."

Walking back to the counter, she said, "You know girls cannot be apothecaries. I can only assist."

"Lucky for me, or I'd be out of a post."

She tossed the dustcloth onto the rear counter. "Never fear. Even if I could, I should not want to work here all my life."

He looked nearly stricken. "But, Lilly, with your abilities—"

She cut him off. "You heard Father—even he realizes I shall not always be here to help."

Much to Lilly's relief, the shop bell rang, putting an end to the uncomfortable conversation.

When nearly an hour had passed and her father had still not come out from his surgery, Lilly grew concerned. His afternoon naps never lasted for more than half an hour.

She knocked softly on the surgery door. There was no answer. She pushed the door open anyway. "Father?"

Her father sat at his desk, head in his hands.

"Father, what is it? Are you all right?"

"No. I don't believe I am."

Alarmed, Lilly stepped inside the small room, closing the door behind her. "What has happened?"

He lifted his head. "I've had a letter."

Lilly regarded the fine piece of stationery upon his desk. "So I see." She swallowed. "From . . . Mother?"

The look he gave her held equal measures of surprise, incredulity, and pain. "No."

She bit her lip and waited.

He sighed. "It is from Mr. Jonathan and Ruth Elliott."

"Elliott?" None of their acquaintances bore that name.

"Your aunt and uncle Elliott. Your mother's brother."

She almost blurted, *Have they seen her?* but thought the better of it. She did not want to conjure that look upon her father's face again.

Instead she said, "I do not remember an aunt and uncle Elliott."

"How could you? You have never laid eyes on them. But you shall. They are coming all the way from London to pay a call this Friday— whether I like it or not."

"Why should you not like it? They are family, are they not?"

He looked away, toward the surgery window. "I suppose that depends upon your definition of the term."

"But you have met them?"

"Yes, many years ago." He frowned. "It was not a happy occasion."

"Do they know . . . ?" There was no need to spell out the painful subject her father habitually avoided.

"Yes. I wrote to them some time afterward."

"What do you think they want?"

Her father's features were pinched. "I shudder to think."

Seeing his distress, she laid a reassuring hand on his shoulder. "Perhaps they merely wish to reestablish bonds with us."

He looked up at her, his blue eyes glinting in the late afternoon sun slanting through the window. "I admire your hopeful outlook, my dear. But I would caution you against it. Mark my words, Lilly. We will rue this visit for years to come."

When [Jane's brother] Edward was 16,
the Knights adopted him as their heir.
It was not uncommon for wealthy relatives to take in a child
from a less fortunate branch of the family.

—JANE AUSTEN SOCIETY OF NORTH AMERICA

CHAPTER 2

Lilly watched from an upstairs window as a post chaise pulled by two matched bays came to a halt before the shop. When the postillion clambered down from his mount and opened the carriage door, a tall, portly man in hat and greatcoat stepped out. He then turned and assisted a dainty woman in fur-trimmed cloak and hat. Lilly hurried down the stairs and peeked through the door of the laboratory-kitchen as Father opened the shop door.

"Elliott. Ruth," he said. "Welcome."

The man took her father's measure. "Haswell. You are looking fit, I must say."

"Benefit of the profession, I suppose. Do come in." He took their coats and gestured them inside.

Taking in her surroundings, Ruth Elliott asked tentatively, "You live here, in your shop?"

"Why, yes—behind and above it."

"Is that common with men of your trade?" she asked.

"Yes. I believe it is common with men of most professions. Now, please, come into the sitting room."

Taking her cue, Lilly hurried to precede them up the stairs. Straightening her mother's miniature portrait on the end table, she stood nervously behind the settee as her father escorted their guests inside.

"Here we are. Do be seated—anywhere you like. Oh, there you are, my dear. May I introduce my daughter, Lilly. Lilly, this is your aunt and uncle Elliott."

Lilly curtsied. "How do you do. I am pleased to meet you both."

"Lilly?" Ruth Elliott repeated skeptically, arranging herself in an armchair.

"Yes," Lilly said. "Short for Lillian."

"Ah, yes, after Mother," Jonathan Elliott said, taking a seat. "That is, your grandmother."

Lilly smiled. She had not known. "But almost nobody calls me that."

"Lillian, a young lady ought to use her given name," her aunt said. "You are too old for pet names, do you not think?"

Lilly felt her smile waver. "Well, you must be tired and hungry from your journey. Will you have tea?" She gestured toward the tea service and tray of assorted tarts, scones, and biscuits.

"You employ a cook, then?" Aunt Elliott asked.

Lilly nodded. "Mrs. Fowler cooks and cleans, but these were provided by a kindly neighbor. An old friend of Mother's, actually. Here, let me pour the tea." Lilly began to serve, hoping to put into practice all that her mother had taught her long ago. She had even rehearsed yesterday, heeding Mrs. Mimpurse's gentle admonitions, but still her hands shook now.

She felt her aunt's gaze upon her every move as she handed her the first cup.

"And where is the boy?" Uncle Elliott asked. "A young Charles, I believe, you mentioned in your letter?"

"Yes," her father answered, accepting a cup from Lilly. "I expect him any moment."

27

"And young Charles is what age now?" Jonathan Elliott asked. "Thirteen? Fourteen?"

When Father hesitated, Lilly supplied, "Fifteen."

"Fifteen," Uncle Elliott repeated. "And do you plan for him to take over your shop one day?"

Charles Haswell studied his teacup. "I had hoped, but now I am not certain."

The Elliotts glanced at one another, and Jonathan Elliott smiled. "Well, that is good to hear."

Her father frowned. "Why on earth would it be?"

"Well, Haswell. We need to meet the boy first, of course, see how we three get on, but I can say that it has occurred to Mrs. Elliott and myself that it might be time to adopt an heir. Providence has not blessed us with a child of our own, and I at least"—he smiled at his wife—"am getting up in years. One must think of the future."

Lilly nearly spilled her tea. "But Charlie has a family," she said quickly. "Us."

"Of course he has, my dear," Aunt Elliott soothed. "And that would not change."

"It is done, you know," Uncle Elliott said. "Legal adoption for inheritance purposes. Quite common."

Lilly murmured, "I had not realized."

"It is not as if we would take him from you completely," Aunt Elliott assured her, then shifted her gaze to her brother-in-law. "Between us, we could determine a visiting arrangement that suits us all. Assuming you and young Charles are amenable, of course."

"Have you no other close relatives?" Lilly asked, feeling panic begin to rise.

Uncle Elliott shifted uncomfortably on the saggy settee. "I do have one young cousin who might suit—if he were not such a despicable character. But a nephew would be my first choice. And, well, Charles is my sister's son." He beamed at them both, as if this would dissolve their disbelief and despair.

As Lilly looked at the smiling face of Jonathan Elliott, she thought how odd it was that this portly man of middle years was her own mother's brother. He appeared years older, for Rosamond Haswell had always been so youthful, slender and pretty. Beyond the man's dark hair and brown eyes, she could find no resemblance to the portrait— nor her memory—of her mother.

The thought of Charlie leaving them, visits home not withstanding, filled Lilly with dread. Her little brother living in London without their father? Without Mary or Mrs. Mimpurse? Without *her*?

She looked to her father for help, expecting at any moment for him to refuse the Elliotts in no uncertain terms. Hoping he would. But then another line of thought presented itself. Might this be the opportunity she had prayed about for Charlie? With her aunt and uncle's resources, could they not find a specially equipped school, although Father insisted none existed for boys like Charlie? Or even a learned tutor who might help Charlie grasp new ideas, adapt to his limitations, and, well . . . grow up?

Lilly stood. "Father, might you help me downstairs a moment?"

"Hmm? Oh, of course." He rose. "Excuse us a moment."

He followed her down to the laboratory-kitchen.

"I know what you are thinking, Lilly," he began, speaking in low tones.

"Do you? I am thinking this might be a wonderful opportunity for Charlie."

He looked at her askance.

"Yes, I know," she continued. "My first instinct was to refuse them and keep dear Charlie here with us. But that would be selfish, would it not? Should we not give Charlie every opportunity to learn, to improve himself? Mr. Marsh did little for him. You and I try, but in London there might be new schools, new tutors, or methods that will take decades to reach us here in Bedsley Priors. Please do not reject their offer for the sake of revenge."

He snorted. "Another man might seek revenge for his wife being cut off from her family simply for marrying him." His voice began to rise. "Followed by nearly twenty years of cold silence, only to have them show up now and ask for one of his most treasured—" He broke off, ran a hand through his thinning reddish-brown hair, and forced his voice back down to a whisper. "But if I truly thought they would do Charlie good . . ."

"Father, I know you will worry, but—"

He grasped her arms. "Lilly. I do not worry about Charlie. Not in the way you mean. I do not worry about him leaving us, for he never shall. Rather, I worry about his hopes being raised and his feelings crushed."

"But—"

"Lilly. The Elliotts will never adopt him as heir. Not once they realize—"

"Hallo, Father!" Charlie bounded through the garden door, dirt on his sleeves and a smile on his face. "Mrs. M. said I was to hurry home. I was at Mr. Fowler's. He has a litter of puppies. Are 'em very nice?"

Lilly bit her lip and smiled gently at her brother. "They are very nice. Now do wash your face and hands and put on a clean shirt. All right?"

Her father moved to the door. "Then join us in the sitting room."

"And Charlie?" Lilly added. "Do your best to remain calm and speak slowly. Let them see how sweet and polite young Charles Haswell is."

Her brother wrinkled up his face. "Who's he?"

"Here we are." Lilly brought in another plate of tarts and currant scones, though no one had touched the first. "May I pour more tea for anyone?"

"None for me." Aunt Elliott touched a linen cloth to her thin lips.

Uncle Elliott held out his cup. "Thank you. I know it must be quite a shock—Rosamond's family showing up after all this time. If it is any consolation, we both regret having remained distant so long."

Father, taking his seat again, nodded. "I will say I was surprised to receive your letter, especially when I had written to let you know that Rosamond was . . . no longer with us."

"Yes. . . ." Uncle Elliott looked down at his hands, and his wife studied her own as well, leaving Lilly to wonder if they knew something about her mother or had been in contact with her.

Father cleared his throat. "I believe your intentions toward Charlie are sincere and honorable, but I must tell you, I do not think an arrangement likely."

"But why?" Aunt Elliott raised her eyes, clearly stunned. "Surely you realize what you are denying your son?"

"I deny him nothing. You see, my son is the dearest, sweetest-natured boy you will likely ever meet, but—"

The sitting room door banged open and Charlie strode in, looking quite presentable in a clean white shirt tucked into his breeches and a wide smile on his boyish, handsome face. He had even combed his coppery-blond hair.

Her father rose. "And this is my son, Charlie. Charlie, say hello to your aunt and uncle Elliott."

Charlie stuck out his hand toward Aunt Elliott. She smiled, but eyed it skeptically, finally touching it with gloved fingers.

"Hallo," Charlie said. "I've never had an aunt and uncle before. Our friend Mary has two of each, if you can believe it."

The Elliotts smiled and exchanged pleased glances.

"So, young Charles," Mr. Elliott began, "your father has been telling us that you are fifteen years old."

" 'At's right. But all the lads say I look younger—act it too." Charlie laughed as though he'd made a fine joke.

"Well, you have a good many years ahead of you to grow up. Have you given any thought to what you will take up?"

Charlie tilted his head. "Take up?"

"Yes, for your profession. The law, for example, or the church?"

"Oh, no. I can barely fink what I am to do tomorrow, or remember what I did yesterday. But Lilly remembers everyfing." He turned to her. "Don't you, Lilly?"

She began to demur. "Well . . ."

" 'Tis true," Charlie insisted. "Francis—he's Father's apprentice—tested her, like. Picked a number from one of Father's books and she remembered everyfing on the page!"

"Not everything, Charlie, I am sure," Lilly said, embarrassed. "Aunt and Uncle Elliott have not come all this way to hear fibble-fable about me. Now, do tell them about your work in the physic garden."

31

He shrugged. "I just do what Father says I ought."

"But our garden has never looked as fine as it did this year." She looked at the Elliotts. "If it were not so late in the season, I would show you." She squeezed her brother's shoulder. "You have a way with plants, Charlie. Do not be modest."

Before he could respond, Mrs. Elliott asked, "Are you in school, Charles?"

"I was. But I guess I learnt all Mr. Marsh knows, for he said 'ere was nofing more he could do wi' me."

"Yes, well, Charlie," Father said kindly, "some lads are gifted at book learning and others at working with their hands. That is where you excel, my boy. I show you how to do something in the garden or in the laboratory, and you work harder at it than any lad I know."

Charlie smiled at his father's praise, and Lilly felt tears prick her eyes. Her father did not praise him often enough. Nor did she.

Aunt and Uncle Elliott did not smile, however. They looked at each other, then at her father with question—and disappointment—in their expressions.

Charles Haswell took a deep breath. "Charlie, why don't you run over and thank Mrs. Mimpurse for her delightful sweets?"

Charlie eagerly stood. "I had better eat one first if I am to tell her how good 'em are!"

"Of course. Take the whole tray."

"Careful!" Lilly rose quickly and helped Charlie pick up one of the trays, then opened the door for him. When he was gone, she closed the door behind him, shutting in the awkward tension in the small room.

From the stairwell came the sound of a crash—metal tray on plank floor. Followed by a muffled call of, "I'm all right!"

When the din faded, Jonathan Elliott cleared his throat. "I am afraid we have been rather hasty. We did not realize . . ."

"Of course you did not," Father interrupted. "How could you?"

When both Elliotts sheepishly lowered their heads, Father hastened to add, "I meant only that, when I wrote, I simply mentioned that Rosamond had left me with . . . that is, left behind . . ." He sighed in frustration. "That she *had* two children—a daughter and a son. I never thought to mention Charlie's . . . limitations. Never dreamed you'd need know." He leaned his elbows on his knees. "You see, Rosamond suffered an extremely difficult lying-in with Charlie. He was far too long in reaching the air he desperately needed. I believe it was this, and no innate defect, that caused his delayed mental development."

"But he isn't, well, an imbecile or anything," Lilly hurried to explain. "Just a bit slow, I suppose you would say. In time, he might very well catch up."

"Lilly, we do not know that," Father admonished. "It would be unfair to offer that hope to others, however dearly we cling to it ourselves."

"But with education, and special tutoring . . ." Lilly looked imploringly at the Elliotts. "I am certain in London, there must be many opportunities for a boy like Charlie."

"I doubt that is the case," Uncle Elliott said, his expression sober. "And even if it were, I must be honest and tell you that I do not feel I can name your son as my heir. While he would no doubt reap some benefit, I have my own estate to think of. I must choose someone who can manage it well."

It was Lilly's turn to hang her head.

"My dear." Her aunt's voice was surprisingly warm. "May I say your concern for your brother is most admirable and touches me deeply. A lesser girl might have begrudged her sibling such an opportunity."

Looking up, Lilly slowly shook her head. "Never."

"I promise you this," Ruth Elliott said. "If we hear of any special school or teacher for boys of Charlie's, well, special qualities, I shall write you directly."

"Thank you."

Her aunt's gaze lingered. "Do not take offense, my dear, but I cannot help but wish that *you* were a boy."

They shared a rueful smile.

"Now, are you really as bright as your brother boasts?"

In Bartholomew Lane, the drink called coffee—
which closes the orifice of the stomach, fortifies
the heat within, and maketh the heart lightsom . . . is to be
sold both in the morning and at three in the afternoon.

—LONDON PUBLIC ADVERTISER, 1657

CHAPTER 3

In the coffeehouse the next morning, Lilly sat on her usual stool in the kitchen. It had been her place for as long as she could remember, which was long indeed. From the adjacent scullery came the rhythmic *rustle, rustle, rustle* of scrubbing and an occasional tinny clang as the kitchen girl, Jane, went about her work. Over this mild clatter, Lilly recounted the Elliotts' visit to her friend Mary, who stood at the worktable, cutting ginger biscuits. Paying no heed, Charlie hunched at the little table in the corner, picking out the caraway seeds from a piece of seedcake. He counted each seed and laid it neatly on a plate beside the others.

"If you don't like it, Charlie, you needn't eat it," Mary said. Her voice and round, pale blue eyes emanated irritation and affection both.

"Ninety-seven seeds, Mary. 'At's fine, fine."

With the back of her hand, Mary pushed a strand of dull strawberry hair from her milky round face. "You know I don't like to see my good baking wasted. At least feed it to the birds, all right?"

Charlie nodded. "Birds likes seeds." He put on his coat, then carried the plate out the door to the kitchen garden.

"Mind you bring back the plate," Mary called after him.

Though it was an autumn day, it was always warm in the kitchen, so the window stood ajar. Lilly realized her brother had settled himself on a bench beneath it, for through it, they heard him begin counting all over again. "One, two, tree . . ."

Lilly shook her head, chagrined.

Mary said quietly, "Don't fret about Charlie. Probably find a post in a counting house one day and end up richer than the Marlows."

From the open window, Lilly heard quick footsteps on the stone garden path. A female voice, in tense, pinched tones said, "Charlie Haswell, you are a sneak and a spy."

Lilly's mouth fell open and she turned toward the door. But Mary placed a staying hand on her shoulder and shook her head, finger to her lips.

"If you tell anybody what you saw—"

"I saw nofing," Charlie said. "I was behind a tree."

"Heard then. Or thought you heard." The girl attempted to whisper, but in her agitation her voice rose. Lilly recognized it as Dorothea Robbins's voice. "I will have you know I did not allow him to so much as kiss my glove. Do you understand?"

"Yes, miss."

"And you must promise that you won't say anything. That you will not even mention my name."

"All right, miss."

Frustration heightened her pitch. "What were you doing in the wood anyway?"

"Nofing. Just sittin' and countin'."

"Counting? Counting what?"

Lilly and Mary exchanged knowing looks.

"Red leaves on the trees."

"What on earth for?"

"Just like to is all."

Miss Robbins sounded incredulous. "But it's not natural."

"Oh yes, miss. Very natural, trees are. 'Tis why I likes 'em."

The footsteps marched away as they had come. When the sound faded, Mary stepped to the door and held it open.

"Everything all right, Charlie?"

Lilly could hear the hesitation in his voice. "Uh . . . yes, Mary."

"Did you get the birds fed?"

"Oh . . . yes."

Lilly rose and joined Mary at the door. She saw Charlie on his feet, dusting seedcake crumbs from his breeches.

"Well, good-bye," he said and lurched away in his awkward gait.

"Charlie?" Lilly called after him.

He turned and looked at her, clearly troubled.

Lilly bit her lip. "Nothing. I shall see you later."

The two young women returned to their places at the worktable.

Lilly began picking at her own piece of seedcake. "The man Miss Robbins was with in the wood. I suppose it was Francis."

Mary kept her eyes on the biscuits as she placed them on the pan. "Do you? I shouldn't think so."

"You would if you saw them flirting with one another in the shop."

Mary shrugged. "It is her nature to flirt, I think. Perhaps after this she'll be more circumspect."

"I doubt it," Lilly said, then recalled that Francis had taken ill the previous day. Miss Robbins had not mentioned when the tête-à-tête had occurred, but likely quite recently. So perhaps it had not been Francis after all. . . .

"You aren't going to ask Charlie about it, are you?" Mary asked.

Lilly hesitated.

"Lill, don't. You wouldn't want him to break a promise to a lady— no matter if the lady is Dorothea Robbins."

"I suppose you are right. Must you always be right, Mary?"

Mary put a dough-crusted hand to her brow in mock melodrama. "It is a curse I must bear up under somehow." She eyed Lilly's plate. "Now, are you going to eat my cake or not?"

⚘

That afternoon, diminutive Jack Dubin stepped into the shop, a wax-sealed missive in his hand.

"Letter by special messenger—that's me—for one Miss Lillian Haswell. You wouldn't know anybody by that name, now, would ya?"

Cheeky boy. Stepping around the counter, Lilly swiped the letter from him. "You know very well who I am, Jack." She tossed him a coin. "Here is a little something for your trouble."

He looked at the coin in his palm. "A very little!"

"Well, try delivering with less wit next time."

Lilly retreated through the back door and took her time slitting open the red wax seal. It was the first time she had ever received a letter by messenger. Or any letter, addressed specifically and solely to her. How she had once longed for a letter from her mother. But none had ever come.

She opened it and saw it was from Aunt and Uncle Elliott, written from their lodgings across the canal in Honeystreet, just a short stroll away.

My dear niece,

> *We very much enjoyed meeting you yesterday, though the circumstances were no doubt trying for you all. Would you please do us the honor of dining with us this evening here at The George at seven? We would very much like to deepen our acquaintance with you before we return to London.*
>
> *Sincerely,*
> *Mr. and Mrs. Jonathan Elliott*

Still holding the letter, she wandered back into the shop, and was surprised to see Jack Dubin still there.

"What's it to be, love?" he asked. "I'm to take back your reply."

"Oh." She hesitated. Should she refuse out of loyalty to her rejected brother? For the sake of her long-spurned father and mother? After all, these people were strangers to her—strangers by choice.

But by choice no longer.

"Tell them I accept."

Lilly had eaten at The George before, though not recently. During the first few months after her mother's disappearance, her father, dazed and struggling to care for his children as well as his shop, had taken them to the then-new establishment whenever Mrs. Fowler had a day off. Finally he and Lilly, under the tutelage of Mrs. Mimpurse, had learned to cook simple meals for themselves.

During her mother's absence, the kitchen had slowly transformed into a laboratory-kitchen, as the distillation and compounding apparatus slowly made their way into the room Mother had doggedly declared off limits before. Now, despite Mrs. Fowler's protests, stove, cupboards, and table saw double duty in food and medicinal preparation. Lilly often wondered how long it would be until they accidentally sat down to a meal of arsenic or digitalis while their patients languished with cure-alls of cod and leek soup.

Mary, who had a knack for such things, had come over earlier to dress Lilly's hair, coiling and pinning her long plait atop her head, curls at her temples. Now donning her best gown for the occasion—the printed muslin with lace tips, normally reserved for churchgoing—Lilly descended the stairs at a quarter before the hour, cloak over her arm.

The door of Francis's bedchamber was open and she looked in on the miserable young man, who had lain abed ill since yesterday. Lying propped on his pillows, his brown eyes widened and brows rose when he saw her. "Where are you off to?"

"Supper with my aunt and uncle. At The George."

"Oh. Right." Still, he stared at her.

Stepping into the pantry that had long served as the apprentice's bedchamber, Lilly sat on the edge of the narrow bed and removed the cloth from his forehead. "How are you feeling?"

"Two parts dizzy and a drachm of weak."

She touched his forehead. "Your fever has abated somewhat."

She rose to her feet and dipped the cloth in a basin of water on the room's single chest of drawers. "Your color is better also. I believe Father is right—the patient will live."

"Is he relieved or disappointed at that prognosis?"

"Relieved, of course." She added with a grin, "Otherwise he should be obliged to return your apprenticeship fee."

He did not grin back. "I thought he might be disappointed, considering I am not the cleverest apprentice he has ever had."

"Shh. You improve every day." She wrung out the cloth.

"And you, Lilly, are you relieved not to be rid of me?"

She cocked her head to one side. "Well, it would be nice to have this pantry back, and I should not mind a better balance of males to females in this house. I am sorely outnumbered."

Francis, whom she was so used to teasing, did not seem to find this amusing. Instead he looked crestfallen.

"Francis, forgive me. I see you are not your old thick-skinned self at present, ready to serve up your own share of teasing in return. Of course I am pleased you are feeling better. And that we shall have you with us for years to come."

Francis smiled ruefully and closed his eyes. "You are never so kind to me when I am well. I shall have to fall ill more often."

"I pray not, Francis. You know what Father says. . . ."

He ducked his chin and mimicked Charles Haswell's low, stern voice, " 'It does not do for a medical man to take ill.' "

"See? You remembered." She replaced the cool cloth on his forehead. "And as soon as you are fully recovered, we shall have you remembering herbals and remedies as well."

When she entered The George's dim, lamplit dining room, her uncle rose from a table in a quiet corner. Jonathan Elliott was tall enough that when he stood to greet her, his head rustled the dry hop flowers hanging from the beamed ceiling. "Lillian, we are so pleased you could join us."

Still seated, her aunt extended her hand and Lilly took it in hers. "I am pleased to do so."

"How nice you look. Your hair is lovely like that."

"Thank you. My friend Mary arranged it." Lilly took her seat and Uncle Elliott pushed in her chair.

Sitting once more he said, "We have taken the liberty of ordering supper. I hope you like beefsteaks and artichokes?"

She could not remember the last time she'd had either. "Sounds delicious."

Two old farmers sitting near the fire with tankards of ale were the only other patrons. Mrs. Dubin, who looked from Lilly to her well-dressed companions with unconcealed curiosity, served them with pragmatic efficiency.

Once their meal was before them, her aunt began. "As you know, we came here with intentions toward your brother which, sadly, are not feasible. However, your uncle and I both believe that we have not made the trip in vain, for meeting you—and of course your father and brother—has been delightful. We are especially impressed with you, my dear."

"Thank you." Lilly felt undeniable pleasure at this warm praise.

"Now, as you know, your uncle must name a male relative to inherit his entailed property. However, we do have some discretion in the distribution of personal effects, such as jewelry, furniture—even an annual allowance may be left to, say, a special young lady. I do not mean to bribe you, Lillian, but I would like you to consider an opportunity. We would like you to come live with us in London. We would hire the best tutors for you in deportment, drawing, language, and dance, and teach you all you need to know to be a proper, accomplished young lady."

Lilly's pulse accelerated. Her own days at Shaw's private girls school had ended when her mother left. Might she now finish her education as she'd longed to do?

Her aunt continued, "You might even bring that friend of yours as lady's maid if you like. We would count it a privilege to host you through a London season or two and introduce you to society . . . and perhaps even to your future husband."

"Now, Ruth, let us not get ahead of ourselves," Jonathan Elliott admonished.

Lilly's heart and head were pounding with such exhilaration, hope, and fear that she found herself speechless.

"Would you not like to see London?" Aunt Elliott asked. "To fill the gaps in your education? See the best museums, hear the finest concerts, dance at the most exclusive balls? Perhaps even travel to Italy or Spain?"

Travel. An image flashed before her mind's eye. Her younger self and her mother, heads bent over an old world map . . .

Still Lilly said nothing, just stared at the kind face of her aunt as though the woman were speaking a language Lilly could not quite make out.

Finally Lilly managed to sputter, "W-why?"

"Why?" her aunt repeated, not understanding.

"Why would you do this for me? Why would you want to? I have nothing with which to ever repay you."

Her aunt's delicate features became earnest. "I do not believe that, Lillian. Not for one moment. Your happiness, your success shall be all the repayment we ever need." She reached across the table and took her hand. "If you come to feel some fondness for us, well, that would be more than we could ask for."

Lilly battled to contain the excitement building within her. Was this not what she had long wished for? But would Father ever allow it? Tentatively, she asked, "Have you spoken to my father about this?"

Uncle shook his head. "There was no need to until we knew if you were even interested. But we shall, if you think you might be."

Aunt Elliott studied her, obvious hope in her eyes. "Shall we, Lillian? Shall we speak to him?"

Lilly took a deep breath, inhaling the hundred questions warring within her. She asked only one.

"When?"

An apothecary first of all should be a lover of piety,
one that fears God, void of envy and malice, of good competency . . .
and not given to corpulency.

—C. J. S. Thompson, *Mystery and Art of the Apothecary*

Chapter 4

Upon her return from The George, Lilly found her father standing in the laboratory-kitchen, using a scraper of horn to clean one of his mortars. He set down the instrument and wiped his hands on a cloth.

"Lilly, good. You're home. I need you to come with me to Marlow House."

Whatever excited words she might have spoken died on her lips. "Marlow House? Whatever for?"

"Sir Henry's man summoned me. Seems his master is in a great deal of pain."

"But, Sir Henry has been calling for Dr. Foster of late."

"Yes, but Foster is home in bed with the very malady that has laid our Mr. Baylor low." He added a vial to his medical case and snapped the lid shut.

She took a deep breath and blew it out between puffed cheeks. "I see."

"Why so forlorn? This is good news for us. Have I not told you that it does not do for a medical man to fall ill? It costs business—patients. Which is why I never get sick." He grinned at her, but she did not return the gesture.

"Perhaps I ought to stay here in case Francis—or Charlie—needs anything."

"Mrs. Mimpurse is on her way over. Come along. You need only carry two species jars. I cannot have them jostling about the gig while I drive."

Her natural curiosity trumped her trepidation. "What remedy do you propose?"

"I prepared traditional gout powder, of course."

Unbidden, her mind flashed the ingredients: *birthwort, red gentian root, leaves of germander, and centaury.*

"But depending on his symptoms," her father continued, putting on his greatcoat, "I may need to prescribe something stronger."

"James's Powder?" she asked.

"Too strong."

"Compound powder of ipecacuanha?"

He narrowed his eyes in thought. "Do you mean . . . ?"

Opium, potassium nitrate, vitriolated tartar, liquorice, ipecacuanha. She gave him the outmoded name. "Dover's."

"Ah. Right. I have both."

Lilly looked about her, intertwining and twisting her fingers. "I could transfer smaller amounts to vials, Father. Then you could carry them in your case."

"I prefer not to delay."

"But—"

He eyed her keenly. "You are not still afraid of Sir Henry's son, are you?"

"No. That is, not as long as you shall be there with me."

Mrs. Mimpurse, buxom and energetic, arrived from next door

and shooed them out, clucking like a mother hen. Lilly climbed up into the gig, and her father handed her the clunky jars, then circled the rig and climbed up into the seat beside her. Urging Pennywort, their mare, into a trot, he drove through the dark, windy night the short distance to Marlow House. Unlike his daughter, Charles Haswell was not fond of walking. Especially in chilly weather.

Lilly thought of a dozen ways to bring up the astounding offer her aunt and uncle had made, but she could not force out a single syllable. Not yet. In any case, the howling wind would only swallow her words. There would be time later, once the current crisis was passed and she'd somehow found the courage to withstand the hurt that would surely appear in her father's eyes when she told him she longed to accept.

When they arrived, Sir Henry's butler, Mr. Withers, greeted them and took their coats. He then led them through the large manor and up the long curved staircase. Following her father, Lilly carefully carried the two pottery jars. At the far end of the corridor, Withers knocked softly on a closed door and then opened it to them.

They passed through the outer dressing room and then entered the inner bedchamber. From the canopied bed, the baronet lifted his arm in a weak gesture of welcome.

"Haswell, good of you to come."

"Of course, Sir Henry. And this is my capable assistant, Miss Haswell."

Even in his pain, the grey-haired man smiled politely to her, the expression lifting the bushy silver sideburns. She knew the baronet was in his fifties, yet he looked older. "Ah yes, your daughter. How do you do?"

Lilly dipped an awkward curtsy.

"Very pretty," Sir Henry said, then shifted his gaze to her father. "More and more like her mother, is she not?"

Her father looked at her, then quickly away. "Yes, rather."

Sir Henry studied her father's averted face. "Still no word?"

Setting down his case, her father drew himself up briskly. "No word. Now, let us see what we can do to alleviate your discomfort. . . ."

Lilly waited at a polite distance from the bed while her father questioned the baronet in low tones about his symptoms. Twice at her father's bidding she retrieved vials or instruments from his case and once filled a water glass at the bedside table.

When her father began lifting the blankets from the man's legs, he paused.

"Lilly. I think you've done all I need. Perhaps you might take yourself to the kitchen and wait for me there? If Mrs. Tobias is still awake, she might offer you a cup of chocolate. And if not, at least the fire will keep you warm."

"Very well, Father."

"Take a candle."

Nodding, she took the candle holder and let herself from the room.

She did not admit she did not know the way to the kitchen from Sir Henry's room. She had been to Marlow House before but had always waited in the kitchen while her father went up to see Sir Henry, or Lady Marlow, before her passing.

Lilly held the candle high and started down the dark, broad corridor. High upon its walls were formal portraits of Marlows past—men in coat and cravat, or military regalia; ladies in fine gowns and jewels—as well as paintings of the hunt, rearing horses, hounds with bared teeth, and foxes with hideous wide-eyed expressions of pain and fear.

In the light of the candle, those eyes seemed to glare at her. The dogs, to growl at her. She shivered.

She passed the main staircase and continued to the corridor's end, assuming she would there find the servants' stairway down to the kitchen.

Suddenly she heard a noise behind her. She spun around, holding her candle before her like a sword. But the corridor was empty.

She continued on until she heard footsteps to her left. She whirled. But her candle only illuminated more paintings and tapestries upon the wall.

She walked faster.

Nearby she heard a scrape, saw a dark stab of movement before her, then felt a rush of air. Her candle was out before her mind could identify what she had seen. And then she saw nothing at all. Nothing but blackness.

"Who is there?" she demanded in an airy croak.

She took a tentative step backward, toward her father and safety, but an arm grabbed her from behind and a hand cupped her mouth, catching her cry and rendering it useless.

"Shh . . ." a male voice whispered. "Did you hear something?"

For one tense second, the arm remained clasped about her waist and the other hand covered her mouth, but then, as quickly as it came, the contact was broken, the hands gone from her.

Indignation chased away fear. Those had not been phantom hands touching her. "Yes. I heard something. You, no doubt. You enjoyed frightening me, did you not?"

A door opened nearby; footsteps receded and promptly returned. Roderick Marlow appeared in a doorway, carrying a glowing candle lamp he had apparently retrieved from the nearby room. With it, he lit a wall sconce. In its light she could see that he was taller and broader than he had been when she had last seen him. His hair and brows just as dark. How old was he now—three and twenty? Four?

"Why are you wandering about in the dark?" He cocked his head to one side, regarding her. "Are you lost?"

"No. Merely on the way to the kitchen."

One dark brow rose. "And where you live, the kitchen is above-stairs?"

She exhaled sharply. "Of course not. I was on my way down."

"You passed the staircase."

"I was looking for the servants' stairs—"

"Are you a servant?"

"No. The apothecary's daughter."

"Ah, I remember. The bran-faced thief."

Irritation surged at this ungentlemanly reference to her freckles.

Before she could respond, he continued. "That explains why you are sneaking about. Perhaps I shall have to search your pockets." He took a step closer. "See if you have helped yourself to any valuables."

She backed away again. "I have never stolen anything in my life!"

"Except a peony?"

"Except a peony," she allowed.

He parted his lips, then paused. "What is your name? I forget."

"Lilly Haswell."

"Ah. Haswell. Of course."

He continued to step forward while she backed away, as if in some slow, inelegant dance.

"And do you do miracles, Lilly Haswell, as your father supposedly does?"

She hesitated, shook her head. "No."

"You do not believe in miracles?"

"I do."

"Why? Have you not prayed for your mother's return?"

She swallowed the painful lump in her throat. "Yes."

"And has she?"

"Not as yet."

He barked a laugh. "Still hoping?"

"Every day."

He stopped where he was. "Such faith . . . such fervency. And yet, nothing. Is it any wonder I do not believe?"

"No wonder. But sad if true." She ceased moving as well.

"I prayed for my mother, too, you know. But that did not stop her from dying. Where were your father's miracles then?"

"I am sorry," she whispered. "We can only do so much."

"Which is why we must take what we want in this life, Miss Haswell. Make our own way. Not wait for some fat, hairless angel to deliver our whims on a silver platter." He lifted the candle lamp and peered at her. "Do I offend you?"

"Yes. As you no doubt intend to."

He laughed again. "True, I am a skilled offender. Whereas my father is a skilled . . . ingratiator. And yours a healer or pretender—I am not certain which. And you, Miss Lilly Haswell, what are you?"

When she hesitated, he smirked and turned away dismissively, clearly not expecting an answer from a frightened girl.

"A rememberer."

He turned back to her, studying her face in the flickering light. Surprised, perhaps, to see how serious and somber she was.

"How so?" He asked, his smirk gone.

She swallowed and answered quietly, "I remember everything. Whether I wish to or not."

They stared at one another. He took another step closer. Suddenly a door opened far down the corridor from which she had come. He grasped her wrist and pulled her through a narrow door she had not even known was there. She gasped, but did not scream.

"This old place is full of secret passages and trapdoors," he whispered, leading her along a dark narrow passageway, holding the candle lamp to light their way.

"Where are you taking me?"

"You said you sought the kitchen."

He pushed open a timbered door and paused to light the lamp at the top of a steep set of stairs. Growing anxious about being alone with him, Lilly stepped around and preceded him down the narrow stairs, even though her own shadow made it difficult to see. When she reached the bottom door, she lifted the latch but could not make it release. When she turned, he was right there.

"It sometimes jams." But he made no move to open it. He brought the light closer to her face. His eyes glinted oddly in the candle's glow, the right eye appearing a deeper shade than the left. "You know, Lilly Haswell," he said in a low voice, "freckles or no, you might be handsome one day."

He reached around her to give the latch a sharp jerk, the action bringing his hand close to the small of her back and his face near to hers.

Feeling the door give behind her and imagining the safety of a bright fire and no-nonsense Mrs. Tobias beyond, she smiled sweetly up at him and said, "Well, that makes one of us."

She pushed her way backwards into the kitchen. Her smile of triumph immediately fell away. The kitchen was empty, the fire but embers.

In two strides he was before her, anger in his eyes. She took a step back. He, another forward.

"Lilly?" Her father came into the kitchen and Roderick stopped midstride.

"Oh! Father! You frightened me."

"Did I?" He looked from her to Roderick and his brow furrowed at seeing the young man looming so close.

"Are you . . . all right?"

She swallowed. "I am perfectly well. My flame blew out, but Mr. Marlow kindly lit another and showed me the way."

Her father looked at her, then turned to scrutinize the young man. "Did he indeed?" He held Roderick Marlow's bold stare a moment longer, then clasped Lilly's hand. "Come, my dear. It is time we took our leave."

On the ride home, her father was quiet but obviously not at peace. The wind had died down, but she still had not found the courage to bring up her aunt and uncle's offer.

"The Elliotts," her father said suddenly. "They want you to go to London?"

Nerves quaking, she forced her gaze to meet his and nodded solemnly.

But instead of the arguments and cautions she expected, he returned his eyes to the road. He drew in a long breath and said, "Perhaps it is well that you leave for a time after all."

She studied his profile for several moments, but he did not explain further. Giving up, she laid her head on his shoulder for the rest of the journey home.

DALBY'S GENUINE CARMINATIVE
Superior to all other remedies for the wind. . . .
This invaluable cordial medicine
is prepared by Frances Gell, daughter of the late
Mr. Joseph Dalby, apothecary.

—THE EDINBURGH EVENING COURANT, 1815

CHAPTER 5

O n Monday morning, Francis was feeling like his old self again and joined Lilly in the shop. She watched as he worked with the mortar and pestle, ineffectively swishing and tamping the simples within. *Must I again demonstrate proper technique?*

"Hold the pestle with a light grip, Francis," she said. "Like a quill. And press firmly in a circular motion." The swishing continued. Frustrated, she stood at his shoulder and reached her right hand over his. "Like this." She held his larger hand beneath her own, guiding his motions.

Though a year younger, he was already taller than she. When he looked down at her, standing close as she was, Lilly felt his warm breath tickling the hairs at her temple. He leaned closer yet, his brown eyes alight, and whispered, "I so enjoy your demonstrations."

She pulled away, irritated at his cheekiness, and decided now was a perfect time to tell him of her plans.

"Leaving?" Francis's voice rose. "Only two days ago you said, 'We'll have you remembering herbals and remedies in no time.'" He repeated her words with syrupy sarcasm.

She had never seen Francis so agitated and was relieved the shop was empty. "I cannot help you forever, Francis. I know you can succeed on your own if you only take your post more seriously."

"I try."

She huffed, "You spend more time learning to amuse Dorothea Robbins than learning your trade."

He ignored that. "Remember what else you said . . . ? Of course you do, for you remember everything. You said, 'I am glad you will be with us for years to come.' What about that?"

"How could I have guessed the Elliotts would offer such an opportunity?"

"An opportunity for what? To wear silk frocks and drink tea with your small finger in the air—and your nose as well?"

"No! I want to see the world, or at least London. I want to learn new things. I want to sleep in a room that does not smell of cat mint, comfrey, and rue." She thought of adding, *I want to find my mother*, but left those words unspoken. "It is different for you. You *want* to work here. I do not want to stay here my entire life, forever the apothecary's daughter, cutting pills and sweeping Father's shop. I thought you would understand. *You* left your home to pursue what you wanted. Are you sorry you did not stay in Saltford all your life?"

"No, I am not sorry to be here. At least I have not been, until now."

His reaction surprised her. "I do not understand you, Francis."

"No, Lilly. Clearly you do not."

Mary Mimpurse came into the shop that afternoon without her customary apron. Her mother's coffeehouse closed at one o'clock on Mondays, giving her the afternoon free. She dragged a stool beside the dispensing counter and watched as Lilly counted liquorice pastilles and packaged them into small paper boxes. Mary reached out and popped a liquorice lozenge into her mouth.

"These are for medicinal purposes." Lilly feigned reprimand. "You do not appear to me to have a cold, Miss Mimpurse."

Mary blithely shrugged. "Put a fancy label on it and call it medicine. I call it a sweet. Sugar or honey?"

"Honey."

"Delicious."

While Mary enjoyed her liquorice, Lilly shared her London plans and the proposed departure after Christmas. Like Francis, Mary responded with less enthusiasm than she had expected.

Eyeing her friend's piqued expression, Lilly asked, "What is the matter?"

"Nothing. I am happy for you. Truly." Mary's tone was snappy, her mouth a thin line. "You'll no doubt have a grand time and forget all about us."

"Nonsense. I don't forget anything and certainly not my oldest friend."

Mary would not meet her gaze.

Lilly laid a hand on Mary's forearm, strong, she noticed from all her stirring and kneading, much as Lilly's own were from many hours spent with mortar and pestle. "I shall miss you, Mary," she said.

Mary acknowledged this with a nod and briefly laid her hand atop Lilly's. "And I you."

"Come with me, then." Lilly slid a box toward Mary and began sealing one herself. "Aunt Elliott said I might bring you along as lady's maid."

Mary froze mid-seal. Her small mouth gaped. "Did she? Well . . . I am surprised. Surprised your aunt even knows who I am."

"She admired my hair. I told her you had done it—and about your many other talents." Lilly reached out and tweaked Mary's nose.

Her friend did not smile or seek playful revenge. Instead she rose and said officiously, "Then you must have also told her that I am much too busy slaving away in a poor coffeehouse to come to London. In fact, I had better hurry." She turned toward the door. "No doubt the *mistress* needs floors scrubbed or potatoes peeled. . . ."

"Mary! Do not take offense. You know I do not view you as my servant."

Mary turned back. "Do you not? I know you've always thought yourself above me, when in reality—"

"I do not!"

"How ironic." Mary shook her head, eyes clouded. "That *she* would suggest such an arrangement, I do not mind, but that *you*, my own—"

"Mary. I did not think. I only wished you might come with me. I am sorry! Please forgive me. . . ."

But sweet, docile Mary had already stalked from the room.

Ignoring the October chill, Lilly stood on the Honeystreet Bridge, staring far off down the canal in the fading light of evening. A ginger tabby lay curled up on the bridge, enjoying the warmth the bricks had absorbed during the day. Enjoying, too, the occasional scratch Lilly administered to its furry chin. She sighed. *If only my day had been as pleasant.*

She could see lantern light gleaming on the water, though she could not make out the shape of the vessel. Was it a narrowboat approaching, or a barge already moored for the night? She would stand there just a little longer in case it came closer. A sudden thought startled her. Perhaps she should not leave. What if Mother finally returned, only to find her gone?

She sensed someone beside her and looked over to see Charlie, his elbows on the bridge ledge, his eyes trained on the distant light.

"Were you looking for me?" Lilly asked.

"I always look for you here." He glanced at her, then away. "I want you to stay."

Father must have told him. "But, Charlie, I cannot always live with you and Father, keeping house for the two of you. I know it sounds selfish, but I want more. I am only going to Aunt and Uncle Elliott's in London. You liked them, did you not?"

"Very nice," he mumbled.

The cat rose, arched its spine, and rubbed itself against Charlie's arms. Lilly was grateful for the interruption. When Charlie reached out to stroke its back, she reminded him, "Gently."

He nodded, petting and addressing the tabby, "I know you. You're Mrs. Kilgrove's puss."

The cat relished the attention with purring and half-lidded eyes. Lilly smiled. "He likes you."

Watching her brother pet the cat, Lilly remembered something she had not thought about in a long while. Perhaps it was seeing the cat and Charlie together, here on the bridge. Here where she searched the boats.

As if the same memory had also been invoked in him, Charlie said, "I had a cat once. Ran away."

Not wanting to dwell on the sad aspect of the memory, she asked, "Do you remember that Christmas when Father gave you the little cat? I think you were eight years old."

"Yes! In a bandbox. Holes cut for air. And his little paws pokin' out, lookin' to play."

Lilly knew her father had mostly wanted a mouser for the shop, but she had rarely seen Charlie as happy as he had been that day.

Charlie bit his lip. "Then he ate the leg off the Christmas goose, and she was angry."

She? It had only been three years since Mother left, but Charlie's memory was often poor. How much did he recall? "Do you remember what Mr. Mimpurse said, when you showed him your new cat?"

"Mr. Mimpurse . . ." Charlie suddenly looked troubled. "He's gone now."

"I know."

Mr. Mimpurse had died more than six years before. Hoping to divert Charlie, she continued, "But do you remember what he said?"

When Charlie shook his head, she supplied, "He said, 'That's a jolly good puss, Charlie.' Remember?' "

" 'At's right."

"And so you named him Jolly."

"Jolly," Charlie breathed, his eyes growing soft at the memory.

Poor Jolly, Lilly thought. How Charlie had clung to that cat, always trying to hold it on his lap, to make it sleep in his bed, forever picking it up and squeezing it so tightly, Lilly feared he'd suffocate the increasingly skittish creature. Charlie was not cruel; he merely tried too hard. Cats want to come *to* you. They need time alone, time to hide away, time for daytime naps and nighttime hunts. But Charlie was young and Charlie was Charlie, and he didn't understand, no matter how often and gently their parents had tried to explain.

Lilly started. *Is that what we did?* she wondered. *Did we try too hard to hold on to Mother? Fail to give her the solitude she needed? Suffocate her with affection?*

When spring had come that long ago year, and the windows and doors began to open more often, Jolly had darted outside and was never seen again.

Not a week had passed before Charlie began bringing home strays with a vague resemblance to Jolly, or sometimes even a neighbor's cat, to the garden door for Mother to inspect.

"Is it Jolly?" he would ask, eyes shining with hope.

"No, Charlie, I am afraid not." Mother would smile with sympathy and return to the kitchen.

Soon he was presenting tabbies, then striped cats, then cats with spots. It was clear he no longer remembered what his cat had looked like. But Mother did and continued to inspect and renounce the would-be Jollies that Charlie dragged to the door all that summer and fall.

Lilly remembered wondering what it would really hurt for Mother to lie just once and say, "Yes, Charlie, you found Jolly," the next time he brought home some stray. But she never did.

Now, on the canal, the distant boat began to move. As it drew near, Lilly saw it was a narrowboat, its lantern casting flickers and shadows along the canal bank and bridge as it passed beneath them. Lilly watched carefully, studying the crew of work-roughened men talking and jesting with one other. From their boisterous laughter it seemed clear they had been moored at The George for some time, drinking a few too many ales.

No women were aboard.

It struck Lilly then. She was as pathetic as Charlie had been back when he was eight or nine, searching out every cat in the village and beyond, hoping to find his lost Jolly. Here she was, eighteen years old, still inspecting the faces of every woman she saw, hoping to find the mother she had lost. But even Charlie had eventually given up and quit searching. Father and Mother had never given Charlie another pet for fear of repeating the drawn-out melodrama. Soon they had all put it from their minds and gone on. Why could she not do the same? She would, she decided. She would go to London. Right after Christmas.

In silence, she and Charlie turned and watched the lantern light until it disappeared.

Suddenly Charlie reached over and grasped her hand—a rare gesture. "Stay."

Tears filled Lilly's eyes. "You are not making this easy." She squeezed his hand. "Do not be sad, Charlie. It won't be forever. I will come back and see you."

He stared off in the distance once more. " 'At's what she said."

Lilly's pulse quickened. "What?"

Charlie kept staring, but did not reply.

"Do you mean Mother? *She* told you she was leaving?"

"No more leaving," he whispered.

"What else did she tell you? Do you remember?"

"Don't leave, Lilly."

Lilly was torn, wishing she might extract every fragment of her brother's memory, yet not wanting to further upset him.

She drew herself up. "Come, Charlie. Father will be wanting his supper."

She returned home to find the laboratory-kitchen in more disorder than usual.

"Father, you left the large alembic on the stove again!" she called. "Please help me move it if you want any supper tonight."

Charles Haswell wandered in from his surgery, hands full of rumpled letters and bills of lading. "Sorry, sorry. Lilly, where is that order for Shipton's?"

"I put it on your desk two days ago." Lilly brought the soup pot from the cold cellar.

"Did you? I cannot find the dumble thing."

"Perhaps if you put things away instead of stacking them all over your desk."

"But I have looked everywhere."

"Father. I do not wish to spend two more hours writing it again."

"Then would you please find it for me?"

"Yes, yes. After I heat our soup. Can you find the ladle?"

He began clanging around, removing the alembic and pulling out pots and kettles from the cupboard. "I cannot find a thing in here! Heaven help us after you leave."

Lilly sighed. "Not you, too, Father. I have argued with three of the people I care about most today. I cannot stand to disappoint you as well. If you want me to stay, just say so."

"Stay? Stay here and clean after me and sort my mess because I am a disorganized fool? Absolutely not. Go."

"You truly want me to go?"

"Well, I don't want you to stay and become like your mother."

Lilly gasped. "Father!"

He paused in his search to look at her earnestly. "What I mean is—I do not want you to stay here and always wonder, always long for what you might have missed. Find out now, before . . ."

"Before?" she asked.

He sighed. "Before there is a husband—and children—to leave behind."

"Oh, Father." Tears filled her eyes for the second time that evening. She squeezed his arm, and the two shared a rare moment of silent empathy. Then he cleared his throat and resumed his search.

Lilly moved to the cupboard and pulled out a quarter loaf of stout brown bread. She forced a light tone. "Charlie told me that Mother spoke to him before she left. Said she would come back, that she would not be gone forever. Do you think it possible?"

"That she planned only a short absence?" He shook his head. "I do not know. She was here one day and gone the next. Told me nothing. Perhaps she lied to Charlie to ease her conscience. Or Charlie might have remembered incorrectly or imagined the exchange. I doubt we shall ever know."

Finding a clean wooden paddle, Lilly used it to stir the soup, but her mind was far away. "I think perhaps she did lie, only meaning to comfort him. For I told Charlie I wouldn't be gone forever, and that was a lie as well. Was it not? For I really do not know that. If I return soon, it will only be because I am an utter failure. Unable to learn what the tutors try to teach me, an embarrassment to the Elliotts."

"Which of course you will not be."

"I pray not, but what if the opposite is true. If I succeed, even modestly, will I not stay two years or more? She mentioned two seasons."

"And if you have the ultimate success . . ." He let the thought trail off.

"What do you mean?"

"Why, to find a suitable husband, of course."

Lilly felt a thrill of anticipation at his words. "I had not thought of that as my principle aim, but I suppose you are right."

"In your aunt's eyes, what else could it be? If you are a success that means you will be sought after by several eligible men and married to the richest or best connected among them. And assuming he is a London man, you might very well live there forever."

Still blindly stirring, Lilly bit back a smile. Her daydreams of a handsome gentleman falling in love with her no longer seemed so foolishly fantastic.

"Which is a sad prospect for your old father, but that is life, and we cannot stop it. Thankfully there are decent roads between here and London, and there is always the canal." He pulled out the ladle from the cupboard with triumphant flourish. "Now, when are you to depart?"

PART II

The apothecary of this country is qualified by
education to attend at the bedside of the sick, and,
being in general better acquainted with pharmacy
than the physicians of English universities . . .
is often the most successful practitioner.

—JEREMIAH JENKINS, OBSERVATIONS ON THE PRESENT STATE OF
THE PROFESSION AND TRADE OF MEDICINE, 1810

For seeing that our frail mortal bodies are subject
to a vast multitude of diseases,
it hath most graciously pleased almighty God,
of his infinite mercy, goodness, and compassion to sinful man,
to plant remedies in our gardens, before our doors, and even on
every side of our paths, in order that we might
put forth our hands, and duly receive the healing balm. . . .

—CULPEPER'S COMPLETE HERBAL & ENGLISH PHYSICIAN

She was certainly not a woman of family, but well educated,
accomplished, rich, and excessively in love. . . .

—JANE AUSTEN, PERSUASION

CHAPTER 6

In the room that had been hers for more than a year, Lillian Grace
Haswell stared at herself in the dressing table mirror. Her aunt's
lady's maid placed the last ornament in her elegant crown of russet
hair, copper highlights gleaming in the candlelight.

"There you are, miss."

"Thank you, Dupree."

Rising, Lilly smoothed the bodice of her jonquille gown where
it skimmed over her slight figure and flowed to the floor. The maid
handed her long white gloves and helped arrange a light mantle over
her shoulders. A heavy cloak would not be needed on such a fine
early-May evening.

As she carefully descended the stairway of the Elliott home, her
aunt and uncle watched from the hall with evident delight.

"My dear Lillian, how lovely you look!" Aunt Elliott cooed.

"Very handsome indeed," Uncle Elliott added, his hands grasping lapels which did not quite cover his girth.

Aunt Elliott smiled at her husband. "Is she not a vision of perfection?"

"A vision to be sure. But not quite perfect, dear lady."

Her aunt tilted her head to one side. "Oh?"

"Something is missing."

Lillian paused on the landing, looking down at herself. She considered the gloves, the reticule, the slippers peeking from under her skirts. What had she forgotten?

"I know just the thing." Jonathan Elliott turned to the hall table behind him and a moment later walked purposefully toward Lilly.

He stood before her and brandished a brown velvet case. "Now, mind your expectations, my dear. It is not the 'latest thing,' as they say. I am afraid it is rather old."

The Elliotts shared a smile that revealed her aunt's awareness of her husband's intent.

He opened the hinged lid of the jewel case and displayed its contents.

"How lovely!" Lilly's exclamation was sincere. For within the silk lining was a stunning saffron-yellow pendant on a gold chain with a matching topaz bracelet.

"These belonged to Lillian Elliott," her uncle said. "Your grandmother."

Her heart squeezed at this show of affection. "They are beautiful. I wish I had known her."

"I have no doubt she would have been very fond of you."

Her aunt stepped behind her and fastened the necklace while Lilly slipped on the bracelet.

"I shall take great care and return them safely."

"They are yours now, my dear. Although it would be wise to lock them in the jewelry chest when not in use. One can never be too careful."

"I am happy enough to be borrow them, Aunt—you needn't give them to me."

"Nonsense. We have had every intention of giving them to you for some time. Why do you think I counseled you to select a gown of this color?"

"They *are* perfect together. Thank you, Aunt. You are very kind." She kissed Ruth Elliott's soft cheek. "And you too, Uncle." The big man leaned down to receive her kiss.

"There, there. You are most welcome, my dear. Now, shall we be off?"

The Price-Winters family was hosting the ball, and Lilly had long been looking forward to it, for she had become acquainted with both son and daughter during the previous season.

"Mr. and Mrs. Price-Winters, good evening," Jonathan Elliott began. "You remember our niece, Miss Haswell."

"Of course. She and our Christina often enjoy one another's society."

Lilly noticed Mrs. Price-Winters had not included their son, William, in her mention of *society*. Aunt Elliott had tried to match her with Christina's brother last season and was disappointed when he married another. Still, Lilly curtsied and smiled at the parents of her friend. The sole friend she could claim after sixteen months in London.

She followed alongside her aunt and uncle, past their hosts and around the perimeter of the crowded ballroom. Lilly smiled and curtsied her way through a long series of introductions, her eyes straying around the room in hopes of seeing Roger Bromley, a current admirer whom her aunt highly favored.

A silver-haired gentleman in uniform bowed before her. "Miss Haswell. You probably do not remember me, but—"

"Admiral Asher, of course I do. How fares your Dora?"

Admiral Asher was uncle to Roger Bromley, Lilly knew, and she was careful to speak kindly to him. The older man smiled and informed her that his daughter had just presented him with a charming granddaughter and that both were getting on extremely well. Lilly assured him she was happy to hear it and moved on.

Her aunt joined her at the refreshment table. There, they were approached by an elegant matron. Lilly did not miss the wrinkle between Ruth Elliott's eyebrows as she began, "Lillian, have you met—?"

Lilly smoothly supplied, "Mrs. Langtry. Of course. We met at the Willoughbys' last summer."

The matron's eyebrows rose. "How kind of you to remember. And I am pleased to see you again, Miss . . ."

"Haswell."

"Quite."

When her uncle went off to acquire something other than punch or ratafia to drink, Lilly also excused herself, stepping away from her aunt and Mrs. Langtry to greet her approaching friend.

"Christina, there you are. What a lovely gown."

"It is nothing to yours, and you know it."

"Nonsense."

A year older than Lilly, Christina Price-Winters was plump and well-endowed, and her mauve dress dipped low to reveal more cleavage than Lilly would have felt comfortable exposing—even had she that much to expose. Christina's face was broad, with prominent eyes and expressive brows that often rose and fell in dramatic punctuation during conversation. Her wide mouth was given to smirks and sardonic one-sided grins.

"Zee gown eez mag-nee-fee-sawwnt," Christina said, mimicking her French dressmaker. "Ew-la-la, eet transforms *votre fille*, madame. So svelte. So graceful . . ." Christina snorted. "She is more skilled in opening Mother's purse than in stitching seams—that much is certain."

"That explains why your neckline is so low," Lilly quietly teased. "Or perhaps Madame Froissant ran out of material?"

Christina grinned. "This is my current scheme to encourage Edward to propose. Do you think it will succeed?"

Lilly glanced at the balding but highborn lord who was staring at Christina with frank admiration. "I believe it already has."

Though not a beauty, Christina's family, connections, and deep dowry supplied her with a promising number of most eligible suitors. Far more than Lilly enjoyed.

Christina's ginger-haired brother, William, walked across the room toward them. Secretly, Lilly had shared her aunt's keen disappointment when he had announced his plans to wed last year. He had been the first man in London to catch her eye and raise her hopes. She found him amusing and sweet-natured and had briefly believed he admired her as well. Perhaps he had. But with Will, and the few suitors that followed, she had quickly learned that she had neither the rank nor wealth to hold the interest of a gentleman of quality—nor of his parent with the purse strings. Men enjoyed dancing with her and flirting with her, but in the end went on to marry girls with better connections and richer dowries.

Will Price-Winters bowed before her. "Miss Haswell."

She curtsied. "Good evening, Mr. Price-Winters. What a fine ball this is. And where is your lovely new wife?"

He shrugged. "Some earth-shattering calamity with her hair, I understand. No doubt she shall be down directly." He frowned at something over their heads. "I say, who is that?"

Christina followed his gaze and rolled her eyes. "Mr. Alban."

"Your old tutor?"

"And recently Lillian's as well." Christina hunched over, rubbing her hands together in imitation of Mr. Alban, parroting his stammering speech. "Miss . . . Miss Has-s-s-well. Do decline the vairb *to be* onc-c-ce more."

"Christina, please," Lilly admonished. Christina's imitation was spot on, but Lilly did not wish to injure the man's feelings or reputation.

"What is he doing here?" William asked.

Christina shrugged. "He all but begged an invitation, and Mother hadn't the heart to refuse him."

Mr. Oscar Alban was educated, mild-mannered, and patient. He was also short, balding, and wore thick spectacles and ill-fitting clothes. It was little wonder parents trusted him with their daughters.

Mr. Alban bowed before Christina's parents, who now stood

conversing with Lilly's aunt and two older couples. "Mr. and Mrs. Price-Winters. Thank you for your generous-s-s invitation. I cannot remember when I've enjoyed mys-s-self more."

Mrs. Price-Winters was reserved in her reply. "You are welcome, Mr. Alban."

The tutor turned to those assembled around his host and hostess. "I had the privilege of instructing Miss Price-Winters s-s-some years ago. And now Miss Has-s-well also. It as been a rare honor indeed to teach two s-s-such fine and gifted ladies."

"Thank you, Mr. Alban."

"Miss Has-s-well's progress with the romance languages has s-s-surpassed every expectation, although Miss Price-Winters can proudly claim the s-s-superior accent."

"That is Christina," Mr. Price-Winters interjected. "Our little myna bird."

"But Miss Has-s-well has memorized French and Italian vocabulary more quickly than any s-s-student I have ever had the pleasure of teaching."

William leaned near Lilly and teased quietly, "Bluestocking."

"I s-s-suppose her background and her familiarity with Latin—"

Aunt Elliott interrupted abruptly. "Mr. Alban, why do you not dance with my niece? I am sure she would benefit from instruction there as well."

"Ah . . . well . . . I do not claim to be a dancing master. But, of course, I s-s-should be pleased to dance with Miss Has-s-well." He turned toward her. "If she would oblige me."

Lilly forced a smile. "Of course."

As he escorted her to the dance floor, he asked quietly, "What was it I s-s-said to offend?"

"Please forgive my aunt, Mr. Alban. It is only that she prefers as little as possible said of my background. Not everyone sees knowledge of Latin and physic as a credit to accomplished young ladies."

"I s-s-see."

"I ought not to have mentioned my past to you. It was just . . .

you struggled so to account for my progress, and I didn't want you to think—"

"That I am a more gifted teacher than I truly am?" he wryly supplied.

"No! I did not mean—"

"There, there Miss Has-s-well. I understand. Do not fret—I shall take all the credit for your amazing progress from here on."

When the dance ended, Lilly excused herself from Mr. Alban and rejoined Christina and her brother.

"And where is Mr. Bromley this evening?" Christina asked.

"I have yet to see him," Lilly said. She still held out hope for this suitor. Roger Bromley did not seem put off by her lack of title or sizeable income. But then again neither he nor his parents likely knew her father was in trade, nor were they aware of her mother's disgrace. Lilly wondered how long his interest would last once they knew.

"I see the swell," Will said, "there by the door."

Lilly followed Will's gaze and saw Mr. Bromley, stylishly dressed in black tailcoat and white waistcoat. He stood before a willowy blonde in blue satin with an overdress of white netting. "Who is that he is talking to?"

"Susan Whittier . . ." Will breathed, staring.

Lilly stared as well and felt a stirring of dread. "I have never seen her before."

"She was away much of last season," Christina explained. "Touring Italy, I believe."

"She is very beautiful," Lilly acknowledged, and swallowed a lump of envy.

"Is she?" Will said innocently. "I had not noticed."

Lilly was unsuccessful in restraining her sarcasm. "And neither, I see, has Mr. Bromley."

With a dismissive wave, Christina said, "Oh, he tried to engage her affections two years ago but was soundly rebuffed. You have nothing to fear from her, Lillian."

Had she not? Lilly saw Mr. Bromley's awestruck expression and did not feel reassured.

As they watched, Roger Bromley offered Miss Whittier his arm. She patted it as though it were the head of a child, laughed, and twirled away in a flutter of blue satin. Even from across the room, Lilly could not miss the man's crestfallen countenance.

He glanced their way.

To pretend they had not witnessed his rejection, the three quickly feigned engrossed conversation. By the time Bromley had crossed the room and stood before them, a bright smile had transformed his handsome face.

"Price-Winters, you old hound," he began. "Monopolizing the two handsomest ladies in the room, I see. The missus would not approve." He bowed to Christina. "Miss Price-Winters."

"Bromley."

He turned toward Lilly. "And Miss Haswell. What a delight. I do hope you have saved at least one dance for poor me?"

She answered warmly, "Of course I have."

Mr. Bromley had become one of her most frequent partners. He was an elegant, slim young man of middling height and excellent bearing. Straight brown hair framed classic English features. He was also the only son of a wealthy family, as her aunt often reminded her. As though Lilly needed reminding.

"Excellent," he said. "Then I shall have the next and the last and as many as I can in between, when the chaperones aren't looking."

She smiled at him, and his answering smile almost reached his eyes. She studied his face, wondering just what was between him and the lovely Miss Susan Whittier.

At the end of the evening, Lilly found herself alone, surreptitiously searching the crowd for Mr. Bromley, who had requested the last dance with her. The first notes of a slow, ceremonious minuet began.

William Price-Winters hurried by. Seeing her, he paused. "Miss Haswell. Not sitting this one out, I hope? Oh, that's right. Bromley claimed the final. Where is that chap?"

"I do not know."

At that moment Roger Bromley and Susan Whittier walked past and joined the dance.

Will saw them too. "Oh. Well, I say."

"She has agreed to a dance after all," Lilly said. "How nice for Mr. Bromley."

Will was not fooled. "I am sorry, Miss Haswell. My wife is waiting, or I—"

"Think nothing of it, Mr. Price-Winters. I have enjoyed a great deal of dancing this evening."

"Wait," Will said triumphantly. "Graves here will dance with you."

"Really, I am fine—"

Will grabbed the arm of a nearby man she had never seen before and turned him around to face her. And a very handsome face it was. Thin nose. Pale blond hair swept over his right temple. A faint moustache, not in present fashion, shadowed his upper lip. "May I present Adam Graves. We were at Oxford together. This is Miss Haswell. Most sensible girl in the room, I assure you." Will winked at her. "Even if she is my sister's friend."

Lilly curtsied to the newcomer. When she looked up, the blond-haired man still stood as he was, stiffly staring at her with startled blue eyes. After a tense moment, he gave a jerky nod.

Will clapped Graves on the shoulder. "Good man." Will walked away to find his wife, who had finally made an appearance.

Still the man made no move. Did not offer his arm nor open his mouth. An awkward silence followed, and Lilly felt her cheeks burn. *How mortifying.*

She turned slightly so that she was facing at an angle between Mr. Graves and the dance floor. Blindly, she gazed toward the other couples moving gracefully through the delicate steps of the dance.

"It is all right, Mr. Graves," she said without looking his way. "You needn't dance with me. Mr. Price-Winters was only acting the part of protective brother. I do not mind sitting out."

"Graves!" Will hissed as he and his wife stepped near, then away again.

Finally, Mr. Graves woodenly offered his arm. "Will you dance?"

She had long ago promised herself never to reject a man who'd gathered his courage to ask for a dance. The automatic response, "I'd be delighted," would not come forth, however. She took a deep breath and forced out a quiet, "Very well."

They joined the minuet in progress. He led her to an open space in the ballroom and took up the movements with stiff, minimal precision. She tempered her own steps accordingly. He kept his gaze averted.

She sighed inwardly. Throughout the previous season and now this new one, she had danced with dozens of gentlemen she secretly found disagreeable or unappealing. But never, she hoped, had she made her disinterest as plain as Mr. Graves made his now. Everyone in the room undoubtedly saw how loath he was to dance with her.

She discreetly glanced around at the other dancers. There at the front were Roger Bromley and Susan Whittier. Roger beamed at his partner, though Susan stared aloofly off in the distance. *Miss Whittier and Mr. Graves ought to be dancing together,* Lilly thought, since both appeared to be enjoying themselves equally.

Suddenly, over Roger's head, Lilly glimpsed a familiar profile. She started, drawing in a breath and turning her face away quickly. There was no mistaking that imposing figure nor those sharp features. *Roderick Marlow?* Here? Now? To witness her humiliation? To reveal, to her aunt and uncle's mortification, her identity as an apothecary's daughter, which to most in attendance, granted her the status of a mere shopkeeper's daughter?

On the next turn of the dance, she stole another glance. Roderick Marlow stood talking to Mr. and Mrs. Price-Winters. On his arm was a stunning woman with splendid maple-leaf-red hair. Mr. Marlow glanced up and his eyes narrowed. Again she averted her face. Had he seen her?

As the musicians reached the final stanzas, Lillian stepped closer to her partner. "Please excuse me, Mr. Graves. I fear I must take my leave."

He stopped dancing and stood there. He opened his mouth, but she was already turning away. She was several yards away from him when his "Of course" reached her ears. Normally she would have hated to be so rude, but in this case she assumed her partner would be relieved to be free of the duty to escort her back to her place and falsely thank her. She again glimpsed Mr. Marlow's face above the heads of the crowd. She could not be certain, but—was he trying to weave his way toward her? She walked quickly away to the safety of the ladies lounge.

Her aunt found her there several minutes later. "There you are, my dear. Are you all right?"

"Yes. Merely tired."

"Your uncle and I are ready to depart, if you are certain you do not wish to remain longer?"

"I am ready."

Gathering their wraps, they made their way to thank their hosts near the door. A man's hand touched her gloved arm and she started. But it was only Will Price-Winters. His usually cheery face was serious. "Miss Haswell, I hope you will not take my friend's reluctance as an affront toward your lovely person. Graves is the most reticent chap I know."

She quickly skimmed the crowd around them. "Think no more of it. Good night, Mr. Price-Winters."

He eyed her closely. "You are certain you are all right?"

"Quite, I thank you. Do say good-bye to Christina for me."

"I shall."

On the carriage ride home, Aunt Elliott squeezed Lilly's hand. "Well done, my dear."

"Pray what do you mean?"

"Roger Bromley favored you with more dances than any other lady present."

Perhaps not by choice, however, Lilly thought. "Yes, he was very kind."

"More than kind, my dear," Aunt Elliott said. "He is evidently quite taken with you. And as a gentleman of means, Mr. Bromley is under no compulsion to find a wealthy wife of the ton. I know we were disappointed last season, my dear, but I trust we shall prevail this time."

Lilly only smiled meekly. She had thought so, too, before tonight. Before she had seen the way he looked at Miss Whittier. Had her aunt not noticed? Had she seen only what she wished to see?

Ruth Elliott continued, "I *was* a little concerned when I saw you dancing with that fair gentleman at the last."

"Were you. Why?"

"Chap with the moustache, you mean?" Uncle Elliott interrupted. "Someone ought to tell him it isn't all the crack, no matter what some officers seem to believe."

Her aunt continued undeterred, "Have you met him before?"

"No. Christina's brother introduced us. A Mr. Graves, I believe. They were at Oxford together."

"Ah . . . Graves," her uncle said. "Mr. Price-Winters told me he is awaiting licentiateship in the Royal College."

She stared at her uncle, not comprehending.

"The Royal College of *Physicians,* my dear," Uncle Elliott clarified.

Lilly felt oddly stunned. "I did not even realize."

"Good gracious, I trust the two of you did not spend the evening discussing ailments and diseases." Her aunt shuddered.

"We discussed nothing," Lilly said. "We barely spoke."

"Good." Her aunt relaxed against the seat. "Then no harm done."

So modern 'pothecaries, taught the art
By Doctor's bills to play the Doctor's part,
Bold in the practice of mistaken rules,
Prescribe, apply, and call their masters fools.

—ALEXANDER POPE

CHAPTER 7

The following evening, the Willoughbys hosted a musicale in their stately Grosvenor Square home. The performer was a young soprano Lilly and the Elliotts had heard perform the previous season. Lilly did not appreciate the ingenue's cathedral-high vibrato but resisted comment. She knew her aunt would never dream of declining an invitation from the Willoughbys.

Dressed in an elegant gown of pearly nacre satin, her upswept hair ornamented with pearls, Lilly followed her aunt and uncle into the impressive home. Several servants were kept busy taking guests' wraps, and by the time Lilly turned after handing over her hooded cloak, she realized she had become separated from the Elliotts in the throng. No matter. She knew where to find them. Front and center before the soprano.

Following slowly with the crowd, Lilly made her way through the double doors into the great drawing room. There the crowd thickened as gentlemen greeted one another and ladies searched for the best seats to regard one another's gowns and to spy potential suitors for their daughters. Lilly paused and stepped to the side, out of the flow, while she searched the room for her aunt and uncle. From the corner of her eye, she glimpsed a gentleman standing against the wall, arms crossed. She glanced over and was disconcerted to see Mr. Graves standing there, looking at her. One could not miss his pale blond hair.

Not knowing what else to do, she nodded at him and returned to her search. Where *were* they? A moment later, she still felt his ponderous eyes upon her. The last thing she wanted was for him to believe she loitered there in hopes he would take notice and address her.

She glanced coolly at him over her shoulder. "I am looking for my aunt and uncle. We came together, and I seem to have lost them."

He nodded stiffly but said nothing.

"Why do you stare?" Lilly asked tartly. "If you are trying to place me, I am the lady you danced with last evening."

"I had not forgotten. But nor would I call what I did *dancing*."

She looked at him sharply. "Dancing it was, though you were coerced into doing so."

He blinked his blue eyes. Opened his mouth. Blinked again.

Crossing her own arms, she turned her back to him, attempting to resume her search, though anger coursed through her and she felt unable to focus with his cold eyes pricking her.

A moment later she was surprised when he stepped to her side and said quietly, "I meant only that I am aware my poor attempt can hardly be called dancing."

"You seemed familiar enough with the steps," she challenged.

He dipped his chin. "True. I can claim no lack of training."

"But you clearly did not enjoy it."

"No. I am—" He cleared his throat. "Miss Haswell, please forgive my conduct of last evening. There is not a man alive who should require coercion to dance with you."

She looked at him, stunned. She felt her lips part, but now it was she who could not seem to speak. And by the time she could, he had already slipped away into the crowd.

It was all Lilly could do to keep from wincing as Miss Augusta Fredrickson hit the climactic note of her aria. However, she could not keep one eyebrow from lifting higher and higher with each screeching half step as the soprano trilled up the score in a piercing octave. The scream, when she first heard it, sounded like more of the same. It took her a few seconds to realize that the scream came from behind her and from a more pleasing voice. She whirled in her seat as the soprano sang on. Clearly others had not realized the shriek had not been part of the performance.

Lilly left her chair and, ducking a bit, hurried to the back of the room. A woman screamed again, this time adding words to her emission. "Somebody help! Call a doctor!"

It was Mrs. Price-Winters, kneeling beside her husband, who lay prone and gasping on the floor.

The singer broke off at last.

The hostess, Mrs. Willoughby, rose. "Is there no doctor in the house?"

Crouched beside Mr. and Mrs. Price-Winters, Lilly searched frantically, but there was no sign of Mr. Graves.

One liveried footman ran to send for a doctor. A second stood nervously at the double doors of the drawing room.

"You there," Lilly called to him. "Please bring me the house medicine chest."

The footman stared at her.

"The mistress does have one?"

He nodded.

"Then hurry!"

The young man rushed away, and Lilly bent to examine Mr. Price-Winters.

In less than a minute, the footman ran back in and set a mahogany box beside the prone man. Kneeling there, Lilly threw open the hinged lid. Square bottles with labels on their shoulders proclaimed their contents—*turkey rhubarb, fever powder, ipecacuanha, laudanum*. Lilly recognized the chest as an older model of one they sold in their shop at home. She pulled open the bottom drawer—lancet, blistering plaster, double-ended measure, and . . . There! The probang. A long flexible device used to dislodge anything stuck in the gullet.

The first footman rushed back in. "Doctor's on his way."

"How long?" Lilly asked.

"A few minutes yet, I'd reckon."

Mr. Price-Winters's face was turning blue.

"He hasn't got a few minutes! Here, help me roll him onto his side." The servant complied. Mrs. Price-Winters was too hysterical to help, and the others seemed frozen—an audience transfixed. It was left to her. She knew what to do. Had done so for Mary more than once. Inserting the probang, she used it first to fully pry open the man's mouth, then to peer down his throat. "Step aside, please. I need more light!"

Someone held an oil lamp above her. There it was. A white object lodged in his throat. She gently but quickly slid the device alongside the obstacle, careful not to push it further down his throat. Pressing the top of the device like a lever, she pushed and pulled simultaneously. This, combined with his gag reflex, was enough to expectorate the obstacle.

"There," she announced, as the object—a round peppermint by the looks of it—popped out.

Mr. Price-Winters coughed and gagged and sucked in a breath, quickly regaining consciousness. His wife embraced him awkwardly there on the carpet. "Oh, thank God!"

Amen, Lilly silently added, grateful Christina's father not been denied life-giving air any longer.

She became aware of murmuring voices, of people staring at her with looks both censorious and amazed. She glanced up, hoping to see her aunt and uncle, but instead saw Mr. Graves. Standing in the back, stone-faced and pale. Had he been there all along? Why had he not come forward?

A distant voice shouted, "Doctor's here!"

A foppish gentleman in evening attire bustled in, carrying his black leather case. "Make way, make way!"

His eyes widened as he took in the open medicine chest, the probang, and the young woman kneeling beside his patient.

"What has happened here?"

Lilly smelled alcohol on the doctor's breath. He had clearly been called away from a supper or party.

"Mr. Price-Winters had a peppermint lodged in his throat," she calmly explained. "He could not breathe."

Mrs. Price-Winters gestured with a limp hand. "She used that thing and got it loose."

"A probang? Good heavens, girl, what were you thinking? You might have punctured his esophagus!"

"I am all right," Mr. Price-Winters whispered hoarsely. "Throat hurts like hades, though."

"And no wonder!" The doctor turned on Lilly. "Who do you think you are to operate on a man?"

Lilly was stunned. Why was he so angry? Was inebriation clouding his judgment?

"I am sorry, Dr. Porter," Mrs. Willoughby soothed. "None of us knew what to do."

Lilly hesitated. Surely she had not done anything so wrong. "I saw no other alternative—"

"Had we known you would arrive so soon," Mrs. Willoughby continued, sending a cool glance her way, "we might have stopped her."

Dr. Porter glared at Lilly. "You could have killed him."

"On the contrary, sir." Adam Graves now stood above them. "He could have died had she not acted."

"Graves . . . you approved this?"

"Not exactly . . ."

His words trailed off and were lost in Dr. Porter's mutterings and instructions for a heavy dose of laudanum, which Lilly thought quite more than necessary.

The crisis past, the crowd began to drain away toward their coats and carriages.

Mrs. Price-Winters offered Lilly her hand. "Thank you, my dear."

Lilly leaned forward and embraced her friend's mother. "I am only glad he is all right." Then she added quietly, "Have him rinse with salt water and a drop of laudanum thrice daily and his throat shall heal quickly."

"Come, Lillian," Aunt Elliott called. "Let us depart."

Even as she stepped away, she heard Dr. Porter ask, "What did she tell you?" Lilly did not hear Mrs. Price-Winters's answer but did hear the doctor call after her, "Who do you think you are? First to operate on a man and then to prescribe treatment?"

Mr. Graves cleared his throat and began weakly, "I must say, Dr. Porter, the young lady acted more quickly than I, but she acted well. Do not abrade her for saving the man."

Lilly silently wished Mr. Graves had found his voice earlier, when the critical crowd was still around to hear it.

"Saving the man? The chit near skewered him."

Her aunt took her arm and said between clenched teeth, "Keep walking, Lillian."

In the carriage, Aunt Elliott sighed emphatically. "Lillian, I know you acted from the heart, but really, could you not have resisted?"

"What would you have had me do? Sit by and do nothing? No one came forward to help, or I would have gladly stepped aside."

"One of the men would have come forward were you not so . . . forward. That Graves fellow was there, it turns out, and the doctor was on his way. You usurped their rightful position as learned medical men."

"He might have died."

"Do not be so dramatic. It was only a peppermint, for goodness' sake."

"Probably choked on it when that soprano hit her high note," Uncle Elliott said dryly. "I know I almost did."

"Mr. Elliott. There is nothing amusing about this. All the dress-makers and dancing masters, all the hours of language, drawing, and deportment. All our efforts, ruined."

"Dear lady, now who is being dramatic? It cannot be as bad as all that. Our Lillian will be a heroine, at least among those with brains in their heads."

"You don't know what you are saying, Mr. Elliott."

"Come now. Even if a few mavens look down on her actions of one evening, they shall forget soon enough."

"I would not depend upon it." Her aunt's voice was haughty and defeated at once. "In that regard, society and Lillian have much in common. They both remember everything."

The art of medicine consists of amusing the patients
while Nature cures the disease.

—Voltaire

Chapter 8

On a fine afternoon two days later, Lilly joined Christina Price-Winters for a drive through Berkeley Square in a sleek open landau. Tall trees stood sentry around the square, their trunks ringed by daffodils. The air was filled with low laughter and birdsong.

Christina joked and shared confidences as though the coachman were deaf, or as intelligent as the two horses he reined. Lilly shifted uncomfortably on the fine leather seat.

"Look!" Christina pointed across the square. "There's William!"

Christina waved and, beside her, Lilly followed suit. William came jogging across the green toward them. She was surprised to see Mr. Graves striding more sedately several yards behind.

"Hold there, Barker!" Will called to the driver, who halted the pair of bays. Reaching them, Will grasped the landau's door and beamed up at them. "I told Graves we'd find you two trolling the park for admirers."

"We are doing no such thing," Christina snapped playfully.

Mr. Graves joined them and appeared decidedly uncomfortable. Will looked at Lilly and teased, "Or has Miss Haswell been saving lives again?"

Lilly glanced at Mr. Graves, then away. "No, nothing of the kind."

Will did not seem to notice her discomfort: "We've just come from Father, who, I am happy to report, is in excellent health and spirits."

"Yes," Lilly said. "I paid a call this morning and was relieved to find him so."

Will grinned. "Checking on your patient, were you?"

Again she glanced at Graves, who had remained silent throughout the exchange.

"No. Simply to assure myself he is well."

"And he is, thanks to you." Will slapped the edge of the landau. "He confided he was perfectly able to be up and about, but was enjoying Mother fussing over him too much to make the effort. If Father's throat is sore, it is because he cannot cease singing your praises."

Lilly felt her cheeks flush.

"Do come down, and let us go into Gunter's for an ice," Will urged. "What do you say? Perfect weather for it."

Christina looked at Lilly, eyebrows raised hopefully.

"As you like."

Will opened the carriage door and offered a hand in helping the ladies down.

"Wait for us, Barker," he instructed the coachman. "We shall want the carriage for the return home."

"Very good, sir."

Mr. Graves stood awkwardly silent. Will glanced at him, then offered his arm to his sister. "Come, Chrissy. Let us you and I go in and purchase an ice for each of our friends here."

Lilly began to object. "You needn't—"

"The least we can do," Will assured her. "That is, unless you plan to send us a bill?"

Lilly again felt her cheeks burn. "Of course not."

Brother and sister left—Christina sending a look over her shoulder that was part confusion and part speculation over her brother's maneuverings.

Lilly prepared for an awkward wait.

"Shall we walk, Miss Haswell?" Mr. Graves asked suddenly.

She inhaled, relieved. "Thank you. Yes."

Carefully skirting parked carriages and sidestepping horse droppings, they left the paving and walked into the square's central garden. There they strolled under the scant shade of young maple trees, hands behind their backs.

After several minutes, Mr. Graves said, "You are to be commended for your quick actions the other night, Miss Haswell."

She looked up at his handsome, unreadable profile. "Thank you."

"May I ask how you knew what to do?"

Lilly hesitated. Her aunt had long counseled her not to offer details about her upbringing nor her father's trade. And who knew how this Oxford-trained physician would view an apothecary, let alone his daughter. Besides, her actions during the concert were not informed by her life as an apothecary's daughter. At least, not directly. Had the man's heart seized and she'd had to administer digitalis, that would have been another case entirely.

She settled for the most relevant truth. "My dearest friend suffers from falling sickness."

"Epilepsy?" His quick glance was grim. "I am sorry to hear it. Is she in an institution?"

"Heavens no. Why should she be?"

"It is very common here in London, depending on the severity of the fits."

"Well, it is *not* common in Bedsley Priors to lock away a lovely, clever person just because she has been, on rare occasion, seized by fits beyond her control."

Mr. Graves had to hurry to catch up with her agitated strides. "I did not mean to give offense."

"How can I not take offense at such an idea? Mary Mimpurse is a blessing to all who know her. She helps everyone and hurts no one."

He asked gently. "No one but herself?"

Lilly sighed and forced herself to slow down. "On occasion she has fallen and sprained or bruised a limb. Or has been eating and had something lodge in her throat. Twice I've had to pry out obstructions when her mother was not at hand."

"I see. That explains *how* you knew what to do for Mr. Price-Winters." He paused. "But not *why* you did so."

Lilly was confused by the question. "My friend's father needed help."

He stopped walking, and she halted as well, turning to face him.

"I think, Miss Haswell, that any friend of yours is lucky indeed."

She studied his expression and found it sincere. With his pale hair, perfect nose, and golden-lashed eyes of delft blue, Mr. Graves had the face of an angel. The only flaw she noticed was a pair of vertical lines between his eyebrows. He evidently squinted or frowned a great deal.

"I would have done the same for anyone," she said.

"Even someone like me?" Dimples framed each side of his wry grin.

"Even you." *Goodness.* If not for the unfashionable moustache, he might have been prettier than she was.

They resumed their stroll, walking in silence for several moments, relishing the sunshine and the fairlike atmosphere of the popular park.

He cleared his throat. "You were kind not to expose me."

"You were kind to defend me."

He breathed in through his nose. "I am not kind, Miss Haswell. I felt morally compelled to speak. Still, I almost did not, fearing recrimination for my inaction. I believe Dr. Porter was too angry with you to realize."

Or too intoxicated.

"Why was he so angry?"

"I fear most physicians are defensive these days. You are not likely aware, but there is a great deal of contention between the various branches of medicine—physicians, surgeons, apothecaries. Physicians are the most qualified to treat and prescribe, but that does not stop the others from horning in on physicians' rightful domain."

Lilly bit down on her lip, hard, to keep from speaking up, from defending her father's rights and skills.

"Even now," Mr. Graves continued, "Parliament is debating who should be allowed to do what. If men like Dr. Porter have their way, apothecaries will be able to do no more than fill the scripts given them by physicians. They can throw in their lot with the chemists."

Anger rose up in her, but she held it in check. "And do you agree with this assessment, sir?"

He lifted a shrug. "I am not yet certain what to think. Physicians alone are university-educated. Why, anyone with a mortar and pestle can hang a shingle and call himself an apothecary."

She shook her head. "But there are long traditions of apprenticeship, and training with a master at the Apothecaries' Society, which has its own laboratory and physic garden. . . ."

He stopped walking and stared at her.

"Or so I understand."

Quickly, she walked on and changed the subject. "May I ask . . . why did you *not* act when Mr. Price-Winters fell?"

He sighed. "Fear again—my old nemesis."

"Fear of what?"

He shrugged. "Fear of authority, fear of failing, fear of consequences . . . even fear of dancing with a beautiful woman."

Her stomach fluttered. "Goodness," she said breathlessly. "I wonder you want to be a physician at all."

"It is what my father wants. He determined each of our professions. My elder brother will take over the running of Father's estate, though he would have preferred the church. My second brother is a reluctant solicitor here in town. And I shall be a physician."

He took a deep breath before continuing. "I am not yet licensed,

Miss Haswell. I resolutely grasp the hope that when that document is in my hand, proclaiming for all the world that I am a fully qualified, capable physician, I shall finally be just that."

Oh dear. She asked gently, "And if not?"

"It does not bear thinking about. My family, my father . . . No. I must overcome and succeed."

Dipping her head, she said, "Then I shall pray for you, Dr. Graves."

She saw him wince.

"Is it the prayer you object to, or the form of address?"

"Forgive me. You may address me as *doctor* if you like, but I fear it will be some time until I am accustomed to it."

Will Price-Winters hailed them, and she and Dr. Graves turned to join brother and sister, each bearing two glass licks of red barberry ice.

❦

The following week, Lilly attended a rout with her aunt and uncle, and again wore the jonquille dress and topaz jewelry. The affair was grand, but her aunt was suffering from a headache, and Lilly from speculative and often cold glances, so they did not stay long. There seemed little point, as Roger Bromley was not in attendance.

Upon their return home, Lilly helped her aunt to her room before slipping downstairs to prepare a remedy. When she returned several minutes later, Dupree was just coming out, her aunt's dress in arms.

"Is she still awake?" Lilly asked.

"Yes, miss."

Seeing the tray in Lilly's hands, the maid knocked on the door for her. Lilly smiled her thanks and entered.

Ruth Elliott sat at her dressing table in her nightdress and dressing gown, brushing her long brown hair, which bore only a few strands of grey. When she laid down her brush and stood, Lilly swiftly set down her tray and took her aunt's arm to help her into bed.

"Thank you, my dear."

"How is your headache?"

"I shall be fine by morning."

"I hope you do not mind, but I have taken the liberty of preparing the Haswell remedy for headaches." *Peppermint, blessed thistle, feverfew, willow bark.* How long had it been since she'd thought in such terms?

Her aunt closed her eyes and released a breath. "My dear, you cannot have failed to notice the coolness, the speculation and gossip about your actions at the Willoughbys' last week. You know I would prefer—"

"I know you wish me to set aside that part of my life, but certainly it can do no harm here at home."

Her aunt looked up at her.

"Here in *your* home," Lilly awkwardly amended.

"No, my dear. I like hearing you saying that. This is your home now, for as long as you like."

"Thank you, Aunt. You are most kind." Lilly kissed her aunt's cheek. "Now, please, drink this." She handed her a teacup from the tray.

Accepting it, her aunt eyed the cup speculatively. "Dare I ask?"

"Merely peppermint and blessed thistle tea." Lilly held out two pills as well. "It is these you need worry about. Rather bitter, I am afraid."

"What are they?"

"Better not to know," Lilly teased. "Don't fret, I have put plenty of treacle in the tea to help you drink them down."

While her aunt swallowed the pills and sipped the tea, Lilly retrieved two cloth bundles from the tray. "And I've brought some wrapped ice."

Lilly arranged one bundle on the pillow and her aunt lay back against it. "There you are. One for your neck and another for your eyes." She settled the second iced cloth over her aunt's eyelids and temples.

"Heavenly," Ruth Elliott murmured.

Standing there, Lilly silently asked God to ease her aunt's pain.

Touching her fingers to her throat and finding the necklace there, she said, "I had thought to return the topaz pieces to the jewel chest, but shall we leave it till morning?"

Her aunt's voice was drowsy. "Would you mind setting your things in there yourself, my dear? I prefer not to stir again this night."

"Of course. You rest. Shall I put your rings away as well?"

"If you would not mind. Thank you, Lillian. If you have any trouble, ask your uncle." She waved a limp hand toward the key on the bedside table. "He will likely be awake for some time yet."

"Very well. I shall."

Walking casually through her aunt's dressing room, Lilly opened the jewel chest with its many tiers of velvet-lined drawers—opening one, then another, looking for an empty compartment. Her hand froze. Her stomach lurched. *What on earth?*

Gingerly, she laid aside her jewelry and picked up what surely was a mirage. A specter of her imagination. Her fingers touched the cool metal, the glossy black onyx, and trembled. Her eyes widened and her heart pounded as she lifted the necklace with its unusual webbed, burnished chain and octagonal onyx pendant. She would have known it anywhere. It was the necklace her mother had always worn. The very one she was wearing the last time Lilly saw her. How had it come to be in the chest?

She longed to rush to Aunt Elliott and demand answers, but her aunt was feeling ill. Taking the necklace with her, she went to find her uncle, but contrary to her aunt's prediction, she found him asleep in his favorite chair in the library. Retracing her steps to the dressing room, she carefully returned each piece and locked the chest—its contents now more valuable and bewildering than before. Her questions could wait.

But not for long.

Run into Bucklers bury, for two ounces of
Dragon-water, spermaceti, and treacle.

—WESTWARD HO, 1607

CHAPTER 9

I n the morning, her aunt was no better and stayed in bed.
"But you must still go shopping as we planned," she said. "Take
Dupree with you."

"Shopping can wait." Lilly set aside her gloves and sat on the edge
of her aunt's bed. "I shall stay and read to you."

Her aunt patted her hand. "Sleep is all I want, my dear. And I
shall feel better if you are out enjoying yourself."

"Are you quite certain?"

"Yes, my dear. I am afraid your uncle has taken the carriage,
but—"

"I shall hire a hackney. I do not mind in the least." In fact, she
was relieved. This way only one servant would know where she'd
spent her day.

With her aunt's maid to accompany her, Lilly climbed into a

hackney coach and directed the jarvey to take them to Bucklersbury, to a row of shops known as Apothecaries Street.

Dupree looked at her in surprise. "I thought we were going shopping."

"We are. Just not for bonnets and ribbons and such."

"Are you unwell, miss?"

"I am quite well. Only curious."

She had thought of visiting the street once or twice before, though she had always dismissed the idea. But somehow her discussion with Dr. Graves about physicians and apothecaries—as well as the previous night's discovery—left her feeling unsettled and missing home.

When they reached Bucklersbury, near the east end of Cheapside, the two ladies alighted and Lilly paid the driver.

As she turned, she noticed Dupree craning her neck to look down a narrow street leading away from the shops.

"What is it, Dupree?"

"I know this place, miss. My sister lives just up that lane there."

"Does she indeed? Then you and she must have a nice visit while I peruse the row."

"On your own, miss?"

"I shall be quite safe and will venture no further. You can find me right here. Say, in an hour's time?"

"But the mistress . . ."

"We shall keep the specifics about how we spent the day to ourselves. Agreed?"

Dupree grinned. "Very good, miss."

Lilly watched as Dupree hastened up the narrow cross street. Then Lilly closed her eyes and breathed in deeply. Smells familiar and foreign reached her. Sounds too. Her father had told her about London's Apothecaries Street, where nearly every shop housed an apothecary, chemist, or grocer. He had spent a great deal of time on the street during the two years he had lived in London, apprenticed at the Worshipful Society of Apothecaries. She longed to see Apothecaries' Hall, as well as the society's garden in Chelsea, but would settle for Bucklersbury for now.

She began to slowly walk down the street, looking in bowed shop-windows so much like theirs at home. She took in signs advertising the latest patent medicines. She smiled in delight at the displays of the exotic—a shark hanging from one shop awning, a blowfish from another. There a statue of an Indian from the Americas, there a carved rhinoceros—one of the symbols on the Society's coat of arms. A mother, in fine promenade dress and fruit-sprigged hat, held her toddler atop the wooden creature. The little boy grabbed for the horn on the rhino's back. A second horn graced its nose.

Unlike at home, she heard callers barking out their wares, offering free samples, and promising cure-alls. The further down the row she walked, the louder the clamor rose. She was about to turn back when a corner shop caught her eye. Its flaking window trim, its simple sign, reminded her very much of Haswell's. Stepping closer, she read the sign, *L. Lippert, Apothecary,* and peered through the window. Very similar indeed—traditional displays, neat counters, even an ancient alligator hanging from its beams. Her heart started at the sight of a young woman bent over a ledger at a tall clerk's desk in the corner. She was alone; there were neither customers nor an apothecary to be seen. Then, from the back, a man entered in waistcoat and apron. He wore spectacles and was older than her father but had the same competent bearing. When the man paused and spoke to the young woman, reached out and tugged affectionately at a loose strand of her hair, tears filled Lilly's eyes. She was happy with the Elliotts but suddenly felt nostalgic. How she missed her father. How she missed them all.

As she pushed open the shop door, the bell jangled, a slightly higher pitch than their own. The woman looked up with a pleasant expression. She had fair, delicate features and appeared to be only a year or so older than Lilly herself.

"Might I help you?" she asked.

"I am merely looking."

"You are most welcome."

The man stepped forward. "If I can answer any questions, do not hesitate to ask."

"Mr. Lippert, I presume?"

"The very same."

"I admire your shop. I was quite drawn to it."

"Well, you are alone in that, I am afraid." He stepped to straighten his already tidy counter.

"It reminds me of my father's."

"Ah! Well, I hope his is busier at least."

"Yes. But, after all, he is the only apothecary in our village."

"Indeed? And may I ask the name of this village?"

"Bedsley Priors. In Wiltshire."

"I know it!" He turned to the young woman. "Your grandparents live not far from there, Polly."

"In Little Bedwyn." The girl smiled. "Do you know it?"

"Indeed I do."

"Many a happy hour I spent with my grandparents in that beautiful valley."

Lilly smiled at the genuine warmth of her words.

"When I started out," Mr. Lippert said, brandishing an ancient pestle, " I thought I would return to Little Bedwyn. But the opportunities here in London were just too great. But now you see how it is." He gesticulated toward the window. "My son says that if I am to compete, I must change—update my equipment, displays, and labels; order the latest exotics from the East and West Indies; and stock all the popular patent medicines. Quite a head for business, my son. Unfortunately, prefers the shipping trade to medicine. Unlike Polly here. The draper offered her a position, but she won't hear of it."

"I like it here, Father. Are you wanting to be rid of me?"

"Of course not, my dear. In any case, I think the draper is in greater need of a wife than a clerk."

Polly smiled wryly. "I've no interest in that post either."

Lilly heard a voice shouting outside and walked to the window. She watched with interest a man with a market cart down the street, lifting a bottle high and proclaiming its virtues like a revivalist. "Who is he?"

Polly glanced up. "Just one of those irregular doctors."

"Irregular, indeed," Mr. Lippert said. "I'd call him a peddler at best, or a quack."

"What is he selling?"

"Lady Rutger's Restorative. Won't tell me what's in it. Declares it patent pending. Useless—as far as I can tell."

"You don't sell it here, do you?"

The old man looked chagrined. "I am afraid I do. My son says if customers want it, I should sell it." He walked across the small shop, selected a bottle from his display, and handed it to her. "The fool stuff is very popular."

She looked at the label. "No list of ingredients. No dosage instructions, no warnings."

"Just promises. I have done a bit of study on the stuff. It contains opium to be sure. Its aroma suggests rose, and something else. . . ." He opened the bottle and offered her the cork. She leaned close and sniffed gently.

"Rosemary," she said. "And peony. I'd know that fragrance anywhere."

He raised his brows, impressed. "No wonder Lady Rutger enjoys this restorative. Gets her foxed and fragrant all at once." He grimaced. "Forgive me, that was crude."

"But likely true." Lilly said. "You know, I believe I will trouble you for some feverfew and willow bark pills while I am here. My aunt suffers frequent headaches, and I have used nearly all the pills I brought from home."

"Of course. Though they will require a few minutes to prepare."

"I am happy to wait." She followed him to the back counter. "Have you sea feverfew?"

"No, only corn and common, I'm afraid." He glanced at her over his spectacles. "I am surprised you know the varieties."

"No matter. Common will do nicely. And white willow bark?"

"Very good."

"My goodness," Polly said. "You put this apothecary's daughter to shame."

"Not at all, my dear." Mr. Lippert assured her. Then to Lilly, explained, "Polly concentrates on the bookwork for me. She has no head for herbs and I've no head for numbers."

Lilly smiled. "Then you complement one another well."

The man began retrieving simples and readying his tools. As he worked Lilly noticed his gnarled, arthritic hands.

"I don't suppose you would allow me. I never thought I'd miss it, but . . . for old times' sake?"

"Of course, my dear, if you wish. That I should like to see." With a flourish of his arm, he invited her into his domain.

Setting aside her reticule, Lilly stepped behind the counter. In rapid motions she measured the powders and poured them into the mortar Mr. Lippert provided.

"And for the binding?" he asked.

"Vegetable gum, if you have it."

He handed it to her. Deftly, she added the liquid and picked up the pestle, turning and pressing. When the compound was the right consistency, she transferred it to the work surface, rolled it, then placed it across the grooves of an old gradated pill tile and cut the pills.

"She's a dab hand, she is," Polly said.

Mr. Lippert asked, "Talc, sugar, or silver coating?"

"Feverfew and willow bark are both terribly bitter," Lilly replied.

"Sugar it is."

Using the flat blade, she scooped the coarse pills into the spherical pill rounder, turning it to round the pills and coat them with sugar. After pouring the pills onto a screen to siphon off the extra coating, she scooped the finished pills into a packet.

"My goodness!" Mr. Lippert said. "If you were a lad, I would offer you a post. Oh. No offense, my dear."

She grinned. "None taken. But I should not accept a post in any case. Those days are past for me."

"I am relieved to hear it!" Polly said, but her smile indicated she had felt not the least threatened by her father's praise of Lilly.

"How much for the pills?" Lilly asked.

"Doesn't seem right to charge you full price when you did the work," Mr. Lippert said. "Shall we say sixpence?"

"That is very generous. I can see why you are not the wealthiest apothecary in the row—but I venture you are the kindest."

"Thank you, my dear. Please do come again."

"Oh yes, do," Polly said. "We close at four on Mondays. Come for tea."

"I should enjoy that. Thank you."

Slipping her little parcel into her reticule, she bid farewell to Polly and Mr. Lippert and left the shop, pausing once more to absorb the familiar jingle of the shop bell.

Then she crossed the street to listen to the irregular doctor preach his remedy.

The rotund man stood on a pallet near his cart. He lifted a paper-labeled brown glass jar before the small crowd gathered near. "Lady Rutger's Restorative. It restores the blood, balances the humours, brightens the complexion, and eases the mind."

"Does it balance ledgers?" a young dandy muttered sarcastically, and Lilly bit back a smile.

She raised her gloved hand and called out, "May I ask a question?"

The rotund man looked her way, eyes gleaming. "Of course, lovely lady. I have nothing to hide."

"What is the active ingredient?"

His eyes narrowed, but his smile widened. "Why? Do you plan to open your own laboratory?"

The crowd laughed.

"Not I," she said innocently.

"Of course not. A jest only. Well, miss, I would happily divulge the ingredients active and binding, but I am afraid such knowledge would be difficult to grasp. The world of medicine is the world of learned men, scientists, physicians, masters—"

"And which are you, sir?" the young dandy asked, thrusting his walking stick at the man for emphasis.

The peddler paused, his smile stiffening. "All of the above, I hope."

Lilly added, "And where did you receive your training?"

"The school of life, miss. I have traveled the world, discovered cures not yet known in England. I have treated patients in hut and castle. Farm and court."

"You speak very well, sir," Lilly said in mock admiration. "I should like to hear such a melodious, learned voice list the ingredients of Lady Rutger's Restorative."

"The language of medicine is Latin, miss. Even if I listed the *materia medica*, you would not understand."

"Might I at least try?" she asked.

"Very well." He spoke quickly and authoritatively, "This is a patented aromatic confection consisting of *Rosar, Poeniae, Anthos,* and *Bryonia dioica.*"

He shuttered his brows and lifted one side of his mouth in a patronizing smirk.

She smiled sweetly in return and pronounced, "Or, in plain English—rosewater, peony, rosemary, and common bryony."

His nostrils flared and his mouth slackened.

She felt the stares of the crowd around her but kept her own gaze on the peddler. "In other words, plants these good people might find in their gardens or hedgerows. Or they could purchase from, say, Lippert's Apothecary for a mere fraction of what you are charging. Is that not so?"

The peddler stepped down from his pallet, stalked over, and dipped his face close to hers. "I don't know who you are," he hissed. "But you are coming dangerously close to irritating me. Who do you work for? Old Mr. Lippert? Is this some last-ditch effort to save that musty shop of his?"

She felt a prickle of fear and stepped back, but still projected her voice. "I work for no one and have had the privilege of meeting Mr. Lippert on only one occasion, this very day. But I can tell you, sir, there is not an apothecary—or irregular doctor—that I would trust as completely in all of Apothecaries Street."

"Hey, *Doctor* Poole," an old man called, "I'll have back my eleven shillings if you please."

"And mine as well," called a well-dressed matron.

Poole took a menacing step closer to Lilly, and she stifled the urge to run. She risked a hopeful glance at the dandy, but saw that he and his jaunty stick were backing off in retreat. *Stupid girl*, Lilly silently remonstrated. Why had she dared such a thing alone?

From out of the crowd, Dr. Graves appeared as if by magic, his face a mask of cool confidence. "Come now," he said officiously, "we really must go." He took her arm and led her smartly away from the peddler and the crowd.

Lilly did not resist.

When they had crossed the street, she whispered, "That will do, I think. Thank you."

He paused and released her, expelling a huff of breath. "I must say, Miss Haswell, that was a most foolish thing to do. Safer to stand between a wild dog and his bone. He will only be back again in an hour, and tomorrow and all next week. Do you plan to stand guard at every show?"

"No. But I could not stand by and let those people be taken in by that quack."

"As I saw. I had only come to purchase a few items for the hospital when I glimpsed you nose-to-nose with that mongrel. I could barely believe my eyes." He regarded her speculatively. "Nor my ears. I heard only a few scraps of what you were saying, but your Latin, Miss Haswell, is impressive indeed. I am surprised your tutor included the subject."

She hesitated. "I have learned a great many things since coming to London," she said, which was true enough. Though Latin had not been among them.

He glanced up the street, at the few waiting carriages. "You are not here alone, I trust?"

"No. I came with my aunt's maid in a hackney. She should return any moment."

He looked at her, eyes alight. "Then might I have the honor of delivering the two of you safely home?"

She smiled, relieved. "That you might, Dr. Graves." She cocked her head to one side to regard him. "For someone who owns numerous fears, may I say you acted very bravely today. I thank you for coming to my rescue."

His fair cheeks reddened with pleasure, and she thought his thin frame stood the taller for her praise.

"Well then," he said, "I am excessively glad I roused myself to the task."

Give me an ounce of civit, good apothecary, to sweeten my imagination.

—Shakespeare

Chapter 10

When Lilly entered her aunt's room later that afternoon, Ruth Elliott smiled at her expectantly from the dressing table. "There you are, my dear." She patted the chair beside her. "Come. Show me what you have bought."

"I am afraid I found little I could not live without. Shopping was not the same without you. And you—how are you feeling?"

"A great deal better."

"I am relieved to hear it."

"Sleep is a powerful elixir. One they don't sell in shops. I think I shall even dress for dinner."

"Aunt, may I ask . . ." Lilly's heart began pounding at the mere thought of the black necklace. It was an effort to speak calmly. "May I ask about something I saw in your jewelry chest?"

Her aunt's eyes glinted. "Ah . . . Saw something that caught your fancy, did you?"

"Well, in a manner of—"

Her aunt rose. "Let us have a look. I am sure whatever it is, you shall be welcome to wear it. What is our next engagement? I forget. Dinner at Caldwells'?"

Thoughts elsewhere, Lilly vaguely replied, "I am not sure."

Ruth Elliott selected a key from the ornate chatelaine. "Here we are."

Lilly followed her into the dressing room and watched as her aunt opened the chest. "Now, what is it that has caught your eye, hmm?"

Lilly's palms were damp as she reached into the case and pulled open the compartment. Would it still be there, or had she dreamt it?

There it was. Black filigree. Black onyx. She lifted it reverently and turned to her aunt. Ruth Elliott took it from her gingerly, her brow furrowed. "I would not have guessed. This is rather severe, is it not? Elegant for mourning, I suppose. But not suitable, really, with any of your gowns. . . ."

"I do not wish to wear it. I wish to know how it came to be here."

Ruth Elliott looked at her, confused. Did her aunt truly not know this had been her mother's? Or was she hesitating, trying to figure out a plausible explanation?

"What do you mean, my dear?"

Lilly did not want to believe her aunt capable of deception, and the innocent question seemed genuine enough.

"Where did it come from?"

"I . . . I don't know. I think . . . if I remember correctly, it is a piece your uncle acquired."

"Acquired? From whom?"

The older woman stared at the necklace as though it held the answer, her face stretched in concentration. "I think he said he purchased it at auction. I don't recall where."

"Auction?" Was it possible? Lilly could hardly credit such a coincidence. Unless her uncle had bid on the piece *because* he had recognized it. "When? How long ago?"

"You will have to ask your uncle. But it seems to me that piece has been there for several years. I have never worn it. I really do not know what would possess him to buy such a thing, though I have never had the heart to tell him so."

Her aunt took her by the arms, concern deep in the lines of her face. "What is it, Lillian? Why do you want to know?"

It was on the tip of her tongue to say, *It was my mother's.* But she bit the words back. Should she tell her aunt if her uncle had never done so? Had he his reasons? Lilly swallowed. "It is an unusual piece, to be sure. You are right. I shall ask Uncle about it as you suggest."

"But—"

"Forgive me. I had better hurry or I shall never dress for dinner in time."

"Very well, my dear."

But she felt her aunt's concern follow her from the dressing room.

As they sat at the dining table that evening, each spooning spring soup in polite, silent sips, her aunt broached the subject.

"My dear. Lillian would like to ask you about a necklace in the chest."

"Oh?"

"The unusual black piece with the onyx pendant?"

Her uncle's face looked disturbed, his eyes stared at the tablecloth, unseeing. Or was she imagining this?

"I am afraid I do not have your every bauble memorized, my dear."

"Of course not. But you would remember this piece. Black filigree, octagonal pendant? I believe you said you purchased it at auction several years ago."

"Did I?" He set down his spoon with a clatter and leaned back heavily against the chair. "Let us finish our meal in peace—then you may show me the article in question. All right?"

Her aunt looked mildly stunned. "Yes, of course."

After dinner the Elliotts disappeared into her aunt's room, and Lilly retreated to her own, waiting anxiously. She found herself thinking back to the day her mother had disappeared. Of coming home to find her father pacing and Charlie hiding behind the draperies. She had gone into the bedchamber and begun searching through her mother's drawers and wardrobe, looking for a letter or for some clue as to why she had left and where she had gone. Lilly feared she knew the reason, at least in part. Even now, she couldn't quite dispel the guilt she felt, the awful notion that their argument had been the cause.

During her long ago search, Lilly had quickly surmised her mother had taken her jewelry and better dresses. Then she had realized the map was gone. The world map she and her mother had pored over on rainy afternoons—the rectangle of thick creased paper the color of a tea stain. The print dominated by two spheres—the eastern Old World. The western New. As a girl, Lilly could hardly believe the tiny rabbit-shaped island was England, its ears Scotland. How small her world was compared to the rest of the world. Mother had agreed, and together they dreamt for hours, their fingers tracing latitude lines, underscoring names of faraway places—the Canary Islands, Trinidad, Tobago, the Southern Icy Ocean—and imagining aloud what each might be like. Her mother seemed to know how long a sea journey might take to *Terra Australis*, where convicts were transported, or to the Cape of Africa, or to South America's Horn.

When she had left, Rosamond Haswell had taken the well-worn map with her. Where had *it* taken her? Was she even now using it to chart her course?

Lilly was pacing her room half an hour later when the housemaid knocked and asked her to join Mr. Elliott in the library. Lilly went down directly.

Her uncle stood alone, one hand on the fireplace mantel. "Come in, my dear. Be seated."

She sat in one of the chairs at the library table, hands clasped. An oil lamp glowed upon the table's gleaming mahogany surface.

He stepped quietly toward her, unfurling his palm, and the black necklace uncoiled from his hand. He laid it on the table between them.

He sighed, his eyes on the piece. "In all honesty, I had forgotten it was there—or at least put it from my mind."

She swallowed and whispered, "It was my mother's, was it not?"

He looked at her, sadness heavy in his hound dog eyes. "Yes, it was. Though I am surprised you remember it so clearly. Ah, I forget. Your infallible memory."

She hung her head. "Not *infallible* . . ."

"I meant no censure. I only wish my memory were half so keen." He sat down in the chair opposite and sighed again. "Your aunt did not know it was your mother's. I never told her before tonight."

While Lilly was relieved at her aunt's exoneration, confusion still plagued her. "Why?"

"Your mother did not wish for Ruth to know."

"I . . . I don't understand. What control would she have over an auction?"

"It was not a public auction, although I allowed Ruth to believe it so. Your mother came to see me privately."

"When?"

"Must be nearly four years ago now. I did not know then that she had left all of you. I arrogantly assumed your father had fallen on difficult times. Difficult indeed for her to be willing to come to me, to ask for money."

Lilly found it hard to breathe.

"She said she would rather offer the piece to me than some stranger, since I ought to value it more highly. I supposed she wanted to keep it in the family. Honorable enough, though it did strike me as cheeky to ask for money for something that our parents had given her."

"What else did she say? Where was she living?"

"As I said, I foolishly assumed she had merely come from Wiltshire seeking funds. I did not ask questions. Though I am afraid I said a few cruel things."

"Cruel?"

"About your father not being able to support her—how we had all been right in advising her not to marry him. I am ashamed to think of what I said then."

"I wonder if she was living in London or passing through . . . Was she alone?"

"Yes."

"And she asked you not to tell Aunt?"

"She and Ruth had been girlhood friends. I imagine it embarrassed her to think of Ruth knowing."

"Or perhaps she realized Aunt would ask more questions than you did. Questions she did not wish to answer."

"Perhaps."

"Did she ask for money on other occasions as well?"

He hesitated only a second. "No, my dear. That was the only money she ever asked for. I suppose she had nothing else of value and was too proud to ask for a handout."

Lilly shook her head, imagining the awkward scene between estranged brother and sister.

"I am sorry, Lillian. I never intended to deceive you. It is only that I knew it would upset you. Tell me you understand."

"I do." She stood slowly to her feet. "Does Aunt? Or is she angry with you?"

He shrugged. "Disappointed, perhaps."

Lilly walked to the window on wobbly legs. Outside on the street, lamplight gleamed on the rain-wet cobbles.

"Will you be all right?" he asked.

"Of course. Thank you for telling me."

Her uncle rose as well. "You are welcome to the necklace, Lillian. I am certain your mother would want you to have it."

Lilly was not so sure. Did anyone really know what her mother wanted? "Let us leave it locked away. For now."

In the morning, her aunt came to her room while Lilly was still in her dressing gown. She took Lilly's strong hands in her own delicate ones.

"My dear, I am sorry. I cannot imagine how you must be feeling."

"I don't know how to feel about it."

She squeezed her hands. "How can I help?"

Lilly took a deep breath. "By telling me everything you know."

Ruth Elliott hesitated. "Your mother and I confided a great deal to one another as girls, but I know very little about what happened after she married your father."

"And before?"

"Well, I don't think you . . . I don't think anyone enjoys hearing a parent's romantic history—that is, history not involving the other parent."

"Tell me anyway." Lilly seated herself on the made bed and patted the nearby chair.

Her aunt sat, though she looked far from comfortable. "Your mother fancied herself in love with a man before she met your father. Did she ever tell you?"

Lilly shook her head, and her aunt continued. "A very dashing man. A naval officer. And she believed he planned to marry her."

"What was his name?"

Ruth Elliott twisted her rings. "I suppose it can do no harm. A Captain Ernest Quincy. But everyone called him Quinn."

The name meant nothing to Lilly.

"She used to tell me that Quinn planned to have ships of his own one day and travel far and wide. And that he promised to take her with him."

Lilly nodded thoughtfully. She could understand how such a man—and such an offer—might appeal to her mother. Had she not spent hours dreaming over her prized world map?

"Rosamond was so happy in those days," Ruth continued. "Then, without warning, Quinn's betrothal was announced in the *Times*. He had engaged himself to Daisy Wolcott, a much better match, I suppose, as her father was quite wealthy. Rosamond was devastated.

"But then, not a fortnight later, she told me she had met another man and that this Charles Haswell was everything Quinn was not. Evidently, *he* thought Rosamond the most desirable and perfect creature ever to live. Balm to her wounded soul, no doubt. But as you know by now, the family thought Charles not at all suitable. No wealth. No family to speak of. No connections." She glanced at Lilly with sorrowful eyes. "I am sorry, but there it is." She took a deep breath. "Of course, Rosamond saw none of this. She argued that he would soon have a good income and good prospects. But more than this, she knew your father would take her from London, the scene of her disgrace, as she saw it, and I think this was his greatest attraction.

"He proposed in a matter of days, and Rosamond accepted. We all tried to dissuade her from such a course. Had your grandfather lived, he would never have allowed it, but he had already passed on by then. Rosamond begged Jonathan to purchase a special license so that she and Charles might marry as soon as possible. In the end, she married two days before Quinn's own wedding, with only her mother, Jonathan, and I in attendance. I think Rosamond spent a great deal of time imagining Quinn's remorse at discovering her wed to another. Several times during the wedding, I saw her glance toward the side door, as if she was sure Quinn would burst through it and object at any moment."

Ruth Elliott shook her head ruefully. "Your uncle determined that no one of our acquaintance should learn of your father's trade. When asked, we spoke in general terms of his 'holdings' somewhere in Wiltshire. After the wedding, the two departed almost immediately. Much to Rosamond's—and everyone's—relief, I am sorry to say."

Her aunt stopped speaking, and the room felt suddenly too silent. The clock above the mantel ticked, a door closed somewhere belowstairs, the faint sounds of hooves and passing carriages bled through the outside walls.

Lilly said, "I can see why you hesitated to tell me. It is not a romantic story, is it? I wonder if my poor father had any idea."

"I do not know, my dear."

Lilly rose, agitated, as all the new details struggled to fit themselves into the old and erroneous impressions in her mind. "So . . . did this Quinn ever buy his ships and sail away?"

Ruth remained seated. "Not that I know of. He is still married to the former Miss Wolcott. Though it does not appear to be a happy marriage. I see Daisy now and again, and she is almost always alone. The gossips claim, and I am among them now, I suppose, that he has kept a string of mistresses."

"You don't think Mother—?"

Aunt Elliott shifted, glanced at her, then away. "As far as I know, their connection was severed more than twenty years ago." She paused. "But I confess, when we received your father's letter telling us Rosamond had left him, I wasn't as surprised as I might have been, had I not known about Quinn. I had hoped Rosamond would be happy with your father. But I never really believed she would be." She sighed. "I am afraid I don't know any more, my dear. I have no idea where she went or where she is now."

Lilly stared out the second-floor window, at the passing traffic and the trees of Hyde Park beyond. "I have always imagined her sailing the high seas, or on a grand adventure somewhere."

"Have you indeed?"

Lilly turned and glimpsed some unfamiliar, dark emotion in her aunt's countenance.

"Then your imagination is far more generous than mine."

But if the young are never tired of erring in conduct,
neither are the older in erring of judgment.

—Fanny Burney, *Cecilia*, 1782

Chapter 11

Thoughts and questions coursed through Lilly all that day and night. In the morning, she felt quite restless. She wanted to run. Needed to run. But where in all of London could she do such a thing? Where were there no eyes ready to censure and report her unladylike conduct?

No place.

She sighed, took up the cup of chocolate from the tray on her bedside, and sipped. Chocolate had always helped her moods but did little to soothe her antsy limbs.

After breakfast, Lilly received a letter. She took it with her into the sitting room, planning to keep her aunt company while the dear woman did her daily hour of needlework. Her aunt smiled up at her, and Lilly smiled in return. No conversation was required. They were now comfortable enough with one another to enjoy silence as well as chatter.

The letter was from Mary. As she opened it, Lilly realized mildly that it was the first she had received from her old friend in several weeks.

When Lilly had first come to London, Mary had dutifully written every fortnight, if not weekly. And Lilly had written back, though not always as promptly as she should have. It was difficult that first year, when she was always so busy with her studies. And now . . . Well, she had time in the early mornings, surely, before the day's round of calls began, but then with taking exercise in the park, then tea, then endless evening and late-night social obligations, somehow she rarely made the time to write home.

She skimmed the few lines in Mary's small practiced hand, and experienced the pleasant warmth she always felt upon reading cheerful reports of new biscuit recipes, the topic of the Sunday sermon, or the latest village fete she had attended with Charlie, Francis, and Miss Robbins.

Lilly knew she should write back, but what could she say? She did not wish to describe the new gowns, the balls, shopping with Miss Price-Winters on Bond Street and Pall Mall, the museums, the concerts. She could not describe Roger Bromley nor his kind attentions— not when Mary had never known a suitor's regard.

"From home?" Aunt Elliott asked, eyes on her embroidery.

"Yes. From Mary."

Lilly would·not demur and pretend her days were as ordinary as Mary's countrified life no doubt was.

She sighed.

Her aunt, pulling a thread of bishop's blue through the canvas, glanced up at the sound. "Everything all right?"

"Oh yes. The usual niceties." She began refolding the letter. "I like that blue."

I shall write back tomorrow, Lilly decided. *Or the next day.*

"Mr. Adam Graves," Fletcher announced and backed from the sitting room.

Startled, Lilly stood abruptly, the letter falling to the floor.

Dr. Graves entered and bowed. "Miss Haswell."

She curtsied and awkwardly swiped up the letter as she did so. "You remember my aunt, Mrs. Elliott?" Lilly hoped he would not mention their recent encounter on Apothecaries Street.

"I do indeed. Ma'am." He bowed again, a wave of blond hair falling forward and then returning to place as he straightened.

Her aunt nodded but remained seated with her needlework.

"By your leave, ma'am, I have come to ask if Miss Haswell might accompany me for a drive in the park. Perhaps tomorrow afternoon?"

Her aunt's expression was pleasantly bland, but the eyes she turned toward Lilly were full of both meaning and inquiry.

"I was certain we had an engagement for tomorrow afternoon. Are we not expected at the Langtrys', my dear? Do you recall?"

Lilly recognized her aunt's clever phrasing. She was giving Lilly an excuse—if she desired one. Lilly knew her aunt would prefer she not encourage the man, but she would not forbid her either. He was, at least, an Oxford man, and must therefore be from a family of at least modest wealth.

She swallowed. "I believe you are thinking of Friday, Aunt. I recall nothing on the schedule for tomorrow."

"Indeed? Well, you would know. That memory of yours. Sometimes I am not sure I should like to have one so keen."

Dr. Graves cleared his throat. "Excellent. I shall hire a carriage straightaway. I've not my own in town."

Aunt Elliott's eyebrows rose.

"I have use of my brother's, but it is engaged for the morrow."

Lilly bit her lip. Did he not know hacks were not allowed in Hyde Park? "Dr. Graves, you needn't bother. I would just as soon walk."

"Indeed? Are you quite sure?"

"Quite. At home there was only one thing I liked better than a country walk."

"And what was that?"

She glanced at her aunt, then changed the subject. "What time shall I expect you?"

Dr. Graves arrived promptly to take Lilly for the promised walk in Hyde Park, only a short distance from her aunt and uncle's home. He wore a morning coat of claret with a patterned waistcoat and buff trousers. Her aunt could not complain that his attire was not *de rigueur*.

Lilly wore a walking dress of ivory corded muslin with a lilac satin shawl. At her aunt's suggestion, she wore a large Oldenburg bonnet, perhaps to keep those of Mr. Bromley's acquaintance from seeing her out with another man.

Meeting anyone she knew seemed unlikely, however, as Hyde Park was sparsely populated in the early afternoon. The fashionable set did not show up until half past five, when they arrived en masse in fine carriages and finer carriage dress, and raced and ogled and flirted until it was time to return home and change into evening dress.

Nor were there any military reviews or driving meets to disturb their solitude as Lilly and Dr. Graves strolled along the web of walking paths and around manmade Serpentine Lake. As they did, Lilly did her best to conjure conversation, pointing out flowers in bloom, a chattering squirrel in a tree, and the occasional dandy in a high-perch phaeton. Dr. Graves would nod or murmur assent to whatever she said, but he was clearly distracted.

Finally he said, "Previously, Miss Haswell, you asked about my fears."

"You needn't—"

"I do," he insisted, then exhaled deeply. "I have diagnosed the underlying cause, I believe. Though not the prognosis, nor treatment. I am the youngest of three sons, as I believe I mentioned. We were all sent to a boarding school reputed for its unwavering discipline. But the stern headmaster was nothing to my father. We did as he said or the consequences were severe. To this day I struggle to confront authority or act in the face of opposition. I was five and twenty before I made a truly important decision on my own."

She looked at him and asked tentatively, "And what was it, if I may ask?"

He blinked his startling blue eyes. "Why . . . to court you."

She felt her face flush and her heart pound in sweet heavy beats. They walked in silence for several minutes before he spoke again.

He began abruptly, "I think it only fair to tell you that I was engaged once, but the lady broke it off."

"Oh." She was taken aback. "I . . . I am sorry."

He glanced at her briefly, then away. "She was my father's choice, but I am afraid neither she nor her mother approved of my chosen profession. The thought of hospitals, injuries and diseases . . . all quite disgusted them both."

Lilly nodded her understanding.

"I suppose medicine *is* rather distasteful," he continued. "Boils and growths. Infections and bodily fluids . . ." He stopped, turning to her, face stricken. "Forgive me!"

Lilly said mildly, "Do not be uneasy on my account."

"Such talk does not disturb you?"

"No. Though I own it is not my favorite mealtime topic."

"Of course. But you do not swoon nor faint nor sicken?"

Lilly shook her head.

He paused on the tree-lined path, regarding her with frank admiration. She was tempted to tell him the reason behind her understanding nature. But her aunt's cautioning voice whispered in her mind.

"In that case—" he gave a rare smile—"there is someplace I should very much like to show you."

His smile transformed his features. His frown lines disappeared, his eyes crinkled, his dimples deepened.

Oh my . . . Lilly felt her cheeks grow warm as she gazed at him, glad he could not read her thoughts.

Fade far away, dissolve, and quite forget
What thou among the leaves hast never known,
The weariness, the fever, and the fret
Here, where men sit and hear each other groan. . . .

—JOHN KEATS, POET & LICENSED APOTHECARY, 1819

CHAPTER 12

Dr. Graves hired a hackney to drive them to the southeast of London, to large and impressive Guy's Hospital.

"I would like you to see where I have spent my days and sometimes my nights this last year gone. This is where I 'walk the wards' as we say, to obtain practical experience. Officially I am a perpetual physician's pupil and pay handsomely for the privilege. Or rather, my father does." He gave a lopsided grin, blue eyes sparkling. "I have taken the examination for licentiateship and should learn very soon whether or not I have passed."

When they arrived, he paid the driver and helped Lilly down from the hired coach. She relished the excuse to place her gloved hand in his, however fleetingly.

He led her through the wrought-iron gates into the open courtyard, flanked on three sides by the four-story hospital of grey and drab-brown brick. In the center of the courtyard, they passed the statue of Thomas Guy himself, who founded the hospital nearly a century before.

"Do you know anything about Thomas Guy, Miss Haswell?" She shook her head.

"I cannot but admire him. He was a man of humble beginnings— the son of a coal monger. He became a bookseller, and amassed his splendid fortune from the sale of Bibles, among other things. The list of all he did, all he gave, would run the length of a man's arm."

Passing between columns and beneath an archway, they entered the building. Dr. Graves seemed to come to life within its walls. Gone was the reticent man she had met at the ball. Eagerly, he led her on an enthusiastic tour of the main hall, the chapel, the lecture theatre, and two of the twelve wards.

"This is a teaching hospital," he explained. "Apothecaries, surgeons' apprentices, physicians' pupils, and dressers come here for courses of study."

Her attention was piqued by the mention of apothecaries, but this time she kept her mouth closed.

A young man bearing a stack of books and papers whipped around a corner and collided with Dr. Graves. Graves reached out his hands to prevent a blow, but still the young man's books and papers fell and scattered to the floor.

"I say, Keats, have a care."

"Sorry, old man." Young Mr. Keats sank to his haunches and began picking up his papers. Lilly did the same, picking up the sheet that had landed on the toe of her boot. She glanced at it, surprised to see, in a lovely hand, stanzas of a sonnet. A few phrases leapt off the page. *O SOLITUDE! . . . climb with me the steep . . . flowery slopes . . .*

As he rose, Lilly saw that the man, near her own age, seemed distracted and flighty as a sparrow.

She held out the paper toward him. Eyeing it, his frenetic movements stilled. He lifted his gaze to hers, warily. Without comment, she handed him the paper. He tucked it under the book on the top of his stack.

"Thank you, fair miss."

"Miss Haswell, may I present Mr. John Keats."

The young man bowed. "How do you do."

"Mr. Keats is training to become an apothecary. Are you not, Keats?"

He ducked his head. "Yes . . . and other pursuits as well."

Graves peered at the book Keats bore. "A volume of lyric poetry . . . I do not recall that in the curriculum."

"No, sir. Only in my spare time, sir."

Bowing again to Lilly, John Keats strode quickly down the corridor.

Watching him retreat, Dr. Graves shook his head. "Keen student. But a bit of a dreamer, I'm afraid. Fancies himself a poet. Writes such nonsense in the margins of his work . . ."

Graves then led her up two flights of stairs. "I would not bring you up here were any operations scheduled. But you might find the theatre itself interesting." He pushed the door open and ushered her inside. The air that met her held a sour, cloying odor, which she recognized instantly as blood. The theatre was horseshoe shaped with three rows of benches rising high on two curved sides.

He led her down the steep stairs to the operating pit below. A narrow wooden table stood at center. Light from a skylight and two gas lamps suspended from the ceiling illuminated the scene. Beneath the table was a box of sawdust for collecting blood, she guessed. Beside it was a common dining room chair and a sideboard of instruments. A mop and bucket stood at the ready against the wall.

From this lower vantage, Dr. Graves pointed up to the rows of benches rising around them. "The first two rows are for the dressers, and behind that partition sit the other pupils. All are required to attend, whether future surgeons, physicians, or apothecaries."

Suddenly the door above them, from which they themselves had entered, burst open, and a stream of young men rushed in, filing into the rows with friendly shoving and jocularity.

Graves frowned and looked at her apologetically. "Must be an operation after all. An emergency perhaps. Let us take our leave."

Before they could, the side door opened and two aproned men came in, carrying a draped figure on a litter.

Lilly climbed the steps quickly, but midway up, glanced back. Behind the two assistants came a man she identified as a surgeon by the old frock coat he wore, stained with blood, dried and fresh.

"Miss Haswell," Dr. Graves urged from behind. "Please."

She continued to the top, Dr. Graves at her heels. By now, the pupils were packed in as tight as pills in a bottle and pushing each other and maneuvering to see below.

Whenever their views were blocked, whether by fellow pupil or by surgeon below, calls of "Heads, heads," rang out. The air was filled with anticipation, laughter, and whistles to chums across the theatre— all of which seemed to belong not to this grave occasion, but to some macabre sporting event.

Once the door was closed behind them, her escort said earnestly, "Miss Haswell, please forgive me. If I had any notion they were operating today . . . I . . . I never meant to expose you to such sights."

Moved by the concern in his eyes and voice, she took a deep breath and considered what she had just seen. "I own I was relieved not to witness the operation itself, but I found the theatre, the wards, the dispensary . . . why, the entire hospital, quite interesting."

"Truly?"

"Yes."

He shook his head, eyes wide in amazement or disbelief, she could not tell.

As they walked on, leaving the din behind them, Lilly remarked, "Had I to require surgery, I should not like it above half to be observed by such a crowd."

"Nor I. It is mostly the poor who come here. They are willing to bear spectators because this is the only place they can afford treatment. Wealthier patients are operated on in their own homes. Usually on their kitchen tables, I understand."

She nodded without comment. In Bedsley Priors, people had to call upon the surgeon in Wilcot for such services. Her father did only minor procedures himself.

"Sadly the death rates are shockingly high. Therefore such operations are usually only performed as a last resort. I will be pleased to limit my practice to physic, if I may—though I suppose in smaller villages a medical man might need to do a bit of everything."

They descended the stairs and were once again in the long main corridor.

"*Do* you plan to establish yourself in a small village somewhere? I had not thought it of you."

He shrugged, then asked shyly, "Does the thought displease you?"

"Not at all. Why would it?"

He paused, examining her countenance closely. "Can you really be so perfect?"

Lilly felt her cheeks heat. She darted a look at him and saw his face redden as well.

"Hardly perfect, no." She was again tempted to disclose her father's trade and even her mother's disappearance. Certainly her aunt would not wish her to withhold the truth once a man was courting her, would she?

As they returned to the welcomed fresh air of the courtyard, he said, "If your father were alive, I should ask to meet him."

Confusion puckered her brow. "But he is alive."

He stared at her. "Is he? Well, dash it, what a blunder. I was given to understand that you were a ward of the Elliotts."

"I suppose I am. But not an orphan. My father is alive and well in Wiltshire."

"I see. Well, this changes everything. Do you think a letter would suffice?"

Here he was again, the timid man full of self-doubt.

She did not want to mistake his meaning. "What . . . sort of letter do you mean?"

Again, his face reddened. "I suppose a letter of introduction and, well, to . . . express my interest."

"In courting me?" she asked bluntly. How far afield she was from the subtle language of fans and flirting her aunt had paid so dearly for her to learn!

"Well, yes. For now."

"Then perhaps my uncle is the person to speak with in my father's stead." She thought once more of revealing her secrets. But if her uncle withheld his approval, might they both be spared the telling? "However, I must warn you that my aunt prefers I keep my distance from medical men."

"Why?"

"I am afraid in that, you will not find her much different from the mother of your previous fiancée."

"I see. I take it your aunt would be quite shocked to learn where you spent the afternoon?"

She shook her head. "Shocked, no. But certainly disappointed. I shall tell her the truth—" she grinned up at him—"that we enjoyed a most interesting walk."

He smiled back at her and again his features were transformed. He truly was a lovely man.

The shop bell jingled as Lilly and Dupree entered Monday morning. Polly Lippert looked up from her books and exclaimed, "Miss Haswell!" She rose, smoothing her apron over a patterned muslin frock. "How good of you to come again."

"I hope you don't mind my calling unannounced."

"No, you are most welcome. Any time."

"This is Miss Dupree. Dupree, this is Miss Lippert."

The maid bobbed a curtsy, then turned to Lilly. "Mind if I have a look around?"

"No. Go on."

Miss Lippert led Lilly back to the kitchen—far neater than theirs at home. Lilly realized the Lipperts must keep a separate laboratory.

"I am sorry my father is not here," Miss Lippert said. "He and my brother, George, have gone to the Docklands."

Lilly would have liked to meet George Lippert. A person like herself, skilled in physic but wanting little to do with it.

"Two colliers are just in from the Cape," Polly continued as she set a pot of water to boil. "The advertisement promised an immense shipment of new exotics and a *live* rhinoceros."

"I should have liked to see that," Lilly said, though she could just imagine how her aunt and uncle would cringe at the thought of her venturing to such a rough, dirty place.

Polly pulled two teacups from the cupboard and set out a pot of tea—infused with mint from their shop stores—and a plate of butter biscuits. The two young women enjoyed tea and half an hour's visit. As Lilly and Dupree prepared to take their leave, Polly wrapped up a new bottle of Warren and Rosser's Milk of Roses, which Dupree insisted Lilly use daily to diminish her freckles. Lilly was just tying the ribbons of her wrap when a startling crash rang out, quickly followed by the shattering of glass. Polly rushed to the shopwindow, and Lilly and Dupree hurried to join her there. Through the wavy glass, Lilly saw a man in a blue gown standing in the threshold of a shop on the other side of the street. In his arms he held a crate of Lambeth pottery.

Lilly cried out in shock as he heaved the jars into the street.

The pottery exploded into pieces. Oils and syrups spilled like jeweled blood onto the beginnings of a pile in the street—wood from a broken medicine chest, perhaps, and shards of blue and brown glass.

"What is he doing?" Lilly exclaimed.

"Dash it. Father told Hetta to be careful."

A woman of middle years ran hysterically into the street, shrieked, then grabbed hold of the man's sleeve as he carried out another load. He did not even seem to notice her. This time he held a decorative blue and gold apothecary jar, nearly half his own height.

"No!" the woman cried.

The man seemed to hesitate for a moment, but perhaps it was only an illusion of the wavy glass. His expression stern, he heaved it onto the pile, the priceless piece shattering in a shower of blue and gold.

Lilly ran to the door and opened it. But Polly caught her arm and held her back. "Don't, Miss Haswell."

"Can we not do something?"

"What can we do? He is the beadle, and the man there"—Polly

nodded toward an officious-looking man in black watching the proceedings with cool detachment—"is the master of wardens for the
Apothecaries' Society."

Stunned into silence, Lilly watched from the open doorway.

"They are within their rights," Polly went on. "Everyone knows
Hetta diagnoses and dispenses physic. Last week a boy nearly died
from mislabeled medicine."

"Oh no."

"And it isn't the first time. There have been charges of selling
inferior and adulterated medicine before."

"But why would they?"

Polly shrugged. "Mistakes. To save money. I don't know. Her
poor husband."

Lilly looked at her, brows raised.

"He's under the cat's paw, that one is," Polly explained. "He's
never been able to manage Hetta. Always insists she is as qualified
as any man in the row."

The woman named Hetta covered her face and disappeared back
into the shop. Finally the beadle brought out a large armful of dried
herbs, stuck bunches in crevices among the rubble, and heaped the
rest on top. A few seconds later he returned once more from inside
the shop, this time bearing a smoldering stick of tinder, which he put
to rapid use. The herbs smoked for a few seconds and then, fed by the
alcohol in several of the syrups, leapt to angry life, the fire devouring
the wood and filling the narrow street with pungent smoke.

Lilly stared. The flames and smoke rose to both frame and obscure the
sign hanging above the desecrated shop. *J. W. Fry, Apothecary.* Though
the heated air touched her skin where she stood, Lilly shivered.

*A certain noble lord had brought his health into a very critical state
and the physicians recommended marriage
as the most certain method of restoring his constitution.*

—THE GENTLEMAN'S MAGAZINE, 1769

CHAPTER 13

Lilly flipped through the letters on the silver tray on the sideboard.

"Strange," she muttered.

Her aunt peered at her over the half-spectacles she wore for reading. "What is, my dear?"

"I wrote to my father nearly a fortnight ago and have yet to receive a response."

Lilly had at last written a few lines to her father the same day she had finally sent a note to Mary to wish her old friend a happy birthday.

Her aunt refolded her own letter. "Perhaps he is busy. Or the post was delayed."

"I do hope he is all right." Though she had not seen her father in over a year, they had corresponded regularly. Her planned visit last Christmas had been canceled when her aunt came down with a worrisome fever. Lilly had stayed in town to nurse her, and somehow the visit home had never been rescheduled.

"Of course he is. He would send word if there was anything amiss, would he not?"

"I hope so." Now that Lilly thought of it, his letters had become increasingly infrequent.

Her aunt slit open a second letter and began to read. She looked up at Lilly again, eyes bright.

"My dear, you will not believe it!"

"What is it? I have rarely seen you so animated."

"The Bromleys have accepted our invitation to dine with us on Saturday. They must realize Roger has selected you particularly. This is a most telling attention, to be sure."

"But we invited them."

Ruth Elliott went on undeterred, "Mark my words, Lillian. Roger Bromley will very soon be making you an offer."

"Oh, Aunt, I do not think so."

Lilly had hoped for such from Mr. Bromley since the end of last season. For beyond wishing to please her aunt by making a good match, she genuinely liked him. But now, with Susan Whittier on the scene, Lilly had all but given up that hope. Depressing though it was to lose the man's gallant addresses, Dr. Graves's attentions had served to lessen her disappointment.

"My dear . . ." Aunt Elliott removed her spectacles. "Tell me you will not reject Roger Bromley in favor of that Graves fellow."

Would she? Had she not given him leave to speak to her uncle on her behalf—believing Mr. Bromley lost to her?

Her aunt leaned closer. "Lillian, if Roger Bromley proposes, promise me you'll not let the likes of Dr. Graves spoil your chance at an excellent marriage. Your uncle and I are offering a substantial dowry and annual allowance. The Bromleys will have nothing to object to on that account."

Though on several others, Lilly thought, but forbore to say so. "That is very generous. I had no idea."

"What more can we do to show you our feelings?" Tears

shimmered in her aunt's eyes. "We look upon you as our daughter and desire your every happiness. We will do all within our power to see you well wed."

Moved, Lilly reached across and squeezed her aunt's hand. "Very well. If Mr. Bromley proposes, I shall duly consider." Though she doubted she would need to, for despite the upcoming dinner, Lilly still believed Roger Bromley would soon be directing his addresses elsewhere.

"Wonderful girl!" Her aunt beamed. "Oh, you have a bright future ahead of you!"

On Saturday, Lilly was pacing the hall when she heard a carriage door close. Were the Bromleys early? She hoped not. Her aunt had not yet finished dressing and would want to greet their guests when they arrived. Lilly stepped to the hall window. The sight of the caller was worse than unfashionably early guests. Panicked, Lilly went to the door herself, opening it to the man before he even knocked.

"Dr. Graves! We were not expecting you."

He smiled at her seemingly enthusiastic greeting. "You suggested I call on your uncle. So, here I am."

"Did I? Well, I am afraid this is not a good time. We are expecting guests any moment."

"Oh?" He raised his brows in expectation, but she did not supply a name.

"Yes, so if you would be good enough to return another time?"

He frowned. "But I have spent the day rousing my courage and pressing my best frock coat. I hate the thought of having to start the whole dreadful process over again another day."

"I am afraid you must." She began to edge the door shut.

"Lillian?" Her uncle appeared in the entry hall behind her. "Where is Fletcher? You needn't . . . Oh, good day. Graves, is it?"

"Yes, sir. I had hoped to speak with you if you can spare a moment."

Lilly said, "I have just been telling Dr. Graves that we are expecting guests at any time."

"True, true," Jonathan Elliott said. "But, well, they are not here yet and you are. My wife is still dressing, but I am as good as I get, as you see." Her uncle chuckled. "Come back to the library, Graves, and tell me what this is about. . . ."

A quarter of an hour later, Lilly was still pacing the hall, but now for a different reason. She had hoped to see Dr. Graves out the door before the Bromleys arrived, but he and her uncle had tarried too long. Fletcher was just taking the Bromleys' coats and hats when Dr. Graves and her uncle reappeared in the hall.

"Graves?" Roger said. "I did not expect to see you here."

"Nor I you."

Roger turned to his parents. "May I introduce Mr. Graves, a new physician—attended the same college as Uncle Thomas, I understand."

Mr. Bromley smiled. "An Oxford man. Excellent."

"My parents," Roger continued. "Mr. and Mrs. Bromley."

"Perhaps you would like to join us for dinner, Dr. Graves," Uncle Elliott suggested kindly.

"Thank you, sir, but I would not wish to intrude."

Awkward silence filled the hall. Finally her aunt filled it, saying dutifully, but without warmth, "Of course you are welcome, Dr. Graves."

Mr. Bromley, senior, surveyed her from across the dining table. "Your parents, Miss Haswell. Would I know them?"

Wariness filled her. "I would not think so, Mr. Bromley. My father did live in London for a time, but that was many years ago now."

Her aunt deftly stemmed unwanted inquiries by adding, "And her mother has been gone these several years."

"Oh, I am sorry to hear it," Mrs. Bromley said. "And Mr. Haswell. He is . . . ?" The elegant woman raised her brows in expectation, too polite to ask if her father had a profession or, worse yet, a trade.

Ruth Elliott sweetly ignored the implied question. "I am sure he is faring as well as can be expected on his own."

Mr. Bromley skewered a hunk of roast pork from the nearby platter and set it on his plate. "How does he occupy his time, Miss Haswell?"

Lillian licked her suddenly dry lips.

Her aunt answered in her stead. "Missing our Lillian, no doubt. How long have you been with us now, my dear? Two years?"

"Not quite so long, but above a year, yes."

"And do you enjoy London?" Mrs. Bromley asked, taking the bait.

"Oh yes. The city is fascinating, and I have met so many wonderful people."

"The Price-Winters family have taken special interest in our niece," Ruth Elliott added. "Such close friends the girls are."

"Yes, but from where do you hail, Miss Haswell?" Mr. Bromley persisted, sawing at his meat with knife and fork.

"Wiltshire, sir."

"Wiltshire!" the man enthused. "I have been there. I shall never forget it."

Lilly smiled. "It warms my heart to hear you say so."

"Then you no doubt know of the Wiltshire miracle?"

Lilly's smile faded. "I am not sure . . ."

He set down his utensils and stared off into his memories. "Must be ten or twelve years ago now. Several of us gentlemen went to a house party there, to enjoy a bit of hunting in the country. Well, a bit of gaming, too, truth be known. One evening, after a long day of shooting very ill, we were all well in our cups and pipes, when the man of the house—my chum's father—died. Right there in front of us all. Thomas rushed to him, but said the old man was stone dead. Still, the servants scurried about and called for the local apothecary. In this fellow comes, and the servants carry the body away to another room, the apothecary and my chum following behind. Well, I have to admit, the rest of us returned to our cards and quite put it from our minds. Death making one want to eat, drink, and be merry.

"But then, lo and behold, not an hour later, my chum Marlow rushes back into the room and proclaims the apothecary had worked a miracle. His father was alive and well and asking for his supper! Well, that spoilt the weekend for the rest of us, I can tell you. Nothing like a miracle to sour the taste of port and pipe."

He lifted his glass to signify the end of his story. Murmurs of amused approval rose up from the others.

"Clearly the man was not dead," Dr. Graves declared. "Merely fainted or unconscious."

Mr. Bromley took a drink and set down his glass. "Normally I would agree with you, sir, and take first seat among the mockers, were it not for one fact. My own brother confirmed him quite dead."

"But anybody might mistake—"

"He is a physician, young man, a master at that college of yours."

Dr. Graves faltered. "Wait . . . Thomas Bromley?"

"That is what I've been telling you."

"He is very skilled, very knowledgeable, I admit," Graves said. "I sat under him for several courses."

Mr. Bromley nodded, sealing his point. He turned to Lilly. "Being from Wiltshire, I imagine you have heard the tale?"

Lilly had barely parted her lips when she saw her aunt's eyes flash warning. Ruth Elliott shook her head in the slightest of rebuttals, urging her to do the same.

"I forget the man's name," Bromley went on. "Something with an *H*, I believe. Howard, or Hatfield . . ."

Her aunt half rose from her seat. "Why do the ladies not withdraw and leave the men to their port?"

"Come to think of it, the apothecary had a scrap of a child with him. A little girl."

"Miss Haswell?" Dr. Graves turned to her, frowning deeply. Lilly swallowed.

"Do you know this man, this apothecary?"

"Uhh . . . yes."

"Well, it sounds as if everybody in Wiltshire knows the man," her aunt said, stepping to the door. "Come, Lillian."

"But do you remember his *name?*" Mr. Bromley persisted. "I do so detest not remembering a name."

Lilly paused where she stood at her place. She glanced at her aunt, but Ruth Elliott looked away. There was nothing for it.

"His name is Charles Haswell, sir," Lilly said. "My father."

She glanced over and glimpsed Roger Bromley staring at her and Dr. Graves shaking his head.

At the conclusion of the unsettling evening, Lilly walked Dr. Graves to the door.

"Well, a night of surprises all around," he began. "An apothecary's daughter . . ." He took a breath. "It all makes sense now. Your actions with Mr. Price-Winters, your familiarity with Latin . . . Why did you not tell me?"

"My aunt prefers I not speak of it."

"Why? So you might capture a gentleman under false pretenses?"

She turned to look at him, anger and resolution kindling in her chest. "Please do not consider yourself captured, Dr. Graves. You are perfectly free."

He opened his mouth but closed it again, saying nothing. He seemed about to try again when Roger Bromley let himself from the dining room, quietly closing the door on the gentlemen still within. Her aunt and Mrs. Bromley were still in the drawing room, her aunt no doubt doing her best to minimize the damage.

Dr. Graves bowed stiffly. "Then I will bid you good-night. Miss Haswell. Bromley."

When the door shut behind Dr. Graves, Roger Bromley took her arm and gently led her to a padded bench near the stairs. Once she was seated, he sat beside her.

"Sorry about that. I don't think my parents meant to badger you. Big on pedigree, my mother. Father is actually impressed. 'The daughter of a real miracle worker,' he said. 'Handy to have one of those in the family.' " He glanced at her as the implication of his words registered. "I have to say I quite agree." He took her hand in his. "I don't care about any of it."

But he doesn't know it all, Lilly thought, *or he might care a great deal.*

"I like you as you are, Miss Haswell. So free from all the snobbery and airs of my set." He grinned. "And not a trial to look at either."

Her heart momentarily surged, but then she thought of her unspoken secrets, and his unresolved feelings for another. She smiled gently. "Mr. Bromley, thank you. But you said it yourself. You like me. And certainly I like you. But there is another, I think, whom you love."

"Miss Whittier, you mean?"

She nodded. "You cannot deny it. Your face gives you away whenever you look at her."

He grimaced. "But she will never accept me. She has already said as much."

"She might. You mustn't give up hope. She hasn't married anyone else, has she?"

He all but groaned, "No."

"You are a true gentleman, Mr. Bromley. Any woman would be blessed to own your heart."

"Miss Whittier would not agree with you."

"At least not yet."

She squeezed his hand before extracting her own. "Perhaps there is something we can do to help things along."

The recipient paid dearly . . . there was a fourpenny charge
for the typical letter consisting of one large sheet of paper
folded several times and sealed with wax.

—SHARON LAUDERMILK AND TERESA HAMLIN, *THE REGENCY COMPANION*

CHAPTER 14

Her uncle came into the library the following Monday and sat in the chair opposite her. His shoulders were hunched, elbows on his knees, and his face was wrinkled in deep thought.

She lowered *The Family Robinson Crusoe*, which she had acquired from the nearby circulating library, and steeled herself for another reprisal of Saturday night's failures.

For several moments, he seemed to study his clenched hands. "Lillian, when we spoke about the necklace, you made it clear you would like to know everything possible about your mother, even if it were . . . unpleasant?"

"Yes." Lilly leaned forward. "Have you heard something? Did she contact you again?"

He shook his head. "What I have to tell you happened some three years ago now." He held up his hand, forestalling her protest before it could form. "I know—but until the business with the necklace I never considered telling you."

He met her eyes directly. "I told you the truth, my dear. Your mother came to see me only that one time, but—"

"She wrote to you?"

"No, Lillian. If I had a letter from her in my possession I would not keep it from you. She did not write to me, but I did receive a letter concerning her. That is, concerning lodgings she was hoping to let. The landlord required a reference, and she must have given my name."

"Did you supply a reference?"

"I did. I made it clear I had no knowledge of her recent occupation or conduct, but that in her younger days she was a good girl from a respectable family."

"And that was all?"

He shrugged. "I assume she secured the lodgings but, of course, had no way of knowing."

"Have you the address of these lodgings?" Lilly's voice rose in excitement.

"I am getting to that, my dear. Before I brought this to your attention, I thought I had better see if I still had the letter. I could not find it, but my clerk did find, in an old ledger, a listing of the postage he paid to receive the reference request."

He handed her a slip of paper. "The street name and number of the lodging house."

Lilly stared down at the few numbers and words inked on the page in her uncle's small precise hand.

Her own hand trembled and her heart pounded. Could she really go and knock on her mother's door? Pay a call as to an old friend? Would she even be received? Her hand began perspiring at the thought of it, and she laid the paper on the table to keep from spoiling it.

"Will you go with me?" she asked in a voice she barely recognized—the voice of a very young girl.

The address was in a court off Fleet Street, in an area of narrow, modest houses.

Her uncle used his umbrella handle to rap on the door, as if he feared touching the surface would soil his gloves. Lilly held her breath. After a few tense moments, the door opened and a woman with silver-streaked black hair answered, dressed in a gown that had once been fine but appeared to Lilly to be nearly a decade out of fashion.

"Yes?"

"Good day, madam. We are looking for a lodger of yours, a Mrs. Rosamond Haswell?"

"No one 'ere by that name."

"Perhaps she used her maiden name, Elliott?"

"Look, this ain't no tenement slum, mind. We just has the one lodger at a time, see, in the rooms upstairs. Helps us live comfortable, now the children are gone."

"I understand, but you wrote to me and asked for a reference for Rosamond—"

"Oh, mayhap you mean Rosa? She is long gone. It's Tommy Baker now."

Rosa? Disappointment tinged with relief washed over Lilly. "How long ago did she leave?"

"Must be above two years now. Maybe more. Couldn't keep up with the rent, see. She took in pupils while she were here—merchants' daughters and the like—but the pay weren't much. She ain't in any trouble, is she?"

"Not that we are aware of. Do you know where she went?"

"Heavens no." The woman's brow wrinkled. "She got herself married, I believe. To some officer, I think it were."

Married? Then it cannot be her. Can it?

"This *husband* of hers," her uncle asked through gritted teeth. "Do you recall his surname?"

"I'm lucky to recall what I 'ad for tea, let alone something what happened years ago."

"Was it Quincy, perhaps?" Lilly asked, avoiding her uncle's startled look.

The woman's eyes narrowed in thought. "Don't ring no bells, no."

"Here is my card," Uncle Elliott said. "Should something come to you, please send word. I shall reimburse you for your trouble."

Lilly thought the woman's murmur of agreement lacked conviction.

As they walked away, Lilly's mind was reeling. Her mother, "married" to another man? She could not credit it. Her uncle strode stiffly at her side, face grim. If this was difficult for her to believe, what a blow it must be for a man such as he to learn that his sister may have sunk so low.

"Perhaps the woman had it wrong," Lilly began. "She said it herself, she has a poor memory. Perhaps 'Rosa' wasn't Mother at all."

He shook his head. "Do you now see why I was reluctant to come? Why I have avoided involving your aunt in these affairs?"

"I do see. Still, I am thankful to you. Painful as it was."

"Shall we speak of it no further?"

"Very well."

His eyes fixed on a shop across the street. "I know. Let us stop in that library there. I think you've read every novel in the one near us. A new book might be just the diversion we need after today's errand."

Lilly nodded her agreement. She already had a new book but could always use another. She gathered her uncle needed this diversion as much as she did.

He opened the door for her and she stepped inside. The lofty room was filled floor to ceiling with books. This library was not as elegant as the one they frequented, but it certainly held a wide selection.

In her peripheral vision, she saw a clerk hail her. "Mrs. Wells! How good to— Oh, forgive me." The thin young man faltered. "I thought you were someone else."

Lilly was instantly alert. "Who?" she prompted. "A Mrs. Wells, I believe you said?" *Who was Wells?*

He shook his head, bemused. "You do look a great deal like her. Henry?" he called to an associate who stood on a rolling ladder, replacing a book on a high shelf. "Come here, man."

The second clerk, somewhat older and rounder, clambered down and joined them.

"Does this lady not look a great deal like our friend Mrs. Wells?" the first asked.

"Indeed she does. Though younger to be sure."

Lilly met her uncle's gaze.

"Haven't seen that lady in some time, though," Henry said. "Have you?"

"No. Must be above a half year since I saw her. Thank you, Henry."

The second clerk returned to the shelves, and her uncle excused himself to peruse the history section.

"Now." The first clerk rubbed his palms together. "Is there something I can help you find, miss?"

Curious, Lilly asked, "What would your Mrs. Wells want?"

The young clerk thought. "Fanny Burney is a favorite of hers. Though she has also borrowed every volume of Scott and Coleridge we've had in. Never knew a keener reader. I believe she is a schoolmistress of some sort."

"And have you records of what she last read?"

He looked at her, clearly perplexed. "We have records, of course, but—"

Embarrassed, Lilly said quickly, "Never mind. I only thought that since I favoured her in appearance, I might enjoy reading what she did. That is all." She laughed sheepishly.

"Well, normally our records are private. But I do not see any harm in this case." He crooked a finger, and she followed him to the center desk. There he opened a wooden file box and walked his fingers through the cards inside. "Here she is. Last borrowed Fanny Burney's *The Wanderer*."

How apt, Lilly thought. "Well then, I shall have the same if I might."

The clerk was still skimming the card. "Oh dear, an outstanding balance of two p—"

Lilly lifted her reticule. "Allow me."

"No, miss, there's no need."

"Yes there is. It is the least I can do for her excellent book recommendation."

He dipped his chin in acquiescence. "That is very kind. When I see Mrs. Wells, whom shall I name as her benefactor?"

Lilly paused. It seemed unlikely Mrs. Wells, her mother or not, would return here, but even so, she hesitated. "You needn't say at all."

Her uncle reappeared beside her. "There you are, Lillian. Are you ready?"

The clerk grinned and made a note on the card.

"Actually, I have thought of one more thing," Lilly said. "Have you Steele's Navy Lists?"

The clerk's eyes widened. "Why, yes. The new one for this quarter has just arrived. Do you know, Mrs. Wells often had a look at those as well."

"Did she indeed?" Lilly was struck by the coincidence, if coincidence it was. "Do you keep older editions as well? From five or so years past?"

"I am afraid not. Only the most current editions. And here it is." He handed her the slim volume.

"Thank you. I shall borrow that as well."

Her uncle's eyebrows rose, but Lilly did not explain.

Men have the sword, women have the fan,
and the fan is probably as effective a weapon!

—JOSEPH ADDISON, EIGHTEENTH-CENTURY ENGLISH WRITER

CHAPTER 15

Lilly was surprised when Dr. Graves paid a call a few days later. She had not expected him after their less-than-cordial parting. Her aunt was breakfasting in her own room, so Lilly was alone in the sitting room when Fletcher announced that a Dr. Graves was at the door. She was tempted to utter the socially acceptable prevarication "I am not at home at present" but could not bring herself to do so. While she dreaded seeing him again, she had lied more than enough to the man, even if in omission.

When Fletcher showed Dr. Graves in, he entered top hat in hand. Fletcher held out his hand to take it, but Dr. Graves did not seem to notice.

"Won't you sit down?" Lilly offered.

"Thank you, no." His gaze focused on the carpet. "Miss Haswell, I have been thinking. I wanted to say . . . that is, I believe I understand why you were not forthcoming about your background. Of course you would respect your guardian's wishes in the matter. I want to apologize for my . . . unfortunate reaction."

"I am sorry for keeping it from you for so long," she said. She was attempting to form the words to tell him of her other secret when he forged ahead.

"But now I think . . ." He looked at her. "Well, do you not see? It makes such sense. Is it any wonder I think you and I so perfectly suited?"

Lilly felt her mouth gape open and quickly closed it. She stared at him, saw his pale cheeks redden.

"That is . . . I do not view your father's trade as necessarily a disadvantage. Your experience lends you a level of understanding . . . of the hours and time away required of my profession."

It was not the most flattering of offers. *Was* he offering for her? Or merely expressing interest in continuing to court her?

On some level, the idea appealed to her. That she might be able to understand her husband's struggles and even help him in his work. Might this not make for the best of both worlds? Whom else could she marry and not count those years in her father's shop as absolute loss? As a physician, Dr. Graves would make a good living and still be considered a gentleman, welcome in her aunt and uncle's world. If not by Ruth Elliott herself.

"Speaking of my profession," he said awkwardly, "I had better take my leave. I do not wish to be late for my shift at hospital. But I do hope we might speak further soon. Will you be attending the Bromleys' rout and card party? They have kindly included me."

"I believe we will be," Lilly said. *If their invitation was not withdrawn after recent revelations.*

"Then I shall see you then."

❧

Lilly had no interest in cards, but she was interested in the Bromley home, which the family seemed forever to be redecorating or improving—knocking down walls, adding or connecting chambers, retiling floors. Currently the home followed the Greek Revival style, though the gallery and main floor rooms also displayed exotic Egyptian art, Chinese lanterns, Italian oil paintings, silhouettes and etchings, all of which imbued the place with a museum-like atmosphere.

Lilly entered the crowded vestibule Friday evening in time to see Susan Whittier shake her head and turn from Roger Bromley. As the lovely blonde walked away, she slowly fanned herself, the gesture signaling, *Don't waste your time. I don't care about you.*

The pitiful look on Roger's face worked on Lilly's heart. She wove her way through the crowd and smiled at him in empathy. "At it again, is she?"

"Miss Haswell. What a delight." He sighed. "Yes, I am afraid so. If only every woman could be as agreeable as you are." He bowed deeply. As she curtsied in return, she felt her aunt and uncle's eager eyes upon them.

"Will you walk with me?" He indicated the long gallery with a sweep of his hand.

"Very well."

He offered his arm and she took it. She hoped Susan Whittier was watching.

He led her along the gallery, pointing out two new paintings his parents had purchased during their last holiday in Rome. "You are right, of course," Roger began quietly. "I cannot deny I have long and ardently admired Susan Whittier. I suppose everybody knows it and pities me. Including Miss Whittier herself, who seems to enjoy tormenting me."

Lilly could not contradict him.

Progressing further along the gallery, he paused to show her a primitive wood carving brought back from Jamaica by his mother's brother, Admiral Roth.

He then led her into the library, where woodwork and leather spines gleamed softly by the light of suspended oil lamps as well as two candle lamps on the desk.

He turned to face her, keeping hold of her hand. "But I do have a strong regard for you, Miss Haswell," he said in plaintive whisper.

"I don't suppose you would accept my suit while my heart is fettered elsewhere?"

How kind he was. How gentleman-like. For a moment she was tempted, but then she thought of her mother and Quinn and felt a chill run up her neck. Sadly, she shook her head. She would not marry a man who would always pine for another.

"Roger, there you are."

Roger's mother stepped inside the library. Behind her, Susan Whittier entered the room and, seeing Lilly, hesitated. Lilly could well imagine the tableau she and Mr. Bromley made, standing hand in hand in a candlelit tête-à-tête. She hoped the scene had a desired effect.

Mrs. Bromley smiled thinly. "Susan and I wondered where you had gone."

Miss Whittier passed her fan from hand to hand. *I see you are looking at another woman.* Did Roger notice this expression of jealousy as well?

Mrs. Bromley begged Lilly's pardon, but insisted Roger come and stand with her to greet guests, as his father had already abandoned his post for a game of faro in the saloon.

Roger Bromley smiled apologetically and excused himself, both of them knowing that his mother was relieved to have reason to call him from her side.

Alone, Lilly slowly walked the perimeter of the library, pausing to admire a beautiful globe on an ornate wooden stand. As usual, the sight of a globe brought to mind the spheres on her mother's creased world map.

Moving on, she scanned the impressive collection of volumes, which would rival any subscription library, and was astonished to see an entire shelf of Steele's Navy Lists. Would the Bromleys mind if she perused them? She could not think of any reason why they should. Running her fingers along the narrow spines, she found the dates she was looking for. She pulled several from the shelf and carried them to the candle-lit desk. Opening the first volume, she skimmed the listing of commissioned officers of first one edition, then a second, then a third. In the last she found the name, Captain Ernest Quincy, and a number. Paging through, she found the corresponding ship name and its list of officers. Captain, Lieutenant, Paymaster, Surgeon, Gunner, Boatswain, Midshipman . . .

She returned the volumes to the shelf and pulled an older edition and repeated the process. Again she found the name Ernest Quincy and the corresponding ship upon which he had served. And there it was. Captain: Ernest Quincy. Lieutenant: James Wells.

Was this *the* Wells? Or was it merely coincidence that a Wells had served under Captain Quincy? Lilly was not sure she believed in coincidence anymore.

Footsteps startled her, and she closed the book as though a thief, caught.

"Miss Haswell." Dr. Graves bowed, looking quite dashing in his black tailcoat and white waistcoat. "Mrs. Bromley said I might find you here."

Lilly could well imagine the woman's eagerness to send another man to divert her attention. As she curtsied, she pressed the book against the folds of her skirt, hoping to conceal it.

"What is that you are looking at?" he asked. Reaching out, he turned the volume in her hand to better read its title, his fingers brushing hers.

She lifted it as though just remembering the book was there. "I was just curious," she said and backed away from him, returning the book to its place on the shelf. "Admiral Roth is uncle to Roger Bromley, you know."

"And what, may I ask, is Roger Bromley to you?"

Two aging spinsters entered the library, sparing her the need to reply. The four exchanged polite greetings and praised the Bromleys' collection for several moments, until Dr. Graves cleared his throat.

"Miss Haswell, I understand the Bromleys are eager for their guests to walk their maze. Would you like to give it a go?"

Understanding he wished to speak with her alone, she agreed. "Indeed. It sounds fascinating."

They excused themselves, then walked without speaking into the gallery and down a second corridor. While cards were being played in the saloon, in the other rooms—dining room, sitting room, and both drawing rooms—the furniture had all been taken away or moved to the walls, to allow hundreds of people to stand and mingle about. As they passed the open doors of the dining room, Lilly saw Roger Bromley hand Susan Whittier a glass of punch and stand close to her in intimate conversation.

When she and Dr. Graves neared their destination, they passed a couple just leaving, the man whispering in the lady's ear, the latter giggling. Dr. Graves frowned at the oblivious couple and ushered Lilly into the gothic conservatory. A dozen wax candles flickered in the darkness, reflecting back on the windows and illuminating the maze of red and black floor tiles.

Lilly looked with fascination at the pattern. "Where does one begin?"

"I am not certain. You begin there and I shall try from this point. Mind your gown near the candles." He walked around to the opposite side.

Lilly began tiptoeing the narrow path outlined by black tiles amid the red, arms gracefully extended as though she traversed a circus high wire. Dr. Graves's polished shoes filled the width of the path, and he took the corners none too neatly.

Lilly bit back a smile. "They say it is a rectangular version of the Hampton Court hedge maze. In miniature, of course."

He narrowly missed kicking over a candle lamp. "Do they. I say it is a colossal waste of time."

Keeping her focus on the tiles, she began, "I have thought about what you said, Dr. Graves. That with my background I might be of some help to you as you treat patients and seek to establish yourself in the medical profession."

"Well—dash it." He came to a dead end in the tiles and had to turn back around. "That is, of course, an agreeable, suitable wife can only help a man—medical or otherwise."

She felt an odd flutter at hearing him say the word *wife*.

She continued to delicately walk the line, reaching the center of the maze before he did. He retraced his steps, then chose another path. Realizing she had halted, he stopped where he was, a few steps away. He stood there, considering the tiles of the maze between them.

"Mustn't cross any lines," she warned in a whisper.

He looked at her intently. "Mustn't we?" He took a step closer.

Around them, the candles flickered, casting shadows on the perfect planes of his face and light on his golden hair and bottle-blue eyes.

Drawing near, he looked warmly at her, his gaze lingering on her hair, her eyes, her lips. She expected him to kiss her at any moment. Willed it. For though the lines of the maze were merely flat tiles on the floor, she felt something very real between them.

"What unusual eyes you have," he whispered. "Green and brown both."

He leaned closer still, and she felt her eyelids flutter closed of their own volition. *What would it be like to kiss a man with a moustache?* she wondered fleetingly. Or any man, for that matter?

A throat cleared. Lilly turned her head and saw Will Price-Winters in the doorway, watching them with marked interest. Lilly felt her entire face heat in a blush. Beside him was a tall, dark-haired man she recognized with a start.

"I thought I saw you passing by with golden boy here," Will began, barely suppressing an amused smirk. He turned to his companion. "May I introduce Sir Roderick Marlow."

Sir was his father's title, but Roderick did not correct him.

"This is Dr. Adam Graves," Christina's brother continued, and the men nodded to one another. "And this lovely creature is Miss Haswell."

She curtsied and Roderick Marlow bowed, though he kept his eyes on her all the while. "Miss Haswell and I are already acquainted."

"Well, dash it," Will said peevishly, "Then why did you insist we find her and beg an introduction?"

"I thought my eyes deceived me," Mr. Marlow said. "She is far more handsome than I recall."

"But how are you acquainted?" Will asked him. "You are not a London man, I understand?"

"Indeed no. I make it to town but rarely. Miss Haswell and I grew up together in the same village."

Together? Lilly thought incredulously. *Hardly that.*

"We be Wiltshire born and bred, ey?" Roderick Marlow's exaggerated accent surprised her, yet was music to her ears. " 'Ow bis en', my lovely?"

She laughed appreciatively.

"Miss Haswell and her father have often been guests at Marlow House," Roderick Marlow explained to Will, with a pointed look at Dr. Graves.

Not unless one counted house calls, Lilly thought, but forbore to comment.

Will shook his head. "She and my sister have been friends for, what, well over a year now, and I had no idea."

"Well, Miss Haswell is known for her secrets," Marlow said, grinning wickedly. "And other crimes."

"Mr. Marlow," Lilly exclaimed. "I must protest."

"Very well, Miss Haswell, I shall keep your secrets for you. Though I suppose your Dr. Graves is already privy to all?"

She felt her lips part, but couldn't form an answer.

"No?" Marlow leaned closer but made no attempt to whisper. "P-W here hinted there might be something between the two of you. I am glad to hear that is not the case after all."

"I never said—"

In full view of the other men, Marlow tapped his forefinger against her lower lip. "Shh . . . Your secrets are safe with me, Lilly."

He turned and sauntered from the conservatory, Will Price-Winters at his heels.

She and Dr. Graves stared after them, both bewildered.

"Lilly?" Graves repeated the name with equal parts distaste and question.

"Yes," she said resignedly. "Lilly."

"A childhood pet name?"

She sighed, suddenly very weary. "My name, period. Until my aunt changed it."

"You have given that man leave to use your Christian name? Even I—"

"No one gives that man *leave* to do anything. He does as he pleases and always has. You need not mind anything he says."

He studied her face. "Indeed?"

WIDOW WELCH'S PILLS
The particular nature and symptoms of female complaints
are given with every box of pills,
and worthy the perusal of every person
who has the care of young women. . . .

—*The Edinburgh Evening Courant*, 1815

Chapter 16

When next Dr. Graves called, Lilly decided it was time to tell him all, though she feared the consequences. They were again alone in the sitting room, for Aunt Elliott was sleeping in after a late night at the theatre. Once he was seated, she began in low tones, "At the Bromleys' rout the other night, Mr. Marlow accused me of keeping secrets."

His raised his brows in expectation.

"There *is* another secret I should tell you." She pressed damp palms to her knees to still their trembling.

He nodded slowly, warily. "Something to do with that man?"

"No. Only that he knows of it." She took a deep breath. "It is about my mother."

His brow wrinkled. "Your mother is gone, I understand."

"Gone. But not dead. At least not as far as we know."

He stared at her, clearly stunned.

"She left us nearly five years ago now. Disappeared without word or letter. We don't know where she went or where she is." She glanced toward the door to make sure no one was listening, then said quietly, "My aunt and uncle prefer not to speak of her. They allow those of their acquaintance to believe she is still living in obscurity in Wiltshire— or dead. I cannot blame them. If it were generally known, their name and mine would be besmirched."

His expression was incredulous. "Simply because your mother disappeared? She might have been abducted—merely gone on some errand when unspeakable mishap befell her."

She raised one brow high. "Are you trying to make me feel better?"

His mouth drooped. "Forgive me."

"In any case, I doubt that." Swallowing a cinder of shame, Lilly whispered, "She was seen leaving Bedsley Priors with a uniformed man. It is only hearsay, and he may have simply been another passenger traveling on the same narrowboat, but as she was in love with a naval captain before she married my father, it seems too great a coincidence."

His expression grew serious, nearly alarmed, the lines deepening between his eyebrows. Still, she steeled herself and continued. "I have recently learned a few things about her. I know she came to London and saw my uncle. I know she lodged off Fleet Street for a time and took in pupils." A choked laugh escaped her. "I know which library she frequented, but I do not know"—her voice cracked—"why she left us, and if it was my fault, and why she never once wrote to tell us she was all right. . . ."

Her throat too tight to continue, she bit her lip to ebb the flow of tears. Finally, she continued. "I lied to you when you asked why I was looking at the naval lists. We believe my mother may be living under another name—as a *Rosa Wells*. It may simply be a false name, short for Haswell. But I wanted to see if a man by the name of Wells had served with the officer my mother once hoped to marry."

"And?" he asked, though a quick glance told her he dreaded the answer.

She exhaled deeply and nodded. "A James Wells did serve with him in at least one commission. I have no real proof he ever met my mother, but still it seems a strange coincidence."

"Will you contact this James Wells?"

She shifted, ill at ease. "I don't know. The connection seems so unlikely." She shrugged. "I don't even know how I would find him."

He nodded, and the two were shrouded in awkward silence for several moments.

"Well," Lilly said, squaring her shoulders. "I thought you had the right to know. Should my mother's desertion—or worse— become known, I would be tainted by scandal, as would my aunt and uncle. As would you, should you . . ." She let the thought trail away unfinished.

"My father detests scandal," Graves said, as though to himself. "Always has." He ran agitated fingers through his pale-blond hair and cleared his throat. "Well, thank you for telling me, Miss Haswell." He rose and eyed the door with apparent longing, his words coming in clipped phrases. "I had better take my leave. Much to ponder. Be in touch soon."

No you shan't . . . Lilly thought sadly, fatalistically, as the handsome golden man turned on his heel and hurried away. Hadn't she always known it would end this way, with any gentleman of quality? *I have finally succeeded in scaring off the last of my suitors,* she thought, and the realization pained her more than she would have guessed.

Fletcher handed Lilly a letter as she passed by him on her way upstairs. She needed to quickly finish dressing, for her aunt would soon be ready to begin paying calls.

But a quarter of an hour later, Lilly still sat on her bed, dressed only in her white muslin morning dress.

"Lillian?" her aunt called from the corridor. "Are you ready? I have the carriage waiting."

But Lilly remained where she was, the letter in her hands beginning to shake.

Her aunt let herself into the room, pulling on her gloves. She was

00

fully dressed in striped carriage dress, vest, and cap. "Lillian? We are late, my dear. Lillian! What is the matter?"

She pushed the paper into her aunt's hand. Lilly already knew what it said, not because of her keen memory, but because of its cryptic brevity. *Come home. Your father is not himself.*

"But you do not know that anything dire has happened," Ruth Elliott insisted while Lilly paced the room. "Your father is 'not himself.' What does that mean?"

"I do not know."

"You do not even know who wrote the letter, if letter it can be called."

"I suppose it was Mrs. Mimpurse. Our neighbor."

"Then why did she not tell you what the matter is?"

"I don't know!" Lilly's voice rose, and her aunt winced at the unusual sharpness of her tone. "Forgive me, Aunt. I am only very worried. I have had no replies to my recent letters, and now this!"

Lilly bent and drew her valise from under the bed.

"What are you doing?"

"Of course I must go."

"But . . . what about Mr. Bromley?"

Lilly exhaled sharply. "Mr. Bromley hopes to engage the affections of Susan Whittier."

"Are you certain?"

Lilly nodded and threw back the lid of the worn valise. It was the only item her aunt and uncle had not thought to replace with a new one, perhaps hoping there would be no need.

"Oh no." Panic swelled in Ruth Elliott's voice and eyes. "There are only six weeks left in the season. Very little time to start again, and by next year they will say you have been passed over—on the shelf."

Lilly hesitated. "Is that really the end of the world?"

"No, my dear. Merely the end of your best opportunity for securing an advantageous match."

"I cannot think about that now." Beneath the brave words, these were the very thoughts plaguing her as Aunt Elliott's worries fed her own. For in spite of Lilly's ideals of marrying for love, or of using her

skills to aid her husband, the truth was a good marriage was impera-
tive to any woman's happiness and comfort, not to mention social
standing.

She began to fold and pack her clothing—Dupree's job. Lilly knew
how distressed her aunt was when she did not correct her.

But surely all was not lost. She would be back soon. She had not
failed her aunt, nor her goal in coming to London. Not yet.

"Surely twenty or even one and twenty is not too old. Unless—
Forgive me. I should not presume you would wish to host me here for
another season."

For once, her aunt's perfect posture melted into a dejected slump.
"In all truth, I am weary. And to see my hopes fall apart all over again.
All the work, the expense . . ."

Lilly felt chastened. She said quickly, "Please forgive me. I did not
realize I had become a burden, but of course I must be. I have been
very selfish, and I am sorry for it."

Her aunt sighed. "I do not mean to threaten or frighten you, my
dear. But with all our failures this season—the gossip, your father's
trade becoming known, Susan Whittier diverting Mr. Bromley—I
simply hold little hope for another season, when a whole new harvest
of accomplished young ladies will come out to compete for the same
string of gentlemen."

Lilly ceased her packing long enough to grasp her aunt's hand. "I
am only going for a visit. A week, a fortnight at most. That will still
give us the better part of a month when I return. Will it not?"

Her aunt looked into Lilly's eyes, her own brimming with unshed
tears, as if she very much wanted to believe her, but could not quite
succeed.

The human heart, at whatever age,
opens only to the heart that opens in return.

—MARIA EDGEWORTH, 19TH CENTURY NOVELIST

CHAPTER 17

I
f Lilly expected things to be the same as ever in Bedsley Priors, she
was much mistaken. During the year and a half she had been gone,
the village as well as neighboring Honeystreet had grown with the
boom of canal traffic. New businesses and thatched cottages had been
built to accommodate additional sawmill workers, barge builders, and
their families. Huntley's Yard, bordering the canal, was now a bustling
enclave of saw pits, paint shops, and even a cobbler and undertaker.
The two villages had developed and spread until all that divided the
once separate communities was the narrow Sands Road.

All this Lilly took in from the coach window, the startling scene
narrated by a kindly passenger who introduced herself as the proprietor
of a new millinery shop in town.

Lilly was too stunned to say much of anything. Was this why her
father had not answered recent letters? Had his shop become so busy
that he simply had no time to write?

Stepping down from the coach in front of the Hare and Hounds, she waited until the coachman handed down her valise and carpetbag. Then she walked around the tall coach, her eyes hungry for the first sight of her father's shop, the Haswell sign, the many-paned window. Eager, too, for the smells and sounds, the pleasant hum of cures discussed and remedies heeded. She walked quickly across the green, and there it was. The bowed window, flaking white paint, the sign hanging from one chain. She wondered when the other side had fallen. She hesitated at the window, noticing the display inside was sparse and dusty. Her brow furrowed. Where were all the customers, all the new villagers she'd heard about? It was not Sunday—why was the place empty?

Concern filtered through her mind. Her hand on the door latch, she breathed a prayer and then pushed the door open and closed her eyes to absorb the jangle of the bell. Same as always. She breathed in. Smells flooded her senses all right, but something damp and foul overrode the dried flowers and herbs.

"Hello?" she called tentatively, and then more loudly, "Father? Charlie?"

No answer. Alarm began pulsing in her veins.

She walked through the shop, noting with dismay the soiled dispensing counter, and the back counter cluttered with pill dust and used mortars, tools and tiles all in need of a good cleaning. *What on earth?* Why had Charlie let off with the sweeping and dusting?

A mouse skittered somewhere in the corner. She shivered. With mounting fear and dread, she opened the rear door into the laboratory-kitchen and private quarters. A foul smell charged out to repel her. Dirty dishes, scummy pots, dank mortars and funnels were piled in disarray on the sideboard. Had Mrs. Fowler given notice? Or been sacked? She had always kept their private rooms clean, if not orderly. She heard more skittering. Rodent or insect, she could not be certain.

"Fa-ther?" She tried again, her voice breaking. "It's Lillian— Lilly."

She passed the narrow chamber where Francis slept and peeked inside. Her heart lurched. The cot wore no bedclothes, the wall pegs were bare, as was the chest of drawers.

She called up the stairs but heard no answer. Remembering the surgery, she returned through the shop and pushed open the surgery door. Papers, bills, and parcels were piled high and obliterated the surface of her father's desk. Soiled plates and a half-eaten roll sat atop the highest stack.

Lilly stopped, hand over her breast. She had found her father at last. Lying on the surgery cot in shirtsleeves and rumpled breeches, jaw unshaven. His mouth hung open, drool forming rivulets at its corners. One arm was flung over his eyes, the other arm hung to the floor, hand clasping an empty bottle.

Dear Lord in heaven . . . "Father?" She tentatively touched his shoulder. She shook him gently, then with more urgency. "Father!"

He jerked. "What? What is it?" He wiped his mouth, then mumbled, "Be right with you."

His eyes were blurry slits, which opened wider at the sight of her. "Lilly?"

"Yes, of course it is me. What has happened, Father? Are you ill?"

He groaned. "Just a nap."

"It is more than that, clearly. Shall I call for Dr. Foster?"

"No. Not Foster." He rolled to his side and pushed himself up, only to fall back against the thin mattress.

Lilly's heart ached to see him in such a state.

"Just need to sleep."

To sleep it off? she wondered.

Her father had never been given to drink. What had happened to drive him to it? She hoped it had not been her long absence. But if so, why hadn't he written? Unbidden, she thought back to Mr. Bromley's declaration of "the Wiltshire miracle." Famed for having once raised a man from the dead, Charles Haswell could now not even raise himself from the bed.

"Where is Charlie, Father? And Francis?"

He mumbled something, his eyes halfway open and eerily unfocused.

"Where is Francis?" she repeated.

"Old tailor's shop."

"What?" Why would her father's apprentice be at the old haberdashery? It had been closed for years. Perhaps it had reopened during her absence. But even so, why would Francis be there?

Realizing she would get no more answers from her father for a few hours at least, she left him in the surgery, replaced her hat, and stepped back outside, careful to turn the shop sign to *Closed*.

She saw the coal monger walking on the green and hurried across the High Street to speak to him

"Pardon me, Mr. Jones," she said. "Have you seen Francis Baylor?"

"I did. In the apothecary's."

He must be mistaken, Lilly thought. She had just come from there.

Dipping her head politely, she walked on across the green, passed the coal merchant, and rounded the butcher's shop. Behind it, she turned down narrow Milk Lane, which housed the old haberdashery— and stopped midstride. Hanging there on two sturdy chains was a shiny new sign declaring, *Lionel Shuttleworth, Surgeon-Apothecary.*

Heart pounding, she forced one foot in front of the other until she stood just to the side of the big front window. She felt like an awkward spy as she leaned and peered inside. The scene that met her was very like the one she had imagined seeing at Haswell's. Ladies reading labels on blue bottles and brown jars. Men standing around the center counter, waiting to be advised or bled. The shelves spotless, the displays overflowing with patent medicines. From the ceiling hung a shark and a blowfish, glistening in magenta and gold.

She saw the back of a tall gentleman wearing a green fitted coat and buff trousers. He wore his brown hair short at the sides and back, his sideburns neatly trimmed. He cut a dashing figure, this man, who must be the new surgeon-apothecary. He turned, and she saw his profile was handsome indeed. . . .

Lilly put a hand over her mouth, catching a gasp. For the man was Francis Baylor—older and taller and better dressed—helping a customer as though he were a doctor himself.

She spun around, but not before she saw him glance up and his eyes widen. She strode away even as she heard the shop door open and rapid footfalls follow her. "Lilly! Miss Haswell!"

She'd wanted to see him, had she not? But perhaps what she had seen answered her questions without a single word being spoken.

Still, she took a deep breath and turned to face him. "Francis," she said coolly.

"Thank heaven you've come. You've seen your father?"

"Yes."

"So you know."

"Know what, exactly? That the apprentice he mentored for years has abandoned him? Gone to work for his competitor? Put Haswell's out of business?"

"No! It isn't like that!"

"Then what is it like? Were you forced to come here?"

"In a manner of speaking, I was. Your father was unable to pay me—"

"Fickle loyalty! You had a roof over your head, did you not?" She critically eyed the broad shoulders and chest beneath his fitted coat. "You don't look to be starving. Nor dressed in rags. Could you not extend a bit of grace?"

"I did. He hasn't paid me a farthing in six months. My apprenticeship is over. I am a journeyman now, entitled to wages. I stayed as long as I could, but I must have some means, mustn't I?"

"Why? Your mother makes a tidy living as tallow-chandler, I understand, and she and your sister must have got by well enough all those years you earned nothing as an apprentice."

A young lady in fine flowered bonnet and gown came out of the shop and walked past, a brown-paper-wrapped parcel in her gloved hand. Lilly recognized her at once.

"Mr. Baylor. You disappeared before I could thank you. Most helpful as usual."

He cleared his throat. "You are welcome, Miss Robbins."

My goodness, she's prettier than ever, Lilly thought, relieved to be wearing her nicest carriage dress and fitted spencer. The girl looked her way and curtsied. Lilly stiffly returned the gesture.

"Miss Haswell, hello. Do you know what a wonderful dancer Mr. Baylor has become?"

Lilly dumbly shook her head.

"I have never enjoyed a village fete as well as I did the last. Well, until next time, Mr. Baylor."

He bowed briefly before returning his attention to Lilly.

Watching Dorothea Robbins saunter gracefully down the lane, Lilly shook her head in disgust. *Some things never change.*

She said, "I see why, or shall I say for *whom,* you are acquiring means." With that, she turned and stalked away.

She hurried back up Milk Lane and followed the High Street to the coffeehouse, hoping desperately that it too had not fallen into disrepair. What would she do if it were abandoned? If Mrs. Mimpurse and Mary were gone? *Please God, please God.*

She turned the corner and breathed a sigh of relief. Old Mrs. Kilgrove and another matron were coming from the coffeehouse, and candle lamps glowed in the windows. Walking quickly to the door, she pushed it open and stepped inside. She savored the sight of tables filled with customers, the stoked fire, the hum of conversation, the smell of coffee and cinnamon and life.

"Lilly Grace Haswell!"

And suddenly Mrs. Mimpurse was there, ample arms around her, floured bodice pressing close, aromas of nutmeg, ginger, and woodsmoke enveloping her. Lilly embraced her in return, feeling tears fill her eyes.

"I knew you would come, Miss Lilly. I knew it. Thank the good Lord."

Mary came out of the kitchen and stood on the threshold, wiping her hands on a cloth. She hung back, eyeing her almost warily. Lilly disentangled herself from Mrs. Mimpurse and walked close to Mary. "I have missed you."

"Have you?"

Lilly nodded and opened her arms, and Mary accepted her embrace. "And I you."

"Mary, my lovely," Mrs. Mimpurse said quietly, "I am afraid I must ask you to mind the place alone for a few minutes."

Mary nodded in grim understanding. Mrs. Mimpurse took Lilly's hand and led her up the stairs into their small sitting room. She moved with youthful energy and grace, though she was a contemporary of her father. "Be seated, my dear. Can I get you something to eat? Coffee? Tea?"

Lilly shook her head, a lump rising in her throat and hands perspiring at whatever news Mrs. Mimpurse hesitated to impart.

"You've been home?" she asked.

Lilly nodded.

Mrs. Mimpurse gave her head a stern little shake. "I would have written sooner, but your father forbade it. Said to leave you be, and not to worry you. But . . . well, have you seen him?"

Again Lilly nodded.

"The shop has been all but closed these last days. If you don't put it to rights, I fear Haswell's will never recover."

"So this has been going on for some time?"

"I am afraid so."

"What has brought it on?"

"I do not quite know. He hasn't been himself for months. Then the new surgeon-apothecary came, and it seemed to lay him very low."

"But, is he . . . Is he really . . . ?"

"Tippling? I don't know what all ails him. He refuses to see Dr. Foster."

"I know. I suggested it also, but he was quite adamant against it."

"Such bad blood between the two of them."

"And now Francis has left him. How could he?"

"Do not judge him harshly, my dear. Your father was very cross toward the end. I think he wanted to be rid of him. Let Mrs. Fowler go as well, so he could sink and stew himself in private. Wouldn't let anyone help."

"I don't understand."

"Well, you're home now." Mrs. Mimpurse smiled bravely. "And if anyone can set Haswell's to rights, it's you."

Lilly did not share the woman's confidence.

Mrs. Mimpurse insisted on going home with her, carrying a pot of stew while Lilly carried two loaves of cottage bread. They crossed the narrow mews between the two establishments and entered through the garden.

"Good *gracious*," Mrs. Mimpurse said, as they stepped into the laboratory-kitchen. "It is worse than I thought."

Lilly took off her hat as she made her way to the surgery. Her father sat on the edge of the cot, head in hands, in the same wrinkled clothes.

"Father, are you feeling any better?"

"As I said, I am quite well. Why have you come?"

She was taken aback by his dour demeanor.

Mrs. Mimpurse stood in the doorway behind her. "I've brought a nice chicken-and-leek stew for your supper."

"I've told you—don't fuss over me, Maude." Her father's voice was rough and sharp. "I don't need your charity."

Maude sniffed. "Charity, indeed. I'd not waste it on a sour cabbage like you. The food is for Miss Lilly here, home after these many months. And if you were half a gentleman, you would come to the table and take a proper meal with your daughter to welcome her home."

"I've never claimed to be a gentleman."

"As well I know, and no wonder."

He looked up at her, irritation and pain in his expression. Still, when Mrs. Mimpurse came and took one elbow, instructing Lilly to take the other, he allowed the two women to help him up and into the laboratory-kitchen. He sat heavily in the chair.

"Happy?" he asked.

"Deliriously." Mrs. Mimpurse matched her father's sarcasm.

"Now will you be gone, you meddlesome woman."

"With pleasure, you ungrateful ogre."

Mrs. Mimpurse hesitated at the door, looking back at them, the pained concern in her eyes not quite concealed by her tart barbs.

All the bowls were dirty, but Lilly managed to find two mugs that would suffice for their stew.

"She wrote to you, did she?" her father asked.

"Yes, and I am grateful she did."

"What did she say? Must have been pretty bad to bring you home with the season still on."

"She only said that you were not yourself. Which appears to be the understatement of all time. What is wrong, Father? What has happened?"

"Food is getting cold."

They ate a few bites in a silence broken only by the ticks of the clock. Lilly glanced up at the old wall-mounted timepiece. "Where is Charlie? Why is he not home for supper?"

Even as she asked, she guessed there hadn't been much supper to come home to for some time. Was he eating with Mary and Mrs. Mimpurse?

"Charlie doesn't live here anymore."

Her father could hardly have stunned her more. "What? Where is he?"

"Gone to Marlow House. Works as an undergardener there."

Her spoon clanked against the mug. She shuddered to think of her sweet, simple brother under the power of Roderick Marlow or his rough, angry gardener.

"But why, Father? When you obviously need his help more than ever. Especially with Francis gone."

He shrugged and laid aside his spoon.

"Eat more, Father. You are as thin as I've ever seen you."

He shook his head, his thoughts clearly far from food. "I am sorry you've come."

Her heart fell.

"Sorry and glad together," he amended. He reached across the small table toward her hand, then hesitated short of touching her. He pulled back and rose shakily from the table. She hurried to her feet and took his elbow to steady him, helping him back to his makeshift bed in the surgery.

"Father, I—" She determined to leave any judgmental words unspoken. "I have never seen you like this."

"I wish you had not. Or anybody else for that matter." He sat heavily on the cot. "I shall master it by and by. I must."

"Is there anything you need?" she asked.

"Just quiet. And time alone."

Lilly went to the door, then turned back to look at him. She saw him bring a new bottle to his lips, recork it, and hold it close to his chest as he lay back on the bed. The terrible act sliced at her. He embraced that bottle like a treasure. While he had not embraced her at all.

The greatest pill taker on record appears to have been one Jessup,
who died in 1814. He is stated to have swallowed 226,934 pills and
40,000 bottles of mixture, all supplied by an apothecary of Bottesford.

—C. J .S. Thompson, Mystery and Art of the Apothecary

Chapter 18

L illy tossed and turned for hours, unable to sleep. At least her
 chamber was reasonably tidy, although she doubted anyone had
dusted or aired the bed in some time. Still, she could not get comfortable. She had been spoiled, she supposed, by the high, luxurious
feather bed she'd enjoyed in London. Or perhaps it was only that
her mind could not rest. What was she to do about Charlie? About
Father? About the shop—her father's only livelihood? If she spent a
fortnight cleaning and restocking it, would it only fall to shambles
again when she returned to London? Even if Charlie helped and she
somehow convinced Francis to return, could they compete with the
new surgeon-apothecary and his modern, fully stocked shop?

She sighed heavily, overwhelming dread filling her. There was just
too much—too much uncertainty and too much to accomplish in too
little time. A floor-to-ceiling cleaning of the shop and living quarters
was needed, and who knew what shape the garden was in. There were

many orders to be placed, but was there even money to pay for stock? Or had her father drunk it all away? It was too much for one person to manage. Too much for her at any rate. Finally, the heavy weight pressed down on her, and to escape it, she found sleep at last.

In the morning, she arose early, dressed in her simplest frock, pinned up her hair in a plain coil, and went downstairs. First things first. A great deal of hot coffee for her father and hot water for a bath and shave.

She walked quietly across the shop in the dim light of dawn. Again the enormity of the task ahead weighed on her. *Hopeless.*

She gingerly pushed open the surgery door. Her father lay sprawled on the cot, much as she had left him the night before. The bottle she had seen him clutch now lay empty beside him in bed. She crept closer. And in the light beginning to seep through the window, she noticed that the bottle bore no label. *What is his poison of choice?* she wondered. She bent low, gently tugged the bottle from his grasp, and brought it to her nose and sniffed. She knew little of liquor, but this biting acrid smell baffled her.

She heard a sound, the rattling of a door, and started. She was not ready to face any would-be patients yet—and the embarrassed explanations that would certainly follow. The door rattled again.

"Father? Father, wake up."

"Hmm?"

"Father, time to get up. Someone is at the door."

He did not respond.

Sighing, she stepped from the surgery into the shop, rehearsing the words to turn whomever it was away. Through the shopwindow, she saw Mrs. Mimpurse standing there. Why had she not come to the garden door as usual? As Lilly crossed the shop, she was surprised to glimpse two others, no three, no four others with her. Was Maude trying to help by bringing customers? Did she not realize neither the shop nor her father were in any condition to serve anybody?

She opened the door. Before she could say anything, Mrs. Mimpurse bustled in, followed by her kitchen maid, Jane, each carrying a mop and bucket. Behind them, Mary bore a basket of biscuits and muffins. Then came sharp-tongued Mrs. Kilgrove; Mr. Baisley, the vicar; and old Arthur Owen with a hen under his arm.

"Put that bird in the garden, Mr. Owen," Mrs. Kilgrove ordered. "We are here to right the place, not foul it with fowl."

Lilly was too speechless to say anything at all.

Then came her brother, bounding through the door.

"Charlie!"

He stretched his arms as though he might embrace her, but ended by awkwardly patting her shoulders instead.

"Mrs. M. sent word you'd come home, Lilly. It's happy I am to see you."

"And I you, Charlie. How you have grown!"

" 'At I have. And I am to see what I can do to right the garden. I've only my half day, but I'm a fast worker, I am."

There was so much she wanted to say to him, to ask him, but he was already walking through the shop on his way back to the garden. As he passed, Mrs. Kilgrove greeted him, her voice full of rare warmth.

Lilly was about to shut the door when one more caller approached. It was a sheepish Francis Baylor, hat in hand.

"Might I help as well?" he asked.

Again she marveled at how changed he was. Gone were the wild waves of hair in constant need of cutting. Gone the gangly limbs, the ill-fitting clothes. In their place stood a handsome, well-turned-out traitor.

She asked in her haughtiest voice, "What about Shuttleworth's?"

"I've asked for the day off. Mr. Shuttleworth is very obliging."

"Is he?"

He bit his lip. "I am sorry, Lilly."

"It is Miss Haswell, if you please, Mr. Baylor."

He tilted his head in question.

"We are too grown for Christian names."

"I do not expect you to call me *mister*."

"Why not? Miss Robbins did."

"You are not Miss Robbins."

"I am quite aware of that." He had never treated her with such gentlemanly deference. Nor such foolish awe.

"I meant only that you and I are old friends. At least I hope we are."

"Yes, well," she huffed. "I am in no position to refuse anybody's help, so do come in."

They worked steadily for several hours, Maude directing and Lilly answering questions as best she could as to where things went and what could be salvaged and what must be thrown away.

At one point the vicar asked quietly, "Your father, Miss Haswell. Is he ill, I wonder? He assures me he is perfectly well whenever I call but we have not seen him in church these many months."

"I am sorry to hear that." Though who was she to judge when she and her aunt and uncle had rarely attended church either, save for holidays. "Perhaps you would be so kind as to pray for my father, Mr. Baisley."

"Indeed I have. Is he here that I might pray for him now?"

She hesitated. "Well . . . Let me pop in first, to see if he is . . . dressed for callers."

She walked to the surgery door, then paused to paste on a false smile. "Father! It's wonderful," she said as she stepped inside. "Several of our neighbors have come to help tidy the place. Charlie is working in the garden, and Mr. Owen has even brought us a hen!"

"Has he an outstanding bill he cannot pay with coin?" he asked dully.

"No. Just being neighborly. And Mr. Baisley is here and would like to pray for you. May I send him in?"

He pulled a grimace. "I don't need some cleric mumbling incantations over me. I only need a few more days to get my strength back."

"But—"

"No."

She bit her lip but saw it was futile to argue further. She took a deep breath and let herself from the room.

She stepped toward the vicar. "He is not dressed for callers, I am afraid. But please, do include him in your prayers."

"Indeed I shall, Miss Haswell." He looked at her kindly. "And you as well."

After a long day of cleaning, sorting, and disposing of spoiled remedies and stale herbs, Lilly's back and neck ached. Mrs. Mimpurse invited the volunteers to the coffeehouse for an early supper, and they all filed out. Francis worked on, taking inventory and jotting in a small notebook. If she did not know him so well, Lilly might have thought him stealing the Haswell recipes.

Eyeing his list, she asked, "How bad is it?"

"You'll have several large orders to place, to bring the simples up to par—not to mention the patent medicines you've run out of."

"*I* have run out of nothing. It is not *my* shop." Still, she held out her hand, and he placed two sheets of paper on her waiting palm. The list was long indeed.

"So much?"

"The first column are necessities, I think. The second might wait if you don't have . . . if you don't have time to order all at once."

She understood his meaning. "Thank you."

"If there is anything else I can do, you need only ask."

Such as return to work here? she thought, but she could not ask it of him. She did intend to get Charlie back to the shop, however. He'd returned to Marlow House before she'd had a chance to talk with him at all.

"There is one thing you can do," she said, lifting a finger to indicate he should wait while she walked quietly to her father's surgery.

She returned directly, an empty bottle in her hand.

His eyebrows rose.

"Can you keep this between us?" she asked.

"Of course. Your father's?"

She nodded and held out the bottle. "What is it? Can you tell?"

With grim expectation, he accepted the bottle, regarded the unmarked surface, then swiped it quickly beneath his nose, as though assuming the smell would be readily identifiable. Instead he frowned and held it under his nose again, sniffing once, then again.

"I thought . . . But I don't know. What do you think?"

"I don't know either."

"I am no expert at this sort of thing. That is, assuming . . ." He broke off and began again. "I shall take this and see if either Freddy Mac or Mr. Shuttleworth can identify it."

Freddy McNeal was the proprietor of the Hare and Hounds, the village public house, a tiny place compared to The George on the canal in Honeystreet. "Do not say where it came from, all right?"

"You can trust me, Lill—Miss Haswell."

Already she felt foolish for insisting on her proper name.

"Are you coming to the coffeehouse?" he asked.

"No. But you go on. I had better stay and see if I can get Father to eat something."

He nodded, then cocked his head to look at her closely. "It is good to have you back."

"Not back, only visiting. For a fortnight."

He continued to study her, and she grew uncomfortable under his scrutiny. Had she changed so much? Was he about to tell her she looked well? "Is something amiss?" she asked.

Grinning a little, he said, "You have a bit of cobweb in your hair."

Embarrassed, she brushed at her temple. "Where?"

"Allow me." He reached out and gently drew his fingertips along her hairline. "There." He held up a wispy web and blew it from his fingers.

Her scalp tingled oddly from his touch. She did not even consider reprimanding him for blowing the web onto the just-cleaned floor.

Aloft in rows, large Poppy Heads were strung,
And near, a scaly Alligator hung. . . .
The Sage in Velvet Chair, here lolls at Ease,
To promise future Health for present Fees.

—Sir Samuel Garth, Dispensary

Chapter 19

Using some of the money her aunt had given her for the journey home, Lilly hired a laundress to attack the pile of dirty clothes and linens in her father's room. She placed an order with the coal monger, then visited the chandler to replenish a few necessities—candles, soap, and such. She would worry about meals later. With the amount her father was eating, Mrs. Mimpurse's stew and Mary's bread would last a solid week in the cold cellar.

Late that afternoon, Francis returned to the shop and, seeing the surgery door ajar, gestured her over. "Mr. Shuttleworth would like to speak with you."

"Whatever for?"

"About"—he lowered his voice—"the bottle you gave me. Freddy Mac couldn't place it."

"And Mr. Shuttleworth?"

"Said he needed more information before he could hazard an assessment."

"A guess, you mean."

Francis shrugged. "You can come by the shop, or—"

"I cannot go there. It will look like I am spying, or worse, disloyal to my father."

Francis looked uncomfortable.

"And I cannot invite him here, for Father might hear us. Perhaps the coffeehouse?"

"Good. Mr. Shuttleworth frequents it."

"Does he?"

"He's a bachelor and keeps no servants."

For some reason his status surprised her. Still, she did not like the thought of Mrs. Mimpurse serving her father's rival.

Lilly was ill-prepared for the man who stood to greet her when she entered the coffeehouse and approached the table where he and Francis sat. He was not a tall man, but had a large presence. She guessed he might be as old as thirty, but it was difficult to tell. Though he was of average build, there was nothing else average about him. His black hair stood in three-inch prickles all over his head. His eyebrows formed sharp black peaks over dark eyes that sparkled impishly. His clothes were startling. A gold-and-black waistcoat shone between the lapels of a plush burgundy frock coat with yellow cuffs. His cravat was not white or ivory like every other she'd seen, but gold.

He followed her gaze. "Do you like it?" he asked, touching his cravat.

"Yes." She hesitated. "I have a gown that very hue."

"A lady with exquisite taste. How charming." His teeth, she noticed when he smiled, were quite long.

"Miss Lillian Haswell, may I present Mr. Lionel Shuttleworth."

She was surprised Francis thought to use her full given name.

She curtsied and Mr. Shuttleworth bowed. His grin, the light in his eyes, communicated deep delight. It gave her an odd feeling of warmth and discomfort at once.

"Miss Haswell. What a pleasure. I have been hearing such wonderful things about you, both from young Mr. Baylor here as well as the Mimpurse ladies."

Mary appeared, as if she'd heard her name. She set down a basket of breads and a pot of tea. "Chicken and vegetables will be coming out soon."

Lilly noticed Mr. Shuttleworth's eyes following Mary's every move. Her friend's fair round cheeks were flushed from more than just the kitchen fires, Lilly guessed. Dressed in her blue frock and white apron, with her hair loosely pinned, Mary might not be beautiful, but she made a pretty portrait indeed.

When Mary had disappeared back into the kitchen, Mr. Shuttleworth returned his attention to Lilly. "I do hope you will come by my little shop sometime. I would be honored to show you about the place. I have a new mounted tiger shark, a shrunken head, and several Egyptian scarabs. The colors, Miss Haswell, are like the finest gemstones. Really, quite exquisite."

"And do you use scarabs and sharks in your physic?" She did not ask about the skull; she knew all too well that many apothecaries used powdered bone—it was supposed to heal wounds and treat falling sickness. Her own father abhorred the practice, said it was blasphemous somehow. Lilly agreed. And it was certainly not something she wished to discuss while dining.

He ignored this question and went on, "I was right there on the deck when the crew hauled in the shark. No catalogue-purchased prize for me. And the scarabs I captured and lanced myself."

She could not keep the surprise from her tone. "You have been to Egypt?"

"Egypt, Italy, the West Indies, Africa."

"My goodness. May I ask how you came to travel so far?"

"Indeed you may." He leaned his elbows on the table. "I worked as a ship's surgeon on a merchant vessel for several years. My employer imported exotic things from exotic places. I found it all fascinating. Not only the unusual plants and animals—even people—but especially the healing practices of different cultures. Most interesting."

"Then I must ask the obvious question, sir," Lilly said. "How in the world—why in the world—would you choose to set up shop in a little inland village like Bedsley Priors? Have you family here?"

He shook his head. "I have no family." He stared off over her head, apparently in deep thought or memory. "I grew weary of shipboard surgery and living among coarse men. I quit my post and took passage on one of the canal boats transporting our wares from Bristol to London. There I served with a master apothecary for several months and then decided to stay a few years, London town having such a varied and rich culture."

"London I can understand, sir. But Bedsley Priors?"

She felt Francis's silent censure and amended, "It is a lovely place, and I am partial to it, having grown up here and having family here."

"You are fortunate to have family and friends, Miss Haswell. And indeed it is a lovely place, occupied by lovely people. In fact, when I passed Bedsley Priors on my way to London, I saw three reasons which compelled me to decide then and there that I would return to Bedsley Priors one day."

Lilly raised her eyebrows. "Three reasons, sir?"

Mary came out of the kitchen again, bearing a tray of dishes. Mr. Shuttleworth said softly, "And here comes one of those lovely reasons now." He rose. "May I assist you with that tray? Looks heavy."

Mary blushed. "I can manage, sir."

He beamed at them all. "And strong of limb as well." His gaze moved from Mary's face to Lilly's. "You might be sisters. So lovely are the both of you."

The platter of chicken clunked heavily onto the table. "Sorry," Mary mumbled. Biting her lip, Mary set out the bowls of vegetables with a return of her usual grace. Lilly hoped she wasn't about to have one of her bouts of falling sickness.

Breaking away from the man's steady gaze, Lilly asked, "Join us, Mary?"

"Can't now. Maybe for coffee and pudding later."

Lilly forked a piece of stewed chicken onto her plate and passed the platter to Mr. Shuttleworth. He stacked several pieces beside his mound of leeks and potatoes. "Well, now the food's arrived, let's dive into business, shall we?"

He leaned in close across the table. "The bottle. I extracted a few remaining drops of liquid. Definitely contains alcohol."

Her heart fell. She felt shame flush her features.

"As well as laudanum."

She looked down at her plate, all appetite fleeing.

"But I believe its primary purpose is not to intoxicate, but rather to tranquilize."

She looked over at the man.

"I surmise the bottle is your father's and is one of many?"

She darted a look at Francis, but Mr. Shuttleworth raised a hand. "Mr. Baylor did not tell me, but it seems fairly obvious. I have been aware of your father's reclusive state. Have even called in, only to have my concern rebuffed."

"I am sorry."

"Never mind." Mr. Shuttleworth dismissed her apology with a wave of his fork. "I saw him on the street several weeks ago, and his features were quite pinched. I wondered then if he was in a great deal of pain. And I am more convinced now. The mixture is a pain reliever to be sure, but what else it is, I am not completely certain."

"But it is physic, you think? Not simply . . . drink?"

"I believe so, yes. Perhaps some new patent medicine, or more likely, something of his own creation. You might look and see what simples he leaves about or is running low on." He leaned back expressively, "Or, you could simply ask him."

Lilly took a bite of chicken in lieu of answering. Mr. Shuttleworth did not know her father.

In the morning, Lilly observed her father carefully, more objectively, she hoped, now that the shock of so many changes had passed. He was unshaven, his cheeks bristling with a few days' worth of grey and ginger whiskers. The skin of his neck hung looser than she remembered, his jowls more slack. His hair was somewhat thinner and in disarray, with new strands of silver at his sideburns. His eyes had lost some of their blue color, it seemed, and much of their light. When she looked at him, she felt repelled and tender all at once. Even though she had not seen him for over a year, he was still the only parent in her life—her security, her constant. Her father had always been strong and capable. It unsettled her to see him seem so weak, so . . . diminished.

She approached and greeted him gently. She sat on the cot near his legs, so that she might speak with him nearer to his eye level.

"Morning." His voice was rough.

"And how are you today?" She found herself speaking to him in a calm, sweet tone one normally reserved for a child. He was no child. Neither was she, but still the thought of losing him filled her with the emptiest quiver of loneliness. She thought of the Chinese kites she had once seen in Hyde Park coming untied and floating away. Like she and her brother would. *Oh, Charlie . . . What would poor Charlie do without Father?*

She cleared her throat and tried again. "Are you very ill, do you think?"

He looked at her sharply.

"The bottles. I am ashamed to admit, but I at first believed you were foxed. And I doubt I am the only person in the village to think so."

"When have you ever known me to drink more than an occasional glass of port?"

"Never—before. But a great deal has changed since I've been away."

He looked away from her, shaking his head despondently.

"What is it, Father? Do you know?"

"No. Some days I am nearly myself, and others I can barely rise. The latter have become frightfully frequent. But I *know* I have only to come up with the correct combination of herbs and elixirs, and I shall conquer this thing."

"Without a diagnosis? When have you ever been successful treating an illness that way?"

"Rarely, but it does happen. Sometimes we are not sure what the underlying problem is, but we stumble upon a remedy after much trial and error."

"But this is foolishness! When you have not even consulted with another medical man. Let me send for Dr. Foster."

"That man! He would be the last I would crawl to for advice. He would waste no time advertising my weakness and failure—that I can tell you."

She knew old Dr. Foster had often resented her father for visiting and treating *his* patients. But bad blood notwithstanding, he was a professional, was he not?

"Mr. Shuttleworth, then."

"My new competitor? Shall I help him drive me from business once and for all? Shall I hand him the shovel to bury me?"

"I have met the man. He seems very decent. Besides, he is a fellow apothecary. He spent several months with the Worshipful Society, just as you did."

"I spent nearly two years there, between my time with the society and my summer working in the apothecaries' garden. Several months indeed."

"Father, please. I insist you see a doctor. If you refuse the two at hand, then I shall . . . I shall write to my uncle and ask him to bring a man from London."

"Your uncle? Who already believes me a useless failure? I'll not prove him right."

"You are not useless. Merely ill."

"Same thing."

"It isn't! Now, Father, I insist—"

He pinned her with an ice-blue gaze. "I am afraid, lass, that you have no right to insist upon anything."

"Do I not?" she asked, refusing to be cowed. "Is my father not acting irrationally? Damaging himself and his beloved shop, passed down from father and grandfather before him? A shop he would once have done anything to protect?"

"I am trying to protect it!"

"No, you are trying to protect your pride. And it is too late for that. I am calling for Dr. Foster or Mr. Shuttleworth—you have your choice."

"Just . . . just give me a little more time. I know I can get back on my feet. Just another month. By then I shall figure out what treatment I've overlooked . . ."

"Two days."

"A fortnight."

"A week—and no longer."

He sighed. "Very well."

"Good," she said briskly. But she wondered if they had that long.

J. & A. PEPLER, beg respectfully to inform the Ladies of DEVIZES
and its vicinity that J.P. is returned from London,
where she has selected a choice assortment of
MILLINERY DRESSES, Straws, & Fancy Bonnets.

—Devizes & Wiltshire Gazette, 1833

Chapter 20

In the morning, Lilly was just making up a breakfast tray for her
father when a rap on the shop door startled her, causing her to spill
hot tea on her hand. Blowing on the scorched skin, she walked from the
laboratory-kitchen through the shop. She was surprised to see Francis at
the door. She opened it and saw that he carried a crate in his hands.

"This is heavy. Might I . . . ?"

"Of course. Come in."

He carried the crate back and settled it gently on the counter.

"What is this?" she asked, eyeing the array of jars and packets.

"Bare basics. Hopefully enough to keep you going here until you
can place and receive an order."

"But . . . how?"

"I made a second list for myself when I completed that inventory
for you. I pulled this from Mr. Shuttleworth's stock."

"But we cannot accept this."

"This is not charity, Miss Haswell. It has all been accounted for. You will pay it back as you can."

"But I won't . . ." Why could she not finish the sentence, *I won't be here*? Dread and cold realization sifted through her. Orders to place, debts to pay, a shop to repair . . . but what of her plans for a stay of only a fortnight?

"Of course I shall see you are repaid," she said officiously. "Thank you." She turned abruptly and retreated to the laboratory-kitchen so he would not see her brave face fall.

❧

The next day, Lilly and Charlie attended services together. How inviting the church looked that bright morning, sunshine streaming through colorful stained-glass windows, candles lit, happy voices filling the chapel. It felt good to be there, sitting in her old place, listening to the fine Kentish voice of Mr. Baisley.

During the singing of a hymn, Lilly was distracted by a deep male voice coming from somewhere nearby. The pleasing baritone filled in the reedy melody carried by so many women and old men. Lilly glanced discreetly over her shoulder and was surprised to see Francis Baylor two rows behind her, eyes on the vicar, singing intently and with feeling. *His voice has changed as well.*

After the service, many villagers made a point of coming over to greet Lilly and to welcome her home.

Undeniably handsome in his Sunday coat, Francis bowed briefly to her. "Miss Haswell. Charlie." He would have turned away without lingering had Charlie not called after him.

"I saw her again today, Francis."

Francis paused. "Who—the red-haired angel?"

My hair is not red, Lilly thought automatically. Russet brown or even ginger—the tawny brown spice—but not red. A moment later her cheeks were no doubt the very color she despised, for they were not speaking of her at all.

Charlie nodded. "Up early she were. I hoped maybe she were coming here."

"Ah well. Plenty of other angels about the place, Charlie."

Francis did not walk out with them but instead turned to greet Miss Robbins and her parents.

Once outside, Charlie put on a dingy hat. "I'd better to get back to Marlow House."

"Charlie, wait. Sit for a minute, will you?"

He hesitated but allowed her to lead him to a bench in the churchyard and sat down beside her.

She asked, "Do you not wish to return home and help Father and me?"

He shrugged.

"What is it, Charlie? Are you afraid? Has someone at Marlow House frightened you?" She resisted the urge to put her arms around him, to protect him from would-be bullies, as she had when he was a child.

"No. I like it 'ere, I do. Mr. Timms is a bit gruff, but I am learning ever so much from him."

"But Father needs you. You do want to help Father, don't you?"

"I do. But—" Charlie lowered his head. His wrists protruded from the sleeves of his old Sunday coat. Just as his ankles showed between trousers and boots. An overgrown little boy. But this streak of stubbornness was something new.

She forced a gentle tone. "I shall speak to Sir Henry, shall I? And explain?"

Again he shrugged. "He won't like it. And I don't like to break my word."

She hesitated. "You've an official agreement, then? A contract of some sort?"

"I'm an apprentice now, I am. Like Francis were." He sat up a little straighter, clearly proud of the fact.

Oh dear. That did complicate things.

She asked Charlie to come home for tea at least. He agreed, but as soon as they entered through the garden gate, he was distracted by a new hornets' nest hanging from the eaves near the back door. And there he sat. Lilly knew better than to try to cajole him while he was counting, especially objects in flight. She sighed. Maybe it was just as well. She could speak to Father alone first.

Over tea, she asked her father about Charlie's position.

Her father nodded. "I'd heard they were looking for a lad. Told Charlie he might try for it."

"But why?"

"I haven't been able to look after him properly, Lilly. Shames me to say it, but there it is." He rubbed a hand over his whiskered cheeks. "At least there I knew he'd not be wandering about the county, getting himself in some scrape or other with his strange ways and spying and I know not what."

"He does not mean to spy."

He waved her words away. "I know, but it does look it. Bedsley Priors has changed, Lilly. Lots of new people have moved here, some of them quite rough. Most don't know how harmless Charlie is. He might be caught eavesdropping on some shady affair and pay a high price for it. I don't so much mind if they say he's off in his attic, but I could not bear to see any harm come to the boy."

"Of course not."

"At least at Marlow House he's kept busy. And has regular meals, which is more than I can say here."

She pushed his plate of bread and jam nearer to him. "Go on."

He bit off a small morsel. "Mr. Timms took him on as an apprentice of sorts. Marlow waived the apprenticeship fee, in lieu of wages. Though he'll start earning after six months' time, and it's been nearly three already."

"But surely now—"

"I'd hate for him to break the contract. No telling what young Marlow might say to that. Might demand the forfeited apprenticeship fee since Charlie didn't earn out his service, at least some settling up for room and board. It isn't done, Lilly. It would look very bad if Charlie quit, especially without proper notice."

"But, perhaps if I talked with him."

"You are going to talk sense to Roderick Marlow?"

"I meant Sir Henry."

"He leaves all of that to his son." He lifted his cup with a shaky hand. "Sir Henry is in better health than I am at present. But during his last illness he gave up the running of things. Roderick Marlow is master of the estate for all intents and purposes."

"Well, even he can't be devoid of all natural feeling. Once I explain the situation."

"And exactly how will you explain the situation?"

"With great tact and discretion—you may depend upon it."

He shook his head. "I have no doubt you learned a fair dose of that in London, my dear. Go on then, but don't take it to heart if he isn't swayed."

She found Charlie still sitting beside the back door. "Charlie, I am going to see Mr. Marlow in a few minutes. See if we cannot work out some arrangement for a leave for you. Can you harness the gig, please?"

He hesitated, then nodded. "All right."

She stepped quickly across the mews to the coffeehouse. Mrs. Mimpurse and Mary were at the small kitchen table, enjoying a rare time of idle talk over tea.

"Mrs. Mimpurse, I'm riding out to Marlow House to see about getting Charlie released from his contract. Can you stop by and check on Father in the next hour or so? I shouldn't be gone long."

Mrs. Mimpurse looked her up and down. "You are going to Marlow House dressed like that?"

Lilly glanced down at the plain morning dress she had put on after church. "It isn't a social call. I merely wish to discuss business."

"Do you hope to sway Roderick Marlow with your words alone?"

"Well, yes."

Mrs. Mimpurse shook her head. "Tut, tut, Miss Lilly. Has your time in London taught you nothing?"

Two hours later, Lilly stood from her dressing table and pulled on her gloves. She wore one of her London gowns, a walking dress of jaconet

muslin with lovely pink embroidery up the front and three flounces at
the hem. Over it, she wore a cottage mantle of grey cloth lined with pink
silk to cover the low neckline and provide some protection from the slight
chill in the air. She had hoped to take care of her errand earlier in the
day, but it had taken time to bathe and dress in her petticoat, stockings,
and boned stays. Mary had come over to help tighten the stays and then
remained to dress her hair. Now rich auburn curls showed at one temple
beneath a straw gypsy hat trimmed with ribbon. Mary had wanted her
to wear one boasting fruit or ostrich feathers, but Lilly would have felt
too self-conscious driving through the village in either of those.

"Thank you, Mary."

"Nervous?"

"Definitely," Lilly allowed.

"The worst he can do is say no."

Lilly drew in a breath. "Is it?"

"And who could say no to you, looking as pretty as you do?" Mary
hesitated, then added gently, "I know you and your father need help,
but it wouldn't be so bad if Charlie stayed there. I think he likes it."

"You are trying to comfort me, should I fail, I know. But I worry
for Charlie. Would worry for anyone under such masters."

"But . . . Well, never mind," Mary said and adjusted the curl
nearest Lilly's cheek one last time.

Lilly descended the stairs and went out the back door, only to see
Charlie sitting in the slanting rays of late afternoon sunlight, much as
she had left him two hours before. She looked out into the mews but
saw no sign of the gig.

"Have you harnessed Pennywort to the gig?"

"Wheel's broke."

"Is it?" She bit back her frustration. "But you knew I was hoping
to take it. You might have said so before."

"You're only going to Marlows'. 'Tisn't far."

She huffed. "Oh, very well. I shall walk."

"Shall I come along?" He lurched to his feet. " 'Ere's a pretty red-haired lady about the place now. Wouldn't mind clapping eyes on her again. All the lads say she's gurt handsome. Even Francis."

Lilly wondered if the red-haired lady was the woman she had seen with Roderick Marlow in London. "Please stay with Father, Charlie. If he needs anything, run over and ask Mrs. Mimpurse."

"All right." Still, he looked uncomfortable.

"Come on, Charlie," Mary said, joining them outside and clearly sensing his unease. "How about a game of draughts before I go?"

Charlie looked up eagerly at this suggestion.

Lilly smiled her gratitude at Mary, then let herself from the gate.

Charlie was correct. Marlow House was not far. She had walked, even run that distance many times. But never in such fine dress, such delicate slippers, nor such tight stays.

She walked rather stiffly, hoping her hair, piled high on her head beneath her hat, would stay within its pins.

She approached Marlow House from the side and stopped abruptly. There, on the lawn, a man stood as still as a garden statue. She hesitated, then walked a few steps closer, staring at the man whose profile grew more familiar with each step.

No doubt hearing her footsteps on the gravel path, the man turned to look in her direction. "I say, you gave me a start."

Roger Bromley, here? In Bedsley Priors? Though she felt awkward and uncertain of how he might react to her presence, she was pleased to see him. She had always liked the man. She smiled at him, cocking her head to one side. Feeling the weighty crown of curls shift dangerously in that direction, she quickly righted it again.

"Miss Haswell?" Roger Bromley smiled in recognition and stepped to meet her. "I did not expect to see you here."

"Nor I you."

"What a pleasure." He bowed to her and she curtsied. "I have just come out for some air and a respite from silly females. I did not know you were joining the house party."

"Oh . . ." she faltered. "I am not. I live here—in the village, that is."

"That's right! I'd quite forgotten you were from the same rustic country as Marlow."

She took a breath, her anxiety rising at the mention of his name. Hoping to disguise it, she asked brightly, "Is Christina Price-Winters here?"

"No. She is busy buying wedding clothes. Engaged herself to Stanton. Had you not heard?"

Lilly shook her head. She had guessed Christina would not keep in touch. Still, it hurt that she had not written with such significant news.

"But there are at least two others here of your acquaintance," Mr. Bromley continued. "Toby Horton and Miss Whittier."

"How nice for you."

"Is it?"

"Oh dear. Has she thrown you over again?"

He eyed her wryly. "I would not say that, exactly, but yes, she has reverted to being quite cold to me."

"I am sorry to hear it. Perhaps you ought to invent another imminent engagement?" She bit back a smile. "Seemed quite effective the last time."

He laughed. "How deliciously forthright you are, Miss Haswell. I have missed you, though I know I have given little evidence of that."

"That is all right, Mr. Bromley," she said, relieved to feel no sting of regret. "I had no reason to expect correspondence."

"That's right, after throwing me over so heartlessly." He smiled at her, a teasing light in his eyes.

"Were you going in?" He offered her his arm.

"I do not wish to interrupt."

"No harm. Dinner will not be served for some time."

She had just laid her hand on his offered arm when Susan Whittier stepped out onto the veranda.

"Roger? I wondered where you had gone. Oh. Hello."

"You remember Miss Haswell, do you not?"

"Yes. How do you do," the pretty blonde said. "I did not know you would be joining us."

"I am not—"

"Miss Haswell is neighbor to Marlow. Why do you think I was so eager to come to . . . Where are we again?"

"Bedsley Priors."

"Bedsley Priors. Charming place." He winked at Lilly.

"Did you not find him?" The familiar voice of Roderick Marlow caused Lilly's smile to fade. Her heart began to pound uncomfortably when he strode out onto the veranda in evening dress, his cravat and dark hair in elegant disarray.

Susan Whittier said, "I did. But he is occupied, as you see, with your Miss Haswell."

Marlow turned to stare at her, dark eyebrows rising before lowering in perplexity . . . or was it annoyance? Lilly felt her cheeks redden.

"*My* Miss Haswell?" Mr. Marlow repeated.

"She is your neighbor, is she not?" Miss Whittier all but accused.

He cocked his head, considering. "Well, I suppose she is. Miss Haswell, what a surprise." He bowed.

"Forgive me. I did not know you had guests."

"No matter. I did not mean it was not a pleasant surprise. You are most welcome. I had forgotten you had friends among us."

"We enjoy only a limited acquaintance," Miss Whittier corrected. "Excuse me. I shall see you at dinner." At that, the blond woman turned and marched away.

Laying his hand over hers, Mr. Bromley escorted Lilly onto the veranda, where Mr. Marlow stood. There, Roger paused to beam down at her. "Miss Haswell quite broke my heart, Marlow. Did you not hear of it? She rejected me most cruelly."

"Did she?" Again Mr. Marlow's dark eyebrows rose.

Roger sighed dramatically. "Yes. But still, how pleased I am to see her again."

Feeling Mr. Marlow's eyes on her, she rushed to say, "I only wanted to speak with you for a few moments. I shall come again another time."

"Nonsense. You must stay," Roger insisted.

"Yes, of course," Marlow said politely. "Come, Miss Haswell." He gestured toward the door. "Shall we speak in the library? Then you may rejoin your most ardent admirer." Marlow cast a shrewd look at Roger Bromley. "Although I had hoped to win back my ten at whist."

"Another time, my friend." Roger grinned. "Who desires gaming when such beauty is before us?"

Lilly all but rolled her eyes.

"Come, Miss Haswell." Roderick Marlow opened the door for her with a flourish, as though welcoming the queen herself. Was he mocking her?

Once they were closed in the library, Lilly swallowed, wondering if seeking privacy had been a good idea.

Mr. Marlow remained standing but leaned back, propping himself against the edge of a massive desk, arms crossed. He dipped his chin, indicating a chair nearby. "What did you wish to speak to me about?"

She stepped closer but remained standing. "My brother, Charlie." When he appeared not to apprehend her meaning, she clarified, "Your new undergardener?"

"Ah, yes. Stedman mentioned something. In fact, he reported the lad was working out rather well. Is there a problem?"

"Not a problem, exactly. But while I appreciate the offer of employment for him, Charlie is needed at home at present. Having both of us gone has left my father shorthanded, and there is much work to be done."

"Yes, I had heard something about Haswell's falling into disrepair."

She bit back a defensive rebuttal. He was right, after all, but it hurt her pride to hear him say it so matter-of-factly. "Yes, well. I understand you waived an apprenticeship fee, but my brother is very conscientious and doesn't want to break his contract, nor hinder his opportunities for future employment." She was relieved when he didn't ask why she was negotiating on her brother's behalf. Was he aware of Charlie's limitations?

He straightened to his full height and waved her concerns away as though a midge before his face. "Think no more of it, Miss Haswell. I understand. I will speak to Stedman and to Timms. Your brother may return to your father's shop without worry. He may even have a reference, if you like. And he will be welcomed back here, should the situation change and he is no longer needed at home."

She was stunned at how easily it was done. Was he really so kind, or simply eager to return to his guests? She had certainly asked at an opportune time.

"Thank you, sir. That is most magnanimous."

He stepped to the door, opened it, and looked back at her. Her invitation to leave.

She walked toward him but was surprised when he held out his arm. She looked up at him in question.

"May I escort you to the dining room?" he asked.

"But I . . . No. I did not intend nor presume . . ."

He looked at her closely. "Did you really refuse Roger Bromley?"

She took a deep breath. "I suppose I did. But only because I knew he loved another."

He nodded thoughtfully. "And you believe people should marry for love, Miss Haswell?"

"I do not know about all people, but I should."

"Shall we?"

"Shall we what?"

"Go in to dinner."

"Oh, of course." *Of course* he'd meant dinner, not *of course* she would stay for it.

Roger Bromley appeared in the corridor. "Enough village business. I'd hoped to escort Miss Haswell to the dining room."

"Too late, Bromley." Marlow actually took her hand and laid it on his arm. "I am afraid you shall have to escort Miss Whittier and her chaperone instead."

Across the hall, Susan Whittier stood with a faded, weary-faced woman of fifty or so years. Susan looked rather vexed. "Has everyone forgotten me?"

"There, there," Roger soothed, striding across the room and offering his arm. She actually smiled and laid her hand on his sleeve. Roger looked at Lilly over his shoulder and winked again.

Before she could protest further, Marlow was leading Lilly across the grand hall.

From above, a flash of green caught her eye. She looked up and saw a woman gliding down the staircase in gleaming layers of emerald silk. Her bearing was elegant, her crown of red hair regal, her porcelain features flawless. Yes, this was the woman she had seen on Roderick Marlow's arm at a London ball. How beautiful she was. Lilly felt horribly underdressed in her walking frock and straw bonnet.

The butler, Mr. Withers, appeared and offered to take her wrap. She swallowed. Should she stay? She wasn't properly dressed for dinner. Nor invited. Nervously, she removed her hat and handed it to Mr. Withers. Then she untied the bow that released the mantle from her neck and shoulders, and the butler took that from her as well. Roderick's gaze surveyed her throat and neckline before returning to her overheated face. Why did he want her to stay? Was not this woman, now pausing before them, his intended?

"Miss Lillian Haswell, Miss Cassandra Powell."

Miss Powell dipped her head politely but reservedly. Lilly returned the gesture. Closer now, Lilly realized that Miss Powell was older than she appeared from a distance. Perhaps a few years older than Roderick Marlow himself.

"I believe I saw the two of you in London together." Lilly meant it as an indication that she understood they were a couple and she posed no threat. But neither reacted as she'd expected.

Roderick cleared his throat, and Miss Powell looked away. "I do not recall such an occasion." She flipped open her lacquered fan. "Well, I shall just see myself in."

"Nonsense, Cass—Miss Powell." He offered her his left arm, his right still trapping Lilly's hand to his side. Miss Powell coolly accepted. And Lilly was taken in to dinner, feeling very much like the proverbial lamb being led to slaughter.

I will not dwell upon ragouts or roasts,
Albeit all human history attests
That happiness for man—the hungry sinner!—
Since Eve ate apples, much depends on the dinner.

—LORD BYRON

CHAPTER 21

The evening passed more pleasantly than Lilly would have guessed. Roderick Marlow was a gallant host, skillfully including everyone in a conversation that ranged from the London season to fashion, books, parliamentary affairs, and the war with France. Roger Bromley was also a master conversationalist, and managed to compliment both Lilly and Susan in equal measure, so that by the second course, Susan Whittier was smiling with genuine warmth at both Roger and Lilly. Miss Whittier's chaperone ate silently but voraciously for such a small woman. Toby Horton drank too much and spoke his opinions too loudly, but otherwise the meal passed very agreeably. Even red-haired Cassandra Powell made an effort to show interest in the others, as though she were already mistress of Marlow House.

The meal was finer by far than the plain fare—soups, stews, beef and kidney pies—she'd either prepared or been given since returning home. Finer even than most of the tables she had seen laid in London.

For the first course they were served green-pea soup, crimped perch with Dutch sauce, stewed veal and peas, lamb cutlets and cucumbers. Then came a second course of haunch of venison, boiled capon in white sauce, braised tongue and vegetables. Finally, there arrived a third course of lobster salad, raspberry and currant tart, strawberry cream, meringues, and iced pudding. Lilly took only tiny portions from the serving dishes nearest her but still could not eat everything on her plate. Giving herself a respite, she paused to touch a linen serviette to her lips.

"Is the meal to your liking, Miss Haswell?" Roderick Marlow asked, raising his goblet.

"Indeed, sir. Mrs. Tobias is to be commended. I had not a finer meal in all my time in London."

Roderick Marlow dipped his head appreciatively.

"And how long were you in London?" Miss Powell asked. "A fortnight?"

Lilly ignored her pointed condescension. "A year and a half."

"Miss Haswell lived with her uncle and aunt, Jonathan and Ruth Elliott," Roger Bromley said warmly. "Fine people and friends of my parents."

Even Susan Whittier added a kind word. "Miss Haswell was quite a favorite with the Price-Winters family, Cassandra. You were guest in their grand home on at least one occasion."

Miss Powell nodded slightly but sipped from her wine glass in lieu of responding.

When the ladies withdrew to allow the men to drink port and smoke their pipes in private, Miss Powell led the way to the drawing room. Lilly followed reluctantly, knowing it would be rude not to join the ladies for at least a short time. Miss Powell went directly to the pianoforte and sat gracefully upon its bench. She ran her fingers over the keys with a flourish, then began playing a dramatic piece. Susan Whittier followed her chaperone's example and sat on one of the set-tees. She picked up a book lying on its arm but quickly laid it back down. She and Lilly exchanged an awkward smile. It was difficult to speak over the music, but Lilly sat on a chair near Susan and attempted it anyway.

"Your gown is lovely," Lilly said, eyeing the evening dress of willow-green crepe with gauze flowers around the hem.

"Do you think so? When I saw Cassandra's silk was green too, I feared we would clash horribly."

"It is beautiful, truly."

Miss Whittier smiled self-consciously. "Thank you."

Lilly could almost believe Susan an agreeable young woman, when not jealous, vexed, or bored. She hoped so, for Roger's sake.

Susan leaned closer. "Do not mind Cassandra. I am afraid she wields her disappointments like claws."

Her tongue as well, Lilly thought.

"She was engaged once, you see, but her fiancé was—"

Miss Powell halted mid-stanza, the chords fading under her words. "How amusing to see the two of you sitting together—all politeness. Two rivals under the same roof."

"One might say the same of two others, Cassandra," Susan said cryptically.

What did that mean? Lilly wondered. *Two sets of rivals?*

Miss Powell's eyes narrowed. "Careful, Susan dear."

Susan Whittier rose. "Please excuse me, ladies. I am just going to dash to my chamber and freshen my toilette."

"Good idea." Miss Powell smiled archly. When Susan and her matronly companion had gone, Miss Powell resumed playing—this time a quiet, moody piece. "Poor Susan. Only wants what she cannot have."

Lilly thought this quite perceptive. Susan Whittier certainly seemed to only want Mr. Bromley when she thought she could not have him.

"You are a shopkeeper's daughter, are you not?" Miss Powell asked.

"An apothecary's daughter."

Miss Powell lifted one hand from the keys in a dismissive wave.

"That explains a great deal." She played a few more bars, then paused. "But not everything."

Lilly rose, deciding she had better take her leave before she said something foolish.

"I shall bid you good-night, Miss Powell."

Cassandra dipped her head slightly, but kept her eyes on the sheet music before her. "I shall be going up in a moment myself. I want to visit Sir Henry. The baronet was up and about all day yesterday. Bested us all at archery, went riding. Quite exhausted himself, I am afraid. Such a pity he was not feeling well enough to join us tonight."

"A great pity. Do greet him for me."

Cassandra paused in her playing. "You are acquainted with Sir Henry?"

"Yes, although I have not seen him in nearly two years."

She nodded, though Lilly had the distinct impression the woman would not bother to pass along the greetings of a mere *shopkeeper's* daughter.

Lilly let herself from the room, closing the door behind her.

She asked a housemaid, a girl she did not know, where Mr. Withers would have put her wrap. The girl bobbed a curtsy and ducked through a door. A moment later, the butler himself appeared, holding her mantle while she put on her straw hat. Roderick Marlow appeared in the hall and, seeing her there, quickly strode over.

"Leaving already, Miss Haswell?"

"Yes, I must be getting back."

He took her wrap from the butler and arranged it over her shoulders himself. She swallowed, uncomfortable with his familiarity, especially in front of Mr. Withers.

She self-consciously took a step away from Mr. Marlow as she tied the bow around her neck.

"Well, good evening," she said. "Thank you for including me so generously."

"You are more than welcome. Has Withers called for your carriage?"

Roger appeared in the hall and walked toward them just as Miss

Powell came out of the drawing room. So much for slipping away quietly.

Lilly said, in what she hoped were low tones, "No. I walked actually. It is not far."

Even so, Roger heard her. "Marlow, send for your carriage, will you? I shall escort Miss Haswell home."

"Never mind, Bromley," Marlow said. "I shall see Miss Haswell home myself."

"Really, Roderick," Cassandra Powell said, passing by on her way to the stairs. "You have guests. The groom can take her perfectly well."

"Yes, please," Lilly urged. "I do not wish to trouble you further. I can walk, or if Cecil has time . . . ?"

"Cecil?" Cassandra swung back around, brow arched.

"Cecil Briggs. The groom."

"Ah," she said. "Do you know all the servants?"

Lilly lifted her chin. "Yes. I know everybody in the village. Or at least I did at one time."

"How quaint."

"As host, I insist on escorting you home," Roderick Marlow said. "Bromley, if you will be so good as to entertain Miss Whittier while I'm gone. Horton is out cold, I'm afraid. I shall have Withers and Stedman see to him."

"Oh, very well," Roger said, as though it were a burden to have Miss Whittier all to himself. His warm gaze fastened on Lilly. "I cannot tell you what a delight it has been to see you again, Miss Haswell. Shall we have the pleasure of your company again tomorrow?"

"No. But I do hope you enjoy the rest of your stay, Mr. Bromley." Lilly curtsied and he bowed.

Cassandra Powell was already halfway up the stairs without a backward glance.

Roderick called for his curricle and waved off the groom. "I'll handle the ribbons myself."

Discomfort flooded Lilly. Alone, unchaperoned with Roderick

Marlow, at night? Did he not realize, or did he simply not care? She said, "I think, Mr. Marlow, that given the hour . . ."

"Of course. You are quite right. The landau, please, Withers, and Briggs to drive. No use rousing the coachman at this hour."

Lilly might have walked home in the time it took to harness the horses and bring the carriage around, but Mr. Marlow would not hear of it. When hooves sounded on the crescent drive out front, he escorted her outside. Cecil Briggs helped her up into the seat, and she did not miss the groom's speculative expression. He and Charlie had been boyhood friends. When Mr. Marlow leaned close to the groom and delivered some low instruction, Cecil darted a look at her that she could not quite decipher. Surprise? Worry?

As soon as Mr. Marlow was seated beside her in the front-facing bench, Cecil climbed up to his perch and started the horses into a mild pace, seeming in no great hurry. It was quite late, but the moon shone brightly on the summer night, and she could see both men quite clearly.

"When I first saw you in London," Roderick Marlow began, "I thought I was imagining things. Why did you run from me?"

"I should think that somewhat obvious."

"Is it?"

"Well, I worried you might . . ." She darted a look at him. "That is, I thought you would . . ."

"Ah." He nodded his understanding. "You thought I would stand on the orchestra stage and tell the venerable assembly that Miss Haswell was not the privileged, accomplished young lady they imagined her, but rather the cleverest, loveliest, most loyal lady in all of Wiltshire."

That was not the response she'd expected. What had come over the man? Was he foxed? Did she need remind him of the exquisite redhead waiting at Marlow House?

She acted on this notion. "And when I first saw you in London, you were with Miss Powell."

"I suppose she is rather hard to miss."

"She is very beautiful."

Marlow looked off into the passing countryside. "Yes, and very aware of that fact."

"All the lads in the village are quite agog, I understand. My brother and my father's apprentice—that is, his former apprentice—are both quite taken with her."

"I suppose the young men in this county have rarely seen such a woman."

"Will they be . . . seeing her often?" Lilly was curious about the former fiancé Miss Whittier had mentioned, but knew it would be impolite to ask him.

He looked at her and smirked. "If she has her way, yes. I believe they will see a great deal of her. You know we Marlows live to please the villagers."

She raised her eyebrows.

Feigning indignation, he said, "My father is highly respected among them—do you deny it?"

"Of course not. Sir Henry is admired by all."

"It is only me you take issue with?"

"You do seem improved with age. You certainly *appear* charming."

"You find me charming. I am pleased to hear it. But you think it only a surface charm? That beneath this façade, I am . . . ?"

He looked at her, waiting while she studied him. She thought of the pills they made in her father's shop, with their sugar pastes and silver coatings. Pretty to look at, sweet on the surface, but still just as bitter within.

"I pray I am wrong."

Surprisingly, he let that go. "Pray often, do you?"

"Not as often as I should." *Nor as often as I once did.*

Cecil turned the horses toward the north, she noticed, toward Alton. Why was he not simply driving straight into the village?

"What do you petition for, Miss Haswell? What worldly troubles press themselves upon your heart? Starving orphans in London? Slavery in Spain, perhaps? The war with France?"

"No, I am afraid my small prayers are of a far narrower scope. My father. Brother. My dear friend Mary." She did not mention her mother, though she could have. She was still distracted by the unexpected detour.

"What about *dear Mary* moves you to pray?"

"She struggles with epilepsy . . . falling sickness. Do you not remember?"

"Oh yes. That girl who has fits."

Her concern was instantly replaced with irritation. "She is not *that girl*. She is Mary Helen Mimpurse. The cleverest girl I know. The gentlest, truest friend. The daughter of a war hero and the finest woman in Bedsley Priors—well you are acquainted with her mother."

"Maude Mimpurse's daughter? I had forgotten. Forgive me, I meant no disrespect to your Miss Mary Mimpurse. My, how diverting to say that. Miss Mary Mimpurse. Miss Mary Mimpurse . . ."

She found herself chuckling with him and noted they were now driving on a narrow track east.

He suddenly sobered. "By your own admission, the list of beneficiaries of your prayers is quite small. Would you consider adding another?"

"You, sir?"

He pulled a frown, brows raised, "You think I need prayers?"

"We all do, sir. Some more than others."

"Miss Lillian Haswell, I do believe you are teasing me."

She grinned.

"Actually, I meant my father. He has fallen ill again. That smug Dr. Foster spent half the morning at his side."

How foolish she felt now. "Of course I shall pray for your father."

"Thank you." They rode on in silence for several moments. Lilly realized that after their brief detour, Cecil had again turned south toward Bedsley Priors.

Marlow said, "But if you happened to mention my name to God now and again, I should not object."

She smiled. "I shall ask Him to give you humility."

He cleared his throat. "Let us not ask for a miracle right off, shall we?"

She laughed.

"But of course . . . you Haswells call down miracles at will—is that not right? Your father, the legendary healer and all that. Bringing my own grandfather back from the dead, as they say."

Lilly bit her lip, then whispered, "That was a long time ago."

They made the final turning down the High Street.

"Well, here we are," he said. "I cannot remember when I've so enjoyed a carriage ride."

"Nor I. But then, we haven't a proper carriage."

He gave a dry bark of laughter. "Here I think I am about to receive a compliment, and she pulls the chair out from under me at the last."

Cecil reined in the horses in front of the shop.

"Hold there, Briggs." Marlow alighted from the carriage, lowered the step himself, and offered his hand to her. She swallowed but placed her gloved hand in his. With a gentle grip, he assisted her down and walked her to the front door.

Retrieving her hand, she looked up at him squarely. "Then here is a genuine compliment. Thank you for your fair treatment of my brother. More than fair. And for your gallant behavior toward me this very evening."

He bowed. "You are most welcome." He leaned near, and she felt his warm breath on her cheek. Quietly, he added, "Now go inside before I attempt something less than gallant."

She hurried to comply.

In the morning, Lilly walked over to the coffeehouse, letting herself in the kitchen door as she always had.

"How did it go last night?" Mary asked, pouring her a cup of coffee.

"It was really very pleasant. Mr. Marlow was quite gentlemanly, even though he had a house party in progress when I arrived uninvited. He even insisted I stay for dinner. I was so glad you'd dressed my—"

"I meant how did it go about Charlie?"

"Oh." Lilly felt foolish but continued on, "Fine. Perfect. He was quite magnanimous about the whole situation."

"Magnanimous," Mary repeated, somewhat skeptically.

"He said Charlie would be welcomed back at any time."

"*Roderick* Marlow said that?"

"Yes. He was very agreeable."

Mary narrowed her eyes. "Really."

Lilly stirred sugar into her coffee, waiting until young Jane passed by with brush and blacking before adding, "And a former suitor of mine was there as well—you remember the Mr. Bromley I told you about?"

Mary leaned her elbows on the worktable and studied her, slowly shaking her head. "I don't think Mr. Bromley put that blush in your cheeks, love."

"Mary, no. I can guess what you are thinking, but—"

"Can you? And worrying about?"

"Do not be uneasy. Roderick Marlow is a very handsome man—I do not deny it. And for some reason he was exceedingly charming last night. But I know what he's capable of. And I'm not foolish enough to think he'd have any serious intentions toward an apothecary's daughter. I experienced my share of that in London. Men happy to flirt and dance with me, all the while planning to marry another lady of their own class."

"Oh, you'll marry one day," Mary said wistfully. "Lovely, healthy girl like you."

Lilly looked up at her friend, sensing her sadness. "I could say the same of you, Mary. Mr. Shuttleworth can barely take his eyes off you."

Mary shrugged the idea away. "It is only because he doesn't know."

Seeing her discomfort and not knowing how to reassure her, Lilly changed the subject, telling all she had learned about Rosa Wells in

London. She concluded by saying, "You and I have both seen unhappy marriages firsthand. I am in no hurry to end up in one of my own, no matter my aunt's machinations." She rose and rinsed her coffee cup in the basin. "In any case, Mr. Marlow has all but said he will marry that red-haired beauty."

"Charlie will be brokenhearted," Mary said in jest.

"Probably." Lilly paused. "Cassandra Powell is a bit older, I think, than she looks. And I am told, suffered a broken engagement, poor thing."

"Poor thing, indeed. I cannot get over how sorry I'm feeling for the picture of perfection who's turned the head of the county's most eligible bachelor. Yes, I think I must take the poor thing to prayer."

Lilly bit back a smile. "Mary Helen Mimpurse! That is the first nearly unkind thing I believe I've ever heard you say about anyone."

Mary smirked and said dryly, "Stick around, love, stick around."

England is a nation of shopkeepers.

—NAPOLEON BONAPARTE

CHAPTER 22

With surprising reluctance, Charlie moved his things back into the bedchamber next to Lilly's. He resumed the sweeping up and his work in the physic garden. She would have liked to ask Mrs. Fowler back as well, and would, as soon as they could again afford to pay her wages.

Lilly was poring over ledgers and unpaid bills when Francis stopped in on his afternoon off. He hopped up onto the high counter, swinging his legs. It reminded her of the Francis of former days. All arms and legs and more energy for cricket than studying. Now those arms and legs had filled out with masculine muscle beneath his white shirt and breeches. He had certainly changed during her absence, but she wondered if the changes were only physical.

"How fares your mother, Francis?" she asked.

"Well enough."

"And your sister?"

"She has engaged herself to Tom Billings at last. That curate she had long pined for married someone else."

"Was your sister laid very low?"

He shrugged. "She caddled about for days at Christmas. But she seems to have recovered rather well."

Lilly closed the ledger and thought back. "I met your sister only the once, but I recall she was very pleasing in manner and countenance. Quite handsome."

"Do you think so?" He grinned. "You said *I* was very like her."

She chose to ignore this statement, true though it was. Thinking once more of her parents, she asked, "Does Mr. Billings know she preferred another?"

"He knows but overlooks her foolishness. That's the way love is, I suppose."

"Is it? I am not sure I would be as understanding if the man I loved pined for another."

His legs stopped swinging. "Do you . . . that is . . . did you form an attachment while you were in London?"

"Only two."

His eyebrows rose.

"But both ended just before I left. I doubt either will come to anything, even when—or if—I return."

He looked at her expectantly, clearly waiting for her to explain.

"One was a physician, of whom my aunt disapproved. He was reserved and uncertain. Still I thought, perhaps . . . The other was a gentleman whom my aunt advised me in the strongest terms to accept. Wealthy, an heir, good-looking, kind . . ."

"No wonder you refused that swell," Francis rued. "I detest him already."

Lilly shot him a wry grin. "No. I refused him because, while he admired me, he did not love me."

Looking at her, Francis said quietly, "He would have, in time."

She met his gaze for a moment, considering his words, then continued. "Perhaps—did he not love another."

"Is there no chance this other woman will accept him?"

"I believe there might be. If she believes she cannot have him."

"Ah . . . yes," Francis said. "I have seen that before—not realizing what one has until he—or she—has lost it."

Nodding thoughtfully, Lilly looked around the shop. "This feels very much like days gone, when you and I would sit here together, wondering where Charlie had got to, wagering on what he had found to count. Wondering where all the customers were, but glad for the respite too."

Francis picked up the thread, "Your father napping in his surgery or grumbling about something I'd forgotten to distill."

"And you forever teasing me. Like brother and sister, we were. I shall never forget it."

"I wonder," he said gently. "Do you remember, Lilly?"

She wrinkled her brow. "Of course I do."

"Clearly, I mean?"

She tilted her head and looked at him. "I am sure my memory will fail one day, but I am hardly in my dotage yet."

He hopped down from the counter, stepping closer as he continued, "What I mean is, you and I seem to remember those days differently. You could not leave here quickly enough when the chance came, but I hated to see those days end. I still remember being here with you . . . living under the same roof, taking meals together, talking and laughing together." He looked steadily into her eyes. "It was one of the happiest times of my life."

Charlie came in, the door slamming behind him. Lilly pulled her gaze from Francis to greet her brother as he carried in an armful of peppermint for her to bunch and dry. Francis moved to the door to take his leave.

Hand on the latch, Francis turned and looked at her. "And I never once thought of you as a sister."

❧

Lilly stood upon the Honeystreet Bridge for the first time since she'd returned from London. She had crossed it several times, of

197

course, but had never tarried. Yet she felt drawn to do so now, as though she might find answers in the slowly flowing water of the canal. She knew she must make a decision, difficult as it seemed. Her aunt's recent letter weighed on her mind. She had written to ask if Lillian would return in time to attend the Langtrys' annual ball.

> *Don't forget the new gown we had made for the occasion and how much we were all looking forward to it. And Mr. Alban has just acquired a new Italian novel he knows you will enjoy. It will sharpen your command of the language before we travel to Rome this winter. . . .*

How Lilly longed to travel to Italy! To see the Coliseum and Pantheon, the basilicas and squares, to stay in a little pension, to speak Italian with Italians. . . .

She sighed, knowing that if she stayed in Bedsley Priors any longer she risked her future with the Elliotts. She would forfeit her last season, her best chance of finding a proper husband and residing in London as a lady of quality.

Her aunt had also written a piece of unexpected news.

> *Your uncle insists I mention that Dr. Graves called. Seemed quite surprised to find you had quit London without a word. As you had not told him anything, I did not think it my place to do so and sent him on his way.*

Why had he called? Lilly wondered. She had guessed he would be relieved to be rid of her after the revelation about her mother. Had she been wrong? If she returned soon, might he still be interested in courting her?

Part of her was ready to jump aboard the next coach to London. After all, Haswell's was not her responsibility. She was only a young woman. Her father had made it clear he did not want her to give up her London life for him.

But she also knew that if she left again, there was little hope her father would survive. If nothing else, his shop—his only livelihood—would fail. And what about Charlie? Her father was in no condition to look after him.

Lilly detested the thought of disappointing her generous aunt and uncle. She felt disloyal, ungrateful. She cringed to imagine the hurt that would cloud their features. Would they feel as though they had wasted their time, money, and attentions on her, only for her to leave them without warning with a roomful of gowns, hats, and hopes that none of them had use for any longer? All so she could . . . what? Attempt to keep her father's shop going when it was obviously failing, along with her father's health? Everyone knew women were not allowed to be apothecaries.

"You are a picture, Miss Haswell."

Startled from her musings, she turned and saw Mr. Shuttleworth standing on the canal bank, this time wearing a red velvet frock coat over the same gold waistcoat and cravat. He circled his hands into a tube and looked at her through it, as a captain might look through a ship's glass. "This is exactly how you looked the very first time I saw you."

"You are mistaken, sir. You were not even living in Bedsley Priors the last time I stood here."

He walked up the bank and onto the bridge.

"Ah. But do you recall my telling you I traveled by narrowboat on this very canal from Bristol to London?"

She nodded.

"I passed Bedsley Priors, of course, and in fact we tied off there near The George for several hours. That's when I saw the first of the three enticements I mentioned."

He rested his elbows on the bridge a few feet from where she stood.

"She was a lovely young lady in white, strolling along the canal near the mill. A beauty among workmen. A blossom in the mud."

"Miss Robbins, no doubt," Lilly said. Did everyone idolize the girl?

"Yes, though of course I did not know her name at the time. I stood watching her until she disappeared. By then, the crew had all gone into The George, and I realized I needed a good meal more than a belly full of smoke and ale. I walked into Bedsley Priors. Into the coffeehouse. And there was served most kindly by the lovely Miss Mimpurse. Your oldest friend, I understand."

"She is indeed. We grew up together."

He nodded his understanding. "But it was only later, after a good meal, and back aboard that cramped narrowboat, that we passed under this bridge and I saw the loveliest enticement of all. Standing here, looking sad and a bit lost, much as you do now."

She felt her lips part in surprise, but before she could form any response, he continued.

"And then and there I decided that as soon as I could, I would return to this picturesque village. Maybe even set up shop here one day.

"But first, I served my term with the Apothecaries' Society, then I studied at St. Tom's Hospital for the poor, as well as a private institution, to update my surgical skills. I sold a great deal of my own exotics collection to raise funds to set myself up in a place. And in between, spent as much time as I could watching the ships come in. I often counted five or even six hundred collier ships waiting to discharge their cargo. Fruit from Kent and Spain, coal from Newcastle, huge Greenland whales . . . Do you know, I once even saw a group of porpoises come up with the tide nearly to London Bridge?"

She shook her head in wonder. "And after all that, you left London to settle here. I am still surprised you would."

"Are you? I understand you lived in London—experienced its delights—and yet you also have returned."

Have I? Lilly wondered. "I planned only a short visit. But, well . . ."

"Your father needs you."

"Yes."

"And so you will stay."

Holding a breath, she squeezed her eyes shut, then exhaled. "Yes."

"Well, I for one am pleased to hear it. I own I have never stayed in one place so long before. Even in London, I was forever moving from one lodging house to another." He looked at her closely. "Still, I wonder . . . Will you always wish, always imagine what you might be missing elsewhere?"

"Will you?"

He smiled shyly, then returned his gaze to the canal. "It is a bit early to tell."

"I warn you," Lilly said. "If I stay, Haswell's will give you a run for your money."

He grinned at her. "I have no doubt you will prove a worthy adversary—though I do not like to use that term to describe you, Miss Haswell. It will be a friendly competition, I hope. I for one believe there are plenty of patients for everybody, what with Honeystreet's labourers and canal traffic, and Alton so close by."

"You are surprisingly fair and generous, sir."

He shrugged. "I have no longing for great wealth. For great adventure, yes, to travel widely and love deeply—these things I value more than profits. Though certainly one needs enough of those to finance the former things."

She chuckled. "So I am learning."

"And you, Miss Haswell. What is it you want?"

She stared thoughtfully at the turbid water below. Once, she had wanted to experience life and love beyond Bedsley Priors. That, and to find her mother. In London, she had experienced a small measure of each. What *did* she want now? Instead of trying to verbalize her jumbled thoughts, she parroted his own words back to him. "It is a bit early to tell."

My dear Aunt & Uncle Elliott,

I am sorry to disappoint you, but I will be remaining here in Bedsley Priors for the foreseeable future. My father is quite ill and his shop failing. Though he does not ask it of me, and

though much of my heart is still with you in London, I know I
must stay to help Father and look after Charlie. It pains me to
be apart from you and to miss all the events and travels we'd
planned, but I hope you will understand my decision, painful
as it is. I regret the great expense and trouble you have taken
over me, but I for one do not count it wasted. My months with
you will forever be a treasure in my memory and in my heart.
While I enjoyed the education and all the entertainments, what
I valued most was coming to feel as though I were truly part of
your family. I love you both and always shall.

I plan to write to Christina P-W myself, but please give my
regards to others of our acquaintance, as you judge best.

With love & gratitude,
Lillian

She did not write to Dr. Graves, knowing it was improper for
an unmarried woman to write to any man not of her family, unless
they were formally engaged. Had Dr. Graves asked, her uncle might
have given him permission to write to her, though her aunt would
not approve. But as the weeks passed without correspondence, she
realized anew that Dr. Graves did not wish to continue their relationship, regardless of the call her aunt had mentioned. Lilly had already
guessed as much but still felt the silence keenly.

She did write to Christina, congratulating her on her engagement
and asking her to pass along her farewells and warm felicitations to
her family. She knew Christina would not stay in touch. As much
fun as they'd had together, their friendship was not deep like hers
and Mary's. Lilly did not think the worse of Christina for it. Out of
sight, out of mind, the saying went, and in Lilly's brief experience,
this was a rule effortlessly observed by others. She sometimes wished
she could do the same.

Desperate affairs require desperate measures.

—ADMIRAL HORATIO NELSON

CHAPTER 23

Lilly asked Charlie to scrape the peeling paint from the many-paned shopwindow. He seemed to take to the repetitive task effortlessly. She purchased new paint from the ironmonger in Huntley's Yard, and arose early to paint the window frames herself. Her arms ached from the effort, but she felt satisfaction at doing the work on her own, saving money she desperately needed to restock the shop.

Most mornings, she and Charlie worked in the physic garden, harvesting all the flowers, seeds, and roots they could. She hung the flowers upside down to dry in the herb garret and shop rafters, and ground what root they needed immediately, while storing the rest in the cellar. When the shop bell rang, still unfortunately a rare occurrence, Lilly would hastily lay aside her garden work and jog into the shop, wiping her hands on her apron as she went, fretting over what each patron might require. Recommending remedies for everyday needs—headache powders, laxatives, hair and complexion creams, tooth sponges, and the like—was no problem. But when a person—especially a man—wanted medical advice, that sent her adrift in murky waters.

"Mr. Haswell is occupied in his surgery at present," she would say, "but I shall nip in and ask him what he would recommend." She would indeed ask, "Father, what would you recommend for Mr. James's rheumatism?" Her father would usually try to rouse himself, sometimes asking for clarification and offering sound advice. But when he could not, she would continue on as though he had. "Yes, the same symptoms as before. Do you think he ought to stay with Burridge's Specific, or try another? Very well, I shall let him know. . . ."

Fortunately, she had known what to dispense for the few ailments presented to her so far—mostly by patients they'd had for many years. She would not risk anyone's health. But neither would she send a paying customer to Shuttleworth's or Dr. Foster until absolutely necessary.

In the meantime, she wrote another letter.

Dear Miss Lippert,

I have returned to my father's apothecary shop in Bedsley Priors. Like you, we also now face greater competition. I am seeking to help my father compete against a young new surgeon-apothecary. I remember our discussion about your brother's keen business sense, and I myself witnessed your skills in displays and ladies' items. I wonder if I might I ask your advice—as well as that of your brother and father?

Polly Lippert wrote back promptly, including a kindly penned list of the most popular ladies' items, toilet articles, and perfumes in their shop. The letter included a few lines written in the shaky hand of Polly's father, saying he would be happy to offer what advice he could and that his son, George, would write to her directly. A few days later, she received a letter from George Lippert himself.

On his advice, she ordered new exotics, new patent remedies, and even an "electricity machine," reportedly highly effective in the treatment of epilepsy, gout, and other disorders of the nerves. Following Polly's list, Lilly ordered French perfumes and cosmetics and other pretty things London ladies liked. She got rid of the jar of putrid bear grease and in its place displayed fragrant Macassar oil from India, which promised to "bestow an inestimable gloss and scent, rendering the hair inexpressibly attracting."

She updated all the displays, adding feminine touches like a vase of flowers and a fabric runner in the window display. She set out bowls of dried flower petals and cinnamon to sweeten the air. She offered free samples of ready-made items like skin lotions and breath tablets. She prayed as she balanced the ledgers and then, prayed some more.

Francis Baylor opened Haswell's back door as he had without thought all the years he'd lived at the shop. He supposed he should have gone around to the front, but he already had his foot in the door and wanted to see how Mr. Haswell was faring. Mostly, however, he wanted to see Lilly.

When he stepped inside, he saw her standing before the laboratory-kitchen cupboards. She looked sharply at him over her shoulder. "Oh, Francis! You startled me."

"I should have knocked. Forgive me."

"That's all right . . ." She was clearly distracted, pawing through drawers, crates, and tins.

"What is it?" he asked. "What are you looking for?"

She hesitated, then sighed. He realized she was whispering. "I was sure Father would have plenty of calcium phosphate. I have already searched the drawers and jars in the shop. Have you any idea if he'd begun storing it elsewhere?"

"No. It was always in its jar on the shelves out front."

Lilly pressed her hands over her eyes.

"Lilly . . . ?" Francis grew concerned.

"A new family in Honeystreet has the ague. All six children. The mother is in the shop now. When I did not find any fever powder, I told her I would just step into the back to prepare some fresh for her.

205

Now I shall have to send her to Shuttleworth's. Can you help her? A Mrs. Todd Hurst. In those new lodgings on Chimney Lane?"

"I know it."

Lilly shook her head. "Such a fine prospect. Her husband a trained barge builder. *Six children* . . . I dare not wait any longer. I must admit defeat and hand the family to you."

Francis had not seen Lilly so discouraged since the first few days after her return, and he did not like to see her so now. He held up his palm. "Don't say anything. Get the calcined antimony and sleeves ready."

"But we haven't—"

But Francis was already out the door.

Wringing her hands and pacing, Lilly tried to pray but only succeeded in worrying and feeling guilty. Treating the children promptly was so much more important than who provided the remedy. She should have sent Mrs. Hurst to Shuttleworth's directly. But she was sure her father would have the *materia medica*. Was it so wrong to want to prove Haswell's still viable? Make a sale? She chuckled dryly. If her London friends could see her now and witness her thinking like a tradesman! She should simply march back into the shop and explain to Mrs. Hurst that she would not be able to supply her needs after all.

The back door banged open and Francis barged in, pottery jar in arms. "Come on, we've powder to prepare. You can box my ears later."

"I was not going to box your ears," Lilly whispered. In fact she felt like embracing him. Instead, she turned her attention to the fever powder.

As the two worked side by side, Lilly surveyed his deft motions. "You have become quite good at this."

"You sound surprised."

"Well . . ."

He held out his hand for the sleeves. "I should be glad you went away to London."

The words startled her.

"Turns out your leaving was good for me," he continued. "I had to learn to do things myself. When you were here, it was easier to ask you rather than haul out those cumbersome tomes and find the answer myself. Took more time, but in the end, I remembered the answers."

"I am glad someone benefited from my absence."

"I did not say I was glad you went away. Nor am I sorry you've returned."

How final that sounded. Uncomfortable, she merely nodded.

"If only *you* were not sorry," Francis said wistfully.

She hesitated, but thought of no suitable answer.

Francis rubbed his palms together. "Now, what else do we need?"

In short order, they had the medicine in individual paper sleeves ready for Mrs. Hurst. She squeezed his arm and whispered, "Thank you."

With a faint smile, he covered her stained fingers with his own.

Lilly returned to the front of the shop to apologize for the delay and explain the dosages to the mother. Once Lilly had paid Mr. Shuttleworth for the calcium phosphate, she would make little profit on the sale, but hopefully Haswell's had gained a customer who would return often.

The following week, Lilly opened a letter from her aunt with some trepidation. How would she respond to the news that Lilly would not be returning after all?

Dear Lillian,

Your letter was both bane and balm. How your uncle and I feared you would be drawn in to your former life there. All our efforts in vain. I confess this is the second letter I have begun to you since reading yours. The first was a blatant attempt to convince you to return at once. Filled with details of all you were missing, of all that might be. Utterly selfish, I realize now. Well, not utterly—I sincerely believe you could be a success in town yet. But of course you must stay as long as your father needs you. I witnessed that noble quality in you when we first met—when you were so eager for your brother to have every advantage you have since enjoyed. We admired your selfless loyalty then. How could we think the less of you for the same honorable trait now?

My dear, what balm your kind words of affection delivered. I know I said this would very likely be your last season, but I certainly do not want you to imagine that you have spent your last days here with us. You are ever welcome, Lillian. We hope that when things with your father are in hand, you may yet return to us, if not for securing a suitor, then for enjoying the felicity of society with those here who love and admire you—your uncle and I chief among them.

What is the situation with your father? You were quite vague, my dear, and if that was your intention, I shall pry no further. But if there is anything we can do to help, you have only to ask.

In that light, I am enclosing a bank draft. Please do not refuse it. In all truth, I had every intention of sending this amount home with you to help address whatever situation you found there. But at the last, I withheld all but a token amount, scheming again, I confess, to keep you on a short tether in hopes of hastening your return. You see how we depend on your company! Please forgive my foolishness and gratify me by using the funds as will do you and your father the most good.

Do write back and keep us apprised of your situation there.

We remain,
Your loving aunt and uncle

How kind they were! How the affectionate words—even the admission of machinations—brought warmth and longing to Lilly's heart and made her miss her dear aunt and uncle all the more. And with the much-needed funds they enclosed, she could pay Francis back for the things he'd procured for them, place new orders, and begin chipping away at her father's other debts.

She would be so relieved to fulfill past obligations and start anew. Still, she could not deny that her aunt's letter stirred embers of longing for all she would miss in London. Besides the Elliotts, would anyone in London miss her?

A skillful leech is better far than half a hundred men of war.

—SAMUEL BUTLER, ENGLISH SATIRIST

CHAPTER 24

Lilly was surprised a few days later when Mr. Shuttleworth knocked on the shop door with his walking stick—an affectation she knew to be all the crack in London.

"Mr. Shuttleworth! How do you do?"

He cleared his throat. "As a matter of fact, Miss Haswell, I am . . . concerned."

"Oh? Is there some way I might help?"

"Indeed there is." His signature smile was noticeably absent. "I understand Mr. Baylor has been securing powders and other simples for you from my shop."

She swallowed. "Yes, on a few occasions. When the need was urgent."

"Well, I do not like it at all. Quite insupportable."

She had never known the man to be so somber. Hadn't Francis told her his employer would not mind? "We did pay for the items—full price."

"Yes, yes. I am not accusing anyone of stealing. However, I cannot allow things to go on in this manner."

She felt truly chastened. A sneak—caught. "Please forgive me, Mr. Shuttleworth. You are quite right. I should have asked you first."

"Indeed you should. For I should never have allowed it."

She bit her lip. She had never seen this side of him before. She hated the thought of losing the man's goodwill. Of jeopardizing Francis's position. "It will never happen again," she assured him.

"I should hope not. Next time, come to me and I will give you whatever you need at wholesale. Full price indeed. Are we not colleagues? Part of the same professional society?"

There, she saw it. Just a hint of a twinkle in his dark eyes.

"Yes, I suppose we are."

He took a step closer, and grinned almost sadly. "Moreover, are we not friends? I had rather hoped we were."

She nodded. "You are right, Mr. Shuttleworth. Again, please forgive me."

"I shall. On one condition."

"Yes?"

"I have a proposition for you." He held up his hand. "A business proposition. You acquire what you need from me at cost—assuming you don't empty the crockery. And, in return, you sell me the herbs, flowers, and other garden stuff I need. I understand from Mr. Baylor you have an excellent physic garden."

"Not as fruitful as it once was. But we are working to revive it. In fact, we have been harvesting all week."

He pushed up his hat brim with the tip of his walking stick. "I own I have never been much of a gardener myself. I like clean hands and fine clothes too dearly. I must go to market for everything. It would be a great boon to have fresh Haswell herbs on hand."

"Truly?"

"Truly." He held out his hand. A gesture rare among unwed ladies and gentlemen, but common enough among tradespeople. Among business associates. "Have we a bargain?"

With a rueful grin, she smartly shook his hand. "Indeed we have."

❦

The next day, her father did not even get out of bed. A fortnight had passed since she had made him promise to see a doctor, and still he refused. But she couldn't bring herself to force him against his wishes.

"I think I need to draw off some blood," he said. "Would you mind bringing the leech jar?"

Lilly felt uneasy. "Are you sure that is the best course?"

"I believe so. I would do it myself, but it's a dashed bother to position them from a supine position."

Lilly went to find the leech jar. The simple white pot had a tight-fitting lid and tiny air holes. *Hirudo medicinalis* were known to squeeze through the smallest of openings. An apothecary needed to take care when placing them on a patient's face that none found its way up a nostril.

She pried open the lid. A strong rotten fish smell rushed out and repulsed her. The water was dry. The leeches quite dead. How had she missed it during cleanup?

Lilly groaned. "I find we need to purchase some, Father. I shall help you as soon as I return." She did not wish to rile her father by admitting she planned to acquire the leeches from his competitor. She was relieved when he did not ask.

She went to find her reticule. "Aaron Jones is bringing a load of coal today," she called. "If he comes while I am out, tell him I shall settle up later."

"Very well. Don't be long."

Stashing a few bank notes into her reticule and sliding the small bag onto her wrist, Lilly hung the new hand-lettered *Returning Soon* sign on the door and let herself out. She walked briskly up the High

Street and down narrow Milk Lane to Shuttleworth's. She did not like going there in the middle of the day, but it could not be helped.

"Miss Haswell!" Mr. Shuttleworth greeted her, looking up from his splendid central desk. "What a lovely surprise. Mr. Baylor is out, I am afraid."

"I came to see you, actually."

"Wonderful. How can I help?"

She took a deep breath. "I am in need of leeches."

"You and the entire medical profession. Did you know there is a shortage on? I had to order this last batch all the way from Germany. The French, it seems, are going through them by the barrelful."

"I had no idea."

"It does not signify, lovely lady. My leeches are your leeches." He chuckled. "Now if that is not the most gallant thing I have ever said."

She laughed. "Chivalrous, indeed."

Mr. Shuttleworth stepped over to his compounding counter, where stood an impressive leech jar nearly two feet tall and decorated with elegant floral and scroll work.

He paused to ask, "Have you milk at home?"

She nodded.

"Excellent. Encourages them to bite. Sometimes they seem capriciously determined to resist all attempts to adhere. If you ever have a great deal of trouble, you can always prick the skin with a lancet and draw a little blood. They cannot resist it. Has never failed me."

She hoped it would not come to that.

Seeing her stare at the ornate jar, he explained, "The most exquisite leech jars are made in Staffordshire. I can order one for you if you like."

"Oh. Thank you, no. I shall content myself to admire yours."

Mr. Shuttleworth opened the lid, extracted one wet leech, and held it aloft for her inspection. The wormlike body was murky green with yellow stripes and as thick and long as her forefinger.

"Humble but hardworking creatures like these deserve the most elegant of raiment." He gave a wink and a tug on his waistcoat. "Like me, ey? Now, how will you transport your new friends home?"

Chagrined, she lifted her reticule. "This is all I thought to bring."

He chuckled again. "Why not? I shall just pop a few into a small jar, and you can transfer them to a proper one at home."

"I am afraid our poor jar is nothing to yours."

His long teeth gleamed at her praise. "You are very kind to say so."

A quarter of an hour later, Lilly walked into her father's surgery with their own leech jar, cleaned and filled.

"Here we are. Five fat *H. medicalis.*"

"Only five?"

"There is a shortage on. The French cannot get enough of them. Leeching is all the crack there—doctors using fifty at a time, then salting them."

He shook his head in disapproval. "Makes them regurgitate the blood so they can be used again. But kills them if you salt them too heavily."

"Right. So, we shall make do with five very hungry German leeches, shall we?"

"Very well."

He had already washed and rinsed his chest during her absence. She removed the leeches from their damp jar and let them crawl about on a cloth for a few moments to dry. At the surgery side table, she had a pot of milk, wine glasses, and a lancet at the ready.

She laid the first leech on her father's chest, then a second. She turned to pluck a third from the cloth, only to return to find the first two crawling away. One was heading for her father's neck, the other for his waistband.

Oh dear. The glasses. Right.

One by one she captured each leech under a small upturned wine glass, trapping it in the desired area. She felt as though she were performing a circus act in Astley's Royal Amphitheatre, hurrying to keep the plates spinning before they fell.

Finally, she stood still, both hands splayed. "There."

"Yes, as long as I don't make any sudden moves," her father said. "Or cough."

"Or talk. Steady on."

"Tickles devilish, but no bites."

Frowning, she removed the first wine glass and dabbed a bit of milk on the spot before replacing it.

No good. She hoped she would not need to resort to the lancet. The thought of drawing blood from her father, cutting him even superficially, made her queasy.

Remembering something she'd overheard in Mr. Lippert's shop in London, she turned and hurried to the door. "Don't move."

"Where are you going?"

"To the tea set."

"Tea . . . now?"

She returned with the sugar bowl and mixed a spoonful into the milk. The sugared milk did the trick, and one after another the leeches bit her father, evidenced by his five successive winces.

When she was sure they had each adhered, she removed the wine glasses, returning them to the side table.

"We'll let them take their fill," he said. "Let them fall off by themselves."

"Very well. Are you warm enough?" She picked up a lap rug hanging over a chair and laid it over his legs.

"Thank you, my dear." He sighed. "If only you had been a boy. The son I might have left my shop to."

"Shh. You will be back on your feet, running the shop in no time."

"For how long? For what reason? What good is a legacy with no one to leave it to? There has been a Haswell in this shop for nearly a hundred years. But now . . . ?"

"Father, Haswell's is not going anywhere. But for now you must regain your strength. Which you won't do by fretting."

"Bossy girl. Sound like a physician."

"No. I sound like you." She grinned. "Worse yet."

It has been recommended, to bleed people when they are lying down.

Should a person, under these circumstances faint,

what could be done to bring him to again?

—Mrs. Beeton's Book of Household Management

Chapter 25

Lilly had never seen the woman before, yet there she sat in Haswell's surgery, boldly giving Lilly detailed descriptions of all her feminine flows and woes.

"I feel like a good bleedin' is all I need," the barge pilot's wife said. "There's nothin' like it to balance the humours, I always say. I've been to Dr. Foster, but that man is worse than a cross headmaster. I like the notion of a female apothecary. So much easier to discuss one's flux without embarrassment, if you know what I mean."

Lilly managed a meek smile. She had been the one to insist her father return to sleeping in his bedroom instead of the surgery. She had counted it a small victory when he had finally relented. Not only would he get more rest in his own bed, but it freed the surgery for private discussions and examinations. The idea had sounded appealing. In theory.

"So you have been bled before," Lilly began nervously. "Can you tell me if the blood was let from elbow, ankle, or throat?"

"Had my ankle opened once. If that didn't hurt devilish bad. Not the neck, either, if you please. Don't want to spoil my frock."

"The inside of the elbow it is." Lilly's pulse pounded in her ears. She began to perspire in a very unladylike fashion. Leeches, she could manage. Blisters and plasters, all well and good. But the lancet? Piercing a person? Drawing not a drop of blood but a veritable fount, were she to accomplish it correctly? Or a waterfall, should she use the many-razored scarificator. She winced at the thought.

She began by washing the woman's arm—that she could do. She had her recline in the bleeding chair, in case she swooned. Offered her a sip of water. Positioned her elbow on the small caster table for the purpose. Picked up the lancet and the double-handled bleeding bowl. Sat on the stool where her father always sat to do what she was about to attempt. If only her fingers would cease trembling.

She rose on shaky legs. "Will you excuse me one moment, Mrs. Hagar?"

The woman nodded, eyes closed. "If you have any blue ruin, I shouldn't mind a sniff. Takes the sting out."

Ignoring the request for strong drink, Lilly quickly padded up the stairs to her father's bedchamber. He looked up at her from over the top of a book. "Bloodletting, Father. I cannot do it."

"Of course you can. Seen me do it a thousand times."

"Seeing it done does not mean I can manage it myself." She suddenly thought of Mr. Shuttleworth. Perhaps he would perform the procedure for her.

"And you've no doubt memorized the prescribed method from one of the texts."

"Yes, but remembering the words is not the same as performing the act."

"Lilly, we cannot afford to refuse patients. Nor to send them to our competition."

So much for asking Mr. Shuttleworth. . . . "Then you come down and do it yourself."

He huffed. "Very well." He used one elbow to push himself into a sitting position on the bed. His arm shook from the effort. He sat on the bed, catching his breath, steeling himself for the energy and pain required to stand.

Her heart ached to see it. "Never mind, Father. You lie down. I shall take care of it."

He fell back, panting. "You can do it, Lilly. Just remember—"

"I remember. Now you rest."

Retreating back down the stairs, she prayed with each step. *Please help me, help me, help me . . .*

She started at the sight of a figure standing in the laboratory-kitchen. "Francis! You startled me."

"Forgive me. I hope you don't mind, but I—"

"No! I am so pleased to see you. Might you do me a favor?"

"Um . . . of course. Anything, if I am able." He grinned, eyes sparkling. "What do you need? Dragons slain, villains dueled? Alembics scoured?"

Grasping his wrist, she led the way to the surgery door. "Nothing so arduous, I assure you."

"What then?"

"Just one small hole."

"Who's this, then?" Mrs. Hagar asked when they entered.

"This is Francis Baylor. Our former apprentice. Now a journey-man at—"

"At your service, madam." Francis bowed to Mrs. Hagar and gave her a charming smile.

"My, my." The woman placed a hand over her chest.

"That is, if you do not mind my stepping in? I can understand why you might prefer Miss Haswell—"

She waved this away. "Oh, that don't signify. You will suit just fine, young man."

"You are most obliging, Mrs. Hagar. Now. Are you comfortable?"

"I am."

"Very good. Let's just tie a ligament here. Miss Haswell?"

She sprang to hand him the tie.

"Thank you." He tied the linen tape around the woman's fleshy upper arm. "Firm, but not too tight. How does that feel?"

"Fine."

"Excellent. Now, let us have a look at your veins. My goodness! When have I ever seen such lovely veins? Really, Mrs. Hagar. What a light task this shall be!"

The woman looked down at her arm with sheepish pride. "Indeed?"

Isolating the vein between thumb and forefinger of one hand, Francis held out his free hand toward Lilly. "The thumb lancet, I think, Miss Haswell. Only the finest instrument for such a fine vein."

The woman fairly blushed.

Lilly quickly handed him the thumb lancet with the ornate tortoiseshell case.

"Thank you. And the bowl is here at the ready. Well done, Miss Haswell. Now, Mrs. Hagar, do let me know the minute you feel light-headed or a swoon coming on."

"I own I feel on the verge already, young man, with you holding my hand that a'way."

Lilly met his eye and bit back a grin.

He chuckled. "You flatter me, ma'am. Now, do tell me where you were born."

"Stanton St. Bernard, but I don't see how that signifies."

"Not in the least. I just wanted to distract you from the prick."

"Ohh . . . I didn't even know you'd done it."

The blood ran in a thin, graceful stream into the waiting receptacle. Not a drop went astray nor soiled her frock. Lilly was impressed indeed. Not only at his skill, but at his warm and charming manner with the worn, plain Mrs. Hagar.

When the blood reached the first gradient line in the bleeding bowl, Francis asked. "And how are we feeling, Mrs. Hagar?"

"Floaty. Tingling. Dark."

"Excellent." With swift deft movements, he placed a lint pad on her wound, pressing it with his thumb and lifting her hand in the air. "There. You put pressure on that if you can."

"All right . . ." she said dreamily.

Lilly handed him the linen bandage and sling, and he skillfully wrapped the wound and secured the woman's arm in less than a minute's time. "Now you rest here, Mrs. Hagar. Until you are quite yourself again."

She nodded and asked, "Mr. Baylor, will you be here next I come?"

Francis again met Lilly's eyes. "Perhaps, Mrs. Hagar. But if I am not, either Miss Haswell or her father will be. And I have learned everything worth knowing from them."

Leaving the woman to rest, Lilly followed him from the surgery. "Francis," she called softly.

He turned.

"How can I thank you?"

His smile grew thoughtful. "Quite easily, Miss Haswell."

She tilted her head in question.

Looking at her, he slowly shook his head, lips quirked, brown eyes alight with equal parts humor and longing.

She stared back, eyes drawn to his full lower lip, and felt a shocking desire to touch it with her own. Where had *that* come from? Thank heaven he could not divine her thoughts!

I am merely grateful to him, she assured herself. If Aunt Elliott had disapproved of a physician, she would be scandalized to think her niece attracted to an apothecary's assistant!

The shop bell jingled, and she self-consciously took a step back, putting a proper distance between them.

The next morning, Lilly opened the door of the coffeehouse kitchen and stuck her head inside. "Hello, Mary."

"Come in, Lill. You've caught me elbow deep in flour, I'm afraid."

Lilly stepped to the worktable. "I would offer to help, but I know how you feel about my abilities in the kitchen."

"Indeed. You with your odd apothecaries' weights and measures with *our* recipes . . ." She feigned a shudder.

Grinning, Lilly sat and surveyed the assembled mixing bowls and ingredients. "A cake?"

Mary nodded. "And not just any cake, mind. A Rich Bride Cake."

"And who is the rich bride?"

With a glance toward the scullery door, Mary leaned across the worktable and lowered her voice. "One Miss Cassandra Powell."

Lilly felt an unexpected stab of regret. She had enjoyed Roderick Marlow's brief attentions. She had known he would never ask for her hand, yet could not help being disappointed at the news, for she could not like Miss Powell. "Well, I should be not be surprised. Mr. Marlow intimated they would marry."

Mrs. Mimpurse burst into the kitchen from the dining room, her face flushed. "Girls, you will be most surprised to hear what I have just learned. That bonny Miss Powell is going to marry—"

"Yes, Mamma. I was just telling Lill about the cake order."

"But we have had it wrong, Mary." Mrs. Mimpurse drew near and spoke in hushed tones. "Miss Powell *is* marrying one of the Marlows to be sure. But not Roderick, as we supposed. She is marrying Sir Henry himself."

"No!" Mary's small mouth fell open.

"How can that be?" Lilly asked, stunned. "I saw them together in London and at the house party at the manor. And when I spoke to Roderick Marlow, I had the distinct impression *he* was going to marry her." Lilly's mind whirled over their conversations. He had not actually said the words, but what he *had* said seemed clear enough.

"Maybe he planned to, but she threw him over," Mary suggested. "Why be Mrs. Marlow when you can be Lady Marlow?"

"But Sir Henry must be nearing sixty," Lilly said. "And not in the best of health."

"Still, a charming man," Maude offered. "Always so kind and attentive to the first Lady Marlow."

"Poor Roderick," Lilly breathed.

"Poor Roderick?" Mary repeated in wonder. "Now, there are two words I would never have imagined coming from your lips, Lilly Haswell."

Lilly ignored that. "I wonder if he is heartbroken."

"You allow he has a heart?"

"Of course he has, Mary," Mrs. Mimpurse said.

Lilly amended, "Though one capable of both extreme coldness as well as warmth."

"How warm?" Mary quirked a brow.

Lilly felt her cheeks heat and hurriedly asked, "When is the great day to be?"

"Thursday," Mary and her mother answered in unison.

Lilly shook her head. "Rich bride indeed. Or will be in two days' time."

Mrs. Mimpurse returned to the front room with a fresh pot of coffee, and Mary continued working, sprinkling liquid onto the mound of almonds she had pounded into a fine powder.

"What is that?" Lilly asked.

"Orange-flower water."

Mary left the almonds and began whisking a bowlful of egg yolks.

Lilly ran her gaze over the worktable. "Where is the recipe?"

Mary shrugged. "Around here somewhere. Slice those candied peels for me, would you?"

"How thin?" Lilly picked up a knife and made a trial cut.

"Like that, right. Mind you don't cut yourself."

"Yes, Mother."

Mary hesitated, looking cautiously at her. Lilly pulled a humorous face, surprised she could make such a joke without an answering sting of loss.

Clearly relieved, Mary said, "The Marlows will not want your blood in their cake."

"No indeed. What else does a rich bride get?"

"Five pounds of the finest flour; five pounds currants; three pounds fresh butter; two pounds loaf sugar; one pound sweet almonds; a half pound each of candied citron, orange, and lemon peel; sixteen eggs; one gill each of wine and brandy; two nutmegs; and a titch o' mace and cloves. And two layers of almond-and-sugar icing besides."

"Rich indeed."

"The ingredients alone cost us nearly ten pounds."

Lilly's eyes widened, and she popped a bit of orange into her mouth.

Mary again raised her brows, "Ten pounds tuppence now."

"It was only a *titch*." Lilly helped herself to a currant. "What is a titch, anyway?"

"A dessert-spoonful or quarter ounce, if I took the time to measure proper."

Two fluid drams. Of its own volition, Lilly's mind converted to the apothecaries' system, based on twelve ounces to a pound and eight drams to an ounce. "And you don't need a recipe?" Lilly asked again.

Mary shrugged.

"But you cannot make *this* cake very often."

"Indeed not. The last one I made was for the christening of the Robbins boy." Mary gave her a shrewd look. "Of course, then I called it a Christening Cake."

"How do you remember—not only what goes in it, but the mode of preparation?"

Mary tucked her chin. "An odd question coming from you, of all people."

Lilly chuckled. "We are alike in that ability it seems."

"True. But my concoctions don't save anybody's life."

Grinning, Lilly snitched another currant and popped it into her mouth. "Oh, I would not be too sure."

BITES OF DOGS
Keep the wound open as long as possible. This may be done by putting
a few beans on it, and then by applying a large linseed-meal poultice.

—Mrs. Beeton's Book of Household Management

Chapter 26

Her apron and gloves already black from cleaning the stove and alembic, Lilly decided she might as well clean the shop hearth also. She thought about her recent encounter with Francis, when he helped her with Mrs. Hagar, and realized she had never felt so flustered, so . . . feminine, in his presence before.

As she knelt to her task, she heard a dog barking outside. She thought little of it at first, but then the barking grew louder and more fevered.

"Down, I say!" She heard a man holler in false bravado. "Down!"

She hurried across the shop and unlatched the door, just as a man pushed it open, causing him to nearly topple into the shop, his hat dropping to the floor. She put out her hands to stop his fall—and to keep the man from falling into her.

The Fowlers' wolfhound tried to bound in behind the man, but

Lilly forcibly shut the door on the long muzzle of the shaggy creature, which likely weighed more than she did. The dog raised itself on its rear haunches at the window and continued to bark.

"Go home, Bones!" she shouted. "Go home!"

The grey dog whimpered but dropped to all fours and trotted away.

She turned from the window to look at Bones's latest victim and started.

"Dr. Graves!" She was stunned to see him again. Especially here in their shop.

He cleared his throat. "Miss Haswell." He bowed awkwardly, and she belatedly curtsied. They both reached for his fallen hat at the same moment, their foreheads nearly colliding.

"Forgive me." She straightened. "Oh! *Forgive* me!" she repeated more vehemently. "I have blackened your coat!"

He looked down at his tawny frock coat, one shoulder and sleeve now marked with smeared black handprints, like the claw marks of a wild animal.

"My tailor admonished me to choose the dark green," he said dryly, "but I would have my way."

"I shall have it cleaned for you. I know an excellent laundress."

His blue gaze swept her person. "Take no offense, Miss Haswell, but you are in more need of a laundress than I."

She looked down at her own attire, the sooty apron, the blackened gloves. He took a handkerchief from his pocket and offered it to her. "You have some—ash, is it?—along your cheekbone."

She held up her soiled gloves. "Thank you, but I do not wish to blacken your handkerchief as well."

He hesitated. Was he about to wipe her cheek? Instead, he tucked the piece of fine linen back into his pocket.

"Could be worse," she said feebly. "At least it isn't on my nose."

"Actually—" he winced apologetically—"there is a smudge there as well."

She began to put a hand up to shield her face, but remembered her soiled gloves just in time. She rushed on nervously, "I am sorry about Bones. He is usually harmless but isn't fond of strangers. He did not bite you, I trust?"

"No. All bark and no bite, as they say. Although I rarely find solace in that morsel of wisdom."

"You have been bitten before?" she asked.

"Yes, and still bear the mark to prove it." He pointed to a scar above his upper lip and extending, though faintly, beneath his moustache and nearly to his nose. "It is why I've taken to wearing a moustache, unfashionable as it is."

She nodded, taking in the short golden hairs, a shade darker than the pale blond hair of his head and eyebrows. She *had* wondered.

"It isn't very noticeable," she said.

"The scar, or the moustache?"

She smiled to cover her embarrassment. "Neither one."

He chuckled dryly. "I must say, this is not at all how I imagined meeting you again."

She peeled off her filthy gloves. "I shouldn't think so. What brings you to Bedsley Priors?"

She wished the words back as soon as she'd said them. Her heart beat anxiously and her neck grew warm. She thought she had alienated him with the news of her mother. Had she mistaken the matter?

He ignored her question and looked around the shop, arms behind his back. "So, this is the famous Haswell's."

She sheepishly followed his gaze. "Well, yes. Though Tuesdays are a slow day for us."

"It is Wednesday."

"Oh. Right."

After a moment of awkward silence, a sudden thought came to her. "Might I take you into my confidence?"

He straightened, eyes alert. "Of course."

"My father is ill," she began quietly.

His brows rose. "Is he? I am sorry to hear it." He hesitated. "Is . . . that why . . . you left?"

When she nodded, he expelled a long breath. "I see."

"But he will see neither the village physician nor the new surgeon-apothecary," she continued, "for fear of his weakness becoming generally known."

"I don't follow."

"He believes it will steal his credibility. The proverbial 'Physician, heal thyself.' "

"Ah." He nodded his understanding.

"Would you look in on him? There is bad blood, I am afraid, between the local physician and my father."

"Dr. Foster?"

"You have heard of him?"

"Well, yes. I—"

"He can be difficult at times, I own," Lilly said. "He rather resents my father, I am afraid. And Father fears he would spread his plight only too eagerly."

"Miss Haswell, I think—"

"But if I explain that you are only visiting," she hurried on, "he might be willing to allow an examination."

"But I am not."

She stared at him, feeling slapped. "Not willing? But—"

"Of course I am willing," he rushed to amend. "But I am *not* only visiting. I am settling here."

"What?" Her heart hammered. She faltered, "But . . . oh . . ."

"Dr. Foster is taking a partner, with an eye to retiring in a year or two. I have accepted the situation. It's provisional for now, but if all goes well, I shall remain indefinitely."

"You and . . . Dr. Foster. Oh, dear. I am sure he is a most capable physician. It is only—"

"Miss Haswell, you needn't worry on my account. Your father's condition and your opinions are safe with me."

She sighed. "Thank you. So you are a licensed physician now?"

"Yes." He bowed once more. "Dr. Adam Graves, at your service."

Three-quarters of an hour later, Dr. Graves emerged from her father's surgery.

"Well? Lilly asked, laying aside the blocks of Castile soap she had been wrapping in brown waxed paper.

He closed the door gingerly and joined her at the counter. "He is resting comfortably. I do not think there is cause for alarm at present."

"But what is it? Do you know?"

"I cannot discuss a patient's condition without his consent."

"He is my father."

"And a grown and, may I add, stubborn man."

That Lilly knew only too well.

"I *can* tell you he agreed that I might attend him now I am here," he said.

"I am relieved to hear it."

Dr. Graves turned his hat around in his hands. "Miss Haswell, there is something I would speak to you about. . . ."

Her nerves jingled and she felt a thrill of hope. Had he come to renew his suit? Her thoughts about Francis seemed foolish now.

He hesitated. "But I can see that you have a great deal on your shoulders, and on your mind, at present. I will not press you." He cleared his throat. "Well, I suppose I had better go and unpack. I will be lodging in one of Dr. Foster's spare rooms until things are . . . settled between us."

"Us" meaning he and Foster, or . . . ? She felt her palms grow damp at the thought.

When Dr. Graves had taken his leave, promising to return soon, Lilly knocked on the surgery door and warily let herself in.

"Father, how do you feel?"

He groaned and raised himself to a sitting position on the cot. "Like a lump of bread dough that Maude has kneaded while vexed."

"Thank you for seeing him."

"And to what do I owe such an honor? He said he made your acquaintance in London. Am I to understand he is here to court you?"

She shrugged. "He did once speak to Uncle on my account. But—"

"I thought as much." He chuckled. "I noticed your handprints on his coat."

Face burning, she hurried to change the subject. "I am not here to talk about me, rather you. Dr. Graves would not divulge a thing."

"I should hope not."

"Father, please."

"There isn't a great deal to tell. He spent most of his time diagnosing what it is *not*. Not brain fever, nor typhus, nor several other fates worse than death. He doesn't believe it is anything contagious, although he has not ruled that out completely. So you still need to keep your distance."

Is that why he's been so aloof? she wondered. "What does he think it might be?"

"Perhaps a compound of two fevers—lung fever and glandular."

She sucked in a breath. "Not lung *sickness?*"

"He does not think it the consumption, no."

"I am relieved to hear it."

"Don't go planning my sixtieth birthday party yet, my dear. Lung fever itself can be can be quite serious. But yes, there is reason to hope." He looked at her shrewdly. "And here I feared your London season in vain. A physician, ey? Ah well, as long as he is nothing like Foster."

A tincture of sage will give old men
the spirit and the advantages of youth.

—DR. HILL, *THE OLD MAN'S GUIDE TO HEALTH AND LONGER LIFE*, 1764

CHAPTER 27

On Thursday morning, before beginning her jaunt up Grey's Hill, Lilly stopped in at the coffeehouse to tell Mary the surprising news about Dr. Graves coming as prospective partner to Dr. Foster. She knew Mary was not fond of Dr. Foster, either, but whether out of loyalty to Mr. Haswell or for reasons of her own, Lilly could not say.

"Are you certain it's Foster he's come to partner with?" Mary asked, suggestively raising a brow in a manner that brought Christina Price-Winters to mind.

Lilly made no attempt to hide her bemusement. "I am not at all certain. I had thought things ended between us in London." Promising to tell Mary more later, Lilly continued on her way.

She reached the top of Grey's Hill and stood catching her breath, looking down at the village below. The church bells rang. She could see several fine carriages in front of the church, the first of which began to pull away. This was the morning Sir Henry and Miss Powell were to be married, she knew. Few had been invited to attend the wedding breakfast, which she supposed was not surprising. Considering Sir Henry's advanced years, a private affair was more dignified.

"Miss Haswell."

Lilly started and turned. "Mr. Marlow! I did not see you there."

He rose and dusted off his breeches. "Seems I am quite invisible these days."

"Is the wedding finished already?"

"It is finished. My role in any case, which was to appear publicly in full support of my father and his new bride. They shall now return home for the wedding breakfast, but I find I cannot stomach it."

"I did wonder how you must be feeling."

"Did you? Well, then you are the only one considering my feelings these days."

She took a tentative step closer. "You . . . did hope to marry her, then?"

He shrugged. "Perhaps." He added acrimoniously, "I certainly did *not* hope she would marry my father. Devilish humiliating."

"I am sorry."

"Never fear, Miss Haswell. I will forget by and by."

"Will you?" she asked, studying his dull expression.

"Yes, with concerted effort and time, I shall."

"Perhaps you might teach me that trick."

She had only been jesting, but he looked at her quite earnestly.

"It can be learned. I am quite the master of forgetting unpleasant things. When the memory raises its head, you force it down. It rises again, you supplant it with new and more vibrant memories. It tries once more, you intoxicate the mind, drown it out. You do not allow such thoughts to revisit themselves upon you."

"But then, do we never learn from our past mistakes? Is that not one reason God gave us memory?"

"I do hope not. Pleasant memories are well and good, but I prefer to banish the others. With practice and constant diligence, one may train a memory to remain cowering in the dark reaches of the mind, where it can no longer prick one's conscience. It may not be quite the same as truly forgetting, I grant you, but a near enough imitation."

"You sound as if you have had long practice. What is it you strive so hard to forget, I wonder?" She nodded toward the church below. "Besides recent events."

He hesitated, and a shadow of remorse flickered and quickly disappeared, replaced by a cavalier grin. "I am sure there must be something, Miss Haswell, but I *do not* remember."

Lilly found herself wondering if she ought to attempt the same method with her own memories that brought such disquiet. Of coming home and finding her mother gone, her father pacing and desperately pretending all would be well, that she would return in a few days. Charlie sitting behind the draperies in Mother's bedchamber, running his small fingers over the roses in the pattern, mumbling the same numbers over and over again—"*Seventy-four, five, six, seven . . . ty-four, five, six . . .*"

"In any event," Mr. Marlow continued, "I am certain there is a woman out there who will not throw me over for a man twice my age."

"I have no doubt there are many." She had only meant to console him, but a sudden gleam in his eye sent warning bells ringing in her mind.

He reached out and touched a tendril of hair against her neck. "You are a balm, Miss Haswell. A sweet balm."

She backed away. "I had better go." She turned and made her way down the hill at a rapid clip.

He jogged beside her. "May I walk with you?"

"I am on my way to visit a family recovering from the ague. I do not think you—"

"How noble you are." He captured her hand and tucked it beneath his arm.

Once they reached the village, she pulled away gently, putting a proper distance between them. As they passed the churchyard, now deserted, he suddenly veered through its gate, pulling her in his wake to stand behind the tall privet hedge. He pulled her close, one arm draped diagonally from her shoulder to waist, his jaw to her temple.

He was tall and strong and wounded, and for one brief moment she allowed herself to enjoy the warm strength of his arm around her, before pulling away once more. With his free hand, he tried to capture her chin, to angle her face toward his, but she turned away. "Mr. Marlow, please!"

"You are right. Forgive me."

"I realize you feel betrayed. But do you really think toying with a substitute will remedy your pain?"

"It would dull it, at least."

"For how long? And at what cost to me? If someone had seen us, just then—"

"Your brother, for example?"

She had been thinking of Dr. Graves. "Actually, I meant—"

"For there he sits."

She turned and stared, and there was Charlie reclining against Grady Milton's headstone. "Hallo, Lilly. Hallo, Mr. Marlow."

"What are you doing here?" she asked.

Charlie shrugged casually. "Countin' dead men."

Lilly sighed and thought, *It's the live ones I have to worry about.*

Still, she was relieved to see her brother there. Something told her Roderick Marlow would not have been as easily dissuaded had he not been.

❧

True to his word, Dr. Graves returned late that afternoon to check on her father, promising to stop in regularly and oversee her father's progress. In fact, he seemed to relish the prospect. She supposed if Dr. Graves had come to Bedsley Priors to continue courting her, he could not have invented a more plausible excuse to see her so often. In any event, she was exceedingly grateful to him for taking over her father's care.

Charlie came in from the garden, and Lilly introduced her brother to the new doctor.

"Graves, is it?" Charlie repeated, confused. "I like graves. Queer name for a doctor though, innum?"

She was relieved when Dr. Graves took no offense.

Afterward, Dr. Graves asked her to recommend a hostelry where he might dine. She immediately suggested the coffeehouse, explaining the proprietress was a dear family friend.

He hesitated at the door. "Perhaps you would be so good as to show me the way?"

She bit back a smile. "Happily, sir."

Even taking the time to tie on her bonnet and retrieve her shawl, she stepped out onto the High Street as he held the door for her. He walked beside her across the narrow mews and progressed several steps before realizing she had already stopped at the next establishment.

"Here it is."

She smiled at him, and he smiled back. There were those dimples she remembered so fondly and the blue, blue eyes brightened by the afternoon sun.

She led him inside and introduced him to Mrs. Mimpurse and Mary—her friend studying the doctor with more than customary interest.

Mr. Shuttleworth was enjoying an early supper, and Lilly introduced Dr. Foster's new partner to him as well.

"Dr. Foster speaks highly of you, sir," Graves said to him.

"I am much obliged." Mr. Shuttleworth smiled. "He honors me with his trust."

Francis walked in, hat in hand. He drew up short at seeing the well-dressed man beside her.

"Mr. Baylor, will you join me?" Mr. Shuttleworth enthused. "You come here far too rarely."

"Many thanks, Mr. Shuttleworth, but I am only here to give you a message. Mr. Robbins asks you to call when you can. One of his workers injured his leg. May have broken it."

"I shall go directly." Mr. Shuttleworth rose, shook hands with Dr. Graves, and turned toward Francis. "Have you met Mr. Baylor here, my young right hand?"

Francis greeted the newcomer politely, but Lilly did not miss the speculative concern in his eyes as he looked from the good-looking stranger to her.

GOWLAND'S LOTION
Eruptive humours fly before its power,
Pimples and freckles die within an hour.

—ACKERMANN'S REPOSITORY ADVERTISEMENT, 1809

CHAPTER 28

The rain was relentless. A smoky grey sky poured leaden sheets of water on Bedsley Priors for three days without ceasing. Dr. Graves called on her father, who seemed to be steadily improving, but otherwise the shop and High Street were silent but for the pounding of rain on roof and cobbles. Rivulets streamed down the shop's window-panes, and only occasionally did Lilly see some brave soul dash past on his way to the coffeehouse, where, by all appearances, half the men of Bedsley Priors were taking refuge.

Late on the third afternoon, the shop door burst open, startling Lilly as she sat at the dispensary counter reading a worn volume of Sterne's *A Sentimental Journey Through France and Italy*. Francis rushed inside, carrying a canvas-wrapped bundle. Water streamed from his coat and the brim of his sodden hat.

"My goodness," Lilly said, closing the book. "What has happened to bring you out in this?"

Instead of answering, he asked, "Are we quite sure God has promised never to flood the earth again?"

She smiled. "Quite sure. Not the entire earth."

"Only Bedsley Priors, it seems."

Her father appeared at the surgery door and leaned against the jamb. "Hello, Mr. Baylor. Communing with the ducks again, are we?"

Francis held up the bundle. "I am returning the text you lent me. I did not wish it to get wet."

Charles Haswell's face wrinkled in confusion. "And so you carried it outside in this . . . ?"

"It's the roof, you see. Now I understand why the old haberdashery remained vacant so long. The roof leaks during any hard rain. But after this storm, the ceiling has more holes than a sieve. I've had to roll up the carpets and pack away the bedding and all my clothes and papers. Mr. Shuttleworth is doing the same."

"And the shop?" her father asked.

"We've employed a score of basins and buckets abovestairs, and so far the shop below is fairly dry."

"Ah." It wasn't clear whether Charles Haswell was relieved or disappointed. He said, "You must bring over anything else you don't wish ruined. And you are more than welcome to stay here tonight."

Francis darted a look at Lilly. "I should not like to intrude, sir."

"No trouble. Unless you relish the prospect of sleeping in a puddle?"

Francis shook his head. "I *was* wondering how I would balance the stew pot on my abdomen all night. . . ."

"It's settled, then. You shall spend the night here." He hesitated, then added, "And do invite Shuttleworth as well. You are both welcome."

Three quarters of an hour later, both men rushed into the shop, bumping into each other with cases and bundles in their arms, hat brims pulled low and coat collars high. Their boots left a glistening trail of water on the floorboards.

235

"Not fit for man nor water buffalo," Mr. Shuttleworth panted.

Her father gingerly took the man's valise. "Come, Shuttleworth, bring your things up to Charlie's room. He's gone to Marlow House to help batten down the place. Can't say we've needed him here these last few days. Sold two liquorice draughts and one plaster. How is business for you?"

"Quiet as well."

"Good, good," her father said, leading the way with unusual vigor. "I know a father-son from Alton Barnes who can put your roof to rights at a fair price. Shall I give you their names?"

"Most obliging, Mr. Haswell."

Lilly was surprised by her father's warm reception. Was he so pleased to learn his rival's business fared no better than his own? He turned back at the threshold. "And you may have your old room, Mr. Baylor—if you do not mind the tight quarters."

"Not at all, sir."

As the two older men disappeared through the door, Lilly smiled up at Francis. "It will be just like old times."

His gaze lingered on her. "Will it?"

She hesitated. "Here, let me help you with your wet things." She took his hat while he hung his coat on a peg, then followed her through the laboratory-kitchen and into the stark former pantry. "I am afraid I have not had time to make this bed yet."

"Then I shall help you."

She reached down and picked up the edge of the dust cover. A bed of less than a yard's width lay between them. On its far side, Francis reached down and picked up the cloth's other edge. He brought up his two corners to meet hers. Their fingers grazed as she took the thin material from him. Then he moved to the foot of the bed and took one end while she took the other, and again they brought the corners toward each other, Francis stepping around the bed to close the gap between them. This time when she tried to take his corners, he held on, their hands touching, his face dipped close to look into hers. Taking a shallow breath, she tugged harder until he let go.

He helped her put on the fresh sheets, tucking the corners and spreading the blanket while she plumped the pillow.

The task accomplished, he thrust his hand toward her, as Mr. Shuttleworth might. "You are very kind, Miss Haswell. Thank you."

Hesitantly, she put her smaller hand in his. "You are very welcome, Mr. Baylor."

Instead of releasing her hand, he held it with gentle firmness. His large brown eyes seemed filled with some unspoken message as well as a glint of humor. "How *do* you make your hands colder than the outside air?"

She said with a shaky laugh, "It is a gift."

He lifted her hand and brought it to his lips, his eyes focused on hers. Her heart pounded as he pressed his warm lips to her cool fingers. She felt a rush of pleasure and nervous tension at the intimate act.

He straightened, but kept his eyes lowered. Quietly, he asked, "You and Dr. Graves were . . . acquainted in London?"

At the mention of Dr. Graves, Lilly blinked. The pleasure she felt dissolved. She shook her head to clear away the unsettling emotions.

He mistook the gesture and furrowed his brow. "No?"

"No. I mean, yes."

Tension stiffened his voice and posture. "The physician of whom your aunt disapproved?"

She nodded and gently pulled away her hand. "Well, I hope you will be comfortable. Do let me know if you want for anything."

He took a slow, deep breath, his broad chest rising and falling. "I want a great many things, Miss Haswell."

His eyes were strangely sorrowful.

She did not ask what he wanted. She was not sure she wished to know.

❧

The rain and chilly weather of the previous week brought with it summer colds and ague, which kept Mr. Shuttleworth and Francis quite busy into the following week of sunny, warm days.

They had met Dr. Graves a few more times, when he had entered the shop in the company of Dr. Foster. The younger physician was a bit formal and starched, Francis thought, and suspected his stiff demeanor hid insecurities natural to any new medical man. Francis determined to be as kind and helpful as he could be, even though the new man was treating Mr. Haswell, which Francis could not help but consider a vague snub.

While Dr. Foster frequented Shuttleworth's, his new partner went more often to Haswell's. Francis knew *Mr.* Haswell was not the primary reason. Nor could he blame the man.

He thought back to that rainy night spent in his old bed beneath Lilly's room. What bittersweet memories that had evoked, of all the nights he had slept there before, comforted yet taunted by his awareness of her lying in her own bed above him. Should he have told her how she affected him?

She was so much the same, yet different too. Her face somewhat thinner, her curves somewhat fuller, though that might be due to the cut of the gowns she now wore. She was as clever and charming as ever, yet she seemed less approachable than before, as though painted with a shiny veneer that kept her true self out of reach. He realized dully that she thought herself above him. She likely always had, but her time in London had served to increase the perceived distance. *Maybe it is better this way,* he told himself. He could not allow her return to disturb his carefully laid plans. Besides, what chance did he stand against a handsome London physician?

Early one morning, a rap sounded from the shop door below, while Lilly was in her bedchamber. She ran lightly down the stairs to answer the door, dressed, but with her hair still down.

She unlocked the door and opened it to Dr. Graves. He stared at her, then away, clearing his throat.

She pushed her long hair behind her shoulder. "I was not quite finished dressing."

"No . . . um, your hair is beautiful," he faltered. .

"Thank you," she said, self-consciously pleased, and gestured him inside. "Are you here to check on Father? I fear he is still sleeping."

"No. I shall come back later for that." Again he stared at her.

"Did you need something?"

Glancing around and seeing the shop empty, he went on in lower tones, "Miss Haswell, when I first arrived, I mentioned there was something I wanted to say to you."

Lilly's heart began to pound. "Yes?"

"I have been waiting for an opportune time. I did not wish to spring it upon you when I saw how ill your father was."

She nodded, mouth dry.

"I must tell you, Miss Haswell. I was disappointed when I called on the Elliotts and discovered you gone. Your aunt was rather vague about the reason."

Lilly could well imagine.

"But considering, well, everything," he continued, "I believe I understand why you left without a word of farewell."

"I did not think you would mind, after our last conversation about my mother."

"It is precisely that conversation I wish to speak of now."

Oh dear.

"The day after we spoke, I went to see my brother, a solicitor, as I believe I mentioned. He contracted a runner on my behalf to discover information about the former lieutenant James Wells."

Lilly was taken aback. This was not what she had expected him to say.

Dr. Graves continued, "It seems Wells now works aboard a convict transport ship, and maintains an address in Cheapside, though he can be home but rarely. He . . ."

He paused and Lilly held her breath, trying to guess the thoughts behind his grim mouth, his serious blue eyes.

"He was married two years ago." Graves extracted a small slip of paper from his pocket and glanced at it. "To a German woman, according to the record. A Gertrude Kistinger, now Wells."

He handed her the paper and she silently stared at it. He looked at her expectantly, then cocked his head to one side. Clearly she was not reacting as he had thought she would.

"Is that not good news? Your mother is not with Wells, as you feared."

Was it good news? Just because she was no longer with Wells, did that mean she never was? And where was she now? Her fragile link to her mother, if a link it could be called, had been broken as easily as a spider's web.

"Thank you for inquiring for me." She wondered, though, if he had done so to help her, or merely to gauge the threat of scandal for himself.

"I thought you would be pleased," he said hopefully. "It can no longer come between us."

She looked up into his warm blue eyes and angelic face and felt her own face—and heart—warm in response. Perhaps he was right. Perhaps nothing stood between them after all.

The door bell rang and Lilly stepped back. Hannah Primmel timidly entered the shop.

"Hannah, hello," Lilly said, striding to the counter. She hoped Hannah did not notice her blush, or would at least not read anything untoward in it if she did.

"Hello, Miss Haswell." The poor girl had the misfortune of skin continually plagued with blemishes and had therefore earned the monikers Carbuncle Face and Hannah Pimples from cruel lads. Seeing Dr. Graves, the girl hung her head, as she habitually did, as though that might keep people from noticing her face.

"I am very pleased to see you," Lilly said. "I hoped you would come in."

Hannah glanced up eagerly. "Did you?"

"Yes." Lilly leaned closer, speaking in confidential tones. "I have something I would very much like you to try."

Her eagerness faded. "I haven't much money."

"This is a complimentary sample. Apply it for a fortnight and report on its efficacy. Will you do that for me?"

Hannah smiled. "Of course I will. Thank you, Miss Haswell."

"Thank me later—if you are pleased with the results."

When Hannah left, Dr. Graves approached the counter and asked quietly, "What did you give her?"

Lilly sighed. "Neither Gowland's nor chamomile was bringing about the improvement I had hoped for. I have now given her an ointment of lemon juice, rose water, and silver supplement."

"Culpeper's Remedy," he said.

"Right. Of course, Culpeper also recommended rubbing fresh butter on one's face of a morning. But that always seemed to worsen the problem when I experienced bouts of the same."

"You, Miss Haswell? I would have thought you had always been perfect."

She glanced at him, surprised that his flattery was not delivered with a smile. Instead, his expression was oddly sober.

"By the way," he added, "you might wish to be careful about prescribing physic."

The warmth she felt turned to annoyance. "I was not *prescribing*. It is a simple, known remedy."

"I am only cautioning you. A woman compounding medicines is one thing, but prescribing is another. If Dr. Foster had seen that just now, he might think you were overstepping. He might . . ." He grimaced. "Just be careful."

I like dreams of the future better than the history of the past.

—PATRICK HENRY

CHAPTER 29

Lilly received a letter from her uncle, which surprised and mildly alarmed her, for she had received a letter only a few days before. She hoped the Elliotts were both in good health.

> *My dear Lillian,*
>
> *I know we agreed to speak no more on the subject of your mother, but still I thought you should know. I have received additional information. Do you remember Mrs. Browning, the lady who let rooms to "Rosa" off Fleet Street? And do you further recall that I left my card? I confess I believed that card would come to tinder and that I should never hear from her again. But, behold, I received a letter from her today—if such scrawl can be called such—and happily paid the fourpence postage.*
>
> *As I understand it, Mrs. Browning had long ago given your mother—or at least "Rosa"—a letter of reference, and a prospective employer has recently written to Mrs. Browning to*

verify Rosa's suitability for the post. I suppose you will struggle to credit it as I did. Rosamond—a housekeeper? In any case, the trail is cold no longer, should you like to pursue it. Of course I cannot say for certain whether Rosa was given the post in the end, but it seems likely, given Mrs. Browning's confidence that she'd "writ a lettr shure to inpress and pleas." But perhaps a letter from you to the steward or butler would answer if you are so inclined. I've included the directions below. Do let me know if there is anything you would like me to do in this regard.

Most sincerely,

Mr. Jonathan Elliott

Lilly fingered the postscript, the name of the estate and its direction. In Surrey, south of London. Part of her longed to go. Another part said this was not a good time—her father was unwell, and she could ill afford to close the shop. Still, it would not be so long a journey. She could go by post and return in two days' time.

❧

The hired hackney took her as far as the end of the lane. From there, she walked, through the gates and up the curved stone drive. Craybill Hall was grander than she had imagined. The estate further out in the countryside than she would have guessed.

Lilly clutched her reticule tightly, knowing her damp palms would likely mar the smooth satin but at that moment not caring. She took a deep breath. The nausea she felt, she tried to tell herself, was from the long day of travel—first the long coach journey, then the jarring ride in the old hackney. She pressed one hand to her stomach, hoping to calm her nerves. How would her mother react upon seeing her? At being tracked down when she had clearly made no effort to reconnect with the family she had left behind? Did her mother assume, perhaps, they wanted nothing to do with her? If so, surely her mother would, if not welcome a visit, be relieved to know her daughter wished her well.

Lilly paused at the bottom of the wide steps leading to the main entrance. She prayed for wisdom, for peace, for her legs to quit trembling. She heard a sound in the distance, several voices raised in laughter. Something about the sound was familiar. On impulse, she turned and walked around the manor house, the peals of laughter guiding her like a ship's bell in the fog.

At the rear of the house, she saw a low garden wall. On its other side, a small table and chairs were arranged on a manicured lawn. Two children sat at that table, a little boy with golden hair, and a girl a few years older with ginger curls. And there, standing between them—smiling—was her mother. She was singing along as the children clapped and sang "Pat-a-cake."

How young and pretty her mother looked. She wore a blue-and-white walking dress, and her dark hair was swept back in a high, fashionable coil. *Where is her hat?* Lilly wondered. *She ought not be out-of-doors without one.* Lilly chided herself for her inane observation at such a time. In the midst of their game, her mother looked up from the children and clearly saw her standing there. Saw *someone* standing there, at any rate. She ceased singing, and her expression sobered.

Taking a deep breath and fisting her hands, Lilly walked slowly to the garden wall. Would her mother recognize her as she drew near? Letting the reticule dangle at her wrist, Lilly laid both hands on the waist-high stone wall.

"Yes?" Rosamond Haswell asked, her tone officious.

"Hello, Mother," Lilly said quietly.

She only stared in response.

The little boy asked in an endearing lisp, "Who is da lady?"

The little girl hung her head, so Lilly could not make out her features.

"Sit up straight, dear, and greet our guest," her mother said to the girl. But the girl made no sign of hearing her. She was either very shy or very rude.

Swallowing hard, Lilly said the next thing that came to her mind. "I thought you were the housekeeper here?"

Her mother continued to survey her person, hat to waist and up again. "I was. The governess took ill." She shrugged. "Besides, I like children. Well, some children . . ."

Lilly felt as though she'd been struck in the chest by a heavy mallet.

The little girl looked up then, revealing a face eerily identical to Lilly's own at that age. The girl scowled and stuck out her tongue.

Lilly sat up in bed, breathing heavily and perspiring as the dream faded. Feeling ill, she arose, wrapped her dressing gown around herself, and stepped gingerly to Charlie's door. She opened it inch by creaking inch. In the moonlit chamber, Charlie slept soundly, hands clasped beneath one cheek, fair hair splayed on his pillow and over his brow.

Lilly tiptoed across the room and leaned low. She reached out and gently brushed the hair from his eyes.

She needed to touch someone real.

In the morning, Lilly went in search of her mother's miniature portrait. She found it in a drawer in the sitting room, shrouded in brown paper. Unwrapping it, she blew off the paper dust and looked at the lovely face, so like the one in her dream the night before. It had been painted before her marriage more than twenty years ago. Lilly wondered how much she had changed by now. And knew she would go on wondering.

Lilly slipped the small frame into her apron pocket, wanting it near. She *would* act upon the information her uncle had sent. She would write a letter to start. After that, she did not know.

An hour later, she was already in the shop, bent over stationery and quill, when Francis came by for the Haswell herbs Mr. Shuttleworth wanted. She had the herbs bunched, tagged, and ready in a crate.

"Excellent. This everything?" Francis asked.

"Hmm?" she murmured, distracted.

"Is this everything. For Mr. Shuttleworth . . . ?"

"Oh." She glanced up at him, then at the crate. "Yes." She looked back at the few lines she had written. "Francis, you never met my mother, did you?"

He wrinkled his brow, no doubt wondering why she had asked a question when she already knew the answer.

"No. She left not long before I arrived."

Lilly nodded, tapping the quill against the inkpot as she thought.

"I do remember a little portrait of her," Francis said. "You used to carry it about with you, until your father asked you to put it away."

Lilly nodded again, thinking how she had found the portrait wrapped and tucked in a drawer. Out of sight.

"I remember thinking she was quite lovely," Francis continued. "And that you were very like her."

Silently, she pulled the framed miniature from her apron pocket and slid it across the counter toward him. He leaned down and peered at it. "Very like her indeed."

She told him about her mother's necklace and *Rosa Wells*. As she spoke, he took her hand in his and pressed it, his brown eyes warm with compassion. The laboratory-kitchen door creaked open and Francis stepped back. Seeing her father in the doorway, Lilly slipped the miniature under her writing paper.

"Good morning, Mr. Haswell," Francis said. "You are looking better."

"I feel better. For now, at any rate. Tell me, Mr. Baylor, how is our new physician getting on in the village? Lilly's Dr. Graves?"

She saw Francis wince. His brow pucker. Uncomfortable, Lilly protested mildly, "Father . . ."

Francis glanced at her, then quickly away. "Well enough, I suppose, though you know how it is. Some are slow to accept a newcomer."

Her father nodded, then eyed the crate. "What's this, then?"

Fearing her father's response, Lilly answered, "Mr. Shuttleworth has asked for some of our famed Haswell herbs, Father. That should please you."

He was incredulous. "You are giving herbs to our competitor?"

"Selling, Father. Selling," Lilly said, realizing her father had resumed his curmudgeonly temper toward his rival. "And at a tidy profit." She gave Francis a look, and Francis took the hint.

"It's dear they are, but Bedsley Priors folk will have Haswell herbs if they can. Shuttleworth has little choice but to pay for the privilege."

Charles Haswell nodded, apparently satisfied. "I should think so."

"Well, I bid you both good day." Lips pulled tight in a resigned line, Francis bowed to Lilly, then to Mr. Haswell, and took his leave.

Her father tilted his head to view the paper before her. "Another order?"

She hesitated. "No, a letter. To Mother."

He looked stunned. "What?"

"At least to the estate where she is believed to have a situation."

"What are you talking about?"

"Come, Father," Lilly bid softly. "Sit down and I will tell you."

They seated themselves in the surgery, and Lilly explained once more about the discovery of the necklace and what she had learned about her mother in London and since—in review, very little. Not wanting to hurt him more than he had already been, she did not include the details about her mother's first love.

She asked gently, "Why did she leave, do you know?"

He took a deep breath. "I thought she was happy, at least for a time." He stared out the surgery window. "When you were born, I thought everything would be all right. She was so delighted with you." He shifted in his chair. "But I believe she always regretted marrying me. I know she missed London, and I think she always wondered what might have been, whom she might have married had she stayed."

She squeezed his hand. "You are the best man I have ever met—in London or anywhere."

He uttered a dry laugh. "Did the Elliotts take you *nowhere?*" Shaking his head, he said, "No, my dear, I am afraid I am a very flawed man indeed. Perhaps even more than your mother knew. . . ."

He let the words fade away and then leaned forward earnestly. "I caution you, Lilly, in this search of yours. You may not like what you find."

[The apothecary] is the physician to the poor at all times,
and to the rich whenever the distress or danger is not great.

—ADAM SMITH, 1776

CHAPTER 30

As Lilly and her father lingered over breakfast the next day, Charlie came in and dropped one of their medical cases onto the table before her, nearly toppling her teacup. "Come with me to Marlow House, Lilly. Mr. Timms has a gurt boil and won't see a doctor."

Lilly grimaced. She no more wanted to lance that crass old man's boil than she wanted to manage her father's shop. "Perhaps Father might," she said, spooning jam onto her remaining crust of toast.

Charles Haswell looked up from his newspaper. "I don't think I am equal to it today, my dear."

How convenient, Lilly thought.

"Come on, Lilly," Charlie urged. "Man's hurtin' fierce."

"Oh, very well," she huffed, dropping the toast onto her plate and rising. Seeing brother's earnest face, she hesitated and added grudgingly, "It is kind of you to think of Mr. Timms."

Half an hour later, Lilly stood in Mr. Timms's small kitchen at one end of the Marlow row houses, where several of the oldest servants lived.

"You rest easy now, Mr. Timms," she advised, repacking instruments and vials.

"Rest? You'll not see me lolloping about. Think the goosegogs'll pick their selves? The deer'll overrun the galley-crow afore the day's out, and the garden be dry as a gix."

Sitting beside the man, Charlie said, "I can help, Mr. Timms."

"Nay, yer needed at home now, ey? But I sore miss ye. A good tasker ye are, Charlie Haswell, and don't ye forget it."

Charlie smiled and hung his head, sheepishly proud.

Lilly said, "I am sorry, Mr. Timms, but my father and I—"

"No need to be sorry, miss. I know how 'tis. Yer father's ailin', innum? I know how that is too."

She shut the case, preparing to take her leave. "I hope you shall be right as a trivet now."

"No doubt of it. I'm obliged to ye, I am. And glad to be shot of that gurt ol' boil."

They bid the wizened gardener farewell and let themselves out the door.

"See, I told you he weren't so bad," Charlie said.

"You were right, Charlie. And if he was surly, no wonder! To be in such pain day and night."

The weather was mild, so they strolled across the lawn to the formal gardens, Charlie pointing out this planting and that which he had helped tend. As they did, Lilly heard a dog bark—first a warning, then with more ferocity. A man called out in a stern voice laced with a telling note of fear.

"Back, I say. Back!"

"Oh no." Lilly ran down the lane, and around the bend spotted Dr. Graves, his back against a tree. The Marlows' large-headed mastiff, nearly the size of a pony, stood on its hind legs, massive front paws splayed against the man's chest.

"Dotty, no!" Lilly called with calm authority. "Down this instant!"

Dotty whined, drooled, and leapt down. Charlie jogged over and grabbed the collar of the brindled brown-and-black dog.

Lilly said, "Tether her in the stables, Charlie, will you?"

"Come on, Dotty-girl," Charlie urged and led the great dog away.

"Dotty?" Dr. Graves exclaimed. "Who in their right mind would name a monster of that size *Dotty*?"

"The Marlows have an uncommon sensibility when it comes to humor and most things," she said, stepping near to look him over. Besides two muddy pawprints on his tawny coat, he appeared unscathed. "Are you all right?"

"You mean beyond my utter mortification and the fact that my heart is beating like a cornered hare?"

"Yes."

He extracted a handkerchief from his pocket and wiped drool from his cheek. "I was only come to meet Sir Henry. I had no idea the act would prove so perilous."

She took the handkerchief from him. "You've a bit of mud . . ." She wiped the dirt from his neck and collar. His Adam's apple bobbed and his pupils dilated. Realizing what she had just done, she swallowed and handed back the handkerchief.

His eyes met hers, then darted away. She attempted to keep her expression impassive, lest he guess how forward she felt.

He cleared his throat. "You are a singular woman, Miss Haswell."

She licked her suddenly dry lips. An awkward silence followed. To break it, she said, "I am afraid your coat is spoiled."

In the act of dusting off the pawprints, he paused. "Are *you* afraid of nothing?"

She considered this. "Everybody is afraid of something. Or someone."

"What are you afraid of?"

She cocked her head to one side to look at him. "Why? Will it make you feel better to know?"

"Vastly." He stooped to pick up his hat and attempted to restore its shape. "Or at least distract me from my humiliation."

"Very well. But I tell you in confidence."

"Of course."

She grinned wryly. "I had rather face that great dog ten times over than his master once."

His hands stilled. "Roderick Marlow?"

She nodded.

He did not return her grin. Instead looked quite alarmed. "Has he threatened you? Harmed you?"

"Well, nothing of consequence, but—"

"He hasn't acted in an untoward manner toward you?"

"Dr. Graves. I meant to comfort you by my confession, not distress you further."

"But, Miss Haswell!"

"There have been a few occasions when I felt mildly . . . threatened, as you say. But these were long ago. Still, I suppose it is the same for me as for you—one bite and I shall ever be wary." She hastened to add, "Of course I meant that figuratively. He did not *actually* bite me." Again she tried to lighten the moment with a smile, but he continued to look quite stern.

He said, "I understand he all but got a man killed once. In a brawl or duel or some such."

Had he? She had never heard such a tale.

"In any case, if he ever threatens or harasses you again, Miss Haswell, you must not allow it to pass. You must tell someone. Me, if no one else."

She wondered briefly what Dr. Graves would do. She could not fancy him fighting Roderick Marlow. Dr. Graves would surely lose any duel not fought with lancets or ear horns.

"Thank you. But as I said, it is in the past. Put it from your mind."

"Have you?"

"Absolutely. As long as he is out of my sight." She smirked. "Or chained up."

Blue eyes sparkling, he grinned—then actually laughed out loud. It was the first genuine sound of mirth she had ever heard him utter. She liked it very much indeed.

ᘯ

When the return letter arrived almost a week later from Craybill Hall, Lilly could not bring herself to open it. To face the rejection that might very well be contained within. How many times had she imagined the possible responses? The cool, detached words: *"I regret to inform you I have no interest in renewing our acquaintance."* Or *"I request that you no longer attempt to contact me; I do not wish to jeopardize my position."* Or even *"If I had wanted to see you, I knew where to find you, did I not?"*

But dared she hope for a warmer response? *"How I have longed to hear of you! But to receive a letter penned in your own hand— My, what a fine young lady you must have become! I would very much like to see you again. I feared to hope you would ever desire to see me. . . ."*

Which would it be?

Turning the shop sign, she jogged to the coffeehouse, barely noticing Jane hunched on the garden bench shelling beans. She dashed through the back door, and thrust the letter at Mary.

"Read it. I cannot."

Mary was grinding coffee beans but paused to study her. She turned to wipe her hands on a cloth. "What is it?"

"From my mother I think. I wrote to the house where she was said to have a situation."

Setting aside the cloth, Mary took the letter. "It is addressed to you."

"Please."

Mary held her gaze a moment longer, then nodded. She slit open the seal and unfolded the letter. As she quickly read the lines, her expression shifted from perplexity to concern.

"She does not wish to see me, does she?" Lilly braced herself.

Mary shook her head.

Lilly winced. *I knew it.*

"It isn't from your mother. It is from the housekeeper, a Mrs. Morton. Here, read it yourself."

Lilly took the letter from her friend and skimmed it quickly, then sank down onto her usual stool and read the critical portion again.

> *We've had no one here by the surname Haswell, but there was a housekeeper by the name Rosa Wells. However, she is no longer employed here, and I am the new housekeeper. I cannot tell you where she went, but I can tell you she left after only a few weeks, without proper notice and without references and that the coachman disappeared on the very same eve. Him, by the name of Stanley Dugan, in case you're wanting to know. If you find them, be sure and pass on that Mr. Dugan left without returning the livery that is rightly the master's property, though the master is a forgiving sort and pressed no charges. Rosa took nothing what didn't belong to her, and Cook tells me she was a fair worker, though not content in her post. This is all I can tell you, as she was gone before I come.*
>
> *Mrs. Morton, Housekeeper*
> *Craybill Hall*

Gone. Again.

Did her mother have some inkling she was being sought? Or was it her nature to move on quickly from situations that did not suit?

"Might it have been someone else?" Mary asked. "With the name Wells, I mean. She could not have married again, could she? With your father still alive?"

Lilly shrugged, feeling numb and empty. "It could be a false name, short for Haswell. Or perhaps she took the name of the man she left us for, and has even now taken another *husband*. It would explain why she has cut all ties to an inconvenient family hidden away in Wiltshire."

"I cannot credit it," Mary said. "More likely it was some other woman."

Lilly said dully, "Perhaps." She crumpled the paper and tossed it among the embers in the cookstove. The paper flamed to life, then just as quickly extinguished.

Like her foolish, foolish hopes.

A man of very moderate ability may be a good physician,
if he devotes himself faithfully to the work.

—OLIVER WENDELL HOLMES

CHAPTER 31

The next morning, when Lilly entered the coffeehouse by the kitchen door as usual, she was surprised to see Mr. Shuttleworth there, seated in her customary stool at the worktable.

She hesitated. "Oh. Pardon me."

He rose and bowed. "Miss Haswell."

"Morning, Lill," Mary said pleasantly, looking pretty in a green frock and seeming perfectly at ease. She walked over to pick up the stool beside the hearth, but Mr. Shuttleworth, perceiving her intention, leapt to assist her, carrying the stool over and setting it not far from his own.

Both ladies thanked him at once. He beamed at them, his gaze lingering on Mary. "My pleasure, ladies."

Lilly perched herself up on the stool, feeling awkward. Mary poured a cup of coffee and placed it before her, then returned her attention to a large basin, stirring its contents with fluid, steady strokes.

"Miss Mimpurse was so obliging as to offer a poor bachelor a bite of breakfast," Mr. Shuttleworth said. "Though the establishment is not yet open."

"Mamma is just opening the shutters now, Mr. Shuttleworth, should you prefer the comfort of soft chairs not dusted with flour."

"And why should I prefer it? Have I not the best seat in the house?"

Lifting the coffee cup to her lips, Lilly said dryly, "I have always thought so."

"Indeed. I cannot imagine warmer fires nor warmer company in any other place in the world."

"And that is saying a great deal, is it not," Lilly said. "Considering all of the many places you have been."

"You are too kind to remember, Miss Haswell."

"Lilly remembers everything, Mr. Shuttleworth," Mary said. "Had you not heard?"

"Dear me. I am obliged to you for the warning."

He grinned, and Mary lifted her eyes from her work long enough to return the gesture.

Lilly smiled as well, though did wonder that Mary should raise the subject of her memory. Knowing how self-conscious Lilly felt about it, her friend usually avoided mentioning it to strangers. Of course, by all appearances, Mr. Shuttleworth was stranger no longer.

Suddenly a pained look pinched Mary's usually docile features, and she grasped her left hand with her right.

"Please excuse me," she said, and Lilly doubted anyone who did not know Mary so well would even notice the tension in her face. "I've just been reminded of something I must attend to."

Mr. Shuttleworth rose, mouth ajar. But Mary had already turned and fled the room before he could say anything.

Lilly rose beside him, concerned.

"I have clearly overstayed my welcome," he said sheepishly. "Do offer your friend a thousand apologies on my behalf."

"Not at all, sir. I am certain it is nothing you did."

"I shall see myself out." He opened the back door and bid her farewell.

As soon as he had gone, Lilly hurried toward the dining room, thinking Mary must have gone upstairs, but a flash of green caught her eye as she passed the pantry. There Mary half sat, half reclined on a ten-stone sack of flour.

"Mary, is a fit coming on?"

Jerking a nod, Mary held her arms tightly, clutching her abdomen as a wounded soldier might hold his innards. Her arms shook and the movement expanded, overtaking her until even her head began to wobble on her neck, tendons corded like angry claws lashing into her shoulders.

Lilly reached for Mary's apron pocket, for the leather scrap she kept there. Empty. "Hold on. I'll try and catch Mr. Shuttleworth."

"No!" Mary cried, voice trembling. "No . . . father."

"But my father is too ill. He has returned to his bed."

"My . . ." Mary began, then her body convulsed, rendering her unable to speak.

Lilly hesitated only a second, then dashed into the kitchen, grabbed the first wooden spoon she saw, and ran back with it. Mary winced but opened her mouth and Lilly slid the spoon between her teeth. Stepping to the door, she glanced into the dining room, where Mrs. Mimpurse was greeting a group of timber men and barge builders, Mr. Robbins among them.

Catching her eye, Lilly jerked her head toward the pantry, mouthing, "Mary." Her pained look must have communicated the rest, for Mrs. Mimpurse quickly but tactfully took her leave of the men and strode toward the kitchen.

Lilly did not wait. With her father ill, and Mary's clear command not to involve Mr. Shuttleworth, she could think of only one place to go for help.

She would even have asked Dr. Foster if need be, but when she pounded on the office door, she was relieved when Dr. Graves answered.

"Please come quickly. It's Mary Mimpurse. She's having a fit."

She half expected him to freeze in the face of an emergency as he had in London, but she silently thanked God when he bent immediately and picked up his case.

Adam Graves's heart pounded, but he did not hesitate. Miss Haswell's practical, no-nonsense commands pushed him into action, and his limbs obeyed her even while his mind struggled to catch up.

She asked, "Have you valerian, or should I run home for some?"

He opened his case and checked its contents. "I have all I need."

"Good. Hurry." She turned on her heel, giving him little choice but to follow.

He had to jog to keep up with her along Milk Lane and then down the High Street. She had somehow learned to run at an impressive pace while appearing merely to glide.

Rounding the coffeehouse, she opened the back door and gestured him inside ahead of her. Mrs. Mimpurse had swept the utensils from the worktable and managed to lay her daughter upon it. The poor girl convulsed, eyes rolled back, wooden spoon protruding from her mouth. Her mother did her best to hold her in place, with the help of a young maid. He surprised himself by immediately rushing forward to aid them.

"Father believes valerian to be the best remedy," Miss Haswell said, appearing beside him at the table. "The trick is to administer it while she's in this state."

"Give me two ounces of the extract, then."

"So much? Is not the regular dose one half to one dram?"

"We shall debate theories later, shall we? With all haste, Miss Haswell."

He continued to help the two women steady Miss Mimpurse while Lilly poured the liquid into a glass measure and handed it to him.

"Help me pry open her mouth." Using the wooden spoon as a lever, the two managed to open her mouth, pour in the foul liquid, and coax it to the back of her throat. Her swallowing reflex did the rest.

"Now, help us hold her until it takes effect. If it does . . ."

"It will. Always has."

Already, the young woman's seizures were gentling, whether from the dosage or the simple passage of time, he could not tell. He did not like that Miss Haswell felt she had to question him, that she could not trust his judgment.

While they held Miss Mimpurse, he endeavored to explain, "You are correct that the accepted *preventative* dose is one half to one dram three or four times as day. But more is required to calm an episode in full force."

"I see."

"In any case, I am not convinced valerian suppresses seizures, and it certainly does not cure the root of the disease."

"What is the cure?" she asked.

He glanced at the white-faced mother, then back at Miss Haswell. "I fear there is none."

Later, after he had helped Mrs. Mimpurse put her weakened daughter to bed, and accepted the woman's gratitude, Adam walked outside with Miss Haswell.

"Do you think she ought to take valerian on a daily basis?" she asked.

"Not at this point. I recommend an infusion of scullcap."

"Mad-dog weed?"

"It works as antispasmodic and relaxing nervine both. Perhaps you would be so good as to prepare it?"

"Of course," she said, clearly pleased to be called upon.

Reaching Haswell's, she paused to look up at him. How earnest her expression, her heart-shaped face wreathed by that splendid russet hair.

"May I ask you to keep this episode to yourself?" she began. "Mary is quite self-conscious about her condition. It has been so long since she's had a fit, the poor dear no doubt hoped she'd outgrown them."

He wondered how he could refuse Miss Haswell anything, when she captivated him so. Though she had not asked, she must know she was the reason he had pursued this partnership in Bedsley Priors.

"Dr. Foster may ask for an account of my time, but otherwise I shall keep it to myself as I would in any case."

"Thank you."

He thought then of the next call he must make. "May I ask a favor of you in return?"

At the cottage door, they were greeted by one of the nine Somersby children and a rush of sharp smells. Inside, Mr. and Mrs. Somersby sat at table, a spread of cheese, pickled herring, and mugs of ale before them. Two toddlers sat on the floor, banging wooden spoons against the floorboards. Four others were blowing and chasing a downy feather about the room, keeping it aloft. The family's cottage was small, their clothes old, but as Mr. Somersby was both poulterer and cheese monger, they always ate well. Perhaps, Lilly thought, too well.

"I beg your pardon. I am Dr. Graves, paying a call on behalf of Dr. Foster. And this is Miss Haswell."

Lilly knew the older physician rarely bothered with house calls now that he had Dr. Graves to send about.

"But we had no intention of interrupting your repast."

"Never ye mind." Mrs. Somersby, a plump woman of forty or so years, lifted her apron hem and wiped her mouth. "Chester here come home from market leer-starved. Why not sit yerselves? I've got a junk o' cheese, good an' aged. Chicken livers, too."

"Thank you, no," Dr. Graves said.

The feather landed on his shoulder, unnoticed by him. Lilly plucked it off and blew it in the air for the expectant children.

Mrs. Somersby rose. "Well then. Let's shut us in the bedchamber away from all these peepers. I'm much obliged to you fer comin' 'ere. Hard to get away with all these young ones aboot."

As she led the way to the cottage's sole separate room, Dr. Graves said, "Dr. Foster described several complaints of a female nature and I have therefore brought Miss Haswell along."

"As I see."

As soon as the three of them were inside the small bedchamber, Mrs. Somersby lowered herself heavily onto the edge of the bed, and

Lilly sat beside her. "Now, tell me," Lilly asked gently. "What ails you?"

"I'm just not my old self of late. My poor nerves are givin' me quiy' a lot of trouble. My Chester don't like how I mump aboot. Seems we 'ave a shandy near ever' night for no good reason. And I'm 'aving pains in my stomach." She leaned toward Lilly and whispered, "And pains in my breast what don't bear speakin' of in a young man's 'earing."

Lilly smiled and said soothingly, "Well, he is a doctor after all, is he not?"

They gave the woman St. John's wort for her nerves and stomach, and a decoction of vervain for the breast pain.

"Now, if that does not bring you relief, you just come by the shop when you can and I shall give you a treatment of tempered figs." Lilly paused, then turned sheepishly to Dr. Graves. "Forgive me. You might prefer to do that yourself. She is your patient after all."

He hesitated, perhaps imagining the awkward scene—pressing figs, tempered as hot as a patient could endure, and applying them to Mrs. Somersby's breasts. He cleared his throat. "Not at all." He said to the woman, "Feel free to see Miss Haswell for that procedure."

They were packing their things away to take their leave when Mrs. Somersby pressed both hands to her temples. "Wha's this? I feel right queer all of a sudden."

Lilly hurried to her side. "What is it?"

"My 'ead . . . aches somethin' awful. Dizzy-like too." Mrs. Somersby used one arm to prop herself upright and moaned, "Wha's 'appenin'?" Then she collapsed onto the bed.

"Dr. Graves!" Lilly exclaimed.

Acting quickly and with surprising calm, Dr. Graves deftly gave Mrs. Somersby a dose of ipecacuanha, and once it had done its work, administered hawthorn and strong coffee.

Half an hour later, Mrs. Somersby was quite herself again, though shaken. Lilly prepared a cup of chamomile tea at Dr. Grave's request, then instructed Mr. Somersby to give another cup when his wife finished the first.

When they finally took their leave, Dr. Graves accompanied Lilly back to Haswell's.

"Do you think it was the St. John's wort?" she asked as they neared the shop. "I've never known vervain to produce such a dramatic reaction."

"Nor I."

He opened the shop door for her and followed her inside.

"A skin rash, perhaps," she continued, "but not collapse. Good heavens. I don't know what I would have done had you not been there. Well done, Dr. Graves."

In her relief, she forgot herself and held out her hand in a congratulatory gesture as Mr. Shuttleworth might have done. Instead of briefly pressing it, Dr. Graves took her hand in both of his own, his countenance quite serious.

"When you are with me, I feel as though I might do anything. You strengthen me, Miss Haswell."

She allowed him to hold her hand but shook her head slowly. "I cannot be your strength, Dr. Graves. That is God's role. I am not fit for it."

"Is it the role you object to, or the man asking it of you?"

She took a deep breath. "At present, I have all I can do to be my father's strength as well as my own."

He let go of her hand and drew himself up. "Of course you have. I would not blame you, in any case. You know my weaknesses too well."

"Have we not all some weakness, Dr. Graves?" Lilly said kindly. "Besides, you seem to be overcoming your weaknesses, as you call them, since coming to Bedsley Priors."

He lifted one side of his mouth in a rueful grin. "Which brings me back to my point, Miss Haswell."

She untied her bonnet and stepped away to hang it on a peg. "We certainly work well together," she allowed. "As evidenced this very day."

"Indeed, though I would certainly not expect you to work alongside me, were we to . . . That is, unless it were a simple case, or involved a female complaint like Mrs. Somersby's."

"Why? Do you not think a woman capable of grasping medical knowledge and skills?"

"Well, I do not say it is impossible, were universities to allow women to study. But . . . they do not."

"I help my father all the time." She moved to stand behind the dispensary counter.

"I understand that. And I admire your abilities." He stepped to the counter and stood looking down at her. "But, Miss Haswell, once you are— Once you are a married woman, you will no longer have need of such skills. Although, certainly as the lady of the house, a knowledge of basic injury care, invalid cookery and the like, will always be useful."

She should have been relieved he would not expect such from her. Had she not wanted to escape such a life? Then why did she feel discounted instead?

I try to avoid looking forward or backward,
and try to keep looking upward.

—CHARLOTTE BRONTË

CHAPTER 32

Lilly stood on the back stoop. She looked out over the garden and breathed deeply of an English summer morn. It had rained in the night, and all smelled fresh and green. Grey's Hill—her hill—was just visible in the distance beyond the garden wall. She closed her eyes, enjoying the warm caress of the sun on her face and arms though she knew she ought not be out-of-doors without a hat. *Ah, what is one more freckle. . . .*

Songbirds chirped happily in the hornbeam and lime trees, and beyond her view, a single horse clip-clopped its way along the High Street. The church bells rang, and when their last peal faded away, all was quiet save birdsong.

She could not help but think back to where she had been and what she had been doing exactly one year ago. She knew she should not let the memory play itself out, knew she should not compare this year to the last, but she gave in and let the memories come.

Many hooves had beat the busy streets outside the Elliotts' Mayfair townhouse. Carriage wheels and church bells had sounded as well. Dupree brought up a breakfast tray bearing a vase of lemon-yellow lilies in honor of the day. Then she helped Lilly put on a new frock of sprigged muslin and dressed her hair with ribbons.

There had followed shopping with Aunt Elliott and Christina Price-Winters. Roger had sent a nosegay and a lovely new fan with his compliments. Later they dined at the Clarendon and then attended the Theatre Royal, sharing a box with Will Price-Winters and his then-fiancée, as well as Christina, Toby Horton, and Roger Bromley. There had been a pearl necklace from her aunt and uncle and a new shawl from Christina. She remembered the presents, of course, but it was not the presents themselves she longed for now. It was the feeling of being special she missed, of being cherished.

She recalled Mr. Marlow's advice on how to tame unpleasant memories and realized there were times when one might wish to stifle pleasant memories as well—when they dimmed the present by comparison.

Stop feeling sorry for yourself, Lilly Haswell, she warned sternly. Purposefully, she strode to the clump of lilies near the garden wall and plucked a lemony bloom. She tucked it behind her ear and felt better immediately.

"You're up early." Francis appeared above the garden wall, and her heart lightened further.

He pushed his way through the garden gate with his hip, his hands full. Spying the wrapped parcel in his arms, Lilly felt foolishly thrilled and bit back a smile.

"I've brought you something. I hope Dr. Graves won't mind."

He would, she thought, but forbore to comment. After all, she'd thought no one had remembered. Her father had not. Nor had Mary said a word. "How thoughtful, Francis. Do come in."

He followed her inside, and Lilly gestured uncertainly toward the kitchen table. "Here, or . . . ?"

"The shop, I think."

She led the way and stood aside as he laid the large parcel on the dispensing counter. He urged her forward with a sweep of his hand. "Go on."

Smiling, she gently ripped back the brown paper. She felt her eyes widen as she stared at what lay beneath. Not a gift box, but a cage. A cage inhabited by a hairy rodent.

She frowned. "It is a rat."

"Not a rat, a cavy. *Cavia porcellus*."

"Looks like a rat." She darted a glance at him. "Though more handsome, I grant you." This long-haired animal had white and caramel markings and close-set eyes.

"Dr. William Harvey himself used several in his research."

"Harvey . . ." Lilly thought. "The first to correctly describe the circulatory system?"

"Exactly."

"I do not recall any mention of . . . What did you call it—a cavy?"

"I believe he referred to them in his writings as *ginny-pigs*."

She peered into the cage. "This little thing is hardly a pig. How odd."

"Mr. Shuttleworth kept one in his ship's surgery. He believed in feeding it new remedies—especially materia acquired in foreign lands—before offering them to the ill among the crew."

"And you thought I could . . . ?"

"Well, since he was working on his own—without colleague to discuss treatments or dosages—he thought it a wise precaution."

Lilly felt herself growing piqued. "And has he a cavy now in that fancy shop of his?"

"No." Francis smiled ruefully. "He has me."

"You know perfectly well many poisons do not show up immediately."

"I do not suggest it as a foolproof measure. Only a precaution against the most harmful of substances."

She huffed and balled the paper tight.

"Come, Lilly, do not take offense. I only thought . . . I know you pretend otherwise, but you are essentially alone here. I know you remember everything you once learned, but some things have changed. There are new exotics, new materia, new methods."

Now she doubted Francis had remembered her birthday at all, but was too self-conscious to ask. Likely he had no idea, the date and the gift coming together in pure coincidence.

He tried another tack. "Mostly I thought he was a sweet little mite. Queen Elizabeth herself kept one as a pet."

"Did she indeed?"

He nodded.

She looked from him to the cavy, then back again. "I would have preferred a cat."

"But cats do not—"

"As a pet I mean. Not a royal taster."

"I did not think Haswells went in for cats."

"That was a long time ago. These days, Haswells are doing all sorts of things we never imagined we would."

His rueful smile returned. He reached out and gently touched her arm. "Well, happy birthday anyway."

❦

Lilly closed the shop as usual that evening and retreated to the laboratory-kitchen to see what she might find in the larder to scrape together for supper. Very little, it appeared. A quarter loaf of bread. A scrap of Stilton. A jar of goosegog conserve and another of sardines.

She took herself upstairs to check on her father and ask if he felt up to eating. Lately, his condition seemed to vacillate by the hour. She knocked, but he did not answer. She opened the door to find the bedchamber empty, the bed made, if haphazardly so.

Where had he taken himself off to? Had he wandered down to the surgery without her noticing? She paused in her own room, to splash water on her face and check her hair in the small mirror. Still reasonably neat. She took off her apron, laid it in the laundry basket, and returned downstairs.

Her father was not in the kitchen, nor the surgery. Had he gone to see Dr. Graves? She stepped out the back door to check the garden. The air was still as warm and sweet as it had been that morning, and she took a moment to inhale it.

Charlie's head appeared over the garden wall, startling her.

"Lilly! Come quick."

Trepidation shot through her. "Is it Father?"

"Father too. Mary says hurry."

What now? Lilly rushed out the garden gate and across the mews to the coffeehouse. She burst through the kitchen door and hesitated in the threshold. Mary looked up at her from the hearth.

"What is it? Charlie said you and Father needed me."

"We do. We're missing something."

"Missing what?"

Mary straightened. "The guest of honor, you goose. Surely you guessed?"

Lilly shook her head.

Mary rolled her eyes, took her by the arm, and led her through the door into the coffeehouse dining room. Charlie followed behind. There, at the large center table were her father, clear-eyed and sitting upright, Mr. Shuttleworth, Francis, and Dr. Graves. Maude Mimpurse stood nearby, reaching over to set a platter of food on the table. An iced cake sat in the middle.

Lilly looked at Mary with surprise and saw her own pleasure mirrored in her dearest friend's face. She squeezed Mary's hand and whispered, "Thank you."

Mr. Shuttleworth cleared his throat. "In ancient Egypt," he began, "at least one pharaoh celebrated his birthday by doing away with his baker."

"Mr. Shuttleworth," Mary scolded, though Lilly did not miss the teasing lift of her mouth.

He winked at her. "No doubt his cakes were not as good as yours."

Charlie hurried over and took a seat next to Francis. "Mary's sittin' next to me," he said. "But your place is here, Lilly." He reached behind Francis and patted the back of a chair at the open place—the place between Francis Baylor and Adam Graves.

Francis met her gaze with a knowing look of his own.

Dr. Graves stood and pulled back her chair. "Felicitations, Miss Haswell."

Walking around the table, she placed her hand on her father's shoulder as she passed behind him. He reached up and grasped it with his own. She looked down at him, saw his eyes crinkle as he smiled up at her. "Happy birthday, my dear."

It was the loveliest gift she could imagine.

After supper, Maude rose to cut the cake. "Now, this is no ordinary cake," she said. "It's an olde English cake, baked with coins and other treasures inside, each one a symbol of something."

"Mind you don't break a tooth," Mary warned, handing plates with generous wedges to each of them.

Looking at each other with nervous anticipation and barely suppressed grins, they began to tentatively fork pieces of cake into their mouths and carefully chew. All except for Charlie, who shoveled in big hunks of cake with abandon.

In a matter of moments, Mr. Shuttleworth held up a coin.

"But not just any coin. Look again," Mary urged.

Squinting, he read, "*Italia*." He flipped it over. "Looks familiar."

"It ought to," Mary said. "It is the one I borrowed from you for the occasion. It means travels in your past or future."

"Ah . . ." He nodded his understanding.

"I also have a coin," Dr. Graves said, holding one up. "A shilling."

"Well then," Mary said, "you shall be wealthy one day."

He leaned in, his expression mock-serious. "Might I have that in writing?"

"I have a sweet!" Charlie triumphantly raised a cake-covered peppermint, then popped it into his mouth.

"What did you find, Charles?" Maude asked quietly.

Her father wiped the find with his handkerchief. "An old Roman coin. Plenty unearthed in these parts. Is this from Harold's collection, or a new find?"

269

Maude didn't respond to the query about her deceased husband, but Mary murmured, "Treasure from the past."

Lilly glimpsed the crumb-coated thimble on Mary's plate, but noticed she made no move to display it. Mrs. Mimpurse glanced over and clearly saw it as well. Looking worriedly at her daughter's face, she whispered, "I am sorry, my love. It is only a game after all."

Mary shrugged and attempted a smile.

"What is it you have, Miss Mary?" Mr. Shuttleworth asked eagerly.

Lilly sent him a warning look, but the man apparently did not notice or understand, for his long-toothed smile did not waver. He leaned closer. "A thimble, is it? What does it mean?"

An awkward silence filled the room.

Lilly opened her mouth but could not form the words.

Head high, Mary said briskly, "It means I shall never marry."

Mr. Shuttleworth tucked his chin. "What nonsense. You must have Graves's piece." He slapped Dr. Graves hard on the shoulder, causing the slighter man to jerk forward.

Lilly knew most people believed epilepsy rendered a woman ineligible for marriage and motherhood. But she did not agree. Hoping to direct the attention off her friend, Lilly asked, "And what did you find, Mrs. Mimpurse?"

Maude Mimpurse blushed and held up a ring. "I got the piece meant for one of you girls, no doubt."

They all chuckled politely.

"I have a key," Francis said. "What does it mean?"

They all looked at Mary.

"I don't know," she admitted. "Couldn't think of anything else to withstand the oven!"

Everyone laughed.

Everyone except Lilly, who was still forking through her piece. And though she looked and looked, she found nothing at all.

I do not know of any remedy under heaven that is likely to do you
so much good as the being constantly electrified.

—JOHN WESLEY, 1781

CHAPTER 33

When Lilly came downstairs the next morning, still securing a final pin into the plait coiled at the back of her head, she was pleased to see her father up and about already. Perhaps Dr. Graves's latest treatments were helping after all.

"I've made tea and toast," he announced with pride. "Had a taste for blood sausage, as well, so I'm frying a few slices if you'd care for any."

She shuddered. "You know I cannot abide the stuff. But tea and toast sounds just the thing." Watching her father potter about the kitchen, Lilly smiled to herself. "You must be feeling some better, Father."

"Indeed I am. And I've had a look at the ledgers, Lilly. First time I've had the courage to do so in months."

Scooping his sausage onto a plate, he joined her at the table. "I cannot express how proud I am. Well done, Lillian Grace Haswell. Well done, indeed."

She ducked her head, hiding her smile of pleasure. "Thank you, Father."

He picked up his fork. "No, my dear. Thank you."

"Shall we thank God, then?" she suggested. "I must say I am feeling quite grateful for His provision of late."

Charles Haswell paused, mouth ajar, and awkwardly lowered his forkful of sausage back down to his plate. "As you like."

Lilly bowed her head and offered a brief prayer of thanksgiving.

Afterward, her Father nodded and quickly moved on. "Once we've eaten, I'd like you to show me everything you've done in the shop. Went out there this morning and scarcely recognized the old place. Smells like a bakery, or a flower shop. But it looks fine, Lilly. Fine."

Lilly bit back another smile and echoed, "As you like."

"I also wonder if it might be time to ask Mrs. Fowler back," he said. "You do far too much on your own."

Lilly heard these words with great relief and pleasure. "I think that an excellent plan. I shall ask her this afternoon."

After they had eaten and done the washing up together, she led him into the shop, telling him about the Lippert family in London and pointing out the new patent medicines, the French perfumes, the ribbons, the rouge pots and other cosmetics.

"Here's one I used myself in London." She picked up a jar of Warren and Rosser's Milk of Roses and read from its label, " 'The most delightful cosmetic in Europe. Recommended by females of distinction for removing freckles and rendering the complexion delicately fair.' "

He glanced at her and coughed. "I'd request my money back, were I you."

"Father," she scolded, but grinned in spite of herself.

He raised his hands in defense. "I like your freckles." He then paused before an unfamiliar contraption. "And what, pray, is this?"

The apparatus, standing on four glass legs, resembled a miniature table. Two wooden uprights stood atop it, holding aloft a cylinder with a crank handle on one side and, on the other, an arm extending to a a small metal ball.

"That is the latest thing in London. Supposed to be all the crack, according to George Lippert."

"But . . . what is it?"

"An electricity machine, reportedly highly effective in the treatment of paralysis, gout, and . . . perhaps even epilepsy."

"Indeed?"

"John Wesley himself called it 'the most efficacious medicine in nervous disorders of every kind.' "

"Ah, that's right. The good reverend fancied himself a healer as well as an evangelist."

She searched for censure in his expression, but saw only mild incredulity.

He asked, "How does it work?"

"The patient holds the ball and, when the arm contacts the rotating cylinder, receives a shock—the strength of which depends upon the vigor with which the handle is turned. I have an explanatory pamphlet, but I own I have not had the courage to try it."

He eyed the device warily. "Let us leave it for another day, shall we? Now, what else have you done?"

They moved on. "Charlie and I repainted the shopwindow. I updated all the displays, as you see. I have also been offering free samples of ready-made items. And . . ."

When she hesitated, he prompted, "And?"

"And I prayed. A great deal."

❧

Lilly and Mary sat on a bench in front of the coffeehouse, half-heartedly watching a group of young men play a scrappy game of football on the village green, Francis among them.

Enjoying the fading afternoon sun, as well as the cheers and shouts of male camaraderie, Lilly and Mary discussed their plans for the coming Sunday.

Across the green, the door to the Hare and Hounds opened and a beefy young man wobbled out.

"There's Nick Clark," Lilly said quietly. "Still won't speak to me."

"No wonder," Mary said, giving a little snort. "He's not likely to forget how you laid him flat before the entire cricket team."

"It was only that once."

"Twice."

"Well, he should have learned the first time."

Lilly had first slugged the loud-mouthed lad for saying Mary's fits meant she was a witch. The second time occurred when they were girls of fifteen, and Nick Clark had said Lilly's mother was a doxy who had run off with the gypsies.

A few minutes after Nick Clark had gone, Roderick Marlow stepped out of the Hare and Hounds. Lilly knew villagers were shaking their heads, agreeing that the baronet's son had been spending too much time in that establishment since his father's marriage.

Lilly was relieved to see him walk quite steadily across the green, adroitly skirting a near collision with ball and player.

"Hello, Mr. Marlow!" Mary called before Lilly could silence her with an elbow in her side.

He crossed the High Street and bowed before them. "Miss Haswell. Miss . . ."

"Mimpurse."

"Of course. How fares your mother?"

"She is well, sir. I thank you," Mary said.

"Gentler on you than she was on me, I hope."

Mary bit back a grin. "I am sure my mother meted out whatever each of us deserved, sir."

"Ah, Miss Mimpurse, you wound me," he teased. "You are your mother's daughter."

Mary smiled, then turned to Lilly. "Perhaps Mr. Marlow would like to go along with us?"

Lilly gave a start. "Oh. . . . um. Well . . . yes," she faltered. "That is an . . . excellent . . . idea, Mary."

He raised his brows in mild expectation.

"We are to have a picnic, Mr. Marlow," Mary supplied, elbowing Lilly.

Lilly hastened to say, "I doubt it will be of a fashion you are used to, but you would be most welcome to join us." She stopped, but he still looked at her expectantly. "So . . . ?"

"When is it to be?" he asked.

"Oh." How foolish of her to leave out that detail. "Sunday afternoon. We are to climb Walker's Hill."

Mary added warmly, "And Mr. Shuttleworth is to bring his telescope, so we may determine if one can truly see the spire of the Salisbury Cathedral from there."

"And Mary is bringing along her famous cakes and sweets," Lilly said.

"Plenty for another," Mary assured him.

Mr. Marlow addressed Mary, "If I were sure Miss Haswell wished me to attend . . ."

They both turned toward her. Lilly swallowed. "Well, I . . . of course would be pleased. After all, you showed such kindness in inviting me to join your guests not long ago."

"True. And so I shall return the favor and accept, though clearly not your original intention nor, I daresay, preference."

"Well, I—"

"In fact, I shall bring a hamper," he interrupted. "I am sure it has been far too long since Mrs. Tobias has had the pleasure of preparing a proper picnic. What shall it be? Cold chicken? Roast of beef? Lobster salad?"

"All of the above!" Mary clapped her hands like a delighted child.

Mr. Marlow laughed. "All of the above, it is. How many shall I ask her to prepare for?"

Lilly answered, "We will be a party of seven or eight, I suppose. Mr. Shuttleworth, of course. And Francis Baylor."

"And Dr. Graves, I presume?" he added in exaggerated nonchalance.

She paused. Why did she feel awkward at his mention of Adam Graves? She lifted her chin. "If he is free." Lilly hurried to add, "And you are welcome to bring someone along if you like."

Charlie suddenly appeared in the open coffeehouse window behind them. "Bring Miss Powell, do. She is ever so nice to look at."

"Charlie," Lilly gently scolded. She had not even realized he was near. "She is Lady Marlow now, remember."

Marlow's jaw worked a few seconds and she feared Charlie had angered him. "Perhaps I shall," he said pleasantly enough. "I shall also bring round the landau—and the gill for the hampers and lads. Just name the time."

They settled the arrangements, and when he had left them, Mary snorted back a giggle.

"Mary Helen Mimpurse!" Lilly reprimanded.

Mary burst into laughter.

Lilly shook her head, biting back a grin of her own. "You are too bad."

A few minutes later, as Lilly knew he would, Mr. Shuttleworth came along after closing up the surgery for the day. Francis had the afternoon off, but he left the game and jogged over to join them as well, clad in grass-stained trousers and shirt-sleeves.

"We've invited Mr. Marlow to join us on Sunday," Mary announced.

"Roderick Marlow?" Francis was incredulous. He was still breathing hard from the game, and his damp white shirt outlined a well-formed chest.

"Take heart," Lilly said. "He may bring the new Lady Marlow you are always gaping at."

At the sound of her name, Charlie bounded outside. "I hope so."

Ankles crossed, Mr. Shuttleworth leaned on his walking stick and looked over at Francis. "Graves, and now Marlow as well. I cannot say I like our odds, Mr. Baylor."

"Nor I," Francis said. "What say you we invite another lady to improve our ratio? Miss Robbins would no doubt appreciate a little variety of society."

"Excellent idea, my boy," Mr. Shuttleworth agreed.

Francis gave Lilly a meaningful look. "And an invitation from Miss Haswell would no doubt come as quite an unexpected pleasure. Unless—is there some reason you would prefer she not come?"

Lilly felt trapped. Indignant. "What reason could I possibly have? Of course she may join us." Francis knew Lilly was now being courted by Dr. Graves. Why should she be surprised he had returned his attentions to Miss Robbins?

Francis nodded his approval, then clapped Charlie on the back. "Come on, Charlie. Come and join the lads."

"Aww. 'Em lads don't let me play," Charlie said.

"They do now."

Francis crooked his arm around Charlie's shoulder and led him to the green.

Lilly watched them go with a warmed heart, ready to forgive Francis his irritating habit of foisting unwanted creatures on her. *Ah well . . .* she could understand why Francis admired Miss Robbins. She was undeniably a lovely, accomplished girl.

"My, our little party is growing by the minute," Mary said, rising from the bench. "I had better bake another cake."

If thy heart fails thee, climb not at all.

—Queen Elizabeth I

Chapter 34

On Sunday morning, Lilly greeted the vicar outside the church doors after the service.

"Good morning, Mr. Baisley."

"Miss Haswell. How fares your father?"

"A little better, I thank you."

Mr. Baisley nodded and cleared his throat. "You no doubt noticed my blunder this morning." He leaned closer. "I believe it startled you awake."

Lilly felt her neck grow warm. "Forgive me. It was only a slight misquotation. I happen to have learned that Scripture as a girl."

He shook his head in wonder. "What it must be like to remember everything you have ever seen or heard or read . . ."

Lilly fidgeted. "Not everything, really. Only what I truly attend to."

"If I had such a gift, what I would store away." He thumped

a broad finger against his temple. "Scripture, hymns, my wife's birthday . . ."

She acknowledged his joke with a polite smile.

He studied her closely. "And what do you store away in that pretty head of yours, Miss Haswell?"

She shrugged dismissively, her discomfort increasing. "Whatever comes my way, I suppose."

A perplexed frown flickered across the kind man's features. "But whatever you take in or, as you say, attend to, it stays with you forever?"

"It seems so."

He shook his head solemnly. "Then, my dear, I hope you will be most careful what you allow in."

Lilly swallowed and attempted another smile, one she feared was quite stiff. *Well*, she bolstered herself, *what is church without a dose of conviction?*

At the appointed hour, Lilly, Mary, Charlie, and Francis were waiting before the coffeehouse when Miss Robbins arrived from neighboring Honeystreet in a lovely white-and-pink gown, French bonnet of tulle, and a parasol. Lilly bit her lip. That parasol would not withstand a half minute atop the wind-whipped pitch. She and Mary had settled for simple bonnets tied securely under their chins and long-sleeved spencers—for even on a summer day, the windy hills of Wiltshire could prove chilly.

The ladies exchanged polite greetings, and Lilly warmed to Miss Robbins when she saw how nervous the girl was.

A man on horseback rode up, and Lilly was surprised to recognize Mr. Marlow. Had he not said he would bring a carriage? It would be a long walk. And what of Mary's hamper?

Beside her, Miss Robbins sucked in her breath and squeaked, "Mr. Marlow!" She turned to Lilly, face stricken, and whispered tersely, "No one told me he was coming."

Was everyone afraid of this man?

Marlow dismounted. Seeing the girl, he hesitated, clearly surprised. "Miss Robbins?"

"I . . . I did not know you were coming," she said defensively.

"Nor I you." He paused, then seemed to recover. "But that doesn't mean it cannot be a pleasant surprise, does it?"

Her mouth hung loosely. "Oh. No . . ."

Francis stepped beside Miss Robbins and assumed a protective, proprietary posture, shoulders back, hands fisted at his sides. For a moment, Marlow regarded the younger man with cynical amusement, then turned at the sound of a carriage approaching.

Lilly heard Francis whisper to the girl, "Do not be uneasy. You shan't be alone."

Her attention was pulled away as a landau, driven by Marlow's coachman and with a footman in the rear, pulled up and halted in the street. The young footman hopped down and jogged over to open the door and lower the step.

But Lilly's eyes were fastened on the landau's sole occupant.

Beside her, Charlie breathed, "Miss Powell . . ." And from the corner of her eye, she glimpsed Francis elbowing him lightly in the ribs.

Lady Marlow was like a print from a ladies' magazine in a promenade dress with ribboned sleeves and a long green vest laced across her ample bosom. A hat of satin straw trimmed with feathers sat at a smart angle upon her head, showing a wealth of red ringlets at one temple.

Francis leaned close and whispered in Lilly's ear. "Now who is gaping?"

Mr. Shuttleworth drove up in his curricle, Dr. Graves beside him. At their arrival, Mr. Marlow made the introductions with practiced ease, as though he had socialized with them all many times before. "Well, now that we are all acquainted . . ."

As if on cue, Cecil Briggs drove up in the low four-wheel gill, hampers stacked in back.

"If the gentlemen would be so kind as to ride in the gill," Marlow said with a sweep of his arm, "the ladies may enjoy the comfort of fine springs and leather seats."

Francis and Charlie climbed in the back of the low wagon, but Mr. Shuttleworth said he and Dr. Graves would take his curricle.

Marlow nodded, then offered his hand to Lilly. "Miss Haswell."

Self-conscious at being singled out first, Lilly stole a sideways glance at the other two ladies. Mary looked as though she'd just sold a Rich Bride Cake—Miss Robbins as though she had a goosegog stuck in her throat.

As he helped her up into the landau, Marlow said quietly to Lilly, "What a diverting outing this is proving to be."

They quickly left the village behind, passing nearby Alton as well. The wild roses were all gone from the hedgerows, Lilly noticed, and the elderberry blossoms had given way to clusters of ripening fruit, which they would pick come October.

A few miles to the north, the carriages halted along the roadside at the foot of Walker's Hill. Mr. Marlow rode back to speak to his servants while the other men alighted. Dr. Graves offered Lilly his hand. Francis, she noticed, hurried over to help Miss Robbins down. She did not miss his reassuring smile nor the lingering press of hands.

Marlow directed the coachman to stay with his horse, the landau, and Mr. Shuttleworth's curricle. Cecil Briggs and the young footman would drive the wagon up the hill as far as they could, then haul the hampers and picnic blankets to the top from there.

While Mr. Shuttleworth transferred his telescope to the gill, the others stood clustered about, staring up at the summit.

" 'At's a gurt big hill," Charlie breathed.

Lilly shielded her eyes with a gloved hand. "A fair pitch indeed."

Miss Robbins eyed the wagon with longing.

"You may ride up if you like, Miss Robbins," Lilly offered kindly.

"All of you mean to walk?" she asked timidly, her parasol already wavering in the breeze.

Lilly nodded. "I believe so."

"Walk?" Francis said as though scandalized. He turned to Mr. Marlow. "What say you, Marlow. Shall we peg it? Have a friendly race?"

"Race?" Marlow's lip curled distastefully.

"What—afraid you'll muss your cravat?"

Lilly winced. *Careful, Francis.*

But Marlow retaliated only with words. "No, afraid you will foul the air."

Francis said easily, "I do not plan on perspiring. Do you?"

Mr. Marlow held his gaze and loosened his cravat.

Francis turned to his employer. "What about you, Mr. Shuttleworth. Are you in?"

"Good heavens." He rubbed his palms together. "Sitting about the surgery all day as I do, I haven't a chance. But why not? I shall be a buck about it." He smiled shamelessly at Mary. "Am I not a jolly buck, Miss Mary?"

She smiled indulgently. "Indeed you are, Mr. Shuttleworth."

He took off his fine coat, folded it, and laid it neatly atop the hamper. Cecil Briggs clicked the horse into action and the gill pulled away. Miss Robbins watched it go with regret.

"If I am very lucky," Mr. Shuttleworth said, "I shall swoon at the top and have four lovely ladies falling to their knees beside me, waving their fans over me and I know not what."

"What a schemer you are, Mr. Shuttleworth," Mary teased.

Stuffing his cravat into his pocket, Marlow challenged, "What about you, Graves?"

Dr. Graves shook his head. "You may count me out. I shall escort the ladies."

"I for one look forward to the climb," Lady Marlow said. "I believe exercise is beneficial for the female figure. Do you not agree, Dr. Graves?"

Dr. Graves cleared his throat.

Lady Marlow surveyed the hill once more. "Pity my husband could not join us. Sir Henry is meeting with his solicitor today, or I know he would have enjoyed this."

Lilly would not have guessed Sir Henry equal to the climb. His health must be greatly improved. Evidently marriage suited him.

Lionel Shuttleworth rolled up his sleeves. "Come on, Graves, don't be a fribble. Give me someone to beat at least."

"I shall walk up and so you shall handily beat me," Graves said.

"Indeed I shall," Shuttleworth agreed with boyish earnestness.

"And I as well, Dr. Graves," Charlie said, adopting an awkward runner's crouch. "I own I'm hudgy, but even I can beat a fellow on a wander."

Lilly bit her lip. She hoped her brother was right.

Mr. Shuttleworth urged, "Start us off, Miss Mary."

"Very well. Ready?" She held up her handkerchief, then sliced the air with a flourish. "Let the race begin!"

The men scrambled forward, Marlow nearly losing his footing on the loose rock at the bottom of the hill. Francis shot forward into an early lead. Shuttleworth ran with an upright, rooster-like stance that threatened to topple him as the pitch steepened. Marlow's long loping strides quickly overtook him. Charlie ran behind, arms windmilling, gait awkward.

"Careful, Charlie!" Lilly called after him. "Mind you don't fall and wrick your ankle!"

The three other women accompanied by Dr. Graves began a leisurely pace up the circuitous path, which climbed the hill more gradually.

Watching them stroll languidly away, Lilly thought, *Fiddle!* She hiked up her hems and ran straight up after the men. She caught up with Charlie easily and had nearly reached Mr. Shuttleworth when she heard Charlie stumble and let out an "Oomph" behind her. She stopped and helped him up, keeping a hold of his hand, thinking to jog the rest of the way side by side. But Charlie pulled away and started off once more, on his own. It stung Lilly, though she knew it should not have.

Reaching the summit first, Francis called down, "Come on, you lollopers!"

"Go, Charlie, go!" Mary shouted her encouragement from the path below.

At that, her brother gave a great burst of speed and reached the top well before her. When she did reach the ridge of flat rocks between her and the summit, Francis reached out his hand to her. Their eyes met. She wondered what he had been thinking to challenge Roderick Marlow. She wondered, too, at the strange mixture of triumph and irritation and something else in his eyes now. Still, she took his offered hand and allowed him to help her safely up and over. Charlie was dancing an ungainly victory jig. Marlow and Shuttleworth were twin bookends, panting figures with hands on knees. She walked slowly over to join them, struggling to catch her own breath. It had been too long since she had run or climbed. Her heart pounded, her lungs burned, her side ached. She felt . . . wonderful.

Tears are often the telescope by which men see far into heaven.

—HENRY WARD BEECHER

CHAPTER 35

L illy and Mary directed the arrangement of blankets and provisions atop Walker's Hill.

"Join us, Mr. Briggs?" Mary asked the groom who helped carry the hampers.

"I thank you no, mum." Cecil Briggs jerked his thumb toward the waiting horses. "My place is with the gristle and rub."

"And mine is in the kitchen," Mary said matter-of-factly, and Lilly felt a pang at her friend's humble self-regard.

"Go on now, miss," Cecil urged. "Enjoy yourself."

Mary's eyes twinkled. "You would not refuse a leg of roast chicken and an apple crowdy, would you?"

He smiled and self-consciously tugged on the brim of his hat. "That I would not."

Mrs. Tobias, the Marlows' cook, had outdone herself. There was enough food for thirty, Lilly guessed. A joint of cold roast beef, four roast chickens, two ham and veal pies, two pigeon pies, and stewed fruit in glass bottles, as well as a basket of fresh fruit, lettuces, cucumbers, and the promised lobster salad. There were also cheeses, bread, butter and jam, three pots of tea, and another hamper filled with bottles of ginger-beer, ale, lemonade, and claret, which Roderick Marlow helped himself to early and often. In her hamper, Mary had brought a large plum pudding, lardy cakes, apple crowdies, jam puffs, and a tin of mixed biscuits.

After they had eaten their fill, the ladies sat primly on the wide blankets while the men lounged at their leisure with legs outstretched.

Francis groaned with satisfaction. "I do not think I can move."

"A fine meal, Miss Mary, Marlow," Mr. Shuttleworth acknowledged, patting the buttons of his snug waistcoat.

"Yes," Lilly added. "Do thank Mrs. Tobias for us."

Marlow nodded and lifted his glass.

Mr. Shuttleworth set up his long telescope, mounted on a tripod of poles, on the ridge facing south.

Mary leaned down, her cheek bunched up as she closed one eye to look with the other through its lens. Mr. Shuttleworth hovered close, a hand lightly on Mary's shoulder to position her just so for the best viewing, clearly enjoying his role as scientific explorer—as well as the excuse to stand so near the ladies.

"There it is!" Mary exclaimed, "At least I think it must be the Salisbury Cathedral, although I have never seen it before."

"I have. Allow me." Marlow bent at the waist and peered through the lens. "Indeed. The spire of Salisbury Cathedral. It is above twenty miles from here. I would not have believed it."

As Mr. Shuttleworth and Mary stood near one another, Lilly noticed his gaze resting upon Mary's profile. He frowned slightly and peered closer yet. "I have never noticed that before."

"What?" Mary asked self-consciously.

"That little scar along your jaw. A burn, was it?"

Lilly saw her friend nod, before looking away disconcerted. Lilly felt embarrassed on Mary's behalf. She was not certain of the burn's origin but could well guess.

"Forgive me, I did not mean to give offense," he said. "Why, it is barely noticeable. It is only my being a surgeon, you see."

"That's all right. It was a long time ago." Mary stepped away. "Who is next?"

They all took turns looking through the telescope—Lady Marlow, Miss Robbins, Charlie, Francis. Lilly hung back, watching the surprise and delight on each face. Charlie likely had no real idea what he was seeing, but he seemed as caught up in the moment as everyone else.

Dr. Graves paused before taking his place at the scope. "Miss Haswell? Will you not have a turn?"

"You go on. I do not mind waiting. I am enjoying seeing it through everyone else's eyes."

Finally it was Lilly's turn. She stepped close and leaned in. She was small enough not to have to lean down very far. "I don't—no . . ."

"Here." Mr. Shuttleworth stepped in very close, nearly cheek to cheek with her, as she tilted her head away so he might take a look. "Must have been jostled. Now, try again." She felt his hand touch her shoulder, much as he had Mary's, but did not mind. There was something likeable and comfortable about Mr. Shuttleworth. And there it was. Britain's tallest spire. Could it really be twenty miles away? She remembered a few years gone, standing on Grey's Hill, wanting to come here, to see this sight, wishing she could actually travel there— travel anywhere. Now she had. She had traveled far more than twenty miles. Had lived in magnificent London. What joys she had imagined in the great *out there.* Had she found them?

She looked up and realized she was alone with Mr. Shuttleworth. Chagrined, she said, "I did not mean to monopolize it. Here. Have a go."

"If you will stay and keep me company."

"As you like."

The others had wandered back to the picnic blankets. Cecil Briggs and the footman had carried the food hampers away, but the beverage hamper and Mary's sweets hamper remained. Shoulder to shoulder at the scope, she and Mr. Shuttleworth turned their heads to regard the rest of the group.

Mary was handing Charlie the biscuit tin, and Mr. Marlow was opening another bottle of claret. Dr. Graves and Francis sat near one another, forearms resting on raised knees. Though both men stared out at the horizon, they were deep in conversation, the light of the westerly afternoon sun turning their faces golden and causing them to squint as they spoke. Miss Robbins and Lady Marlow sat together on the opposite end of the blanket, talking and laughing like old friends. How very unexpected. What a strange party they were.

Quietly, Mr. Shuttleworth said, "We stand apart, do we not?"

She turned to look at him, to search his countenance for the meaning of his odd statement. But he turned as well, so that they faced one another, noses too close together. He did have a prominent nose. She backed up a step, leaving him at the telescope. "What do you mean?"

"We are here but not here," he said softly. He turned away from her to stare out to the west, past Milk Hill to the ridgeline diminishing into the distance, the narrow canal cutting through the vale, and the horizon beyond. He looked without aid of telescope, his hand resting on its surface, chin resting on his hand.

She spoke as quietly as he had, "What do you see?"

He stared without speaking, then took a slow, deep breath. "Tomorrow. The next day. Next year."

She studied him for several moments, then asked gently, "Are you leaving us, Mr. Shuttleworth?"

He inhaled again, seeming to return to himself. "Why would I? I have my work here. I have settled here. I like life in Bedsley Priors. It is what I wanted."

Still he looked off into the distance, and she felt she understood him.

She understood that he spoke to convince himself as well as her. She understood he spoke a truth beyond his grasp.

Adam Graves felt restless at the sight of Miss Haswell and Mr.

Shuttleworth in such intimate conversation. He believed the man harmless but still resented him for monopolizing Miss Haswell. He would not be so obtuse as to join them, but nor could he sit there any longer, no matter how decent a chap Baylor seemed. He rose to stretch his legs and for respite from the incessant chatter of Lady Marlow and Miss Robbins, two lovely but vociferous creatures.

As he walked away from the group, a voice called after him. "Graves."

He looked back and saw Roderick Marlow rise a bit unsteadily to amble after him. Reaching and then passing him, Marlow climbed the steep incline to the ancient burial mound atop Walker's Hill.

He called down, "Do you know what this mound is called?" The man did not wait for a response. "Adam's Grave. Did you know it?"

"I have heard that, yes."

"Climb up with me, ol' boy."

Adam was instantly wary. "Why?"

"I want to show you something."

Adam frowned but climbed up anyway, his boots slipping on the grassy slope.

Atop the mound, Roderick Marlow flopped a heavy arm across his shoulders and laughed. "Adam Graves atop Adam's Grave. Is that not ironic? Mind you don't fall." Marlow crooked his arm around Adam's neck, an embrace bordering on a headlock. "What does Miss Haswell see in you, I wonder?" He leaned in close, nearly nose to nose with him. "You are a pretty quiz, I own."

How much claret has the man had? Adam wondered.

"You are devoted to her, are you not?" Marlow asked.

Adam pulled away, disgusted. "And you are devoted to claret."

"I am. It is my own prescription. Purely medicinal, I assure you." Marlow again peered at him. "Do you *love* Miss Haswell?"

The cheek! "That is none of your affair." He was affronted as well as perplexed. Was Marlow implying feelings toward Miss Haswell? When every patient gossiped about how the man pined for the former Miss Powell? Still, Marlow's question rang in his mind. Did he love her? He believed so. Did he not hope to marry her once he had established himself?

Adam glimpsed Lady Marlow approaching the foot of the mound. She called up to them coyly, "What are you two discussing, pray?"

"Not you, Cassandra," Marlow snapped. "Of that I can assure you."

Adam stepped nearer. "Might I offer you a hand up, Lady Marlow?"

"Thank you. At least there is one gentleman among us."

Adam gently pulled her atop the mound. The wind, even stronger at this height, threatened to loose her hat. Tendrils of red hair escaped from under it, blowing across her cheek. She was beautiful, indeed. No wonder Marlow was perturbed. He felt that man's glare upon him and turned.

Marlow looked from the lady to him. "Careful, Graves. That woman can knock the life out of you faster than any fall from Adam's Grave."

"Pay him no mind, Doctor," Lady Marlow said with a casual smile. "Mr. Marlow enjoys playing the heartbroken lover. But if you were to examine him, you would find he hasn't a heart to break."

"If I did," Roderick Marlow said, eyes hard, "you can be certain nothing you could say or do would touch it."

She seared him with a look that belied her sweet tone. "Indeed? I shall remember that, Roderick. I suggest you do so as well."

AGAINST YE FALLING SICKNESS

Take purple foxgloves and polipodium of the oak. Boil them in bear
or ale and drinke ye decoction. One that fell with [this disease]
2 or 3 times in a month, had not a fitt for 16 months after.

—17TH CENTURY RECIPE, *MYSTERY AND ART OF THE APOTHECARY*

CHAPTER 36

At church a week later, Lilly sat with Mary and Mrs. Mimpurse. As usual, Lilly's father had not felt well enough to attend and Charlie was nowhere to be found, no doubt off on one of his wanders. Even had the male members of her family seen fit to join her, she thought the Mimpurse ladies might appreciate her company on this, the seventh anniversary of the death of Harold Mimpurse.

Mr. Shuttleworth, Lilly noticed, was seated on the other side of the church and often glanced their way. *Mary's way*, she corrected herself and secretly smiled.

As Mr. Baisley was winding down his sermon, Lilly noticed something unusual. Mary's posture, as she sat beside her, was erect yet unnaturally rigid. Even as those around her flipped pages to follow along in the Book of Common Prayer, Mary's book remained perfectly still in her hands. She stared ahead, pale blue eyes unblinking.

Lilly reached over and gently squeezed her wrist. No blink, no response. She squeezed again, harder. Nothing. Around them, people flipped pages to find the final hymn, cleared throats, and upon the vicar's signal, began to sing. Still Mary stared, unmoving. Lilly shuddered. How eerie those unseeing eyes were. As if someone had put out the candle behind them. She reached over Mary's lap to tap Mrs. Mimpurse, who was singing robustly. Mrs. Mimpurse glanced over and instantly became alert. She set aside her own book and gently removed the book from her daughter's stiff fingers. She sent Lilly a pleading look, and Lilly believed she understood it.

The song over, the benediction given, the congregants rose and began to follow the vicar down the aisle. She glimpsed Francis walking out with the Robbins family and Dr. Graves offering his arm to old Mrs. Kilgrove. Only Mr. Shuttleworth showed no sign of leaving, remaining no doubt to greet them. But Lilly knew Mary would not want him to see her in such a state.

She heard a long exhalation and felt Mary go limp beside her. Using her body, Lilly gently pushed Mary toward her mother, and Maude put her arm around her daughter and pressed her cheek close to hers as though deep in whispered conversation. Lilly rose and stepped across the aisle to distract Mr. Shuttleworth.

"Is Miss Mary all right?" he asked with concern.

"She will be. It is the anniversary of her father's death. I think they are both rather melancholy at present."

"I had no idea. I am sorry to hear it. Shall I—?"

"I think we ought to leave them for now."

"Very well. I am sure you know best."

Charlie burst through the doors at that moment, the door slamming against the rear pew like cannon shot.

"Sorry I'm late," he said.

Lilly noticed mud on his face and straw in his hair. "Church is over, Charlie. Perhaps you could show Mr. Shuttleworth where Mr. Mimpurse lies?"

Her brother didn't seem to find this request at all strange, and if Mr. Shuttleworth did, he was too polite to say so.

When they departed, Lilly hurried back to Mary and Mrs. Mimpurse.

She was relieved to see her friend had returned to her senses. "Are you all right?" Lilly whispered.

"I think so. Just tired," Mary said wanly.

Tears glimmered in her mother's eyes. "Oh, my dear girl."

Together they helped Mary to her feet and out into the churchyard.

"I'll be all right, Mamma," Mary said. "Am I not always?"

Lilly spent an hour with Mary in her bedchamber that afternoon. Mary leaned back against the headboard, hugging a pillow to her chest, while Lilly sat in a chair near the window, reading to her from Byron. Finally Lilly could stifle her curiosity no longer. She lowered the book and regarded Mary until her friend's eyes rose to meet hers.

"What is it like?" Lilly asked gently.

"Hmm?"

"You know, when it happens?"

Mary fidgeted atop the bedclothes. "You have seen it yourself."

"I know what it looks like, but what does it *feel* like?"

Mary exhaled sharply. "Oh, I don't know." She looked down at her hands.

"Come on. I want to know."

Mary said brusquely, "Thank the Lord you don't." She rose and went to stare out the other window, posture rigid.

Taking in her friend's grim countenance, Lilly said, "I am sorry."

Mary stood there silently for so long, Lilly wished she had not asked.

On Tuesday Lilly watched as Mary swiftly chopped several carrots at once. The carrots lay side by side, like logs in a raft, and were each as big around as a man's finger, yet Mary cut them as easily as if they were fingers of dough.

"If I could cut pills that swiftly, my father would be rich indeed."

Mary barely seemed to look at the vegetables as she made quick work of reducing the roots into even chunks for stewing. And then her hands stilled. "You asked what it was like."

Lilly had already determined not to raise the topic again and was surprised when Mary did. "I said I was sorry."

"Don't be. Only . . . I don't much like to talk about it." Mary paused, her eyes far away. "I feel as if to even speak the words might bring on . . . well, you know."

Lilly nodded.

Mary returned to her work, chopping in silence for several minutes until Lilly was sure she had said her final word on the subject.

"It is not always the same," Mary began abruptly. "At times, like on Sunday, I just . . . go away. I sit there, eyes open, but I am not there. I feel no pain, no sensation. It is as if I am watching myself from a short distance away. Then everything goes white. When I return to myself, I am left feeling weak and tired." Mary scooped up the chopped carrots and dropped them into a pot.

Tentatively, Lilly asked, "Do you never cut yourself?"

Her friend shrugged. "Rarely. I usually have a bit of warning."

Mary then moved on to a bunch of leeks. "Other times, like when Mr. Shuttleworth was here that day . . . my head begins to ache and my fingers to tremble—or they might go numb. Either way, I usually have time to call Mamma or get to my bed—so I don't fall and injure myself."

Mary leaned her elbows on the worktable. "But then, when that sort overtakes me, I feel as though I might be sick—hot, then cold. Then everything starts clamping up, shutting down, and I find it difficult to breathe." Mary straightened and continued with her chopping. "Then my vision goes black and I wake up a quarter of an hour later to find Mamma or your father looking down at me."

"How dreadful," Lilly murmured, but she could not stop staring at the long, sharp knife so close to her friend's pale fingers. She said quietly, "I pray for you, Mary."

Mary winced. "For what?"

Lilly was taken aback. "Well, for you to be healthy—healed, of course."

Mary shrugged. "You heard Dr. Graves. There is no cure. And Wiltshire has already had its miracle." A grin flickered across her face. "We needn't be greedy."

She chopped the leeks, then looked across at Lilly earnestly. "If you pray for me, pray that I would bear this cross cheerfully. That I would be a blessing to my mother and . . . everyone."

"You already are."

Mary acknowledged this with a nod. "I overheard Dr. Foster once tell Mamma she ought to send me to an asylum. *Once*. He has not been welcome here since."

"Your mother was right," Lilly said hotly. "You do not belong in an asylum—you belong here, with those who love you."

"I know, but . . ." Mary set down the knife and wiped her hands on a towel. "There are times I think it would help to talk with someone who knows how it is. Is my experience the same as theirs, or different? Am I really as strange as I feel?"

Realizing she needed to return to the shop, Lilly rose from her stool. "I can answer that myself." She said mischievously, "You are strange indeed, Mary Helen Mimpurse."

Mary grinned and swiped at her skirts with the towel.

We must trust to the Great Disposer of all events
and the justice of our cause.

—ADMIRAL HORATIO NELSON

CHAPTER 37

L ater that day, Lilly was busy in the laboratory-kitchen preparing a strong decoction of chamomile, which they sold as a hair rinse and, separately labeled, as a wash for ailing teeth and gums. She heard Charlie rattling around in the shop, playing with the cavy most likely.

"Charlie!" she called, opening the large pot on the stove to see if the water was boiling. "Remember to take Mrs. Kilgrove her tablets. They are on the front counter."

"All right, Lilly." A moment later Charlie called, "Cavy likes chamomile, does he not?"

"What?"

"The cavy. Likes chamomile?"

Replacing the pot lid, she called back, "Yes."

Just that morning, she had pressed a bottle of chamomile tablets for Mrs. Kilgrove—they soothed her stomach and helped her sleep.

Most people made a tea of the herb for this purpose, but Mrs. Kilgrove could not abide the taste. "Smells like tobacco, tastes like fodder," she always complained. Lilly did not ask the old woman how she knew.

"Give him some?" Charlie called.

"Yes, all right. Only a few tablets. From the drawer."

Since she had used the last of the dried chamomile they had on hand, she and Charlie had harvested a batch of chamomile flowers from their garden early that morning. Her back still ached from the tedious chore.

Lilly checked the stove. She added more coals to the fire to keep the water steaming. Now she would allow the tiny blossoms to steep for half an hour.

Just in time to give over the stove to Mrs. Fowler to prepare their dinner. She was so relieved to have the dear woman back in service. She not only cooked but also took in the laundry and cleaned their living quarters.

While the blossoms steeped, Lilly spread the remaining flowers on stretched-linen screens. Then she carried the first of them up the three flights of stairs into the stifling hot herb garret, where the flowers could dry out of direct sunlight. Later, she would store the dried blossoms in tightly sealed jars.

As she came back down the stairs, she heard the shop bell ring. Wiping her hands on her apron, she stepped into the shop. Glancing around, she was surprised to find the place empty. That was not Charlie just leaving, was it? She had imagined him ten minutes gone. She checked her memory—no, she had not heard the shop bell ring earlier. What had the lad been doing since she'd asked him to take Mrs. Kilgrove her tablets? Surely it hadn't taken so long to feed a bit of herb to a caged cavy.

Though she had not wanted the animal, Lilly actually enjoyed tending and feeding it. She grimaced wryly. Now she had three males in her care. Thinking of this, she turned and walked out the garden door, striding to the plot of carrots. The cavy would need more than a few bites of chamomile for his supper.

Francis's head and shoulders appeared over the garden wall.

Eyeing the dirt-encrusted root in her hand, he asked skeptically, "Hungry?"

"I am, actually, but this is for that rodent you foisted upon me."

"Aww. Warms my heart to see you taking such good care of him."

She rinsed the carrot in the water pail. "I must. It would not help business should I fail to nurture life in any form."

"I see. Still. If you really don't want it, I suppose I could always give it to Mrs. Kilgrove. She has a cat who is ever hungry."

"You would not dare."

She shook the carrot in his direction, the wet greens splattering him with water. He ducked behind the wall and she returned to the house, swinging the carrot, humming as she went.

Undaunted, Francis followed. "Mind if I pop in and greet your father?"

She held the kitchen door open behind her. "You don't fool me. I know you really only want to see the cavy."

She thought of Charlie again. She hoped he had not gotten sidetracked on his way to Mrs. Kilgrove's. The woman would want her chamomile before supper.

"I have been reading up on lung fever," Francis said. "I trust Dr. Graves has ordered nitrate of potash or spirit of nitre?"

"Mmm . . ." she murmured noncommittally, too distracted to be impressed.

Striding back into the shop, Lilly examined the dispensing counter. The small jar of tablets she'd labeled for Mrs. Kilgrove had been taken—all seemed just as it should be.

Francis paused in the threshold. "Is your father in his surgery?"

She pointed without looking up. "Bedchamber."

Her eye was drawn to a new bottle of silvered pills at the end of the counter. The late afternoon sun shone on the glass and glimmering metallic pills. Then she noticed it. The lid askew, a disparate yellow tablet among the silver.

Dear Lord, no . . .

She turned toward the cage on the back counter. Frowning, she

298

stepped closer. Shock drove a cry from her lips, and her hand flew over her mouth.

The cavy was dead.

Lilly ran.

Pausing only long enough to shout for Francis and grasp a vial of emetic tartar, she dashed down the High Street as fast as she could.

"Charlie!" she cried as she ran. She crossed the Sands Road and followed the narrow dirt track leading to Mrs. Kilgrove's cottage. "Charlie!"

She had to catch him before he delivered those tablets . . . before the woman took them, at any rate. She recalled the labeled dosage: *two tablets with supper.* Two tablets. Two chances. How long had she stood there, speaking foolishness with Francis, while Charlie may have carried the wrong remedy to an unsuspecting woman? *Lord, please. Please. . . .*

Francis caught up with her as she reached Mrs. Kilgrove's gate. There was Charlie just outside the door. How was it he was just now arriving? Had he stopped to visit Mary on his way? Normally, she would scold him for such. Today she thanked God.

"Charlie. Wait. Don't—"

Charlie spun toward her, pale-faced. "Lilly! Somefing's wrong. Mrs. K. is pigged. I don't know what to do. I was coming to find you."

Panic seized her. "Did you give her the tablets?"

He nodded. "She were waiting for 'em like you said."

Oh, God. Oh no.

"What did she take?" Francis asked, still panting from the run.

Lilly pushed through the cottage door without answering or knocking. Mrs. Kilgrove was on the settee, holding her abdomen and groaning. Lilly hurried to her side, and in the woman's pained and confused eyes there was not one spark of recognition. Was she already experiencing delirium?

Lilly opened the vial of prepared emetic tartar and tried to press it to Mrs. Kilgrove's mouth. The old woman batted at her hands, nearly knocking the fragile vial from Lilly's grasp.

"Away!" she cried, waving her hands wildly. "Yellow smart—away!"

"Mrs. Kilgrove," Lilly said officiously, "there are no bees in here. It is Lilly Haswell. You need to drink this. Now. Do you understand?"

Francis knelt beside the woman and put his arms around her in a firm but careful hold. This done, Lilly succeeded in administering a generous dose of the vomit-inducing preparation.

Francis rose and disappeared into the kitchen.

"Charlie, run and fetch Dr. Graves," Lilly said. "Or Dr. Foster. Tell him Mrs. Kilgrove's taken digitalis not meant for her."

Francis, returning with a basin, nearly tripped at the words. He quickly laid the vessel on the floor. "I'll go," he said soberly. "I'm faster."

She nodded and laid Mrs. Kilgrove back on the settee, holding the groaning woman on her side at its edge, knowing she would be sick any moment. Lilly prayed desperately. She prayed Francis would find Dr. Graves. Or even Dr. Foster, though the old man could not run and would take far too long in hitching his gig. Only later did she consider that in coming he would have to know everything.

Several minutes later, Francis ran back in, followed by Dr. Graves, bag in hand. Both men were breathing heavily.

"I've already administered emetic tartar," Lilly said. "Though likely she would have been sick enough without it, poor creature."

"How did it happen?" Dr. Graves asked.

"I am still trying to work that out for myself."

An hour later, Lilly gazed mournfully down at Mrs. Kilgrove. The woman's lined face was grey, her body so lifeless on the bed where Dr. Graves and Francis had lain her. With remorseful tears in her eyes, Lilly slowly lifted the blanket over Mrs. Kilgrove's legs, her torso, then under her chin.

Lilly whispered, "How long will she sleep?"

300

"She is not sleeping, Miss Haswell," Dr. Graves said sternly. "She has lost consciousness."

Lilly nodded, tears spilling down her cheeks.

"Her heart rate seems to have slowed to a more normal rate, but it is irregular. We can only hope this restful state will aid her recovery."

"Will she recover?" Francis asked.

"I cannot say. She is very weak. It is too early to know if she suffered a fatal disturbance of the heart. I've administered the *de viper* antidote. Now we shall have to wait and see."

When they had removed themselves to the woman's sitting room, Lilly sat down on Mrs. Kilgrove's settee, wadding and twisting a handkerchief in her hands. Mrs. Kilgrove's cat to curl up on her lap, but Lilly firmly returned him to the floor, feeling unworthy to be comforted by his warmth. Francis sat in an armchair across from her, elbows on his knees, leaning near. Dr. Graves stood, his hand on the mantel, staring into the empty fireplace.

"I think I know what must have happened." Tears made her cheeks wet and her throat tight. "You know how Charlie is. He would have to count the yellow chamomile tablets. Then the new silvered pills must have caught his eye. We don't often do silver coatings, but Dr. Foster ordered them for Mrs. Robbins's dropsy. Charlie must have poured the pills out and counted those as well. He could not have resisted all those pretty silver pills. When I reminded him to take the tablets over, he must have quickly tried to slide the pills back into their correct bottles. In his haste, he must have mixed one or two digitalis pills in with Mrs. Kilgrove's chamomile. She must not have even noticed. Her eyesight isn't keen, you know. Poor creature! And Charlie—" She suddenly realized she had not seen her brother this hour gone. She looked around the room. "Where is Charlie?"

Francis said, "He was pegging it down the road as we ran in. Thought you must have sent him on some errand or other. And with . . . well . . . everything, I quite forgot."

New tears filled her eyes. Her facial muscles strained. "Poor Charlie! He never meant to harm anyone."

Dr. Graves's expression remained somber, but Francis said quickly, "Of course not. We all know how fond he is of Mrs. Kilgrove."

"Charlie must be frightened to death by all this. Francis, please find him. This will lay him very low, and I fear what he might do."

Francis reached over and laid his hand on hers. "You mustn't think the worst. I am sure he is in the churchyard, or one of his other haunts. I shall find him."

He gave her hand a squeeze, his eyes wide with compassion. Lilly noticed Dr. Graves frown at their clasped hands just as Francis let go and took his leave.

DEATH BY A POISONOUS HERB

Wm. Ross had or pretended to have considerable skill in the
administration of herbs. His daughter had got a root of monk's-hood in
a neighbouring garden. He mistook it for some other plant,
and commenced chewing it . . .

—DEVIZES & WILTSHIRE GAZETTE, 1833

CHAPTER 38

Ttrue to his word, Francis found Charlie—hunkered down in the
churchyard—and gently escorted him home. He had twigs in
his hair and torn breeches but was otherwise unharmed.

For two days, Lilly, Francis, Dr. Graves, and even Mr. Shuttleworth took turns sitting with Mrs. Kilgrove, spooning distilled water
and broth into her dry mouth, turning her to prevent bedsores, doing
whatever they could. By unspoken agreement, none of them mentioned
the incident to Dr. Foster, but Lilly guessed it was only a matter of
time until everyone in Bedsley Priors and Honeystreet knew of it.

Late that second day, just as Lilly feared, a sharp knock sounded
on the door. Rising from Mrs. Kilgrove's bedside, she walked slowly,
dreading to answer it. When she opened the door to Dr. Foster, his
lip curled and he brushed past her without comment. He took himself
into Mrs. Kilgrove's bedchamber, felt the woman's pulse, laid his ear

on her chest, and lifted her eyelids, testing for responsiveness. All the while, Lilly hovered in the threshold.

"So. It has finally happened," he said. "The Haswells have killed someone."

Lilly sucked in her breath. "We have killed no one, sir, and I'll thank you to lower your voice." She was fleetingly tempted to tell him it had been the pills *he'd* ordered that had done this to Mrs. Kilgrove, but she knew that was irrational. If only Dr. Graves had taken Foster's order to Shuttleworth's instead!

"Yes, she lives, but barely. And not for long, I'd wager."

"Is there nothing you can do? Or advise me to do?"

"I will do what I can, but I would not waste my breath on you, girl. You already fancy yourself too much the medical man."

"No, I have—" She hesitated. Wasn't he right? To know that she had injured, possibly even taken the life of another person was the worst feeling she had ever known. Worse even than losing her mother.

"Unprescribed digitalis. Past time that brother of yours was put away somewhere, if you ask me."

Hot indignation rose up in her, only to be quelled by an icy chill as his words registered. This man held the power to do that very thing.

When Adam Graves came to take his shift, he immediately noticed that Miss Haswell's expression was somber indeed. He could easily guess the reason. "Dr. Foster came?"

She nodded and sat heavily on the settee.

Remorse filled him. "He heard it somewhere and asked me directly. I could not lie."

"Of course not." She sighed deeply. "He all but accused us of purposefully harming Mrs. Kilgrove. Charlie would never intentionally hurt a soul. And she, always so sharp with everybody else, dotes on Charlie."

She shook her head, over and over again. Clearly the reality of what they were facing had begun to sink in. "He is so innocent, so childlike. If they were to arrest him, to take him to . . . prison, or an institution . . . I could not bear it. *He* could not bear it."

Tears cascaded down her cheeks, and he felt powerless to comfort her. He recalled how Francis Baylor had so naturally taken her hand. Why could he not do the same?

She pressed a handkerchief against the corner of one eye, then the other. "I must protect him. I love him more than my own life. Please, Dr. Graves. Please, help him."

Dread gripped him. "I will try, Miss Haswell, but what can I do? You must know Foster will report this to the constable."

"That man! Everyone knows Bill Ackers will do the bidding of whoever puts a pound in his pocket."

"But will he not bring the case to the local magistrates to make any official ruling of wrongdoing?"

"But it was a mistake! An accident!"

"Neither of which are allowed in this profession," he said, as gently as he could. "You must know that."

She hung her head. "Tell them it was my fault, then. Charlie was only acting under my authority."

He sighed. "Miss Haswell, I hate to be blunt, but you have no authority. Do you not realize what could happen if you are found guilty of poisoning someone?"

"Poisoning . . . ? What a nightmare this is! But . . . may she not yet live? Oh, God, that she might live. For all our sakes."

He paced behind the settee. "I do not know. She may yet pull through, but you should not rely on it."

She hid her face in her hands. Finally, he reached over and touched tentative fingers to her shoulder.

"I can bear the punishment, whatever it is," she said. "But Charlie must be spared."

Foolish girl! He strode around the settee to stand before her. "You don't know what you are saying. Women have been transported or imprisoned for less. And should your part reach the ears of the Worshipful Society of Apothecaries, they would be well within their rights to tear apart your father's shop, burn everything, and put him out of business for good. The Haswell's you have been trying to save could very well be ruined forever."

"But Charlie is more important than the shop. Father would not disagree."

He stared at her. "You have not told him?"

"Not yet. I fear what it will do to him."

He knelt before her to look into her eyes and gripped her hand. This was not the topic he had imagined discussing from this position. "Tell him, Lillian. You cannot bear this on your own. I will do all I can to help, but I fear it is not a great deal."

❧

Lilly was sitting in a chair beside Mrs. Kilgrove's bed when the woman's eyes fluttered opened at last.

"Mrs. Kilgrove?" Lilly reached out and grasped her spidery hand. The old woman turned watery eyes in her direction.

"Rosamond?" she whispered hoarsely. "I knew you'd return." Her head lolled to the side, and Lilly had to rise and lean over the bed to hear her murmur, "You did the first time, after all."

Lilly's heart hammered. "What do you mean, Mrs. Kilgrove?"

But the old woman did not answer, merely squinted toward the bedside table. "Why do the candles wear blue halos?" Her eyes closed and she said no more.

Mrs. Kilgrove was seeing things, Lilly realized. Had even mistaken her for her mother. No doubt what she had said about Rosamond's return had been wild imaginings as well.

Despite the poor woman's hallucinations, a tentative, fluttering hope filled Lilly's breast. She tamped it down, lest it fly away at any moment. Fearing the old woman might yet take a turn for the worse, she waited and prayed. Her father came, brought by Charlie's racked confession. There was nothing he could do, but it was still a relief to hear him confirm everything that could be done for Mrs. Kilgrove had been done. Later, the vicar came to pass an hour with her at Francis's behest, offering words of comfort and prayer in his mellifluous voice.

That evening, Mrs. Kilgrove again opened her eyes. She turned to Lilly with a weak smile. "How nice to wake with someone beside me. Haven't known that comfort since my John died a day back agone."

"I am glad to be here," Lilly said. "Do you know me?"

Mrs. Kilgrove frowned. "Foolish girl," she whispered. "Have I not known you since an infant?"

"Yes, but you've been unconscious." She did not add *delirious.* "How do you feel now?"

"Queer. My head aches." She slowly moved her gaze across the room. "And everything seems rather . . . yellow."

"Mrs. Kilgrove, do you remember the pills you took—the ones I sent over?"

She squinted in attempted concentration. "I don't . . . to help me sleep?"

"Just so, and to calm your stomach. I am afraid there might have been one or two wrong pills in the lot. Do you remember taking any silver pills?"

She winced. "Lass, I am near eighty years old. I am happy to remember my name, much less the color of a pill I took . . . when was it?"

"Three nights gone."

"Three nights? Some pills . . ." Her eyes drifted closed once more.

❧

The next morning when Mrs. Kilgrove awoke, Lilly and Charlie were both with her. Charlie sat in a bedside chair, the woman's cat on his lap. When he saw her eyes open, his voice shook. "I am dreadful sorry, Mrs. K." Tears filled his wide blue eyes.

Mrs. Kilgrove turned her head toward him and reached out a shaky hand. "No need. I don't blame you, Charlie. You may be small in the attic, but you have a big heart."

Charlie bit his pronounced lip and ducked his head.

"Mrs. Kilgrove, will you take some water?"

The woman turned sharp eyes in her direction. "Why—is there no tea?"

Biting back a smile, Lilly rose to prepare some. While she was at it, she set a pan of broth to warming on the stove, broth Mrs. Mimpurse had kindly sent over, firmly believing the invalid would regain consciousness as well as appetite. Lilly certainly hoped she was right.

Francis Baylor was on his way to visit Mrs. Kilgrove and, if he were honest with himself, to see Lilly, who stayed so loyally by the woman's side. He knew he was a fool. Graves, a good-looking, Oxford-educated physician, was courting her, was he not? Francis sighed. Still, he would do anything to help her.

From the corner of his eye, he glimpsed Dr. Foster disappearing into Ackers Stables and Smithy, the establishment of Bill Ackers, the county-appointed constable of the neighbor villages.

His stomach seized at the thought of what trouble Ackers could bring down on the Haswells, and he knew the man was more than capable of doing so with relish. Francis changed course and crossed the road, stepping surreptitiously near the open stable door.

"Will you fail in your duty, Ackers?" He heard Foster say, voice sharp. "There has been a crime, man. A devilish crime."

Francis blew out a puff of air. *Worse than I feared.*

"You'd like 'at, would'n ye?" Bill Ackers spoke in a voice passed down from generations of family members who'd never ventured beyond Wiltshire. "Haswell's dippin' in yer pockets, innum?"

"No. He is nothing to me."

"Now, long as the woman lives, there's been no murder, mind. And no one's gawpus enough to believe 'at young dummel meant to harm the old ghel."

"It is a fine thing when a body can poison an innocent person in your village, Ackers."

"Now, Foster. Let's not jarl. You know I'll be watchin'. And when summateruther happens, I'll see to it, I will."

"I am very glad to hear it."

There was a pause. Thinking the conversation at an end, Francis was about to move away when Dr. Foster spoke again.

"Perhaps, Mr. Ackers, we might discuss this further at the Hare and Hounds? I for one grow thirsty standing here."

"If yer buying, I'll go along," Bill Ackers said. "Always were a fair-minded man."

A robin red breast in a cage
Puts all heaven in a rage.

—WILLIAM BLAKE, *AUGURIES OF INNOCENCE*

CHAPTER 39

As Charlie was finishing his breakfast of eggs and sausages the next morning, Lilly slipped briefly from the kitchen, then returned with arms full. "I have something for you, Charlie."

Still chewing, Charlie's gaze tracked her progress across the room. At her mother's old place at the table, Lilly set down a bandbox with bored-out air holes. Anticipation prickled within her as she watched her brother's face. Though his memory was poor, she thought she saw a glint of recognition in his blue eyes.

He swallowed his bite and said, "I had somefing very like it once."

"Indeed you did. I am pleased you remember."

A flick of white batted against one of the holes and disappeared. Charlie's eyes grew wide. "Am I to have a puss?"

With effort, she kept her voice calm. "Open it and see."

Still he hesitated.

"Go on."

Charlie carefully removed the lid. A young cat, older than a kitten but not fully grown, lifted his grey head and put two white paws on the edge of the box. He sniffed the air, and when Charlie offered him his fingers, sniffed those too.

"Hallo, boy." Charlie looked up at her anxiously. "He is a boy, innum?"

"I am no expert on such, mmm, identification, but Mr. Fowler assures me this is indeed a male."

"Good. 'Twould be a queer fing to call a girl-cat Jolly."

Her heart warmed and ached at once. "Is that what you will call him?"

He nodded. "Does he look like the first Jolly, Lilly? I can't remember."

"Well, I do remember, and he looks a great deal like your old Jolly. I daresay this lad is his grandson or grandnephew."

"Oh, 'at's fine! Fine!"

But then Charlie's smile faded. He faltered, "But she said I weren't ever to have another."

"She . . ." Lilly hesitated, then said gently, "Mother is gone. But Father and I want you to have it."

"But what if he runs away again?"

Lilly answered thickly, "Then I shall help you find him. And you will love him and care for him better than anyone in Bedsley Priors. As I love you."

The cat put its muzzle close to Charlie's face, sniffing his cheek and mouth.

Lilly smiled through her tears. "He seems to like you a great deal already."

Charlie stroked the cat. "I fink he does. Or the milk I drank wi' breakfast."

"Look how gentle you are with him."

"Mrs. K. taught me."

A movement caught her eye, and Lilly looked up to see her father leaning against the doorjamb. Their gazes met for several ticks of the clock, and she saw that hers were not the only eyes filled with tears.

❧

Three days later, just before closing time, Bill Ackers strode boldly into the shop. Lilly felt her heart jerk as wildly as from foxglove itself. Ackers was a big, broad man in his late twenties with arms strong from his smithy work and years of starting and breaking up fights. Broom in hand, Charlie froze, staring up at the man.

"Charlie Haswell, there thee bist. I've come for ye."

Charlie's mouth drooped open. "She died, did she, Mr. Ackers? Poor Mrs. K. gone to the churchyard?"

"Not yet, she ain't. No thanks to you and yers."

"Thank God," Lilly breathed.

"There's still wrongdoin' to be answered for, lad. That's why I'm come to take ye in."

"To the blind house, Mr. Ackers?" Charlie asked.

"Aye."

"Mr. Ackers," Lilly protested, panic rising. "If anyone is to blame, it is I."

"You poisoned Mrs. Kilgrove then?"

"No one *poisoned* Mrs. Kilgrove. That word conveys such vile intent, does it not? A mistake has been made, I own. She swallowed one small pill of the wrong sort. Not poison. Not for a healthy stout person. But for an eighty-year-old woman . . ."

"I have it on good authority that givin' a person the wrong medcine is a crime, Miss Haswell, no matter the old ghel's age. And seein' how it might yet lead to her death, can ye deny it?"

"No. Of course it is wrong. And I do not expect all consequences to be waived. But it is *my* fault, the shop is my responsibility."

"Is it now? Might yer father have sumat to say about that?"

"Father is recovering from an illness, Mr. Ackers. In his stead, I have temporarily assumed responsibility. It was I who filled the pill bottle and I who left the wrong pills in proximity to the first. Charlie was only the delivery boy."

"Yer telling me *you* put the wrong pill in 'er bottle?"

She swallowed. "Well. Not actually physically put it there, but in effect, by my negligence, yes."

"And who actually, physically, put it there?" A dark glint lit his eyes.

She changed tack. "Am I to be brought before the magistrates, Mr. Ackers?"

"Might come to that, aye. Need to hold 'im till the next quarter session in Devizes. Though in yer brother's case, I'm thinkin' the JPs might forgo county gaol or transportation."

"Oh?" Tentative relief sprouted within.

"I understand there are places for imbeciles like Charlie. Where he'd be kept safe and do no harm to others."

Relief quickly withered. "He is not an imbecile, and he does no harm to others now!"

"I've got a woman courtin' death who just might jarl with'ee. If she lives, that is." He smirked at his macabre joke.

Suspicion filled her. She narrowed her eyes at the man, her head tilted to one side. "How would you know about such institutions? Dr. Foster put you up to this, did he not?"

"I may have asked the man's advice. But I act on my own authority. Maybe I ought to take ye both in till we get this sorted out. Fisherton Anger has a women's prison too."

"No!" The vehemence of Charlie's shout startled her and the broom handle cracked to the floor. "Lilly did nofing wrong. Never has. It was me what done it, Mr. Ackers. Don't know how, but must have done. Leave Lilly be."

"That's to yer credit, Charlie. I daresay there might be a jobbet of man in'ee after all."

As Charlie stepped forward, Lilly took his arm. "Charlie, no."

"Lilly?" Her father appeared in the doorway, fatigue and concern in his eyes.

"He's taking Charlie!" Her voice rose. "To the blind house."

"It's all legal, Haswell," Ackers said. "I'll be holdin' 'im till a hearing is set."

Father slumped against the doorjamb. "Take me, then, Ackers. It is my shop, after all."

"Don't look to me like ye can barely stand, let alone stand trial. Weren't even in the shop the day it happened, now were ye?"

"I . . . don't know. When was it?"

Lilly answered quietly, "You were abed all day, Father."

"Seems every Haswell's in an awful hurry to bear the blame," Ackers said. "Would ye rather I locked yer ghel in the blind house, Haswell? We've only the one drunkard presently—might not go too hard on her."

"Of course not, man."

"It's all right, Father," Charlie said. "I don't mind. Mind less if 'ere were windows."

"Then it wouldn't be a blind house, now would it?" The constable turned harsh eyes on Lilly. "Not an imbecile, innum?"

Her father launched himself from the threshold but stumbled and nearly fell, barely managing to take hold of the dispensing counter for support.

Lilly ran to help him, and Ackers took advantage of the diversion. He grasped Charlie's arm and led him from the shop without interference. He wasn't violent but did stride rapidly, pulling gangly Charlie along behind him like a floppy fish on a line.

Trying to hold her father upright, Lilly called, "Charlie!"

Her brother looked back over his shoulder. "Take care of Jolly. And tell Mary, so she don't fret where I've gone."

"I'll come as soon as I can!" But the door was already closed, shop bell jingling, and she knew he could not have heard her.

Her father slipped lower, and taking his arm, she helped him onto the surgery cot without injury. She knelt beside him, dread filling her anew at the sight of his grey face and trembling limbs. "Are you all right?"

He fell back against the pillow. "So detestably weak . . ."

Indeed he seemed worse than ever. And now Charlie

imprisoned—what a double blow this was! Covering her father with the lap rug, she tried to keep the panic from her voice. "What will they do to him? Will he be whipped? Put in an institution? Transported?"

"I do not know. Which is the least of evils? Which should we pray for?"

She noted his rare mention of prayer, and knew he must feel as desperate as she.

"A miracle. We need another Wiltshire miracle."

Grief and fear overwhelmed her. Tears streaming down her face, Lilly bolted from the shop. Her first impulse was to run to the arms of Mrs. Mimpurse and Mary, but she knew they were visiting Maude's sister in Wilcot. She thought of running up Grey's Hill, but for once the thought of its wild loneliness didn't draw her. She felt too alone already.

As she dashed through the village, the quiet churchyard called to her. She paused at its gate, then turned and walked up the stone path to the old church. The door creaked in her hands as it opened to the dim, quiet interior. She entered slowly, her boot heels disturbing the silence and echoing against the limestone walls. There seemed no one about, and that suited her. It was not a mere human's presence she sought. She stepped through the nave and into the chapel.

She sat in the front pew, where Haswells had sat for a hundred years. Where her mother had once sat in her fine frocks and plumed hats, and her father in his dark blue Sunday coat, Charlie on his lap, little eyes staring at the stained glass, counting the individual panes, no doubt. How long ago it seemed since they had all sat there as a family. They would never do so again.

Lilly fell to her knees on the stone floor, driven there by losses of the past . . . and by probable losses of the near future.

Oh, Lord, please spare my brother and father. I have already lost my mother. I cannot bear to lose them as well. . . .

How long she stayed like that, on her knees, head bent and eyes closed, she could not say. Vaguely, she heard a door open, footsteps echo in the nave, and the clank of something metallic. But the sounds took several seconds to fully register. When she came to herself with a start, embarrassed to be found in such a humble position, she tried to quickly rise. Only to realize she could not.

"Lilly?" a surprised voice asked.

The chapel seemed completely dark at first, but as her eyes adjusted, she saw the faint glow of a lantern or candle somewhere nearby.

Her discoverer knelt before her. Francis.

"Lilly!" Concern sharpened his voice, though it was still hushed in that reverent place. "Here, let me help you up."

"I am afraid my legs have fallen asleep. I cannot feel them."

He took her hands to pull her up but hesitated, holding her fingers more tightly. "Your hands are chilled!" He released them to grasp her arms. "A little at a time, all right?" Gingerly, slowly, he helped her up onto the bench. As he did, she realized the clank she had heard must have been the sound of a lantern being set hastily on the floor. Its light flickered dimly down the aisle.

"Here now, let's get some life into those limbs." He rubbed her hands, first briskly, then kneading them more deeply.

"My knees—"

She'd only meant to comment on how strange they felt, numb yet prickling with pins and needles at the same time. But Francis took her words as plea and began working on her knees as well, massaging her estranged appendages. Though his touch was professional and her modesty secure beneath her sturdy kerseymere frock, still the act felt unquestionably intimate. His administrations at first intensified the pain, but gradually the pins faded and warmth spread through her.

He returned his attention to her hands. "Still cold."

She allowed him to caress and knead her hands, sudden tears pricking her eyes. How nice to feel cared for. An old memory unwound itself in her mind's eye—her father cupping her little face with both palms. *"Patient has no fever, but suffers a fatal case of good looks and freckles."*

"Here." Francis dropped her hands and leapt to his feet. She missed his touch immediately.

He hurried down the aisle, retrieved his lantern, and sat beside her again. "Warm your hands over this."

She eagerly complied.

While she did so, he said, "May I ask what brings you here tonight? Your father?"

She nodded, tears filling her eyes anew. "And Charlie . . ." She told him about the constable taking him away and her father's recent collapse. She felt more than saw him grimly shake his head in the dim light, her hands masking much of the lantern's glow.

Setting the lantern on the floor before them, he pulled off his coat and laid it over her shoulders, enveloping her in warmth and lingering aromas of herbs and woodsmoke. He took her hand in his once more. "All right if I pray for you?"

She hesitated. "Now?"

He nodded.

"Aloud?"

He pursed his lips. "Unless you'd prefer to read my thoughts?"

She bit her lip. "Very well."

Francis bowed his head, the lantern light glimmering on his profile. When had his jaw become so square, and hints of a beard begun to show at the end of day?

"Gracious Father, please look with compassion upon the Haswell family. Have mercy upon Charlie in his present danger. Relieve the pangs of Mr. Haswell's disease, and avert from him all lasting harm. Give Lilly strength to bear these afflictions, and comfort them all. Grant this for the sake of our blessed Saviour, in whose holy name we pray. Amen."

"Amen," Lilly echoed softly, warmed by his words, lofty yet so sincere. She felt a new flutter of hope lift her spirits.

She soon became self-conscious, sitting so close to Francis in the dark, quiet place. Gently pulling her hand from his, she straightened and looked up at the chancel, shadowy in the flickering light. She asked lightly, "Have you not enough of this place on the Sabbath?"

He leaned back against the pew. "Well, with all the page turning and hymn singing and sermon listening—of which I approve, don't mistake me—little time remains for quiet reflection."

"Could you not do that in your lodgings? Now that the roof is repaired, I mean."

He laughed softly. "I attempt it. But as well as Mr. Shuttleworth and I get on, it is tiring to be always in the society of one's employer. And, well . . . the man does love to sing. Often. And with great enthusiasm."

Lilly chuckled. "Most men would flee to the Hare and Hounds or the coffeehouse."

"No doubt. But I cannot afford to go every night like Mr. Shuttleworth is wont to do. I keep a few eggs, bread, and cheese in the larder and do well enough on my own most meals."

"You seem quite concerned about money, Mr. Baylor. Is Mr. Shuttleworth not fair in your wages?"

"He is more than fair. I . . . well, my wages are not for spending."

"Then what?"

He took a deep breath and shifted on the bench. "Let's talk of something else."

"Very well. What do you reflect upon when you come here?"

She felt him shrug.

"Whatever is in my thoughts at the time. My father was such a man. He would always talk over his decisions before he made them."

"With your mother?"

"With her as well. My father was a North Somerset fisherman. He always said if the apostles needed the Lord to tell them where to cast their nets, then he could do no better than to ask the Almighty for direction as well." As the echo of his words faded, he looked over at her. "Do you feel ready to stand now?"

"Of course." She rose tentatively, and he took her hand, deftly moving it to his arm for support.

"I shall walk you home." He picked up his lantern.

"What of your time of quiet reflection?"

"Oh, I think I came here for a different reason tonight."

As they stepped out into the churchyard, she studied his profile in the moonlight. "Are you really so changed?" she asked.

"I hope I am more responsible than I was as a lad, but that is only to be expected." He walked beside her up the High Street. "You know, a decade ago, had a young man and woman been seen coming out of a dark building alone together . . . why, their parents would have seen them married by morning."

"Do not fret, Mr. Baylor," she said on a laugh. "No one will force you to the altar."

"I was not fretting in the least."

His tone was perfectly serious, and she felt oddly disoriented as their light banter fell away, replaced by an awkward silence.

He cleared his throat. "But I . . . understand that may soon be another man's privilege."

She let the comment fade away. It would be indiscreet and premature to confirm such a presumption. Dr. Graves *had* moved from London to be near her, had he not? She was grateful he was not pressing her with a declaration, instead giving her time to help her father, to see him well again. And now to help Charlie too. She was fond of Francis, but could not let him distract her from a gentleman like Dr. Graves.

When they reached Haswell's, Francis said, "I will continue to pray for you and every member of your family, dispersed as they are." He squeezed her hand. "I will also see what can be done."

I once was lost, but now am found,
Was blind, but now I see.

—John Newton, *Amazing Grace*, 1772

Chapter 40

The blind house was like a round, windowless granary with a cone-shaped roof. Most villages in Wiltshire and surrounding counties kept such a building to temporarily confine wrongdoers.

Lilly knocked on the locked door. "Charlie? Are you all right?"

Hearing nothing, Lilly pressed her ear to the door. She heard a shuffle, then Charlie's muffled voice. " 'Tis awful dark, Lilly. Nofin' to see."

"We shall get you out, Charlie. As soon as we can."

"Nofin' to see . . ."

At the distress in her little brother's voice, she pressed her forehead to the wood, blinking back tears.

"Try counting sounds, Charlie," she said, injecting false calm into her voice. "Bird calls, passing horses. Whatever you hear, all right?"

No response. Then a feeble, "All right . . ."

Oh, God, Lilly prayed, *this will not do. Please help us.*

❧

"It is a medical matter. An apothecary matter," Charles Haswell asserted, slowly shuffling across the surgery. "Perhaps we should suggest Ackers report it to the Society and let *them* dole out reprimand or consequence to me as they see fit."

"Would that satisfy Ackers?" Lilly asked, relieved to see her father on his feet. He had even felt strong enough to walk across the village that morning to speak with Charlie through the blind house door. Dr. Graves had given him sweet spirit of nitre, as Francis had suggested. The liquid preparation clearly had some effect, though it remained to be seen how long the improvement would last.

"I don't know. He'd like to get his own pound of flesh, I'd wager. Worse yet, if someone else is pulling his strings."

"Dr. Foster?"

"Would not surprise me in the least."

She'd had the same thought. "Should I call on Mr. Ackers and suggest he refer the case to the Society?"

Charles Haswell ran a weary hand over his stubbled cheeks. "Bill Ackers write a letter? I'd as soon believe the claims of a Cornhill quack."

Lilly was having her tea alone when Maude Mimpurse let herself in the kitchen door. She had been incensed when Lilly had told her the news and had promised to see Charlie just as soon as she could get away.

Over one arm Mrs. Mimpurse bore the straps of a worn leather market bag, in her free hand, a quart jar. A delicious smell of pastry and savory sauce emanated from the bag.

Seeing Lilly eye her burden, Maude explained, "Two gurt meat-and-potato pasties and a jar of honey tea. Charlie's favorite."

Lilly rose from the table. "But do you think Mr. Ackers will allow it?"

Mrs. Mimpurse snorted. "You leave Billy Ackers to me."

Her father was in his surgery with Mr. Fowler. But even if she'd had to leave the shop unattended, Lilly would not miss this chance to see Charlie face-to-face.

A quarter of an hour later, coat and blanket in arms, Lilly strode beside Mrs. Mimpurse as the woman marched smartly along the hedgerow. Lilly kept up easily, but Bill Ackers—whom Maude had cajoled from his smithy—trudged begrudgingly behind.

"Do keep up, Billy. These pasties won't stay warm forever."

Reaching the blind house first, Maude and Lilly waited for the constable to catch up. "Do hurry, Billy. My coffeehouse won't run itself."

"My smithy either," he grumbled. Taking out a pair of old heavy keys, Bill Ackers unlocked the blind house door. "Step back, Charlie," he called gruffly.

Incredulous, Maude said, "As though a lamb like Charlie would run away? Really, Billy."

"All right. Hand 'im 'is supper."

"Indeed I will not. Why can he not sit here in the sunlight and eat his meal with dignity?"

"He's not on holiday, mum."

"Nor is he an animal. Come out, Charlie. I have a nice supper for you."

Charlie emerged from the darkness and hesitated at the threshold, eyes squinting. Lilly's heart ached to see it.

"Poor love!" Mrs. Mimpurse tutted. "You come out nice and slowlike, Charlie. No hurry."

Bill Ackers sighed.

Glancing shrewdly at him, Mrs. Mimpurse handed him one of the pasties. "For your trouble, Billy."

Four days later, when the post came, Lilly received two letters. One was an all-too common request for payment, but the second set her palms to perspiring.

She found her father alone in the surgery, looking through the newest dispensatory Mr. Shuttleworth had loaned him.

"It is a letter, Father, as I feared. From the Worshipful Society of Apothecaries. It appears Mr. Ackers wrote to them after all."

"I cannot credit it."

"Who else could it be? Foster could have nothing to do with apothecaries, could he? When he so clearly loathes the lot of us?"

He shrugged uneasily. She held out the letter, but he waved it away. "You read it."

She broke the seal and unfolded the fine stationery. " 'The Court of Examiners at Apothecaries' Hall, Blackfriars, London.' "

He frowned. "Spare me the friggling and just lay out the worst."

"Very well. 'It has been reported that one Charles Haswell III has dispensed an adulterated, potentially harmful drug.' "

Her father thundered, "They haven't even the facts!"

" 'Upon receiving any further such reports, the Society will have no alternative but to pursue formal action. Proceedings will then be taken against said person.' "

"Said person? Formal action—all the way from London? Fuss and nonsense. What a narration about nothing."

"I am not so certain it is."

"Is that all it is to be, then? A threat? A slap on the wrist from afar?"

"I can hardly credit it," Lilly said. "Can this really be all?"

"I would wish it so."

"Wishing isn't enough, Father. We must pray it so as well."

Her father stared out the surgery window. "Now, if only we could convince Ackers."

The days passed slowly, and Lilly found the wait interminable. Rarely had she felt so helpless, so frustrated, so afraid. She visited Charlie every day, as did Mrs. Mimpurse, Mary, Francis, and her father, when he was able. And she prayed. But as Charlie's imprisonment approached a fortnight, she felt her faith flagging. Had she not prayed for her mother's return to no avail? Her father's healing? Did it really make any difference?

Then, in a moment, everything changed. One minute she and her father were despondently sitting before plates of food neither saw nor wanted, and the next there was Charlie in the doorway. Dirty, odiferous, and wonderful to behold.

"Enough for one more?" he asked, looking at their breakfast.

Lilly gasped, leapt to her feet, and grabbed her brother in a fierce hug. Her father raised himself on shaky legs and squeezed Charlie's shoulder before sinking heavily into his chair. His improvement had not lasted.

"Sit down, Charlie. I can barely believe it. Tell us what happened."

He sat, and they both looked at him expectantly. Charlie eyed her breakfast once more.

"Oh, here." She pushed her untouched plate before him.

They waited impatiently while he took several bites, and then Lilly prompted again. "What happened?"

Charlie shrugged, and said around a bite of cold ham, "Mr. Ackers comes in and says, 'Charlie lad, it's yer lucky day. Mr. Marlow says you work for him and he wants you back. He's responsible for you now, so no more nanny fudgin' about.' "

Lilly shook her head, stunned. "I cannot believe it. Mr. Marlow! And when he had already released you from your contract."

"Must need me straightaway for his gurt garden."

Lilly doubted the garden was in such dire need, but forbore to say so. She did not doubt Mr. Marlow's influence over the constable as leading landowner and future baronet. Beyond that, the two had been boyhood friends. She fleetingly wondered how she had not thought to request his help herself.

"Well," Lilly said, relief flooding her, "we shall have to go and thank Mr. Marlow personally."

After breakfast, she and Charlie hitched up Pennywort and drove the gig to Marlow House. As they drew near, Charlie saw Mr. Timms clipping privet near the fountain and asked to be let down to speak to him. "Very well. But come to the house as soon as you've done so."

She turned the horse toward the stables, but instead of Cecil Briggs coming to take the reins, Roderick Marlow himself strode out, dressed in riding coat and Hessian boots.

Flushed and breathless at his sudden appearance, she burst out, "Mr. Marlow, I have come to thank you."

A smile slowly formed on his aquiline countenance as he looked up at her. "Your brother has been released?"

"Yes, thanks to you."

"I am pleased to hear it." He led her horse and gig into the stable yard.

She stood, preparing to climb down. Lifting his hands, he grasped her by the waist and effortlessly carried her to the ground. She felt her cheeks flush anew. A simple hand down would have sufficed.

"You are very kind. Charlie is with Mr. Timms, but I know he will want to thank you. I'll—" She turned to fetch Charlie, but Mr. Marlow took hold of her wrist, halting her departure.

"Please wait." Hand still holding hers, he led her into the stable office. "I am glad for your brother, but do not paint me a saint. I confess I thought only of you."

She inhaled deeply. Her heart beat with heavy thuds. Would he always have such an effect on her?

"I don't know what to say."

"Miss Haswell, speechless?" He grinned. "I am all astonishment."

She tried to smile in return, but her awe was such that her lips only managed a tremble.

He slowly shook his head. "What a man would do, to have a woman forever look at him the way you are regarding me." He reached out and traced a finger along her jawline and chin. "I should very much like to kiss you, Miss Haswell."

She swallowed.

"I must also own that I have never before asked permission."

She said shakily, "You have kissed a great many women, then?"

He considered this. "I would not say a *great* many. But I have never kissed you, Miss Haswell. That I would remember."

She stared at him, mesmerized by his unusual eyes. One a shade darker than the other. Or was one green and the other brown?

"Miss Haswell?"

"Oh!" She started. "Forgive me."

He leaned down. "Here, now you may examine me more closely."

For a moment, she did just that. Studied his eyes, his dark lashes and brows. His prominent cheekbones and pinpricks of black whiskers beneath fair skin.

"Anything amiss?" he asked. "A sty, perhaps?"

She shook her head, still regarding him, his thin lips and sharp nose, the nostrils which seemed to flare at her close inspection.

When she returned her gaze to his eyes, she saw that they gleamed with suppressed laughter. "Have I need of an apothecary, or might a kiss suffice?"

She bit her lip. "I cannot give you leave to kiss me."

He sighed dramatically. "Which is why I never ask first."

She squared her shoulders. "But perhaps I might kiss your cheek, Mr. Marlow. For saving my brother."

His brows rose. "A gratitude kiss? Not my favorite sort."

Feeling foolish, she began to turn away. "Never mind, then."

He gently turned her back to face him. "No. Please never mind *me*. I dearly long for a gratitude kiss from you, Miss Haswell."

She realized he was likely mocking her, but her thankfulness overwhelmed every other emotion.

He bent low again, face near. She would not have reached him otherwise. His hands, she surmised, were now safely behind his back. Safe enough, she hoped.

She leaned forward slowly, aiming for his cheek. He shifted and she kissed his lips instead. Their lips touched for a lingering moment. One heartbeat, then two. When she pulled away, the laughter had altogether gone from his eyes.

The fashion hails—from countesses to queens,
And maids and valets waltz behind the scenes. . . .

—Lord Byron

Chapter 41

In the coffeehouse dining room, Lilly helped Mary with the heavy task of pushing all the tables to one side and stacking chairs, preparing to mop the entire floor. Surveying the open space, Lilly dramatically stood her mop straight, head up, and curtsied before it.

"I would be delighted to dance with you, sir," she said. With a bend of her elbow, the mop-haired "gentleman" tilted toward her in a bow. Grasping her stick-thin partner with both hands, Lilly performed a spinning dance around the cleared room.

Leaning on a second mop, Mary grinned and shook her head. "You can take the lady out of London . . ." She let the words trail away. She studied Lilly's whirling steps. "I have not seen that dance before."

"It is the dreaded turning waltz."

"No," gasped Mary in feigned shock. "Not the scandalous dance condemned by all the papers."

Lilly halted and propped her mop against the wall. "The very same. Might I tempt you into learning it?"

"Never," Mary said coyly. "I am far too proper for such wickedness."

Lilly raised an eyebrow. "The Mary Mimpurse who spied the cricket team swimming in the Owens' pond? I think not."

Tugging the mop from Mary's hand and standing it beside her own, Lilly grasped Mary about her waist and pulled and spun her around the room, until they nearly collided with the stacked chairs.

"Please, Lill, stop," Mary gasped. "I am dizzy!"

Lilly halted abruptly, still holding on to Mary as her friend regained her balance and breath. "Are you all right?" she asked, concerned.

Breathing hard, Mary said, "I am not having a fit, if that is what you mean. Unless you mean a fit of the vapors."

Assured her friend was all right, Lilly released her.

"That dance will *not* be performed at Wilcot, I assure you," Mary said, refastening a hairpin that had come loose whilst spinning.

"Even so, how I look forward to the country dance." Lilly retrieved her mop and dipped it into the bucket near the hearth. She slanted a glance at Mary. "And I know a certain surgeon-apothecary who looks forward to dancing with you."

Mary bit back a smile of pleasure. "I own a certain gleeful anticipation of that myself."

After the trying days of Charlie's imprisonment, they were all looking forward to Wilcot's end-of-summer fete, which was to include both a fair and a dance. She and Mary planned to attend with Charlie, Dr. Graves, and Mr. Shuttleworth. No doubt Francis and Dorothea Robbins would attend as well.

But on Saturday, her father awoke with a fever, and Lilly felt obliged to stay with him.

"Then I shall stay as well," Mary said, though her countenance was decidedly downcast.

"And leave all those fine partners to Miss Robbins alone? I think not. You know Mr. Shuttleworth and Charlie will be exceedingly disappointed if you do not attend."

Mary grinned. "They would, would not they?"

"Of course. Now go and be danced off your feet, my lovely, as you well deserve."

Mary's eyes sparked with mischief. "I shall benefit from your absence in that regard, shan't I?"

"Oh!" Lilly winked. "I can see how much I shall be missed!"

That afternoon, Dr. Graves called on her father, prescribed fever powder, fluids, and bed rest. He was disappointed to learn she would not be attending the Wilcot fair. "I would not go either," he said sheepishly. "But Dr. Foster requests it. Says I should make the acquaintance of as many potential patients as possible. But I shall not dance, Miss Haswell—you may depend upon it."

"I do not wish to depend upon it! I hope you will dance, especially should gentlemen be scarce and ladies be in want of a partner."

She thought of her own first dance with Dr. Graves and hoped no lady would have to endure such a reluctant performance.

He said quietly, "I did not come all this way to dance with other ladies, Miss Haswell."

She smiled shyly up at him. "Just don't enjoy it overly much and I shall be satisfied."

He grinned. "When have I ever?"

Lilly looked up from her book to the sitting room clock once more. Two hours had slowly passed. It felt like more. Her father was sleeping peacefully and the novel was not engaging. Perhaps she should just give it up and go to bed.

An unexpected knock sounded on the sitting room door. Before she could react, Francis stepped in, looking masculine and handsome in his dark coat and trousers, hat in hand.

She rose. "Francis. What are you doing here?"

"I could not enjoy myself, knowing you were not."

She was pleased and anxious at once. "You needn't have come. There is no use in the both of us missing out."

"I don't mind."

"But Miss Robbins mentioned you were quite the accomplished dancer."

"Mr. Shuttleworth has taught me a few things, I own." His eyes gleamed. "Now, there's a sight not to be missed. Mr. Shuttleworth in purple coat and gold waistcoat, prancing the fancy steps of a cotillion."

She chuckled. "I can well imagine. But I should have liked to see you dance as well. No doubt Miss Robbins was counting on you as a partner."

He shrugged easily. "She was dancing with Mr. Marlow when I left, Mr. Shuttleworth awaiting the next."

She wondered if he was disappointed. Was that why he had returned?

He said kindly, "You have had little entertainment since returning, Miss Haswell, and far too much work. I am sorry *you* had to miss it. I hope your father is better."

"Yes, the fever has broken. He is resting comfortably."

"Good. Good."

They stood awkwardly for a few moments, until Francis said, "Mary told me about the dance lesson you gave her. That *I* was sorry to miss."

Lilly screwed up her face. "I would never have done so with an audience."

He smiled, a warm glint in his chocolate-brown eyes. "As you said, there is no point in both of us missing the evening's entertainment. We might have a dance here."

"Here?" She looked skeptically around the small room.

"Why not? We could try that turning waltz Mary described. Though I am surprised your aunt and uncle allowed such a scandalous dance."

Her cheeks heated. "There is really nothing scandalous in the side-by-side position, only in the closed."

He took a step nearer. "And what is the 'closed' position?"

She knew she ought to refuse and back away but felt oddly drawn to him, touched that he would return, surprised to find she wanted to touch him.

She tentatively reached out. "I would place my hands here. . . ." She lightly gripped his upper arms, feeling the firm muscles beneath his coat sleeves.

He looked into her eyes and asked in a low voice, "And where do I place mine?"

She drew in a long shallow breath, nerves tingling, throat tight. "On my . . . waist." She was relieved her hands were not in his, for he would no doubt have felt how damp they were.

His large hands pressed warmly around her waist, though his eyes never left her face. She had difficulty holding his gaze at such close proximity. "Then you would step forward, and I back."

He stepped forward as directed, but his hands held her fast, keeping her from stepping back, keeping her close to him. His jaw tensed, his brown eyes sparked with longing.

She looked away, focusing on her hand on his arm. "Partners must keep a proper distance apart," she said, parroting the admonition of the Viennese dancing master. "Bodies must not actually touch."

"Pity," Francis breathed, his sweet breath warm on her temple, her ear. He leaned close, his face dipped toward hers, but still she averted her gaze. She did not want this, did she? This was Francis—what was she doing? She knew she had but to look up and he would kiss her. Her heart pounded at the thought.

"Lilly," he urged hoarsely. "Tell me it is not too late for us. That you and Graves are not—"

The door opened behind them, and Lilly pulled away.

Dr. Graves stood there, hand on the door latch, expression startled, bearing rigid. "I came to see how you and your father were faring, but I see I am interrupting." Eyes dull, he backed from the room.

"No, Dr. Graves, please come in! I was merely demonstrating the waltz to Mr. Baylor."

He stared at her, flicked a glance at Francis, then returned cool eyes to her. "Do you think that wise, Miss Haswell?"

The particular dance, or the partner? Lilly thought. "You must forgive us, Dr. Graves. Francis and I grew up together, and find it far too easy to slip back into our former foolish ways."

He stared at her a moment longer, then cleared his throat. "I see. Well." He bowed stiffly. "Good evening."

He did not acknowledge Francis in his farewell.

"Dr. Graves, you needn't leave," Lilly insisted.

"Miss Haswell has done nothing wrong." Francis gestured in vague motions between Lilly and himself. "I instigated this."

"No, Francis," Lilly said. "I have acted thoughtlessly. I ask you both to forgive me."

Her father's voice called from down the passageway, "Lilly? Everything all right?"

Lilly grimaced. "We've woken him."

Dr. Graves said icily, "I shall go and check on him. If you don't mind." He skewered Francis with a look.

"Yes, please do, Dr. Graves," Lilly quickly replied. "You are very kind to think of him. I thank you."

Graves nodded and pivoted on his heel. As soon as he had left the room, Lilly turned toward Francis feeling contrite and chagrined. "Francis," she whispered tersely, "I was wrong to allow this to happen. I don't know why I did."

"Because you feel something for me, Lilly. I know you do."

She exhaled. "Of course I do. But not what you might wish I would feel. Francis, please understand. I do not want the life you do. I do not want to spend mine in an apothecary shop. I never have."

He ran a hand through his thick brown hair. "It is all I know. All I *want* to know. Are you suggesting I give it up?"

"No. Stay. But all *I* want is to help my father regain his strength, put the place to rights, then leave it to him."

"But I've seen you, Lilly—helping people, easing their pain. . . . I know you derive as much satisfaction from it as I do."

She shook her head. "You are wrong. I have done what I've had to do, but I do not enjoy it. Nor do I aspire to any profession. I am, after all, a woman."

He winced. "I am aware of that. Painfully aware. But the Lilly Haswell I knew would never so belittle her sex."

"That Lilly Haswell is gone," she said, more sharply than she'd intended.

His eyes glittered with sadness and irritation both. "I for one am sorry to hear it." He picked up his hat. "I will trespass upon your time no longer. Good evening, Miss Haswell."

On his lips, the formal address sounded nearly derisive, and it delivered an unexpected prick of pain.

I, being of a sound mind, memory and understanding,
knowing the certainty of death when I shall be called to my
wished-for-long home, do make my last Will and Testament. . . .

—WILLIAM PHILLIPS, GENTLEMAN, 1786

CHAPTER 42

Francis opened the kitchen door to say hello to Mary—and hoping to apologize to Lilly, who was so often there in the mornings.

He had been tempted to give up hope when Dr. Graves first arrived in Bedsley Priors. But as the weeks passed and no engagement was announced, he'd allowed himself to believe he still had a chance with Lilly. After their last encounter, however, Francis was almost relieved he would soon be going away.

Mary stood at her worktable as usual, but she did not smile, or even acknowledge him. She seemed to be staring straight ahead. Her hands, still idly chopping something, slowed, then jerked.

"Mary!" He bolted across the room, but was too late. She collapsed where she stood, a sickening crack preceding the thud of her landing.

He knelt beside her on the hard brick floor. A deep gash on her forehead showed white, just before the blood began to flow profusely.

There was blood between the fingers of one of her hands as well—the hand still clutching the knife.

Jane rushed in from the scullery and shrieked at the sight. Mrs. Mimpurse came running as well, no doubt hearing him shout her daughter's name. She gasped and covered her mouth with a trembling hand.

"Clean linen, and quickly!" Francis called.

The kitchen maid rushed to do his bidding while he ran his hands down Mary's limbs and checked her pupils. When Jane returned, he pressed a linen serviette to the gash on her forehead.

"She needs a surgeon. Send someone for Shuttleworth."

Lilly appeared at the back door, as he had hoped she would, though for far different reasons. "I will go." Her face was pale but resolute.

"Wait," Francis called. "I think he will attend her better in his surgery. She has no broken bones, I am sure. Help me wrap her hand, and I shall carry her."

Lilly nodded and deftly assisted him in wrapping Mary's cut palm and finger while Mrs. Mimpurse and Jane looked on, sobbing. Yes, it might be better to treat Mary elsewhere for several reasons.

Mary's eyes fluttered opened. "What's happened?" she mumbled, blue eyes clouded.

"You've cut yourself and need a surgeon," Francis said. "We're taking you to Mr. Shuttleworth."

He did not miss the look of pain, of mortification, which passed over her pale features. Why wouldn't Mary want to be helped by a man she so obviously admired, and who admired her in return? *Unless Mr. Shuttleworth does not know . . .*

Lilly glanced at him, then back to her friend. She said gently, "There's no help for it this time, love."

Resigned, Mary gave the briefest of nods and her eyes fluttered closed once more.

Please let the man be in his office, Francis prayed as he lifted Mary in his arms.

Lilly jogged beside Francis as he carried Mary with impressive strength. Mrs. Mimpurse scuddled behind them, hand to her heavy bosom, face stricken. Crossing Milk Lane, Lilly was relieved when Mr. Shuttleworth opened his door before they had even reached it, likely having seen them run across the lane. He appeared shocked and alarmed to see the patient Francis bore with such determination, the blood already seeping through white linen at her brow and hand.

"She fell. Holding a knife," Francis panted.

For a fraction of a moment, Shuttleworth found and held Lilly's gaze.

Lilly looked away first.

She waited while Mr. Shuttleworth skillfully stitched up the gash on Mary's forehead as well as one of the deeper cuts on her finger. Mary was in a strange dreamlike state, and did not even seem to feel the pain of the stitches, though he gave her laudanum to lessen the pain she was sure to feel soon.

He assured Mrs. Mimpurse that he expected both injuries to heal well in time. He asked Mary's mother more questions about how the injury occurred, and if the like had happened before. And as Mrs. Mimpurse began her quiet explanations, Lilly let herself from the surgery.

A few hours later, Mr. Shuttleworth sought Lilly out, as she had known he would. Finding her alone in the shop, he began in low tones, "I cannot believe I did not know. Does everybody?"

Lilly nodded. "Everyone from Bedsley Priors." She sighed. "We gossip among ourselves freely, but with outsiders, as you have been, we protect our own."

"Why did *you* not tell me?"

Lilly looked away from the hurt in his dark eyes. "She did not wish me to."

"But . . . that's not right. Nor fair."

She forced her eyes to meet his. "Was it so wrong that she wanted to enjoy your company without the knowledge tainting your opinion of her? To be just a lady with a gentleman? She's never had an admirer before."

He frowned. "Had I known, I might have been more circumspect.

Not allowed myself to . . ." His words drifted off, but his meaning was clear.

"But why? It isn't really so dreadful, is it? It has been quite a rare occurrence, at least, until lately."

He blindly gripped the edge of the dispensing counter. "Miss Haswell. I served in an epileptic asylum, two years gone. Not to learn to treat epilepsy, for there is little treatment to speak of and certainly no cure. I was there because surgeons were always in demand in that place. I received a great deal of practical experience stitching cuts and cracked heads, splinting broken bones, and treating burns. . . ."

She thought back to Dr. Graves mentioning such institutions and her adamant rebuttal at the thought of sending her dear friend to such a place. Lilly found she had no strength for such a speech at present. Not with such deep disappointment in the man's voice and expression.

Mr. Shuttleworth took a deep breath and blew it out between his cheeks. "Epileptics were sent there to live. Permanently. And, Miss Haswell, patients beyond the age of thirty were exceedingly rare."

While Mary recovered from her wounds, Mrs. Kilgrove recovered her strength, relieving lingering fears of further penal action. Charlie, seemingly no worse for his captivity, spent all his spare time with the doting, forgiving woman, and with his cat, Jolly.

Lilly's gratitude toward Roderick Marlow did not flag. His father's health, however, did. After enjoying a brief return of vitality in the weeks prior to and after his marriage, Sir Henry had again fallen ill. Her father had been called in to see him a few nights before, and just that morning, Marlow's man had come to the shop to ask Mr. Haswell to come again. But her father had awoken quite weak that day, so Lilly had gone alone. This seemed to agitate Mr. Withers, and upon entering the ailing baronet's chamber, she'd understood why. Never had she seen Sir Henry in such a state. She had actually been relieved to hear Dr. Foster had been summoned as well.

Now, Lilly wearily made her way home from Marlow House,

grieved at this latest turn in Sir Henry's health and her inability to help him. Ahead of her, Lilly heard someone cry out. Picking up her skirts, she ran through the trees separating the road from Arthur Owen's farm. In the clearing, she paused, stunned. There was Roderick Marlow in the Owens' market garden, kicking and punching first the galley-crow, then the fence post. He cried out in unintelligible grief or anger or both.

He must know, she thought.

Owen's pigs scrambled to the far end of the pen. Marlow's horse whinnied, ribbons dangling, trotting this way and that, clearly spooked by his master's behavior. Lilly was spooked as well.

"Mr. Marlow!" she called. "Mr. Marlow, pray calm down."

He spun to face her, expression wild. "Calm down? How can I?"

"Your father is ill, I know, but—"

"Father has been ill for years—in body, but never in mind. Until this!" He thrust a piece of paper high above his head, then crumpled it with both hands, hurtling it toward the pond, though the wad fell short of its mark.

Wary, Lilly walked closer. "What is it?"

"A copy of his new will. He has authored my ruin, or more accurately, the red witch has convinced him to do so. Now should my father die, *she* will take what is rightfully mine."

Her mind whirled. "But . . . I thought the law was quite clear. The eldest son is heir."

"I am to inherit the land, yes. It is entailed. But to raise the staggering amount specified for her jointure, I shall have to sell off the stock, the London house, and I know not what to satisfy it."

"But certainly you would not begrudge your father's widow something to live on."

"Something to live on, I would not begrudge. But the amount is far above that. I shall be unable to pay my steward, the servants, let alone afford to heat that huge place. Father no doubt allowed her to believe he was wealthier than he was when she married him. But in truth we have struggled for some time. You know we keep only two carriages, only a small London house—and that we let out for most of the year. We do not entertain often. We live quietly, and we retrench and retrench again. And so far we have managed, but this is the absolute end."

"But did your father not realize? He has been ill, perhaps—"

He went on as though he had not heard her, "I may even have to let the place out. My own home . . ."

"I am sorry. There must be some mistake. Some misunderstanding."

In two strides, he closed the remaining distance between them. "Perhaps I shall have to enter a trade as you have, Miss Haswell." He looped his arm around her and pulled her close, but the fire in his eyes was fueled by betrayal, not passion. "Do you think I should make a good butcher? Perhaps an apothecary. . . . You would teach me all I need know, would you not?"

"Mr. Marlow, please. I—"

No doubt seeing her stricken expression, he released her, the fire in his eyes fading to dullness. "Forgive my foolishness, Miss Haswell. You have come upon me at a most dark moment." He reached down, retrieved his fallen hat, and stepped toward his horse. "I beg your pardon. I must speak to my father and unwork the devilish persuasion that woman has wrought."

Lilly was confused. "But . . . I have just come from Marlow House. Your father lies in a coma. I thought you knew."

"No!" He whirled back around, hat forgotten. "I have been trapped with Father's solicitor all morning." Mr. Marlow sank to the ground and stared at her, stunned. "When?"

"He might have been in this state all night, but there's no way to know. Withers said he at first thought Sir Henry merely sleeping. When he did not rouse, he sent for my father. My father was indisposed, so I went in his stead."

Cautiously, she sat down on the ground near the stricken man, tugging her skirts around her. "Dr. Foster is expected any time, I understand," she added, hoping to comfort him. "He has long experience with your father."

He sat, elbows on his knees, staring blankly ahead. "Indeed my father has had long association with several of the medical profession, enjoyed their company, but with no benefit that I can see. And now this."

He shook his head. "I argued bitterly with Father when last we spoke. I have not quite managed to forget that, as is my wont. And now I shall never be able to make it right."

He laid his head down, face hidden within his arms. "A coma," he breathed. "Then it is too late. All is lost. . . ."

Impulsively, she laid a hand on his elbow. "Your father may yet rally. He has before, remember."

He lifted his head and regarded her, eyes alight. "Might he come to his senses, then, at any moment?"

"I don't know. But it is possible."

"Then I must be there should he awaken." He rose quickly. "Beg him to change his mind and . . . to forgive me."

With that he turned, leapt on his horse, and galloped away, without farewell or backward glance.

That evening, when Lilly confided Mr. Marlow's tidings in hushed tones to Mrs. Mimpurse, the Marlows' former nurserymaid shook her head, her mouth turned down in a rare frown.

"Him not even in his grave and already they're fighting o'er his money. Fuss and commotion."

"What's this about?" Mary asked, coming in from the dining room, her finger still wrapped but healing nicely.

"Sir Henry changed his will," Lilly explained once more. "So much money is to go to the new Lady Marlow that, in raising the sum, Marlow House may very well be ruined."

Mary's brow puckered. "If she wanted the money and title of Lady, " she began, "why not marry the heir and have both? She had to know Sir Henry could not be expected to live many years."

"Perhaps she really does love Sir Henry," Mrs. Mimpurse ventured. She sighed. "And now the poor man is senseless, and not two months gone since the honeymoon."

Lilly knew Maude was partial to her former employer, but she could not quite believe Cassandra Powell had married the sickly baronet for love alone. "Or perhaps she liked the thought of a widow's jointure to spend as she liked."

Mrs. Mimpurse shook her head. "Most widows get only a small portion of the dowry they brought to the marriage. Beyond that, they must depend upon the generosity of the husband's heir."

Lilly considered this. "Then perhaps Lady Marlow did not wish to depend upon Roderick's generosity, and that is why she worked on Sir Henry to change his will, as Roderick suspects."

That Lilly would believe. But she did not foresee the danger it would mean for them all.

Oh thou, to whom such healing power is giv'n
The delegate, as we believe, of heaven.

—RICHARD CUMBERLAND, *ODE TO DOCTOR ROBERT JAMES*

CHAPTER 43

When the summons came the following afternoon, Lilly was not overly surprised. In the hastily written note, Roderick Marlow bid Charles Haswell to come directly, bringing all medical necessities.

"I did not think I would be summoned, not with Foster attending Sir Henry yesterday." Her father groaned and swung his legs off the side of the bed.

"I shall go again, Father. You are still not fit for it."

He lifted the piece of paper. "He asks specifically for me in the most pointed terms. I dare not refuse."

"Then I shall go with you."

She harnessed Pennywort to the gig and helped her father up into it, then set his largest medical case on the floor.

When they arrived, Mr. Withers opened the door to them. Lilly noticed the man still seemed agitated, and was surprised when he did not escort them up to his master's rooms as he had on previous calls.

She helped her father up the long staircase and down the corridor to Sir Henry's chambers. Holding his arm, she said, "Lean on me, Father. It is not much further."

She pushed open the first door and was surprised and perplexed to see Dr. Graves standing in Sir Henry's outer dressing room.

"We did not expect you to be here," she said.

"I was summoned by Mr. Marlow."

"As were we."

Before either of them could say anything further, her father's knees buckled. Dr. Graves rushed to take his arm, and together they helped him to the stuffed chair. With shaky hand, her father pulled a handkerchief from his pocket and mopped his perspiring brow. "A great many stairs, that."

Moments later, the door opened again, and Mr. Shuttleworth came in, stick in hand. He smoothed down his fine coat before realizing there were others already in the room. He seemed startled to see them there. "Good heavens. The old man must be very bad indeed."

Lilly nodded. Her heart pounded at the thought of the grief and rage she had witnessed in Roderick Marlow the previous day. Whatever was about to happen would not be pleasant.

The door to the inner room, Sir Henry's private bedchamber, opened and Roderick Marlow strode out. He stood, hands on hips, eyes blazing. His face seemed more gaunt than she remembered, and his strange eyes, unfocused and glowering, were like those of a mad dog.

When those eyes lit on her, he seemed to falter. "Miss Haswell . . . you should not be here." He swept his arm toward the door. "You may leave. Go."

She forced herself to hold his gaze without flinching. "I will stay and assist my father in whatever you have summoned us here to do."

He hesitated only a moment. "As you wish." He lifted his outstretched arm and scratched at the back of his neck. "I cannot say I am surprised. Everyone knows the apothecary's clever daughter is all but running Haswell's these days. The master to her father's impotent puppet."

The words felt like a slap after his recent kindnesses. Her father opened his mouth to protest, but then tucked his chin, defeated.

She squeezed her father's shoulder. "Charles Haswell is the greatest apothecary Wiltshire has ever known."

"So he would have us believe. Today, he shall have his chance to prove it. Or be ruined once and for all."

She opened her mouth—stunned—but no words came.

Marlow paced the room maniacally before them. "You medical sorts. You all pretend to such powers, such compassion, but really, all you care about are your own purses. I read the papers, I know about the posturing, the verbal battles about who should be allowed to treat what. You don't care about patients—you care only for your own livelihoods."

He jerked his thumb toward his father's bedchamber. "Dr. Foster was here last night and again this morning. It seems that each of you has treated my father—has filled him with potions that together have rendered him unconscious. You have all treated my father in the last week, have you not?" He paused, scorching each of them with his gaze.

Lilly was flummoxed. Aside from her father, she'd had no idea the others had so recently seen Sir Henry. Why had no one told her?

"Lady Marlow sent for me three days ago," Dr. Graves defended. "I did what I could for Sir Henry, which was little enough, but he was still lucid when I left."

Her father nodded. "I called on Sir Henry that same evening. I found him weak but stable."

Mr. Shuttleworth's dark eyebrows seemed unnaturally high on his forehead. "Sir Henry's solicitor asked me to render an opinion *two* days ago. Said he did not trust his client was getting the best care."

Lilly felt her face wrinkle in confusion. She said, "Mr. Withers summoned me—that is, my father—again yesterday. I came in his stead."

Mr. Marlow paced before them once more. "And so you each plied him with elixirs that in combination worked to send him into a coma. Now you will work together to revive him."

Lilly shook her head in dismay. Sir Henry was already unconscious when she arrived yesterday, but she made no attempt to exonerate herself. In her mind, if her father bore any responsibility, she did as well. When she had last seen Roderick Marlow, he had been looking for someone to blame. Now it appeared he had found his scapegoat. Several of them, in fact.

"I know you will not endeavor to revive my father for pity's sake," Marlow continued. "Nor for mine. Financial reward has not been sufficient motivation to this point, so instead I offer threat. Punishment. I have no power to cure my father, but I have enough to crush each of you. To bring ruination to your practices, your reputations. Is this motivation more suitable, more *efficacious*, as you say? Will you now heal my father?"

Dread filled her like bile. Roderick Marlow must be drunk. Perhaps even mad. She had never seen him like this. She barely recognized this furious, desperate man as the same one she had kissed not so long ago in the stables.

Marlow stopped before her father, shifting his weight to one hip. "Haswell, legend has it that you once raised my grandfather from the dead. How convenient for you—otherwise people would not have been so quick to overlook your fickle wife and idiot son. How the hordes have flocked to you, to lap up your counsel and supposed cures. You have lived off your fame long enough."

Marlow turned. "Shuttleworth, you came to town claiming your worldly experience, your remedies brought from distant lands. Here is your chance to show up your rivals."

"And Dr. Graves." Marlow's lip curled. "You with your privileged Oxford education—about which you constantly remind us. Here is your opportunity to prove your knowledge superior to the less-learned surgeon or apothecary."

His hands returned to his hips. "Personally, I do not care which one of you succeeds. But should you all fail, if my father dies without regaining consciousness, your livelihoods die with him." He looked

once more at Lilly. "You should have left, Miss Haswell, when you
had the chance."

The outer door slammed behind Roderick Marlow, and no one
spoke or moved until the echo died away. Then together the four of
them quietly entered Sir Henry's inner chamber and approached his
bed. How still the man was. How grey.

"Good Lord," her father breathed. "He is far gone indeed."

Dr. Graves bent to listen to the old man's heart. Mr. Shuttleworth
lifted Sir Henry's sagging eyelids and palpated his abdomen. Her
father took up his limp wrist. "Rapid, yet weak."

Together they discussed how each had treated Sir Henry, what
medicines they had given him, and if any of these might have reacted
adversely together.

"I gave him a very low dose of digitalis for dropsy," Dr. Graves
said. "It would not have done this."

"Digitalis?" Shuttleworth asked. "When an infusion of juniper
or briony would have been much less risky?"

"Gentlemen, please," Lilly said. "Let us not place blame. Let us
together find a solution."

"Solution?" Dr. Graves's voice rose, incredulous. "The man is
dying. There is no solution."

Lilly thought, flayed her memory for answers. Could she—could
any of them—find a possible remedy for this impossible situation?
Neither physician, surgeon, nor apothecary knew anything to do for
Sir Henry. Nor for his desperate son.

They needed a miracle.

The door burst open behind them. Whirling about, Lilly saw
Francis Baylor at the threshold, quite out of breath. She felt unaccountably relieved to see him. "Francis! Were you summoned as well?"

Francis surveyed the room and its occupants. "No. But Mrs.
Mimpurse told me about the will. When I couldn't find Mr. Shuttleworth, or either of you, I became concerned. Thought I had better
come. See how I might help."

"Have you some remedy in mind?" Mr. Shuttleworth asked.

Francis walked across the room and laid his hand on the baronet's pale brow. It seemed clear the old man was not long for the world. "I am afraid I don't. Though I may have let Withers believe I did, to gain entry."

Dr. Graves asked, "What's this about a new will?"

Lilly confided, in low tones, what she had learned from Mr. Marlow about the new will—the primary reason, she suspected, for today's threats. Unless . . . Could he really be so desperate to gain his father's forgiveness?

The outer door banged open again and Roderick Marlow strode in. "What is this about a remedy, Baylor?" he challenged.

Francis held up his hand. "I am afraid there is little any of us can do for Sir Henry but pray."

Marlow threw up his hands in angry disgust.

Francis said, "But I suggest you stay in here with your father, Mr. Marlow. Spend all the time you can at his side. Talk to him. He may very well be able to hear you."

For a moment, Marlow's eyes lit. "Do you really think he might?"

Francis nodded. "The rest of us will leave you and Sir Henry in peace."

Marlow crossed his arms, eyes narrowed. "None of you is going anywhere. Not until you have accomplished what I summoned you here to do."

"We are not leaving, sir. Only withdrawing to the dressing room." Francis held Marlow's glare without wavering. "You have my word— we shall not depart until you give us leave to do so."

Roderick Marlow hesitated, staring at Francis, sizing up the younger man. Lilly was surprised when he nodded and returned to his father's bedside.

The rest of them moved to the door. Dr. Graves took one of her father's arms, she the other, and together they helped him to the chair in the dressing room. Francis closed the bedchamber door behind him.

As he helped Mr. Haswell back into the stuffed chair, Adam Graves found himself remembering Lady Marlow's veiled threat to Roderick atop Adam's Grave. Was that somehow related to the present threat? Had the new will—her unexpectedly large jointure—been what she had referred to? If so, no wonder the man was incensed.

Adam forced himself to remain calm and think. Turning to Lillian's father, he began, "Mr. Haswell. If it is true that you once raised a man from the dead, might we ask for a repeat performance?"

"Indeed, Mr. Haswell," Shuttleworth added. "If you could get us out of this muddle, I would be much obliged."

Miss Haswell laid a hand on her father's arm. "We know the truth, do we not, Father? Perhaps it is time we admitted it."

Charles Haswell looked as though he might refuse, then sighed. "I don't do miracles. Never have."

"But word of it has spread as far as London and Oxford," Adam insisted. "It has become the stuff of legends. Dr. Thomas Bromley was here at the time, I understand, and witnessed the event. He attests the man was dead indeed."

Mr. Haswell nodded. "I tried everything I knew, but nothing had any effect. I devised no secret miracle cure. Rather, in desperation, I fell to my knees in this very room and prayed for his recovery." Haswell looked at his daughter, tears shimmering in his eyes. "My little girl beside me."

Miss Haswell took his hand, tears in her eyes as well.

"Perhaps that is what is needed again," Mr. Baylor quietly suggested.

Charles Haswell inhaled deeply. "I own it has been too long since I have done so."

Still holding his hand, Miss Haswell helped her father kneel beside the chair. Mr. Baylor joined them, and together the three bowed their heads.

Adam looked on, feeling sheepish. Beside him, Shuttleworth also looked uncomfortable. For an awkward moment their gazes met. Adam shrugged his response. He considered kneeling beside them, but felt too foolish at the thought. He noticed Shuttleworth had closed his eyes where he stood. He did the same.

Kneeling there beside her father, Lilly felt her legs begin to stiffen and guessed her father must be growing uncomfortable as well. She glanced over, but her father's eyes were still closed, his face wrinkled in concentration. On his other side, Francis also had his eyes closed, forehead resting on clasped hands. As if sensing her scrutiny, Francis looked at her. In silent agreement, they rose and, with a few whispered words, encouraged Mr. Haswell to rise and rest, and together they helped him regain his seat.

"What is happening here?" Lady Marlow asked, startling them all. She had entered without any of them hearing her. Wearing a reserved day dress, her red hair simply fashioned, she stood regally inside the dressing room door, looking from one face to another. Her gaze landed on Dr. Graves.

He cleared his throat. "We were each of us summoned by Mr. Marlow. To see what might be done for Sir Henry."

"Then what are you doing out here?"

When Dr. Graves hesitated, Francis answered, "Praying." He added gently, "I am afraid, Lady Marlow, there is little else to be done for your husband."

For a moment the woman froze, her mouth forming a pink oval of surprise.

"Mr. Marlow is in with Sir Henry now," Francis explained. "Saying his farewells."

Lady Marlow sighed as if suddenly weary, her face drooping into lines that added ten years to her apparent age. "Poor man," she murmured bleakly. And Lilly wondered which man she referred to.

The bedchamber door opened and, as one, they warily turned. Roderick Marlow appeared at the threshold, tears on his cheeks. Ignoring the others in the room, his gaze sought out Lilly's.

"I begged his pardon . . . and he . . . squeezed my hand." His face contorted with emotion. "He knew me. . . ."

Tears of understanding trailed down Lilly's own cheeks as her eyes held his.

The rest of the assembly were equally moved, as well as relieved, to realize Roderick Marlow had returned to his senses. In a matter of minutes, he gave them all leave to go, visibly chagrined at his reckless and irrational behavior. Given the distress of his father's condition, all seemed ready to forgive the future Sir Roderick, Baronet.

Sir Henry did not regain consciousness.

There had been no miracle, no answer to their prayer.

Or had there been? Lilly remembered the look of wonder, and relief on Roderick Marlow's face when he said, *"I begged his pardon and he squeezed my hand. He knew me."*

So perhaps there had been a miracle, after all.

What is a weed?
A plant whose virtues have not yet been discovered.

—RALPH WALDO EMERSON

CHAPTER 44

In the busyness that followed, getting her father home to bed, telling Mary and Mrs. Mimpurse all that had happened, and checking on Charlie, Lilly did not see Francis again. She wanted to thank him for coming to Marlow House and to talk over the events of the day. She had hoped he would come by the shop that evening, but now it was late and he no doubt thought she had already retired for the night. Or had he stayed away in deference to Dr. Graves?

When Lilly finally slipped into her nightdress and into bed, she still could not sleep. Beyond the stress of the day, she could not stop thinking about Francis Baylor. Though the youngest man there, he had been the one to take charge, and the one to suggest praying together. She thought back to his quick actions after Mary's fall and his many kindnesses to her since then.

She thought, too, of his tall, athletic figure, his strong jaw and cleft chin, his chocolate-brown eyes. As she had come to realize, Francis

Baylor had changed a great deal since her return to Bedsley Priors. Or was it she who had changed?

She now understood what Miss Robbins had long seen in Francis, and felt that same admiration herself. When she thought of how she had so soundly rejected him, she was filled with wistful regret.

Lilly rolled over in bed. Still, he was only an assistant—a journeyman—in an apothecary shop. Dr. Graves was a physician and therefore a gentleman. Might he not move his practice elsewhere in a few years? Perhaps even return to London? Somehow, the inner arguments rang hollow now.

Even so, Lilly wondered why she should suddenly feel shy at the thought of seeking out her old friend. Francis would certainly come by the shop on the morrow, would he not? She would thank him then.

In the morning, someone did enter the shop and Lilly hurried out to greet him. But it was not Francis. Nor even Adam Graves. It was Dr. Foster.

He removed his hat and said, "I know it is early and you are no doubt recuperating from a trying day yesterday, but I am afraid I need you to dispense an order for me."

His tone was surprisingly polite.

"Of course." She moved to the dispensing counter and picked up her quill. "What is it you need?"

He fiddled with his hat brim. "A fortnight's worth of St. John's wort, powdered, five grains per day."

She nodded. "For?"

He looked up at her. "I am sure you, being a dab hand yourself, know what the herb is used for, Miss Haswell."

"I do, but—"

"Good. Now, can you figure the sum, or shall I?"

"I meant, who is the patient? For our records."

"My, my. Records too. Haswell's is better managed than I knew."

Was the man being sarcastic? She wasn't certain. "Thank you. We do our best."

He inhaled, then paused. "It is for Mrs. Chester Somersby of Honeystreet. Do you know the family?"

Lilly lowered her quill. "Indeed I do."

"She suffers from nerves, poor creature. Have you sufficient powder on hand, or shall I call round for it later?"

Lilly stared at the man. Did he really not know what he was asking?

"I don't mind stopping back," he said.

"You cannot."

"I can quite easily. It isn't far."

"I mean, you cannot give Mrs. Somersby St. John's wort. She had a violent reaction to it once before."

He regarded her placidly. "I know of no such reaction."

"I do. And Dr. Graves does as well. Ask him if you don't believe me."

His eyes met hers boldly. "Dr. Graves follows my directives and keeps me informed of all irregularities. You needn't trouble yourself, Miss Haswell. Shall I pick up the order at say, four o'clock?" He replaced his hat smartly, turned without awaiting her response, and strode from the shop.

She stared after the man. Anger and fear and dread balled in her stomach. He was either ignorant or pretending to be for his own ends. Either way, Mrs. Somersby was not the only person about to be hurt.

The shop had been so busy that, when four o'clock came, she'd had no time to ask anyone for advice. Now Dr. Foster again stood before her, the dispensing counter between them like a futile shield.

"Are you refusing to fill my order?" he asked.

"You have not had an opportunity to confer with Dr. Graves, I see. If you will only speak with him—"

"Yes or no?" His voice rose. "Will you dispense my prescribed medicine for Mrs. Somersby or will you not?"

"I have no wish to quarrel with you, Dr. Foster. But I cannot in good conscience do what you ask."

"Once more, girl. Do you or do you not refuse to dispense the physic I ordered?"

She swallowed. "Yes. I refuse."

He nodded, clearly angry yet not surprised. And apparently satisfied as well.

Leaving the shop untended, though it was before five, Lilly hurried up the High Street and down narrow Milk Lane to Shuttleworth's. She wanted to make sure Dr. Foster did not turn there for the prescription he wanted for Mrs. Somersby. She found Mr. Shuttleworth standing at his large central desk, drying glass measuring jars with a clean white cloth. When she asked about Dr. Foster and learned he had not been there all day, she sighed with relief. She leaned her elbows on the high desk and confided her confrontation with the old physician.

Mr. Shuttleworth winced. "Oh dear. I am not certain that was wise."

She jerked back, stung. This wasn't the empathy she'd expected. "What was I to do?"

"But to refuse him?" Lionel Shuttleworth whistled under his breath.

"I had no choice."

"Do you not read the newspapers?"

"I barely have time to read bills of lading and ledgers, let alone news."

"You *have* heard about the recently passed Apothecaries Act?"

She frowned. "I believe Francis may have said something, but I own I paid little attention."

Mr. Shuttleworth leaned forward, sober concern in his dark eyes. "Among other things, a clause of this new act imposes severe penalties on any apothecary who refuses to dispense medicines on the order of a physician."

"You are joking."

"I am deadly serious."

"How long has this been generally known?"

"It's been before Parliament for quite some time, but came into effect the first of August."

How easily she had walked into his trap.

Adam Graves walked slowly down the High Street to Haswell's to pick up two prescriptions he had requested earlier. He knew Miss Haswell appreciated that he brought them to her though Shuttleworth's was nearer his offices. Normally he enjoyed the excuse to see her. But today he dreaded the coming encounter and the news he must impart.

When Adam had first learned of a possible partnership in Miss Haswell's home village, he had thought it a godsend. Now it was beginning to seem more like a test. One he appeared destined to fail.

He hesitated at the door to take a deep breath, then pushed his way inside. At the dispensing counter, Miss Haswell acknowledged him with a nod. He waited until Miss Primmel had paid for her purchases and said farewell to them both before approaching the counter himself.

Miss Haswell handed him his order without her usual smile, her features strained. She asked tensely, "Have you spoken to Dr. Foster about Mrs. Somersby? Tell me he did not procure the St. John's wort elsewhere."

"He has not. He pursued another course of treatment."

She released a breath. "I am relieved to hear it. He understood, then?"

"I would not say that." He found himself fidgeting with his parcel. "I did describe Mrs. Somersby's reaction, but he said it was more likely caused by the vervain you suggested for the . . . other complaint."

"But I asked Father, and he agrees. Vervain would not—"

"Yes, yes, I tried to explain that, but he would not hear me."

"You ought to have *made* him hear you."

He looked down at the counter. "Seems I fail at a great many things you believe I ought to do."

Her voice rose to a consolatory pitch. "Dr. Graves, I did not mean—"

"In any case"—he forced himself to continue—"I am afraid he has written to your own society, reporting your refusal."

"To the Apothecaries' Society?" she said. "I can hardly credit he'd waste the ink, so little does he respect the profession."

"I believe there you are wrong, Miss Haswell. It is not apothecaries in general he abhors."

He saw her bite her lip, clearly apprehending his meaning. "Surely nothing will come of it. The last time we heard from the Society, we received nothing more than a warning."

He shook his head. *Can she really be so naïve?* "The law has changed since then."

"What can he hope to accomplish?"

"I should think that all too evident. He wants to see Haswell's put out of business."

She blanched. "Could you not do something?"

There it was again. It was his fault. His failure. "What would you have me do?" His voice rose. "Pilfer his letter from the post?"

A quick glance revealed her chagrin. He took a deep breath and forced himself to speak calmly. "There is little I can do at this point. But I did want to warn you. And I shall apprise you of anything else I learn."

"Thank you," she murmured.

Feeling defeated and indignant both, he turned on his heel and left the shop. Why could she not leave the criticizing to Foster? It appeared neither of his provisional partnerships was working out as he had hoped.

On his way back to Dr. Foster's offices, he saw Bill Ackers leaving. What was the constable doing there? He then saw the man fold what looked to be several bank notes and tuck them into his pocket.

❦

The following week, Dr. Foster brought two men with him into the office.

"Graves, come out here, man."

Adam did not appreciate the way the elder man ordered him about. Still, he put on his coat and stepped from his private office into the reception hall.

"Here you are." Foster addressed his guests, "This is Dr. Adam Graves, the young partner I was telling you about. Not quite seasoned, but working out rather well. So far."

Adam managed not to frown and bowed to the newcomers. One was a man near Foster's own age in dark double-breasted coat and pantaloons, his waistcoat festooned with a lacy cravat. His hair was far too black to be natural for a man of his fifty or more years. He affected both quizzing glass and walking stick.

"May I introduce Mortimer Allen, a very old friend indeed," Foster began. The man inclined his head but showed little interest in the introduction.

"And this is John Evans, his . . . associate."

Mr. Evans was in his forties, Graves surmised, and wore a serviceable but plain coat and trousers. He looked exceeding fit, with a wiry strength rather than bulk. His tawny hair was thin on his forehead.

"How d'you do?" Evans said. This man took his measure, and Graves felt himself standing up the taller under it.

"What brings you gentlemen to Bedsley Priors?" Graves asked politely.

Mortimer Allen parted his full lips, but turned toward Foster in lieu of answering.

Dr. Foster said, "Merely a visit. They are on their way to Bath to take the waters. I don't credit the medicinal benefits myself, but I give you leave to prove me wrong, Mortimer."

"A rare pleasure it would be to accomplish that, I assure you."

"Well, do come upstairs for port and cigars. I have some good cheese and herring as well."

"Lead the way," Mortimer said.

"Thaht's all right. You gentlemen go on," John Evans said. "I'll leave you two to visit."

The man had a mild accent that Graves could not place after such a brief sampling.

"Are you sure, Evans?" Mortimer Allen asked.

"Indeed. I'll do on my own. I expect there's a public house nearby."

"Don't be out late. We've an early start on the morrow."

"I haven't forgotten."

The two older men went up the stairs together to Foster's private living quarters.

Evans looked at Graves. "If you would kindly point me in the right direction, I shall disturb you no more."

"Mind a bit of company?" Graves asked, curious about the man.

"If you like."

As the two walked the short distance to the Hare and Hounds, Graves hit on the origin of the man's accent. The long vowels, the clipped staccato syllables, the *r*'s, nearly rolled. "Wales?" he asked.

Evans smiled. "God's country, yes."

They entered the small, dim public house and took stools at the polished wooden counter. Two old men, one Adam recognized as Mr. Owen, sat in chairs near the fire, their dogs lying at their feet. He was relieved when the curs paid him no mind.

Once Freddy McNeal had served them each a half pint, Graves asked Mr. Evans, "But you live in London now?"

"Had to find work, hadn't I?"

"And what is your work, if I may ask?"

The man paused, considering, an odd smile playing about his lips. "I serve a city livery company, like. But I *work* for Mr. Allen."

Before Graves could ask him to explain, Evans asked, "And you? Who do you serve?"

"I would like to say I serve my patients. But as you said, I *work* for Dr. Foster."

Evans nodded and took a sip of dark ale. "What's he like?"

"A man of strong opinions. An experienced physician."

Evans grimaced. "No offense, mind, but I've never cared much for physicians—and thaht's the truth."

"May I ask why not?"

"Comes to this. In plague years, when the rich fled London for the country, every physician followed, leaving the poor to suffer and die without care. Surgeons followed. But apothecaries all stayed—to a mahn."

"You admire them."

"I do. When a body's ailing, money or no, apothecaries turn up trumps. Which is why it rankles me to . . ."

"To what?"

"Never you mind. Thaht's the half pint of bitter talkin'." Evans rose. "I'm to bed now."

All doctors are more or less Quacks!
. . . and what they talk is neither more nor less
than nonsense & stuff. . . .

—The First Duke of Wellington

Chapter 45

The next morning, Adam Graves jogged down the stairs from his third-floor rooms, but when he reached the ground floor, stopped, stunned. There stood John Evans. Gone were the congenial ale-warmed gaze and the unremarkable suit of clothes. In their place the man wore a gown of vibrant blue tufted with dozens of golden tassels. His eyes were stern, hard, and brooked no question.

What on earth?

Voices followed him down the stairs. There came Mr. Allen, dressed in an unadorned black gown. Dr. Foster followed him, breakfast teacup still in hand. Foster hesitated at seeing his young partner standing there, but the smile did not waver from his whiskered face.

"I shall bid you farewell here, Mortimer." Foster held out his free hand. "Thank you for coming to address the situation as only you can."

Mr. Allen shook his hand. "You are quite welcome. Again, I

apologize for not being able to respond in person to your first letter. But I trust you will be more than satisfied by day's end."

What did it mean? Adam wondered, suspicion gnawing at him.

John Evans opened the door for Mr. Allen, but once they were outside, Graves saw that John Evans preceded the older man down the lane.

"It is going to be quite a day for medicine, Graves. Quite a day."

Adam turned from his place at the window. "How so?"

"Justice, my boy. Justice for the common man and the Royal College both."

"I have no idea what you mean, sir. Has this something to do with your friends?"

"Indeed. Though I count only one as friend. Mortimer and I have known one another since boyhood. His father would have gladly stood him at Oxford, as did mine. I suppose Mortimer had a taste for power—enjoys being a big fish among small. One would think he knew all along he'd end as Master of those beetle crushers and potion pushers."

"What?"

"Yes. Mortimer is Master of Wardens for the Apothecaries' Society."

Adam felt his stomach clench as alarm pulsed through his body.

"We both have well-placed friends in Parliament," Foster continued, "and have helped one another over the years, when a letter to a friend might sway the vote on one medical issue or another. Very broad-minded the both of us, I'd say. That other man is only the beadle of the beetle crushers, who does my friend's bidding."

"Mr. Evans seemed quite well-spoken. A gentleman, I'd say."

"A gentleman? A hired henchman." Foster all but shuddered.

Adam swallowed, his mind reeling. "What are they about?"

"Oh, merely righting wrongs left too long to fester. Really, when one *thinks* of it—the negligence, the arrogance. Refusing to dispense a physician's order? Unpardonable—as the new law makes quite clear." He chuckled into his teacup.

"If you are referring to the Haswells and that order of yours, you know very well they were justified in not filling it."

"So you say."

"I have the patient record to prove it."

"I have the law. And the Master of Wardens of pompous Haswell's very own society."

"The letter of the law, sir, perhaps, but not the spirit. Does not our Hippocratic oath rank supreme? To save a life must be the primary mandate, not the law."

"That's radical politic, young man."

"You brought them here for this purpose, did you not? Journey to Bath, indeed. They stray quite far afield from their jurisdiction, would you not agree?"

"Now who's holding to the letter of the law?"

"It isn't right. In this case, the Haswells have done no wrong."

"Do you not mean *she* has done no wrong? I have not missed your interest in the Haswell girl. But perhaps I *did* miss some new law allowing women to diagnose and dispense physic?"

Adam turned toward the door.

"Hold there, Graves. I advise you—do nothing to interfere. I promise you a bleak future if you do."

Adam Graves reached for the door latch, and felt its cold metallic reality in his hand.

※

Lilly opened the door to Shuttleworth's and leaned across its threshold. The surgeon-apothecary was alone with his ledgers.

"Mr. Shuttleworth, do you know where Francis might be? I have not seen him these two days gone."

He looked up at her blankly. "Do you not know?"

Her senses became instantly alert. "Know what?"

"Mr. Baylor has taken his leave. Quit my employ."

She was stunned. "But why?"

"He has other plans. Did he not tell you?"

"He told me nothing."

"Well . . ." Mr. Shuttleworth awkwardly straightened his cravat. "They're not my plans to tell."

"Lilly!" Charlie ran up Milk Lane toward her, arms windmilling. "Francis is leaving." He paused when he reached her, bending over and panting to catch his breath. "I just seen him . . . carryin' his bag to the canal."

Lilly stared at her brother, yet hardly saw him nor her surroundings as he spoke.

Charlie straightened. "Remember when he first come 'ere? And spoilt Father's shoes?"

Lilly ran.

She arrived at the canal, out of breath, lungs heaving, as much from emotion as the exertion of the run. There was Francis, stepping down onto the stern of his cousin's narrowboat, moored near the Honeystreet Bridge.

"Francis!"

When he saw her, he left his valise and hat on the deck and climbed back up the bank to where she stood, still trying to catch her breath.

"Where are you going?" she asked.

"London."

"London?" She stared at him in confusion, her mind whirling. Had he told her and she'd forgotten? Was this what it felt like to forget something? This disorientation, this disturbing, irrational dread?

He continued, "It is my turn to see something of the world, I suppose. Learn a few things. Better myself."

"Without saying good-bye?"

He nodded, sheepish.

"But I've wanted to talk to you, to thank you." She swallowed a rising wave of panic. "How long will you be away?"

His grin was rueful. "Do not fret, Lilly. You've not seen the last of me."

She thought of her mother's vain promise to Charlie. She thought of Mr. Lippert, the apothecary from Little Bedwyn, who had stayed in

London where the opportunities were too great to give up for village life. "You cannot know that, Francis."

He tilted his head to the side, studying her.

She took a deep breath, forcing herself to remain calm. "If you are determined to go to London, I should like to give you the name of a kindly apothecary I met there."

"An apothecary? At one of your fine London balls?"

"No. In Bucklersbury, where every other shop is an apothecary's or chemist's."

Again she felt his inquiring look.

"I went there a few times, when I was feeling lonely, I suppose. Missing home."

"I am surprised you had the time to miss Bedsley Priors."

"Well, not only the village itself, but my father, of course. And Charlie and Mary and . . . you."

Eyes intent on hers, he took a step forward. "Lilly—"

"Mr. Baylor!" a feminine voice called. Glancing over, Lilly saw Miss Robbins smiling and waving from the lawn of Mill House. "Bon voyage!"

He waved back quickly before returning his attention to Lilly. It stung to realize he had shared his plans with Dorothea Robbins instead of her. Had the two an understanding? She felt her chin begin to tremble.

"In any case," she hurried on, determined not to cry, "the apothecary's name is Lippert. He and his son were very generous when I needed advice on reviving the shop." Lilly darted a glance at the retreating figure of Miss Robbins. "And he has a charming daughter as well."

He raised a skeptical brow. "What is that to me?"

"She is a lovely young woman who adores everything about an apothecary's shop. There is no place she would rather be."

He frowned. "And you wish me to meet her?"

Do I? Lilly hesitated. "Well, if you are ever in need of a friendly face in London."

He looked at her, slowly shaking his head. "Is that what you really want, Lilly? For me to find myself a charming London girl and never return?"

"No. I . . ." She faltered, confused. Of course she wanted him to come back—though not for Dorothea Robbins. *Have I mistaken the matter? Did Francis not renew his attentions to Miss Robbins after I refused him?* Tentatively she asked, "Do you plan to return?"

He expelled a dry puff of air, a bitter pull at his lips. "I don't know. Not until you . . . That is . . ." He ran a hand through his hair. "This is why I thought to leave without trying to say good-bye." He cleared his throat. "Lilly, I know Dr. Graves is a physician, and that he—"

"Come on, Francis!" his cousin called up from the narrowboat. "Must shove off and sharpish. The lockkeeper Reading way goes to bed at eight bells."

Francis lifted a hand to the man, then looked once more at Lilly. "I've got to go."

"But—"

"Francis! We can't wait any longer!"

Francis took Lilly's hand and pressed it with his larger one. "No matter what you decide, I hope we shall always be friends." He turned away and jumped aboard. The crew immediately began casting off.

"Write!" she called as the boat moved away from the bank.

But Lilly knew Francis had never been one to write. His poor mother had received a letter at Christmas and another on her birthday only when Lilly had been there to remind him.

She watched as Francis faded away. He lifted his hand in farewell, and the sight of it caused her chest to ache and tears to burn and well in her eyes. The canal had claimed another dear to her.

She felt bereft. Muddled. Aching. Was he implying what she thought—*hoped*—he was implying? But why did she—when she never wanted any part of the life Francis would likely lead? But she did hope. Too late, she realized she did. But what about Dr. Graves? He had uprooted himself and come to Bedsley Priors to pursue her. Had she not an obligation to him?

She groaned, her prayer inarticulate. She breathed in deeply, exhaled, then breathed in again. She paused. Sniffed the air gently, critically. What was it she smelled? Something sweet and mildly familiar yet too complex to identify. She closed her eyes and breathed in again, relishing the strange, sweet smell. But then something acrid joined the wispy odor.

"Lilly!" Charlie screamed. "Lilllll-leeeee!"

She spun around, eyes scanning the village behind her. A narrow spire of smoke rose above the rooftops, and below, Charlie bounded wildly down the Sands Road toward her.

Fire. Near the shop. Father in bed. *Dear God, no.* Lilly hurried to meet her brother.

"He's burning it, Lilly," Charlie cried. "Burning it all. Grandfather's pretty pots, all broken!"

Lilly ran.

Adam Graves turned the corner and dashed down the High Street. Smoke billowed from a mound in the street before Haswell's door. A small crowd of people had already gathered. Mortimer Allen stood on the opposite side of the High Street watching the proceedings with cool detachment. John Evans came out the shop door, heaved a crate onto the fire, then turned back and disappeared inside once more.

As Adam ran across the cobbles, he saw Mr. Shuttleworth cross the green in his odd upright trot.

Bill Ackers suddenly appeared before Adam, blocking his view and path. "Steady on."

He tried to step around the bulky man, but Ackers took his arm in an iron grip. "Stay back, Dr. Graves. Woe betide ye if Foster hears of ye meddlin' in this affair."

Ackers's bailiff, his brother in size and strength, held Shuttleworth as the surgeon, cravat askew, strained forward. His dark troubled eyes met Adam's over the bailiff's beefy shoulder. "Good heavens, man," he cried. "Do something."

"Nothin' he can do to puh a stop to it," Ackers said. "Haswell's in quiy' a lot of trouble. Gentlemen come down from London town with papers." He nodded toward John Evans, coming back out with an armload of dried herbs. "That man in the queer une-ee-form showed me. All legal an' so like."

"Foster paid you off," Adam said. "You knew what would happen today."

"I am only doin' my duty. Keeping the peace, innum? You'll keep yers, too, if yer a clever man."

Adam stopped resisting, stepping back from the constable's hold.

"That's it. Just go on to yer offices, now. Nothing to concern you here."

Adam stepped back, into the shadows beneath a lime tree on the green. Across the waves of heat and roils of black smoke he saw Miss Haswell, clutching a thick book in one arm, and with the other, holding her father back.

Their gazes caught, and for a moment hers alighted, but then, as he stood there, unmoving, her focus dimmed and finally fell away from him. Adam realized it was happening again. He was once more held in fear's grip. Frozen. He uttered a rare prayer, *Lord in heaven, help me!*

The beadle carried out a tall eighteenth-century jar bearing the Haswell crest, and seeing it sent a jolt through Adam's limbs. As if in boiled syrup, he strode heavily across the cobbled street and stood before John Evans. Recognizing him, the beadle hesitated. His hard eyes grew angry and his Welsh accent lilted his answer. "Not workin' fahst enough for you, is thaht it?"

"Please stop, Mr. Evans—John. The charges Dr. Foster brought are unjust."

"Thought you worked for the mahn?"

"Yes. But I can prove that a person would have died if Haswell's had filled Foster's order."

"Show it to the Master, then." He jerked his head toward Mortimer Allen, across the street.

"No, John. I am showing it to you—a man of honor. Your master and mine are in league together. Would you destroy the livelihood— the legacy—of an innocent man? A noble apothecary?"

Evans hesitated. "I've a writ with two charges—not just the one. Are you telling me there's no truth in either of them? Thaht . . . this"— he nodded toward the pile of broken rubble—"was unjust?" For a moment the man's green eyes looked bleak, urging him to deny it, to renounce his guilt.

"What other charge?" Adam asked warily.

"Thaht one Lillian Haswell, female, has been practicing as an apothecary, unlawfully diagnosing and dispensing physic without legal qualification to do so. Can you prove this charge false as well?"

Again Adam hesitated, held by the earnest, forthright eyes of the man staring back at him. "I . . . cannot."

Mr. Evans blinked.

"But this is a lesser charge, surely," Adam added. "Not requiring such a heavy toll. No charge of adulterated medicine, no harm done. Her father has been dreadfully ill—she has been nothing but a credit to him."

Something in the man's eyes glinted, as if he understood Graves's reasons for interfering were not merely professional. Evans stared at him a moment longer, then shoved the tall jar into his arms and turned away.

"Why do you stop?" the Master of Wardens called after him. "Who told you to stop?"

"We are well beyond our jurisdiction here. I've done all I will."

"We are not finished here!"

"We are."

John Evans strode down the street, his golden tassels flapping against his blue gown. On him, the effect was regal. Adam Graves had no doubt he had just been in the presence of a true gentleman. A man worth knowing.

The Master sputtered with anger and looked as though he might continue the dark task himself. But he seemed to consider the growing crowd of onlookers, and the fact that the burly constable was retreating with his bailiff, and instead followed after the beadle.

Standing there with smoke burning his eyes and lungs, Adam held the Haswell jar in his arms, feeling defeated and useless. He slowly walked toward Miss Haswell, who stepped forward to meet him as he drew near. Tears streamed down her cheeks. He met her eyes and held out the jar toward her. An offering. She took it mutely from him. For a moment, they both held it. Then he let go, turned, and walked away. Tears stung his own eyes, but that was only the smoke, doing what it would.

The past is the beginning of the beginning . . .
the twilight of the dawn.

—H. G. WELLS

CHAPTER 46

M uch had been lost. But they would have lost far more without
Dr. Graves's interference.

Still, Lilly was not surprised when he appeared at the shop door two
days later, carrying both valise and medical case. That he had shaved
off his moustache did surprise her, and she regarded the pale exposed
skin above his lip with a feeling of nearly maternal tenderness.

He cleared his throat. "As you know," he began quietly, "I came
here to see if a provisional partnership would work out." He smiled
wistfully. "It did not."

"I am sorry," she whispered.

He nodded. "I have given up my partnership with Dr. Foster, though
he no doubt would have broken our agreement had I not done so first."

"I do not blame you, for that decision nor for that day."

He looked down at the floor. "There comes a time, Miss Haswell,
when a man must admit defeat."

She knew he was speaking of more than his profession. "Of course you must not yoke yourself with Foster, but might you not set up on your own?" She attempted a wry grin. "I know where you might let a surgery very cheaply."

"Thank you. But I know this village cannot support two competing physicians."

"Does Foster not mean to retire after all?"

He shrugged. "It does not signify. I go to London."

"To practice there?"

"Not private practice. I own now, I am not fit for it." With a lift of his hand, he cut off her objections before she could voice them. "I intend to return to Guy's Hospital. I was offered a teaching post there before and turned it down. Now I shall take it. No doubt I shall be quite content. I excel in academia." He grinned bravely. "It is only real life I fail to master."

He bowed and took his leave of her. She watched him go, regretting that he had come there only to be disappointed. Yet she knew it was not within her power to make him happy. Nor whole.

The shop cleanup continued. Given her father's state of health and their shaky finances, they could no longer fool themselves that they could restore the shop to its former glory. Humpty Dumpty had taken too great a fall. Though clearly grieving its loss, her father seemed oddly resigned to the closing of Haswell's. Perhaps even relieved. Lilly felt a muddle of conflicting emotions herself.

It took days to sort through the rubble and salvage what they could, to sweep up the spilled powders and scrub away the syrups soiling the shop floor, and to make sense of the jumble which had been her father's surgery. Her father had always been disorganized. His desk and sideboard were forever piled high with papers, but now those papers carpeted the floor and were wedged between sideboard and wall, desk and window. Lilly piled and sorted and read and tossed until the dustbin threatened to overflow. *If the beadle must burn,* Lilly thought tartly, *why could he not have burned this lot?* Such calamity was likely the only thing that would have driven them to this frenzy of purging and cleaning.

Charlie's cat, Jolly, had fled the house during the fire, and had not been found. Though discouraged, Charlie did his best to help, splitting his time between Marlow House and home. At the moment he was sweeping the floor near the large front window, its display empty now save for the rescued apothecary jar.

Still in the surgery, Lilly reached down and pulled at a corner of paper sticking out from under the desk like a child sticking out its tongue.

"Charlie, come here a moment, please," she called.

Charlie was not clever, but he was very strong. When he appeared, she asked, "Do lift the corner of the desk for me, will you? Father's papers have flown everywhere, and knowing me, I'd miss the only one worth recovering."

Charlie heaved the heavy oak desk and Lilly snatched the paper out. "Well done, Charlie. Thank you."

He grinned meekly before returning to his task.

She began to put the letter on the stacks remaining to be sorted when the handwriting caught her eye. This was no bill of lading, no chemist's advertisement. Hairs prickled at the back of her neck. Her heart began to pound. She remembered this handwriting. Of course she would. It belonged to her mother.

Trembling, she sat on her father's desk chair and studied the letter. When had her mother written it? The paper was starting to yellow and bore deep indentations like a triangular leech bite, as though it had been pressed under that desk for a long time.

It had been directed to Charles Haswell without return address. The postal markings were faded and unreadable.

From where had she posted it? From someplace exotic, as Lilly had long imagined? From her London lodgings? Perhaps even from some nearby estate where she had a post? Lilly wondered if her father had read it and purposely hidden it from her all these years. Lilly ran a fingernail under the fold; the yellowed wax seal still held. It might very well have been lost in the chaos of her father's surgery, and lain there unread by anyone. Or perhaps the seal had become reaffixed from the pressure of the desk.

What answers did it hold?

Part of her longed to open it right then and there. Part of her was too exhausted to care. Did she really want to know?

She dutifully carried it up the stairs to her father's bedchamber. She was relieved to see him up and dressed, sitting at his little letter-writing desk, quill in hand.

He looked at her over his new spectacles, and she handed him the letter without comment. He turned it over in his hand, then sat still, staring at it, head bowed.

"I found it under your desk in the surgery."

He did not move.

"Do you know its contents?"

He gave a barely perceptible shake of his head.

"Father?"

"No, but I fear it."

"What more can she do to hurt us? After all this time?" Lilly held out her palm. He looked at her for a moment, blue eyes wide, before lowering his head again. He thrust the letter toward her without looking her way.

She took it from him and carried it to the window, where the light was better. She peeled open the shrunken wax seal and carefully unfolded the stiff yellowed paper.

A clue to the letter's age was given in its opening line.

A year has come and gone since I left Bedsley Priors.

Lilly read on silently. Finding out her mother was not traveling the continent nor the high seas as she had often imagined did not surprise her as it might once have done. At the time of this writing, her mother was living in London under another man's protection. But even that was not what shocked her.

"What can she mean?" Lilly murmured, and reread the section once more, this time aloud.

"I do not lay all the blame at your door, Charles. I know that as a wife, I was a disappointment, and that I broke our

*marriage vows even before you did, and in more respects. I had
been unhappy for quite some time, as you well know.*

*"I release you to M., Charles. I know she is the wife of your
heart. And if that poor afflicted girl can grow up with a father, then
I shall take some comfort in that. Comfort I sorely need whenever
guilt over leaving L. and C. rises to stab me in the heart. . . ."*

Lilly felt frozen and overheated all at once. Nerves tingled down
her spine and through her limbs. Her mind spun and spun again, down
through the years of memories, trying to force it all to make sense. *It
cannot mean what it appears to mean. It cannot.*

She looked at her father and saw the shame and grief in his eyes. For
so long she'd assumed him innocent, the victim. She had blamed her
mother alone! Blamed and empathized with and longed for. What good
was an endless memory if what it remembered had all been a lie?

"Is it true?" Lilly asked. "You and . . . Mrs. Mimpurse?"

"It was a long time ago."

The hands holding the letter shook. "How long?"

"More than twenty years . . . long before your mother left us. I
thought we had got past it."

"Where was Mr. Mimpurse?"

"Gone, as he often was, before he left for good."

"Before he died, you mean?"

"You had better ask Maude about that."

"You want me to ask your *lover*? I think not." Never had Lilly
used such a cutting tone with her father.

He winced.

Her mounting anger suddenly faded into a cold, dizzy cloud
that threatened to suffocate her. "What does she mean, 'if that poor
afflicted girl can grow up with a father'? Did she mean she expected
you to marry Mrs. Mimpurse and raise Mary as your own?"

Her father looked at her. Two seconds passed. Two ticks of the
clock. Three. Four.

"She is my own."

The company of agreeable friends will be the best medicine.

—DR. HILL, *THE OLD MAN'S GUIDE TO HEALTH AND LONGER LIFE*, 1764

CHAPTER 47

Lilly burst into the coffeehouse—through the front door, not the kitchen. Mary glanced up at her from where she was wiping off a table, startled by the door banging against the wall. Vaguely, Lilly noticed tears in Mary's eyes, eyes that were bloodshot and miserable.

Lilly faltered, suddenly not sure if, or how, to reveal her own news. Instead she asked, "What is it?"

Mary wiped randomly at the table without seeing its surface. Her finger bore only the smallest bandage now. "I know it is foolish. Did I not tell you he would be quickly shot of me once he learned . . . ?"

Oh no. "I am so sorry to hear it."

"I do not blame Mr. Shuttleworth, poor man. It is my own fault for not telling him I was not the woman he thought I was."

Lilly took a deep breath. She said unsteadily, "You are not the woman I thought you were either."

376

Mary looked up at her sharply, searchingly.

Lilly crossed the room and stood before her. "What do you know of your father?"

Mary straightened. "My father? Do you mean . . . Harold Mimpurse?"

Lilly asked quietly, "Do I?"

Mary stood perfectly still, only her sad blue eyes blinked. Eyes so like Charlie's, Lilly realized.

"Do you know?" Mary tentatively asked.

Lilly nodded. "Do you?"

"Yes."

They heard a sudden scraping of chair legs on the floor above them, and as the two stood there, staring at one another, Maude Mimpurse trod heavily down the stairs. She halted at the bottom step, holding the rail for support, looking from one of them to the other.

Lilly stepped forward and held the letter out to her. She kept her face impassive as Mrs. Mimpurse's wide eyes tried to search her own. Maude's gaze fled to the letter instead, and after a few seconds of skimming its contents, the woman pressed a trembling hand over her heart. She looked again at Lilly, shamefaced. The eyes she turned toward her daughter were filled with trepidation.

"You know?" she asked Mary.

"That Charles Haswell is my father?" Mary said matter-of-factly. "Yes, I know."

"How? For how long?" Maude was clearly stunned.

"My room is above this one, as yours is, and sound carries in this house, as you've just witnessed. I heard the two of you talking once. Arguing actually, about what Dr. Foster said about me. But even if I hadn't overheard, I had the evidence of my eyes, hadn't I? I remember *Papa* well enough to know there was nothing of the man in my veins." She splayed her fingers in the air beside her head. "And where else did this ridiculous hair come from?"

"I never thought it. Not once," Lilly said breathlessly. "Have I not always said you were more clever than I?"

Maude said, "We didn't want anyone to know Mr. Mimpurse was not your father. Your reputation would have suffered."

"Mine, or Charles Haswell's?" At the unusual rancor in Mary's tone, Lilly winced. She could easily imagine her father putting his precious Haswell reputation—and that of his shop—above anything else.

"It's very natural you should be upset," Maude said.

Mary took a deep breath. "I am not. I am glad she knows."

Lilly stared at Mary, a girl she had always known, but had never really known at all.

"Lill finding out we are sisters is the only good thing this day has brought."

Sisters.

"*That,*" Lilly said, "I have always known."

Mary looked skeptical, brows high. "Indeed?"

"Though I may have forgotten, for a year or two."

"Lilly Haswell forgetting," Mary said, smiling tremulously. "A day of firsts all around."

Maude, Mary, and Lilly sat in the kitchen near the hearth, all three indulging in a rare glass of honey wine.

"It was about a year after your father returned to Bedsley Priors with his new bride," Maude began. "I had loved Charles for years and, in truth, thought he would marry me when he returned from his apothecary's training in London. Instead he came home with a beautiful wife."

Tears brightened Maude's eyes even all these years later. "I could not blame him. We were not officially engaged. And Rosamond *was* very lovely, though she seemed to regret the marriage almost at once. I was heartbroken but decided I would go on as best I could. I married Harold Mimpurse, though I'd refused him once before. I had always wanted to open a coffeehouse once my days as a maid were behind me, and Harold promised to set me up. And that's the one promise he kept. He was a goodhearted man but had the constancy of a hound." She glanced at Mary. "Sorry, my dear."

Mary nodded.

"He was gone more often than not, peddling his copper wares once he'd been decommissioned from the army. Met up with a widow in Reading and spent more nights with her than with me. It was during one of these absences that your mother left the first time, before you were born."

"The first time?" Lilly interrupted. "She'd left before?" Lilly instantly recalled Mrs. Kilgrove's seemingly delirious words about her mother's first return.

Maude nodded. "Charles and I were both hurting and lonely, and temptation had its way. I thought perhaps we'd be together after all, Charles and I, after a fashion. But then, Rosamond came back only two days later. As though she'd only been gone shopping. I don't know that she ever told your father where she'd gone or who she'd been with, but I saw how shaken and repentant she was. Charles and I were mortified over what we'd done and didn't speak of it for years.

"Your parents had a real marriage after that, it seemed. For a time anyway. Mr. Mimpurse came back as well, though I cannot say with equal repentance. He soon left again, while Rosamond stayed. How could I tell Charles I was carrying his child? When his marriage looked to finally be on solid ground? Especially when Rosamond soon confided she, too, was carrying a child?" Maude paused to drain her glass.

How difficult that must have been for her, Lilly thought. She had always known her father and Mrs. Mimpurse were fond of one another beneath their sharp words and brusque ways, but she'd had no idea how deep those feelings went.

"When Rosamond was in her lying in, I admit I wondered if the child would look like Charles . . . and I wondered if he feared the child would not." She turned wine-warmed eyes on Lilly. "But one look at you and it was perfectly clear you were Charles Haswell's daughter, with tufts of his reddish hair already gracing your little head. As you grew older, you came to look more like your mother, but are still so like him in many ways.

"After that, I tried all the harder to be a friend to your mother.

Both of us having wee girls so near in age gave us plenty in common we'd not had before. I cannot say I felt *no* resentment, but I prayed God would give me a love for her, and I think He answered."

Maude reached over and refilled their glasses, though hers was the only one empty.

"Things went along quite uneventfully until Charlie was born. Such a hard birth it was. Your poor father. He did all he knew how, but it wasn't enough. He even sent Mrs. Fowler to fetch Dr. Foster. The man was so long in coming, Charles thought he had refused. Foster never gave an excuse for his delay. I don't think your father has ever forgiven him for it."

Lilly shook her head. "I had no idea."

"Finally Foster did come with his gruesome forceps and cold con-descension and pulled the child from your mother at last. To his credit, he also revived the babe. Poor Charlie was nearly blue at birth."

Thoughtfully, Maude shook her head. "Rosamond was cast down after that. Not even your sweet face could cheer her."

Lilly felt the familiar ache of rejection stir in her breast.

"By Charlie's first birthday, it was evident that something was not right with the lad. Very little could hold his attention. He did not want to be held or petted. Was slow to creep, stand, and walk. But still she stayed."

Maude sighed. "Harold did not. When Mary was twelve years old, he announced he would not be returning. I told no one. I confess I was tempted to announce that he had died on one of his trips. The status of widow so less shameful than abandoned wife. When I received a letter from the Reading widow a few months later, I thought I had brought his death down upon him. Killed in a fall from his horse. Can you imagine? Him, a war hero. I'd have sooner believed the pox." She took another sip and stared at the embers in the hearth.

"Rosamond did not leave until some three years later. I saw her walk away with her carpetbag, dressed for travel. I knew your father had gone to see Sir Henry, so I ran next door, to make certain Charlie was all right. You and Mary were already at Mrs. Shaw's. I asked Mrs. Fowler where your mother had gone, but she said the missus hadn't told her a thing, just bid her look after the lad till Charles come home. I hurried after Rosamond in the direction she'd gone. I did not actually see her on the narrowboat that was heading east on the canal, but Mrs. Kilgrove did. Said Mrs. Haswell had embarked with a tall, dark-haired man in naval dress. Of course, Mrs. Kilgrove's sight wasn't keen even then."

Quinn or Wells? Lilly wondered and shifted in her chair. "In London, I learned that Mother hoped to marry a naval captain before she met Father. But the man married another." She thought of what Dr. Graves had told her. Had first Quinn, then Wells disappointed her?

Mrs. Mimpurse nodded her understanding. She looked exhausted from the telling, eyes bleary and troubled. She glanced back at the letter, almost forgotten in her hand. "I always wondered if your mother knew, or guessed, about your father and I. If it had something to do with her leaving. But with so much time passing between, I hoped I was not to blame." She reached over and grasped Lilly's fingers with her free hand, eyes intense. "I promise you, Lilly, your father and I were together those two nights twenty years gone, and never again since."

Lilly nodded, feeling sick and dazed about the whole affair. "I always feared *I* was to blame."

"Oh, my dear, why?"

Lilly took a deep breath, trying to keep her voice steady. "We argued, you see, a few days before she left. She received a letter, which was rare for her, but would not tell me who it was from. She became angry when I kept asking her. Of course, now I wonder if the letter was from a man. This officer."

Mrs. Mimpurse considered this. "A letter might very well explain why she left when she did. But it wasn't your fault." Again she squeezed Lilly's hand. "Why, if every woman left after an argument with her daughter, there wouldn't be a mother left at home in all of England." Mrs. Mimpurse glanced at Mary, and mother and daughter shared a knowing look.

Lilly felt as if a stone had been lifted from her chest. She gently retrieved the letter from Maude's hand and reread its few lines. "It is as if she expected you and Father to marry. But how could you?"

Maude Mimpurse took a deep, shuddering breath. "How could we, indeed."

❧

On a crisp autumn afternoon, Lilly saw Roderick Marlow standing before his father's grave, black mourning cloak about his shoulders. They had buried Sir Henry a fortnight before. The villagers had turned out in great numbers for his funeral, Lilly and her father among them. She had already given her condolences, which were civilly if awkwardly received. Still, seeing him standing there now, alone, she felt compelled to speak to him.

When he glanced over and noticed her beside him, he acknowledged her with a silent nod.

She stood there with him for several moments, looking at the freshly turned soil. The headstone would be several weeks or even longer in the making.

"What will you do now?" she asked gently.

He wiped his nose with a handkerchief and inhaled deeply. "I suppose I shall go forth and find a wealthy wife," he said archly. "So I can afford the widow's jointure and somehow manage to keep the place up. Father would no doubt haunt me if I let the place fall to ruin."

"And what will become of—" she hesitated—"the former Miss Powell?"

He shrugged. "She was my father's wife, no matter what else she be. She will have a place at Marlow House for as long as she wants one. Though I doubt it will be for long. Once she receives her portion, she will no doubt move on, perhaps even remarry. I wish her no ill will."

"You surprise me," she said. "I never took you for a merciful sort. Except when you secured my brother's release, of course."

He looked at her for a moment, then away, off into the distance. "That was your clever Mr. Baylor's doing. He brought to my attention how my old friend Ackers was having his ribbons yanked by Foster. Never liked the man. I suppose Baylor knew that and used it to goad me into action. Anything to put a fly in that man's ointment." He looked at her again. "Though had I known you'd kiss me for it, I might have done so anyway."

Francis.

"Truth is, I owe Cassandra a debt. I wronged her long ago and believe she married my father as revenge. She never admitted it, but . . ." He left the thought unfinished.

"What happened? How did you—?"

He tapped a finger against her lips. "Tut, tut, Miss Haswell. Have I taught you nothing? That memory is long gone, and I intend to keep it that way."

He glanced down once more at his father's bare grave beside his mother's ornate headstone. "I still regret my bitter words to him. How I wish I might see him again."

She said quietly, "But you can see him again someday. After all, you know where he is."

He shrugged. "I confess I have never shared your faith, Miss Haswell."

"I am sorry to hear it."

"I suppose I lost it when I lost my mother. Did not you?"

Lilly took a deep breath, considering. "For a time, perhaps."

He turned to her and gently gripped her shoulders. "Still, might we not share other things?"

Shaking her head, she pulled away. "Let me go, Sir Roderick. And I will do the same of you."

❧

A week later, Lilly hatched her plan for a long-belated gift for Mary.

"It is all settled," she announced as soon as she stepped into the coffeehouse kitchen. "You and I shall go to London. It isn't right that I have been while you have not."

383

Mary's lips parted, but she quickly resumed her work. She kneaded the dough, turning the lump over and pressing it down with the butt of her palm. "No, Lilly. I don't need—"

"Yes you do. You deserve a holiday in London. My aunt has sent a far too generous gift of funds which will see us there in fine fashion."

"I don't know. What about the coffeehouse?"

"Father is doing well enough and has said he will help, as will Mrs. Fowler if need be. We have all conspired against you, Mary, so further objections will only prove futile."

As she separated and placed the dough in pans, Mary seemed lost in thought and Lilly was afraid she was formulating another argument. Instead she asked, "Could we eat somewhere very fine?"

Lilly smiled. "Of course."

"And see a palace or two?"

"Or three! And anything else you'd like."

"I would dearly enjoy that, I think."

"And I would dearly enjoy being there with you. Perhaps we might take in a play, or visit the museums, or the shops."

"And Francis?" Mary suggested.

The mention of his name turned Lilly's stomach into a ten-stone sack of wormwood and regret. "Oh. I am sure he is very busy . . . doing whatever it is he went to London to do."

"You've had no word?"

Lilly shook her head and forced a light tone. "I don't even know where his lodgings are. He did send Charlie a letter on his birthday, but it bore no address." Upon admitting she'd checked this, Lilly felt her ears burn and fiddled with her gloves.

"Never mind," Mary said. "We shall have plenty of other handsome sights to see, shall we not?" She grinned, and Lilly could not resist mirroring the gesture.

They settled on Friday of the following week for their departure, and Lilly posted a letter to her aunt and uncle, letting them know of their coming visit and asking to call at their convenience. She went through her wardrobe and pulled out two gowns she had barely worn since returning home, and two others she thought would do nicely for Mary.

They visited the new village milliner for hats and gloves and the dressmaker in Devizes for warm autumn cloaks. Together they planned an itinerary and packed.

On the night before their departure, they sat down to supper together. Her father looking younger than he had in months, Mrs. Mimpurse, rosy-cheeked and cheery. And Mary pretty in a new frock, her hair curled and pinned high on her head in a fashion they had seen in *La Belle Assemblée*. Even Charlie came, late and mussed, straight from the garden, and they had to send him to the well to wash.

"Goodness, Mary," he said upon his return. "You're as pretty as the portraits hangin' at Marlow House."

Mary smiled with no hint of blush. She clearly felt as lovely as she looked.

They dined on vegetable-marrow soup, fried soles, veal and ham pie, and all manner of vegetables, breads, sauces, and jams. The Mimpurse ladies had truly outdone themselves. But the biggest surprise came after, when Mary carried out a beautifully frosted Rich Bride Cake. Or, Lilly mused, was it a Christening Cake?

"What's this?" Maude asked, perplexed. "Is there something you are wanting to tell us?"

Now Mary blushed. "No. I have not gone and got myself a husband. Or a babe."

"Thank the good Lord for that," her mother murmured.

Mary remained standing at the table before them, and made the first speech Lilly could ever remember her giving. "But I do feel there is cause for celebration. For thanksgiving. For God has added greatly to my family, and I am thankful indeed."

"Here, here," Lilly said as she lifted her small glass. She glanced at her father and glimpsed tears rising to fill his blue eyes. She saw him glance at Maude, and answering tears brighten her eyes as well.

"I have always had the best of mothers . . ." Mary began.

Lilly found herself nodding to this. She too had gained the best of mothers. In many ways, Maude Mimpurse had long been a second mother to her.

"But now I have a brother—"

"Now, Mary, I ain't really." Charlie could still not grasp the change in their relationship, and Lilly could barely blame him, so recently had the facts come to light.

"And sister." She smiled at Lilly, eyes shining. Mary's voice was hoarse when she added, "And Father."

Tears spilled down Charles Haswell's freshly shaven cheeks. Lilly was distracted by Charlie, however, his face bunched up into a grimace of confusion and working himself up to a question. Hoping to divert him from asking about Mr. Mimpurse, Lilly said to him, "You don't like cake, do you, Charlie?"

He looked nearly indignant at this. "Indeed I do. You know I do. Father! Lilly forgot I like cake. Why, it's my favorite."

Sharing a knowing glance with Lilly, Mary said, "Then you shall have the first piece, Charlie. Would you like a little piece or a large one?"

"A gurt big one, Mary, if you please."

The moment was saved.

The evening was the most delightful in recent memory. They all stayed and did the washing up together, and then Mrs. Mimpurse shooed the girls off to bed, saying she would finish putting the dishes away on her own. She reminded them they had a big day ahead of them, and the London coach would not wait, should they oversleep. At the kitchen door, her father gently embraced Mary before bidding her a good night. Lilly wanted to throw her arms around her friend . . . no, sister . . . too, but Mary was already backing away, waving good-bye on her way up to bed. Ah, well. They would have a whole week together in London.

The next morning, Lilly awoke early, taking a great deal of time with her appearance. She felt unaccountably nervous about returning to London. Her gowns would no longer be the latest, and her hands were calloused from long hours with the pestle. Thank goodness for gloves. She wished she might have thought to ask Mary to come over and help her with her hair. Not as a servant might, but as sisters might help one another. She felt giddy at the thought, and at the adventure ahead. She packed the items she had just used—brush and comb, tooth sponge and alum—into her valise and checked once more to make certain her money was in her reticule. Putting on her hat and cloak, she slipped the reticule onto her wrist and left her bedchamber, descending the stairs with no effort to be quiet. If her father was not yet awake, he ought to be rising. He insisted he wanted to be there to see them off. But it was not her father who stood in the laboratory-kitchen, awaiting her noisy descent.

Mrs. Mimpurse stood there, a shawl thrown hastily over her night-dress, hair down, face . . . broken. Tears and anguish marred her countenance and Lilly froze in shocked horror. She knew the truth even before Mrs. Mimpurse could form the world-darkening words.

Part III

Thus ends the story of the apothecary.

Although he has ceased to exist in name,

his art still survives, and though stripped of much of its

ancient mystery, it is likely to live, so long as suffering

humanity has need of drugs and medicines to alleviate

the ills to which the flesh is heir.

—C. J. S. THOMPSON, *MYSTERY AND ART OF THE APOTHECARY*

Sweet Memory! wafted by thy gentle gale,

Oft up the stream of Time I turn my sail.

—SAMUEL ROGERS

Remember Man as you Pasby
as You Are Now So once Was i
as i am Now so Must You Bee
Make Peace with Christ And
FOLLOW ME

—1715 EPITAPH, *WILTSHIRE NOTES AND QUERIES*

CHAPTER 48

M ary Helen Mimpurse had died in her sleep. And according to her mother, and to Mr. Shuttleworth who had attended her, peacefully. No sign of a fit marred her lovely, placid features, nor her pale fingers. Mr. Shuttleworth said he had seen the like before, in the asylum where he once worked, though he did not pretend to understand the cause of death.

Lilly did not think she could have loved Mary more for knowing they were sisters, but she did mourn her loss more deeply, more enduringly, for that knowledge.

How Lilly wished she had known the truth sooner, even while she understood her father's and Mrs. Mimpurse's reasons for keeping it secret. She wished she might have explored, embraced, relished the strange and wonderful fact that she had a sister. Had she not always longed for one? Someone with whom to share frocks and courtship confessions. Someone to favour.

Now Lilly longed to look once more into Mary's dear face and recognize all that she had been blind to. Charles Haswell's features softened by Maude Mimpurse's rounder ones. Charles Haswell's—and Charlie's—blue eyes. The ginger hue of the Haswell hair, though a lighter wash upon Mary's fine silken strands. And what of Mary's infallible memory for the most complex recipes? So like Lilly's with physic.

Now Lilly felt guilty for the slight superiority of situation, intellect, and even beauty she had felt toward Mary over the years. *How mistaken I was!* Mary, she concluded, was the wiser, lovelier woman twice over.

As the days, then weeks, then months passed, regret for the past transformed into pining for a future that would never be. Lilly thought of all she and Mary would miss together. They would have been aunts to each other's children. Their children close cousins. She thought of the hours they would have enjoyed, sitting together in Mary's coffee-house—for it would have been hers—nibbling on scones and village news and the triumphs of their children and grandchildren.

What comfort there would have been in beholding that familiar face and seeing the lines and reeves there, as on her own. They would have grown old together, yet seen in each other the young women they had once been, long after everyone else saw but two grizzled crones. Long after their husbands were gone—men did seem to die the sooner—they would have bided together as they had "a day back agone," as Mrs. Kilgrove would say. Of course all of this was assuming Mary would have been allowed to wed.

Lilly would have seen to it somehow.

Charlie still visited the churchyard, as he always had. He no longer went to count dead men. He went instead to talk to Mary. He sat in the sun, his back resting against Sir Henry's headstone. Lilly did not think the old baronet would have minded.

Poor Charlie, Lilly thought. He had lost another woman he loved. Lilly prayed nothing would happen to her.

Since the fire, they had begun referring their patients to Shuttleworth's—or even to Dr. Foster, as the case required. Several of their oldest patients, Mrs. Kilgrove and Mr. Owen to name two, still insisted they would see a Haswell and no other, and she and her father did what they could for them.

That spring after Mary's death, Lilly and her father tended the physic garden together, and throughout the summer months, sold the herbs and simples to Shuttleworth and other medical men in the county, but also to the proprietor of The George, and other hostelries which had no kitchen-garden of their own. She—and even her father, when he was able—helped in the coffeehouse now that Mary was gone. Though neither her father nor Maude would likely admit it, Lilly thought the two old friends took great comfort in each other's company.

With the arrival of September, Lilly finally received a letter from Francis Baylor. Her heart squeezed at the sight of it and, hand to her chest, she stepped into the garden to read it.

Dear Miss Haswell,

I have only just learned of Miss Mary's death. I was stunned and deeply sorrowed as no doubt everyone in Bedsley Priors must be, but especially you and Mrs. Mimpurse. You have my deepest sympathies. Had I known in time, I would have returned for the funeral, in hopes of being some comfort to your families at such a dark hour.

Though my lodgings seem to change with much regularity, I know I ought to have given you or your father some way to contact me. I had my reasons for not doing so at the time, but they seem foolish now, given what has happened. I hope you will forgive me.

I am here in London studying to become a fully qualified apothecary. Under the Apothecaries' Act, I need to acquire a certificate from the Court of Examiners to practice as an apothecary. But I did not tell you my plans, because in all truth I was not certain I should be able to afford the schooling, nor that I would succeed in passing the examinations. You know I have never been a quick student. . . .

"Nonsense," she breathed. "That was only as a lad. When you did not apply yourself."

> *. . . But I am succeeding. Beyond my five-year appren-*
> *ticeship with your father, the new Act requires instruction in*
> *anatomy, botany, chemistry, materia medica, and physic, in*
> *addition to six months' practical hospital experience. I am now*
> *undergoing the latter here at Guy's Hospital. God willing, I will*
> *set out my own shingle one day, if you can believe it. I occasion-*
> *ally see Dr. Graves about the place, though he is master to my*
> *pupil. I suppose his return to London means you will soon be*
> *returning as well?*
>
> *I have taken your advice and made the acquaintance of Mr.*
> *Lippert and his son and daughter. They have made me most*
> *welcome on several occasions. Miss Lippert is quite as charming*
> *as you led me to believe, and I must thank you for making the*
> *family known to me. The felicity of their society has given my life*
> *in London a congeniality I had not hoped to find. Mr. Lippert*
> *has even offered to sell his shop to me, hinting that I might have*
> *a wife in the bargain. He is only jesting, of course.*

Lilly inhaled sharply. *Is he?* she wondered.

Francis went on to describe his studies at both the laboratory and gardens of the Apothecaries' Society as well as his time spent "walking the wards" at Guy's. He ended by giving his address and asking how her father fared. He sent his best to Mr. Haswell and said he would write to Mrs. Mimpurse himself.

He signed it *FB*.

No *love*, no *warmly*, no *sincerely*. Her spirits sank. But after nearly a year, what had she expected?

Still, Lilly wrote back to Francis, at the address he had given, and described her father's ongoing symptoms. She also told Francis in the most dispassionate terms of the demise of Haswell's as he knew it. She was surprised when he wrote back directly and suggested her father come to London. Thomas Bromley and a master apothecary at the teaching hospital were working with glandular and lung fever and might be able to help him. He said he would have suggested it earlier, but believed Charles Haswell would never consider leaving his shop as long as its doors remained open. Francis even offered to share his lodgings. It seemed there was a small pantry her father might have for nothing. She expected he was teasing with this last part and doubted her father would be interested in submitting himself to hospital care in any case.

She was wrong.

Within a matter of days, she and her father had made plans to travel to London. Aunt and Uncle Elliott had extended several invitations over the preceding months and wrote to say they would be delighted to have her stay with them for as long as she liked, Charles as well. But her father was adamant about going to the hospital directly. He was tired of being ill and wanted to start treatment as soon as possible.

Lilly was relieved they would not be arriving during the height of the season, but rather the quiet of autumn. They traveled by post to London and, from the coaching inn, hired a hackney to take them the rest of the distance to Guy's.

Lilly had worn black and grey mourning clothes for six months, as custom decreed for the passing of a sister. But now, a year after Mary's death, she wore one of her more reserved promenade dresses from her London days, no longer in fashion and creased from the journey. She found she could not care. Her thoughts were of Francis. She longed to see him, but felt increasingly jittery and ill at ease as they neared the hospital.

There it was. The gate, the tan and grey building were familiar. Yet how long ago it seemed since she had been there with Dr. Graves. She wondered if she would see him again, and felt nervous at the prospect. She hoped he held no ill will toward her.

Taking her father's arm and a deep breath, they walked past the columns and arched doorway, and into the main corridor.

She was surprised to find Dr. Graves awaiting them in the

receiving office. His smile was sincere, if reserved, as he stepped forward to greet them.

"Mr. Haswell." He shook her father's hand. "Welcome. And Miss Haswell." He bowed, then faltered. "I . . . trust you are well."

She nodded. "I am. And you?"

He pursed his lips, considering. "Like a fish tossed back in the pond."

She opened her mouth to reply but hesitated. Did he mean that he was relieved to be back in his element, or that he felt rejected? Before she could fashion some suitable reply, he returned his attention to her father.

"Dr. Bromley has been called away, I am afraid. But I have agreed to oversee your case until he returns." With that, Dr. Graves excused himself, saying he would see if the bed for Mr. Haswell was ready.

Francis appeared along the corridor. His pace hastened to a near-jog at seeing them, and he smiled broadly. Reaching them, he shook her father's hand vigorously. "Mr. Haswell, I am so glad you've come. You've arrived just when you wrote you would."

"Yes, we made good time by post."

He turned to Lilly, suddenly more reticent. "Miss Haswell." He bowed, and she curtsied stiffly, surprised at his cool greeting.

Graves rejoined them, and Lilly saw Francis hesitate. "Ah, here's Dr. Graves." She noticed him glance from the physician to her and back again.

"Dr. Bromley has quite a schedule of tests and treatments in store for you, Mr. Haswell," Dr. Graves said. "I trust we shall have you stronger very soon."

Her father nodded. "Excellent. When do we start?"

"Tomorrow morning. Let's get you settled into a room for a good night's sleep first."

Her father turned to her and said warmly, "I will bid you farewell here, my dear. I am sure you will not want to venture into the men's ward."

"Indeed no." She received her father's kiss and embraced him in return. She whispered, "I shall pray for you every day."

"I count on it." He held her at arm's length and looked directly into her face, as though committing her features to memory. As though in final farewell. Lilly felt her lips begin to tremble and forced them into a smile.

"Never fear," Francis assured her. She felt the barest graze of his hand at her elbow. "He will be in excellent hands with your Dr. Graves here."

She felt her smile falter and her brow pucker at his final words.

"Well," Dr. Graves said to her father. "Why don't I show you the way." He glanced back at Francis, brows raised. "Mr. Baylor?"

Francis was still looking at Lilly. "I shall be along directly. I shall just see Miss Haswell out. Hail a hackney for her."

Dr. Graves nodded, stiffly resigned. "Very well." And led her father away.

With a sweep of his hand, Francis gestured Lilly toward the entrance and walked beside her. She was filled with nervous antici-pation at being alone with him. Would he say anything? Should she? Her palms were damp, while her mouth felt suddenly dry.

"Staying with your aunt and uncle?" he asked.

"Yes. In Mayfair."

He nodded. "How does Mrs. Mimpurse fare?"

"As well as can be expected. Still wearing her mourning, though."

Somberly, he reached over and pressed her hand. Her whole arm tingled. "Again, I am sorry I was not there."

She nodded her understanding, disappointed he had released her hand so quickly. An awkward silence followed, broken only by the sound of their echoing footfalls. They had never been so stiff and formal in one another's company before. Had it been too long? Were things irreparable between them?

As they emerged through the columns into the courtyard, Lilly asked too brightly, "And how are the Lipperts?"

He pursed his lips. "Fine, last I saw them." They reached the gutter and Francis hailed a hackney carriage approaching from up the street. "I am afraid I haven't visited of late. I've been busy preparing for exams." He turned to look at her, hesitated, then said, "Your Dr. Graves has never given his reason for leaving Bedsley Priors. I admit I wondered. When I received your letter, I deduced it was something to do with Foster and the fire. I suppose he is waiting until he fully establishes himself here before—"

The hackney driver reined in his horse beside them, the sound of hooves and his "Whoa now" interrupting their conversation.

The jarvey leapt down and opened the carriage door. Francis gave the driver the direction and handed him Lilly's valise. Francis offered her his hand.

She accepted it and stepped up into the carriage. She held on tightly for a fleeting moment, then let go. "Thank you," she murmured. Why could she not find the words? Tell him she'd been wrong?

The driver climbed back to his perch as Lilly took a seat and looked down at Francis from the open window.

Last chance, Lill, she thought. *Say something. Say something now.* Heart hammering, she opened her mouth and managed two breathless syllables. "Francis?"

He lifted his chin to meet her gaze, his brown eyes expectant.

She spoke the words before she lost her courage. "He isn't *my* Dr. Graves."

His eyes searched hers. The jarvey cracked his whip and the carriage lurched away.

When they reached Mayfair, the driver handed her down on her aunt and uncle's street. She tried to pay the jarvey, but he waved her away, saying the gentleman had already done so. Francis, who had always been so careful with his money. Now she realized he had been saving for his education all along. She picked up her valise and paused to take in the tall façade of the building. The stately white townhouse was still familiar, of course. Yet how long ago it seemed since she had thought of it as home.

She walked up the steps and was let in by stony-faced Fletcher, who barely concealed a smile at seeing her. Dupree dashed down the stairs and seemed about to embrace her, then thought the better of it and curtsied instead. Her aunt and uncle did embrace her and welcomed her warmly. How good it was to see them all again.

Stepping into her former room in the Elliotts' home was like visiting a museum of the past. Her best ball gowns, slippers, and hair ornaments were all as she had left them—relics of another age—*a day back agone.* On the dressing table was a clipping from the *Times,* which announced the wedding of Roger Bromley and Susan Whittier. Lilly grinned ruefully. She hoped Roger would finally be happy.

Before going to sleep, she slid to her knees beside the bed. Something, she realized, she had not done a single time while she had lived here those eighteen months. Now she couldn't imagine *not* doing so.

She prayed for her father, far from home, and for the doctors and apothecaries who would endeavor to help him. She prayed for Francis and Dr. Graves. She prayed for Charlie, Maude Mimpurse, and her mother, wherever she was.

Then she climbed into the soft, lofty featherbed with a sigh of pleasure.

Her aunt and uncle had planned a full week of events and outings. Lilly would have liked to visit Guy's again while she was in town, to see how her father was getting on. But he had been adamant that she not worry about him—that she allow the doctors to do their work while she enjoyed herself in London. She would do her best to honor his request.

The dear Elliotts no doubt hoped Lilly would yet return to them to stay. But Lilly knew then that she would not. Not for anything longer than a visit. As much as she enjoyed London, Bedsley Priors was, after all, home.

Remember, it's as easy to marry a rich woman as a poor woman.

—WILLIAM MAKEPEACE THACKERAY

CHAPTER 49

Several months later, on a wet day in late spring, Lilly stood upon Grey's Hill, taking in the damp vale, the canal and the village—her village—below. The bluebells and plum trees were in bloom, and the mist carried the honeyed scents of their blossoms.

She was mildly surprised to see Mr. Shuttleworth climbing the footpath toward her. Reaching the summit, he paused to catch his breath. "I've become too sedentary. This mound seems a veritable mountain this morning."

"Good day, Mr. Shuttleworth."

He bowed. "Miss Haswell. How fares your father?"

"He is doing quite well."

"I am pleased to hear it."

In London, her father had undergone several courses of treatment—aconite inhalation among them—and had returned home greatly restored. The demise of Haswell's had produced that silver lining at least. She returned her gaze to the village below, wearing a veil of mist.

"A haypenny for your thoughts," he said.

Quietly, she admitted, "I was thinking about Mary."

He nodded, his features pinched as if in sudden pain. "You must despise me, Miss Haswell. For I know I disappointed your friend."

He picked up a handful of chalk and pebbles in one hand, and with the other, tossed them as far as he could—not far at all. "I suppose I am a coward. But the thought of becoming attached to any woman, dear though she may be, who might succumb at any moment . . . I could not do it."

Do any of us know the number of our days? Lilly thought, but refrained from saying so. She watched as he dusted his hands, unaware that he had gotten chalk on his usually immaculate coat. "I believe I understand, Mr. Shuttleworth, and I know Mary did. But for my part, I would give anything to have a little more time with her, no matter the cost or risk."

He looked at her, then away again toward the village. He inhaled a long breath. "You were great friends."

"More than friends. Sisters."

He lifted his chin. "Ah. I heard the tale, but was not certain I was supposed to know."

"I am glad you know. Did you not once tell us we could be sisters?"

"Yes, angels the both of you. Sisters in spirit."

He was right in a sense. She and Mary had been like sisters even before they knew they were related by blood.

"She was an excellent girl. Truly. I regret I did not tell her so more often."

Tears brightened his dark eyes, and Lilly felt answering tears fill her own. Impulsively, she reached over and squeezed his hand. "So do I."

He looked down at their clasped hands, then turned his gaze to the canal below. "I should tell you I am leaving Bedsley Priors."

Lilly slowly shook her head. *Must everybody leave?* "I cannot say I am surprised, but I am sorry to hear it."

"Are you? Then perhaps you ought to come with me. See more of the world, as you once longed to do. I feel the sea calling to me and must visit her again. Why not come along? There is less to keep you here now, is there not?"

An incredulous laugh escaped her. "Mr. Shuttleworth! I know you have never concerned yourself with the rules of polite society, but even you must see the impropriety of such a suggestion."

He grinned ruefully, and she smiled in return.

"I do enjoy your company, Mr. Shuttleworth, and will miss it more than you know. But . . ." She sighed. "This is my home. I am at last content here. I wonder," she asked kindly, "if you shall ever be content anywhere?"

She spoke from genuine concern and was relieved when he seemed to take no offense.

"I wonder that as well." He looked out to the horizon. "But I cannot help thinking I will find it. Someday, somewhere, beyond that hill, or the next. In the next county or the next port. . . ."

She nodded thoughtfully. "For my part, I would not wish to live always on the move, a few years here and there. Perhaps once, but no longer. I have become quite attached to Bedsley Priors since my London days."

"Yes, sometimes we must lose something . . . someone . . . before we realize its worth."

She remembered Francis once saying something similar. They were silent several moments, each one thinking of his own losses. Finally she asked, "How soon do you leave?"

"As soon as I can manage it. I've received an offer from the advertisement I placed in the *Times*. If all goes as planned, I shall be selling out and moving on in no more than a fortnight."

She groaned inwardly. *Another new medical man to get used to.* "I daresay your replacement will not realize how fortunate he is with so much less competition now that Haswell's and Dr. Graves have gone."

"Has your father no plans to reopen?"

"None he will admit to. He is, however, expanding the physic garden. He likes the idea of making a tidy profit on his *famous* Haswell herbs."

Mr. Shuttleworth chuckled. "Perhaps he ought to stay on as a chemist, then."

"I think not. Haswells are apothecaries the way we are English. One cannot simply change citizenship at will."

Again he chuckled and nodded his understanding.

For several minutes they stood without speaking. Down on the canal, a narrowboat was slowly making its way under the Honeystreet Bridge. "I remember when I first arrived here and saw you standing on that bridge," Mr. Shuttleworth said. "One of the three lovely entice-ments to settle here."

She nodded at the memory.

"Do you know if Miss Robbins enjoys the sea?"

"Mr. Shuttleworth!" Lilly was incredulous and amused both. "Are you serious?"

"Why not?"

"She is daughter of a boat builder," Lilly allowed.

"My thoughts exactly."

Lilly thought about Francis. "Mr. Baylor seemed to think a lot of her as well."

"Do you think so? He was attentive to her, I own. But nothing to the attention he paid you. In any event, he departed, leaving the field open for me."

She shook her head, grinning in spite of herself.

"You judge me fickle, Miss Haswell? I protest your censure. I have always been completely loyal to whichever one of the three of you I could convince to fall madly in love with me—and did not tend toward seasickness."

Nor sickness of any kind, she thought sadly, but did not say so.

"Now . . ." He rubbed his hands together comically, looking down toward Mill House and the barge yard. "I wonder if Miss Robbins is in the mood for adventure."

Still shaking her head, Lilly watched him go.

Realizing she had lingered far too long, Lilly trotted down the damp, windswept hill to help Mrs. Mimpurse and Jane serve supper. She was enjoying helping at the coffeehouse. For all Mary's teasing, Lilly had learned to convert from her ingrained apothecaries' measurements to the standard with less trouble than she would have imagined. Still, many was the time Maude found her bent over the worktable with a frayed quill and scrap of paper, checking her sums. Lilly was still no great cook, but was steadily improving. She took to baking more naturally. She liked the careful measurements required, the level teaspoonfuls of leavening or pounds of fat. Not the "pinch of this and handful of that" mode Mrs. Mimpurse used to throw together stews, soups, and other dishes with such easy flair.

When she stood in Mary's place at the old worn worktable, Lilly felt closer to her sister-friend. She took pleasure and comfort in mixing, in kneading, in shaping dough. Not so different from mixing and cutting pills, really.

Still, she found herself unexpectedly missing the shop. She hadn't realized how much she had enjoyed knowing how to help people and doing so as confidently as Maude whipped up a suet pudding or pasty. Francis had been right. Lilly even missed the feel of the mortar and pestle in her hands, and when she brought a small one from the shop to use in mixing spices, she saw Maude bite her lip, but the dear woman had not protested.

Now, as Lilly rounded the corner of the vicarage, she slowed her pace according to long habit. When she reached the coffeehouse and opened its door, she paused as she usually did to inhale deeply of the sweet, familiar aromas. Freshly ground coffee beans, cinnamon, nutmegs, ginger, and cloves.

Smells like home . . .

She did not miss the alligator.

LOVAGE

A known and much praised remedy.

—CULPEPER'S COMPLETE HERBAL

CHAPTER 50

L illy remembered it clearly, although it was years ago now. For she remembered everything.

She remembered the day Francis arrived by narrowboat more than seven years before, as a seasick apprentice. She had been standing on the Honeystreet Bridge, as she often did, searching for her mother on every narrowboat that passed by on the canal.

She stood there now on a warm springtime evening, a fortnight after her meeting with Mr. Shuttleworth atop Grey's Hill. *One last time*, she told herself. Once more searching—searching God's will for the future, searching her memory for every moment spent with Francis Baylor, Mary Mimpurse, her mother—even Roger Bromley and Dr. Graves. Dear ones lost to her. Any day now, Mr. Shuttleworth would join that list.

She watched as a barge approached from the east, followed by a narrowboat.

She had given up standing there all those months she had tried to manage her father's shop. She hadn't the time for it then. Now it seemed she had a great deal of time.

Or do I? she wondered. She once thought she had all the time in the world to see the world, enjoy the world. Now she understood what far wiser people had long known—no one is promised the world, nor even the morrow.

Lilly used to long for travel and adventure far from Bedsley Priors. But death and loss had narrowed her sights. Her telescope no longer focused on the horizon, but rather on what was nearest and dearest to her heart. The rest was just so much water boiled away and gone—it might steam the glass and cloud one's view for a time, but in the end it vanished, leaving only the purest essence of life behind. Family. Faith. Friends and neighbors. Health. Things Mary would have given her last breath for, and perhaps had.

Lilly told herself all this, and yet she knew. She knew her heart had never gotten over the loss, the missing of one gone away from her. Should she return to London and begin a *new* search? No. She must let go. Again.

The barge passed under the Honeystreet Bridge, its load of coal sinking the vessel low in the canal's waters. A crewman lifted his hat to Lilly, and she dipped her head in acknowledgment. She knew she should be getting back. Her father and Mrs. Mimpurse were having a few neighbors in for whist and tea—an unofficial end to their mourning—and they were expecting Lilly to join them.

The narrowboat approached then, painted in shades of muted gold by the slanting rays of sunlight. Lilly saw two figures on its tiller deck. One hand rising in salute.

She felt a flicker of recognition. Strained forward to better see in the fading light.

It cannot be. . . .

But it was.

Finally, finally, Lilly saw that cherished face, the much-missed and loved person.

The hand waved. The well-known voice called, "Lilly!"

Her heart leapt within her.

It was Francis, coming back to Bedsley Priors.

Before the boat was even lashed to its moorings, Francis jumped from the deck and scrambled up the bank with no thought to his fine suit of clothes. At the end of the bridge, he stopped and looked at her, his earnest gaze reflecting all the longing she felt.

Lilly stood there, feeling stunned and oddly rooted where she was, some fifteen or so feet away from him.

"You can have no idea how much I have missed you," he said, the angles of his face more defined than ever, his brown eyes large and intense.

Lilly swallowed. "Have you?"

"I've thought of you every day. Why do you think I wanted so badly to succeed?"

Breathless, she could only stare at him.

"I have passed the examinations, Lilly," he said. "I am a certified apothecary."

Her throat was suddenly dry. "Congratulations," she managed.

"I am taking over Shuttleworth's. Did he mention it? He's let me have it for exceedingly generous terms."

"Shuttleworth's?" Lilly asked, feeling slow-witted. "*You're* the new apothecary?"

Francis nodded. "Though I do not plan to call it Shuttleworth's any longer. I was thinking . . ." He took a step forward. "That is . . . How does *Baylor and Haswell* sound?"

Lilly's heart, already beating at an alarming rate, felt as though it had taken a shock from the electricity machine. Dragging in a deep, shaky breath, she feigned a casual shrug. "Or *Haswell and Baylor.*"

He grinned and opened his arms.

Lilly ran.

Francis caught her mid-air and held her tightly against his chest. Slowly, he let her slip down until her feet returned to the bridge. He released her only to cradle her face in his hands. Lilly looked up at him with all the love she felt, and his warm, chocolate eyes seemed to melt into hers. He leaned down as she reached up, and their lips finally met. She leaned into his embrace and together they stood, with no thought to passersby, nor to the canal, nor to a single boat upon it.

EPILOGUE

I walked, as I often did, to the churchyard. My brother, Charlie, was not there this time. He was likely off working in the gardens at Marlow House, counting weeds as he plucked them, or ladybird beetles, or emmets crawling about their hill. And I knew he was content in his own way.

I stood before a headstone, still new, not yet cankered by time and wind and lichen. But in my mind's eye, I was standing before another grave. Her grave.

Uncle Elliott had finally sent the letter I had once longed for: *We have found your mother.* Upon reading those words, I remember thinking that we ought to go to her quickly, before she moved again—again out of reach.

But Rosamond Haswell was not going anywhere. Ever again.

When the Elliotts took me "to her," they took me to a London cemetery. To a plot bearing a temporary cross marker with the name *R. H. Wells* inscribed.

Her searching, and mine, was over.

She died in hospital of consumption, her secrets with her. A scrap of paper with Jonathan Elliott's name and address was found among her things, and the hospital had sent a message—hoping, no doubt, for payment. Uncle Elliott had been away traveling, but upon his return he had paid what was due and located the gravesite, leaving the temporary marker until he might confer with me.

I could not protest that she was not buried here in the Bedsley Priors churchyard, when she had so long wanted to escape our village. But I agreed with the Elliotts' plan to purchase a headstone and have it engraved with her legal name. Rosamond Haswell had disappeared, and Rosamond Haswell had been found. If *Rosa Wells* wished a pauper's grave, we would not oblige her. Cemeteries and headstones are for the living, after all. The ones who need a place to mourn and visit and remember.

We held a brief funeral in London. The service was sparsely attended. Jonathan and Ruth Elliott, Charles and Charlie Haswell, Maude Mimpurse, Francis and I. A small announcement ran in the *Times*, but no unfamiliar men—men named Quinn or Wells or Dugan—appeared. In the end, it boiled down to blood and love.

It always did.

After the funeral, Uncle Elliott led me into the library, pressed something into my palm, and closed my fingers around it, saying only, "I found it among your mother's things." When he left me, I opened my hand. My heart lurched at the sight of my name written in a familiar though shaky hand, on a thrice-folded scrap of paper. I unfolded it and saw that it had been torn from the corner of a larger piece. The smeared ink words it bore swam before my eyes.

> *It is too late to undo what I have done.*
> *Too late to plead forgiveness, or tell you I love you.*
> *But I beg you, do not follow my course.*
>
> *And please, tell Charlie I am sorry I never returned as I told him I would.*

Squeezing my eyes shut, I clutched the paper to my breastbone, and held it there. Only when I held the note aloft once more, tears magnifying my vision, did I recognize the paper itself—the thick, creased paper the color of a tea stain. The curve of a sphere. Torn away . . .

To think I used to covet her *adventurous* life. Even wished she had taken me with her. How foolish I had been.

The memory of my mother's grave receded, and I focused on the one there before me in the Bedsley Priors churchyard. The large headstone my father had paid a dear sum to purchase and a dearer sum yet to have engraved. So many words and flowers and embellishments have not graced a headstone since the first Lady Marlow's. We had feared Mrs. Mimpurse might mind our involvement. But she, dear woman, seemed to understand my need to claim kinship and Father's need for atonement—for though kind to Mary, he had never publicly acknowledged her during her lifetime.

Now I traced gloved fingers along the grooves of the carved-out dates of my sister's life. *1795 to 1815.* Far, far too brief. I sank to my knees before the sun-warmed stone. Tears streamed down my face as I again read the words that ushered in such a bittersweet torrent of pain and pleasure and release.

> *Here lies*
> *Mary Helen Mimpurse,*
> *The Apothecary's Daughter*

I felt a hand on my shoulder and looked up. Francis had come. He offered me his hand and helped me to my feet. In his dear brown eyes I saw love and empathy. He kissed me tenderly and then wrapped his arms around me. For a moment, we stood there, simply remembering. Then together we walked hand in hand back to our shop, back to the endless duties and joys of an apothecary, and his wife.

Author's Note

W hile most people visit the London Eye or Buckingham Palace,
I dragged my long-suffering husband to less-visited places like
the Worshipful Society of Apothecaries and a museum of pharmacy.
While other tourists snapped pictures of the changing of the guard,
he tirelessly photographed ancient mortars and leech jars. I appreciate
his help very much. We did *not* visit Bedsley Priors, for the village
exists only in my imagination, near the real places of Honeystreet and
Alton Barnes, Wiltshire.

I am indebted to John Williams, Beadle of the Apothecaries' Hall,
for his gallant and informative tour and for sharing a history of which
he is justifiably proud. He even donned his ceremonial gown covered
with golden tassels, which represent the posies that beadles of old
pinned on to ward off the odors of the plague years. For fictional purposes, I took a few liberties with the information he gave us. I certainly
hope Mr. Williams won't come after me wearing that gown.

I am also grateful to Julie Wakefield, Assistant Keeper of the
Museum of the Royal Pharmaceutical Society of Great Britain, who
gave us a detailed, fascinating tour through the changing medical

treatments from early to modern times. She also took pity on my "poor soldier" husband, offering him a soft chair and a cool drink while I continued my barrage of questions.

I would also like to thank my colleagues and friends at Bethany House, especially Ann Parrish, Charlene Patterson, Jennifer Parker, and my editors, Karen Schurrer and Jolene Steffer. Deepest thanks to author Beverly Lewis, for her friendship and prayers.

Greetings to the ladies at Curves, who bought so many books, and to Sarah, the pharmacy technician who first brought the apothecaries' system of weights to my attention.

I appreciate all the readers who have taken time to visit my Web site and send kind e-mails about my first novel, *Lady of Milkweed Manor*. Your encouraging words have helped me through many late nights of writing.

Heartfelt thanks to Carlisa, first reader and dear sister-friend, as well as friends Teresa, Berit, Gina, Suzy, Betsey, Patty, Lori, and Mary, who have given me such support—and a great book party!

Finally, thanks again to my husband and sons, who have given me the time and quiet (usually!) to write. I thank God for you.

READING GROUP
DISCUSSION QUESTIONS

1. What does the opening quotation, "Providence has made the most useful things most common, and for that reason we neglect them," mean to you?

2. When is it easy for you to neglect "the most useful things" in life? What distracts you from your priorities?

3. What surprised you about apothecaries in the early 1800s? How are apothecaries similar to and different from today's physicians, pharmacists, and herbalists?

4. Did you grow up "missing" someone in your life (mother, father, sister, brother, grandparents, etc.)? Did you find ways to fill this void?

5. Mary suffered from epilepsy. Do you know anything about epilepsy or anyone afflicted with it? How has public opinion about this condition changed since the 1800s?

6. Charles Haswell was too proud to ask for help. Do you ever struggle to reach out in times of need?

7. Did you want to know more about what happened to Lilly's mother, or were you satisfied?

8. Have you ever been guilty of wanting something (or someone) only when you cannot have it (or him or her)? Have you ever had to lose something before you appreciated its worth?

9. If you had a memory like Lilly's, what would you want to memorize or remember?

10. Which of Lilly's suitors did you most like? Did she choose as you would have?

ABOUT THE AUTHOR

JULIE KLASSEN is a fiction editor with a background in advertising. She has worked in Christian publishing for more than twelve years, in both marketing and editorial capacities. This is her second novel.

Julie is a graduate of the University of Illinois. She enjoys travel, research, books, BBC period dramas, long hikes, short naps, and coffee with friends.

She and her husband have two sons and live near St. Paul, Minnesota.

For more information about Julie, *The Apothecary's Daughter, Lady of Milkweed Manor,* and her upcoming books, visit *www.julieklassen. com.*